Praise for *Suga.*

"When I read Dan Chodorkoff's historically vivid Vermont novel, I thought of Faulkner's famous statement: "The past is never dead. It's not even past." *Sugaring Down* takes place in the turbulent 60's, when the Vietnam war was malignantly in our communal hearts and minds. But Chodorkoff's story is also about the friendships and fateful decisions we made in our flurried passions, at the same time hauntingly sensed that we may never again feel quite so alive."

—Howard Norman, author of *The Ghost Clause*

NO LONGER PROPERTY OF SEATTLE PUBLIC LIBRARY

"In *Sugaring Down* Dan Chodorkoff tells the story of a young couple, of the communal days of 1968 and 1969, of political passions and of a Vermont landscape that exists in its own weathered right. The notion of revolution that animates the young communards has become distant but that is all the more reason to read this compelling, deeply felt novel. Historical moments exert enormous pressure; people make fateful decisions. At the same time, Chodorkoff shows us a world whose natural rhythms cast an almost timeless spell. The northern Vermont village he writes of is to some eyes a nowhere but in Chodorkoff's hands it feels remarkable—an essence that speaks to dark perplexities and calm, sun-blessed mornings."

—Baron Wormser, author of *The Road Washes Out in Spring*

"*Sugaring Down* whisks us back to the late 1960's, another turbulent time in American history when the personal and the political were deeply entwined. The winds of change have swept up David and Jill, a couple who make very different choices in their resistance to the war raging in Vietnam. With his vivid depictions of communal life in Vermont and the radical underground in New York City, Chodorkoff has delivered a mythic tale of love, revolution, and redemption."

—Suzan Ritz, author of *A Dream to Die For*

"David, the protagonist of Dan Chodorkoff's insightful new novel *Sugaring Down*, is conflicted. He has moved to Vermont in 1969 to be part of an activist political collective, but finds himself drawn to the quiet rhythms of the Vermont seasons. The more radicalized his comrades (and especially his girlfriend Jill) become, the more David finds true fulfillment in putting down roots.

David and friends come to Vermont's Northeast Kingdom with very little practical knowledge. Through his closest neighbors, the vividly realized Leland and Mary Smith, he gradually acquires the skills to survive. He must use them all when the collective disintegrates and he faces a winter alone.

Leland and Mary do not pass judgment on the newcomers and become a guide to much more than splitting wood and boiling syrup. They advise David and friends on what not to say to hostile individuals in town, how to behave at Town Meeting, and in general how to act so that - eventually - they might be accepted in their community.

I appreciated that through Leland and Mary, we also learn some Vermont history that predates the counterculture. David has never heard about Barre's radical history (Mary, the daughter of a granite worker, has Italian roots), or the forced sterilizations of Abenaki people during the eugenics movement, or the bulk tanks that forced Leland and Mary's to give up dairy farming.

Chodorkoff is especially evocative as the reader sees each successive season - their glories and their challenges - through David's city-bred eyes. And it was painful to this veteran of the late 1960s to relive the heated political conversations of the time. The book takes place at a time when some on the "New Left" were turning to violence, and Chodorkoff does not shy away from these upsetting themes.

Chodorkoff uses the maple sugaring process as a central metaphor, hence the title. The sap boils off (and there is furious boiling indeed) and we - and David - are left with the essence. *Sugaring Down* is a worthy addition to the growing literature about Vermont during this tempestuous time."

— Rick Winston, author of *Red Scare in the Green Mountains*

SUGARING DOWN

Dan Chodorkoff

Fomite
Burlington, VT

Copyright 2022 © Dan Chodorkoff
Cover Art © David Smith
All rights reserved. No part of this book may be reproduced in any form or by
any means without the prior written consent of the publisher, except in the case of
brief quotations used in reviews and certain other noncommercial uses permitted
by copyright law.

ISBN-13: 978-1-947917-81-1
Library of Congress Control Number: 2020945369
Fomite
58 Peru Street
Burlington, VT 05401
www.fomitepress.com

01-26-2022

To my daughters, Lisa and Rebecca

Acknowledgment

The 1960's were a tumultuous time in America, and in Vermont as well. The state was transformed by an influx of young people seeking an alternative to the consumerism, injustice and hypocrisy that they perceived in the larger culture. Drawn to Vermont by it's human scale, its traditions of tolerance and direct democracy, its natural beauty, and cheap land, they sought community and connection to each other and the natural world. This work seeks to capture that moment, a time of discovery and revolt, a time when it seemed to us that anything was possible

Sugaring Down is a novel. There is no town of Zion in Vermont, and the Zion Farm collective never existed, but the Northeast Kingdom is a very real place and it was inhabited by numerous communes and collectives in the 1960's and 70's. The characters depicted in the story are, purely the invention of the author, and any resemblance to any real person is co-incidental, with the exception of certain public officials.

The book in its present form is the result of several years of development, and could never have happened without the help and guidance of key people who must be properly credited. Marc Estrin, my editor and publisher at Fomite Press worked through multiple drafts of the manuscript with great patience and insight. Donna Bister, publisher and production manager at Fomite slogged through many pages of revisions to produce the final copy. Rebecca Robinson's careful, close reading and copy editing corrected many mistakes I made along the way. Howard Norman's generosity in reviewing the manuscript also helped to strengthen the final presentation.

Writing this novel was a process that drew on history, memory, and imagination. I hope I was able to convey something of the mood of the times, the tensions that existed between the old and the new Vermont, and the relationships that emerged to shape the Vermont in which we now live. While the final form of *Sugaring Down* is the result of a collaborative process, I alone must take full responsibility for any failure, distortion, or inaccuracy in that depiction.

Dan Chodorkoff- 2021

"Two roads diverged in a yellow wood...
and I took the one less traveled by."
—Robert Frost

Spring 1968

THE KINGDOM STANDS APART. We drove north, past Killington, Woodstock, and Stowe, through Morrisville, Wolcott, Craftsbury Common, deep into the Northeast Kingdom; timeless and elemental, shaped by eons of wind and water scouring the glacier-torn landscape, slowly grinding lofty peaks to lonely hills, transforming granite and schist to loam, sand and gravel; carved by ancient rivers meandering through valleys and rushing down mountainsides, draining into kettle ponds and majestic lakes, defining a geography of hope and pain, hardscrabble and demanding, yielding only to the constant toil of people as rugged as the outcroppings of rock that break through the thin soil of the hillsides, making every crop an act of will, every harvest miraculous.

A hard place, snow covered for six long months until life slowly reemerges and finally, for a brief glorious moment, bursts forth into more shades of green than imagination can conjure—and then dies back after a multi-colored spectacle unmatched anywhere on the planet; a place where humanity exists as an afterthought, an asterisk, or, more accurately, a question mark in the larger grammar of the natural world.

Boreal forests, mixed northern hardwoods, dominate this world, slowly reclaiming the hard-won pastures and high mowings, reversing all of the works of men and women in a geological instant. Two hundred years of clearing and cultivating disappearing under their growth; the stone walls that run straight and true through the forest testimony to the inexorable succession, silent monuments to the rigors of this hard land and the futility of resistance. Here, our labors amount to nothing, giving way to the greater forces that condition our lives.

The tectonic plates that shaped this land, thrust mountains up out of ancient seas, are still present, slumbering in the depth of the earth, molten magma bubbling below the surface, but unreachable, beyond our feeble powers, unknowable; perceived only in the realm of theory.

Here reality is shaped by the mountains, the rivers, and the forest, the winds that ceaselessly scour the hillsides, the thin rocky soil, glacial till fit for little but growing grass, and the cycle of seasons that dictates when and how people may live; a hard place, but not without its pleasures, satisfactions, and possibilities.

The farm itself was carved from the forest on a shelf that backed up to Hardwood Mountain, which was really more of a hill. The other side of Hardwood overlooked Zion Lake, which straddled the border with Canada; a corner of the Northeast Kingdom that seemed frozen in time, where a sparse network of dirt roads traced ridges dotted with long abandoned houses and barns; thinned out, populated only by the hearty few who managed to hang on despite the cold, the worthless soils, the plunging dairy prices.

Into this world we came, wild eyed, wandering, searching for a place where the world made sense, or where we could make a world that made sense to us, a place to strive for: home.

When we arrived with our longhair and beards, wearing sandals, bellbottoms, fringes and beads we straggled onto the old hill farm over the course of the summer until we were twenty strong, and the little town couldn't help but notice. Improbable pilgrims to this land of frozen toes, broken hearts, and shattered dreams, we came to build, to redeem the promise of America; to find something real and true. We called ourselves a collective in order to mark us as different from the myriad of back-to-the-landers who were flooding Vermont back then. We came to transform reality, not escape it; to purge ourselves of petite bourgeois individualism and become a revolutionary force, part of the change that we knew was sweeping across the planet—Cuba, Vietnam, China, Mozambique. We stood in solidarity with the Third World.

JILL AND I WERE the first. Her aunt and uncle owned the place, purchased a dozen years earlier from a distressed farmer who could no longer pay the taxes and who now lived with his wife in a modest mobile home at the end of the road.

We arrived the second week of April, expecting spring. "Holy shit!" I said as I pulled my backpack out of the Volvo wagon and surveyed the field, deep with snow. "What the fuck!"

"Come on David, we knew it wouldn't be easy. Where's your sense of adventure? We're the vanguard." Jill used a hand to brush the hair out of her eyes just as a gust of wind sent a patch of snow spiraling into the air. She saw the house perched where field met forest at the end of a long, unplowed drive. It sat there, cold and silent, waiting for us, but hardly beckoning.

"How do we get all our shit up there? We can't drive in." I shouldered my pack.

"Maybe we can get Leland to plow the drive."

"Leland?"

"Our neighbor," She nodded her head in the direction of the small trailer. "Sy and Claire bought the place from him. A really cool old guy."

The aloneness of the place surprised me. The hills rolled away to the horizon, row after row—an empty slate of gray trees occasionally punctuated by snow filled hay fields and puffs of smoke from the chimneys of the few people still hanging on. For a city boy like me it was almost overwhelming. No traffic noise, no honking horns or lumbering trucks, no buildings, houses, or people. I stood a moment taking it in, then looked over at Jill, who had hoisted her pack and begun wading through the calf-deep snow.

"Come on, let's check out the house and get a fire started. We can deal with the stuff later."

"Okay," I said, then took my first steps into my new life; the place austere and somewhat terrifying—an unknown.

We came to change everything. Neither Jill nor I ever questioned that. We were on the crest of a great wave sweeping the planet, liberating the world, awakening the sleeping people to seize their birthright, to arise and revolt! No question about it, the revolution was happening, and we were a part of it, spinning in time with the universe, peace, freedom, love, justice.

And Vermont, remote and placid as it might be, was part of it too. Thousands of kids, turned off to the straight world, seeing the injustice all around them, were moving to the hills and villages, reclaiming the old places and building something new, something communal and caring, almost tribal. Turning the granite hills upside down.

"Fuck, I can't believe we're really here, really doing it!" I was stamping snow off myself on the covered porch of the old farmhouse.

"Yeah, pretty far out!" Jill opened the door and entered a mudroom which had a rough wooden bench pushed against one side and a row of wooden pegs for hanging coats above it on the wall. The slate floor was polished by age and heavy use.

We dropped our packs, opened a paneled door, then stepped into an open space that had been parlor and kitchen until her uncle had torn down the wall that separated them. A large brick fireplace sat in the middle of the room with a wood stove attached. The kitchen area was dominated by an enameled cook stove with porcelain knobs, the type, I imagined, that had been popular at the turn of the century. Exposed, hand-hewn beams on the ceiling revealed the bones of the house, its nineteenth century hemlock frame.

"Wow! What a place!" I dropped my pack on the threadbare couch that sat facing the wood stove.

"Dynamite! Isn't it? They just started the renovation, but—what the hell, it really is great. Plenty of room too, five bedrooms, big living room…"

"Holy shit! I didn't know what to expect."

"Well, it needs lots of work, but there's plenty here to start with." Jill turned and squeezed me.

I looked around the room, as a shaft of late afternoon sunlight illuminated the dust dancing in the wake of our entry. "Kinda cold in here. You said something about a fire?"

"Sure, There's the wood." She indicated an old copper boiler that held a stack of kindling and a pile of newspaper. "There's more outside, on the porch."

"Really? Do I look like a boy scout? I didn't build a lot of fires in the Bronx."

"You're impossible! I'll teach you." Jill bent in front of the ornate wood stove, the words "Round Oak" cast into the top. She opened the door on the front and a small pile of cold ashes fell onto the slate hearth. She crumpled up some newspaper, used it to line the bottom of the stove, lay kindling on top of it and lit a match. As the paper caught fire the room began to fill with smoke.

Jill began pushing and pulling the rods and levers that controlled the stove, but the smoke kept billowing out. The room was thick with it. I finally noticed a wire handle on the metal pipe that connected the stove to the brick chimney, and turned it. The fire gave a whoosh and the smoke began to exit up the chimney. Jill went over and opened the mudroom door and the door to the porch, allowing the smoke to empty from the room.

"Welcome to Vermont." She laughed and used her hand to fan the smoke out. "It's gonna take a while for the place to warm up. Maybe we should go see Leland and start moving stuff up here."

"I'm down for that. I could use some fresh air."

We left the room and stood on the front porch long enough for the smoke to empty out, then loaded the stove with blocks of wood from the pile on the porch, shut the doors and retraced our steps down the drive back to the road.

The wind gusted across the field and I wished I had brought a hat and gloves. But who knew? It was April, after all. Daffodils, tulips and forsythia had all been in bloom when we left the city. I trudged along, trying to ignore the cold blasts that nipped at me.

The little trailer sat just down the road, surrounded by piles of junk covered by newly fallen snow. Not one of those fancy double wides you would see down along the state highway, just a simple trailer that sat on a cinderblock foundation.

It had a faded blue exterior, and a curl of smoke rose from a metal chimney protruding from the top. We climbed the wooden steps that led to the front door.

Jill knocked once, and after a moment a large woman with round cheeks and a shock of short white hair opened the door. "Jill! Wondered who it might be when I heard the car pull up. Not a lot of folks coming up the hill this time of year. Come on in." We entered a small kitchen with Formica counters the same color as the trailer's exterior. "Who's this?"

"Hi Mary." Jill hugged her. "Sorry, this is David, my boyfriend."

"Well, hello, glad to meet you. What brings you kids up here?" Her eyes sparkled.

"Nice to meet you." I extended my hand and looked around the house.

"We're moving up, us and some friends." Jill answered.

"Movin' up? Oh my goodness, you mean your gonna live in the old place? Not just here for skiing, or the lake?"

"Well, that's the plan." Jill saw Mary's eyes widen in surprise.

"Now isn't that something. Wait till I tell Leland...When your aunt and uncle bought it, I guess we had you figured for summer people, I never..."

"Not Sy and Claire. We're going to fix up the house and start to farm." I felt the need to explain, to differentiate us from the "summer people".

"Farm?" Mary threw her arms into the air. "Farm that old place?"

"Well, grow a garden anyway. Some animals."

"Oh, garden, uh huh, I can see that. But I'm being rude, leaving you standing in the doorway. Sit down." She gestured to a small kitchen table with chrome legs and topped with the same blue Formica that covered the counters. Jill and I sat.

"I was just brewing myself a cup of tea. Want some?"

I looked out the small window at a bird feeder where a scattering of small birds, sparrows maybe, were feasting on seeds of some sort, chattering excitedly.

Mary placed three mugs on the table, then turned back to the kitchen and returned with a chipped teapot. "Just let it steep for a minute."

"Thanks, Mary." Jill leaned forward in her seat. "How've you been?"

"Oh, not bad. Really can't complain." She gave a wry smile. "Nobody listens even if I do, so what's the point?"

I laughed, but then Mary's smile disappeared.

"The old man's not doin' so well though. Not that he'd ever mention it to anybody, but the diabetes got worse and he had a heart attack. Tryin' to get him to take it easy, but he's a stubborn one, you know. He still likes his chocolate bars too, sneaks 'em off to the woods with him and thinks he's foolin' me. But other than that…well, things don't change much up here, except for the weather. We sure don't see a lot of new folks. Mostly they leave."

"Mary, things are changing, people are waking up. We're here to stay." Jill swept her brown hair off her forehead. "We're starting a collective." She saw Mary's raised eyebrows. "Like a co-op."

"Oh, I know all about collectives. I grew up in Barre." She gave a knowing look.

"Cool!" I wondered what Barre signified, but didn't want to reveal my ignorance by asking.

We sat drinking our tea, silent for a moment as a bright red bird chased the sparrows, or whatever they were, away from the bird feeder.

"Is Leland around?" Jill took a sip of tea. "We've got a load of stuff in the car we want to move into the house. I thought maybe he could plow a path, or something."

"Oh, he went over to Newport, but he'll be back soon. I'm sure he'll figure something, but driving up there might not be such a good idea right now. Ground's thawed; mud season."

"What?" I had to ask.

"Mud season, you'd just tear up that path, dig some mighty deep ruts and maybe get your car stuck in the bargain." She looked at me. "You know we got five seasons up here; summer, fall, winter, mud season, and then, a little later, spring finally comes around."

"Well, I'm glad to hear this isn't spring." I surveyed the snow-filled landscape.

"Oh, snow just fell a couple days ago, ground was bare before that. It'll melt off soon enough."

While we sipped our tea, I looked over the rest of the trailer's interior. A tin stove glowed cherry red in the corner of the small adjacent living room. A couch covered by a white chenille slipcover was decorated with small colorful patchwork pillows. Two wicker chairs, painted white, sat opposite the couch. A small table piled high with catalogs and ladies' magazines lay between the chairs.

"Well," Mary smiled, "It sure will be nice to have some neighbors up here. A whole collective, huh? All friends of yours?"

"Yeah, friends from college. We were together in the city last year." Jill answered.

I was getting antsy, anxious to settle in. "If we can't drive, do you have a sled or something we could borrow to get our stuff up to the house?"

"I'm sure we do. I think there's one in the shed down here. If not, he's got one out in the barn. He's got that place so crammed full of junk I believe there's at least one of everything ever made and two of most!" She rose and started to pull on a pair of high rubber boots. "Best if I go get it for you. Might all collapse on you if you start pokin' around."

Jill and I rose to join her, but she turned toward us. "You can wait in here and store some heat up. I'll bet you a nickel it's not too warm in that house."

"No, we're coming." We joined her, donning our jackets and following her out the door.

Mary walked to the rough-planked shed that was attached to the end of the trailer. It was filled mostly with carefully stacked firewood.

"Here it is!" She bent over and then stood holding a rope attached to a large old sled with wooden runners.

"Perfect! You sure you don't need it?" Jill took the rope from Mary's hand.

"Just put it back when you're done with it."

"Thanks, Mary. Great to see you!"

"Well, nice seeing you too, neighbor."

We loaded the boxes that filled the back of the Volvo onto the sled. It took four trips to get everything inside the house and by then it had warmed up enough, at least in the room near the stove, for us to feel comfortable.

What had induced us to come to this cold, empty farmhouse, vaguely musty and thoroughly uninviting? Austere didn't come close to describing the setting; the gray woods, still filled with snow despite the calendar's promise of spring; the equally gray sky threatening more snow at any moment.

Jill's memories were all of summers in the farmhouse, glorious, sunny, and green, and they seemed very distant at the moment. The little light that remained was fading fast and the room's details were disappearing into shadows.

Even Jill, usually supremely confident, began to question if this had really been the right move. "I hope we can make this work."

We had no doubt it was time to build a new world. Our question was: where's the best place to do it? After all the protests and rallies, the organizing and community work, we decided to move to Vermont, start a new life and build a new world, one that would let us live our dreams. Freedom, sharing, struggle; our community would be about our wildest hopes, we were building utopia. We'd build a new society on the rubble of the old, a model of how life should be, and at the same time build a base for resistance and transformation, a revolutionary outpost.

David and I had first raised the idea with the collective, spent months debating it, and then, finally, a few of us decided to just do it. More planning and dreaming, and now we were here, the advance party, here to get things ready for the others. It had been easy to get my aunt and uncle to agree. They had hardly used the place since I'd gone off to college, and they weren't getting any younger.

The house is kind of primitive, wood for heating and cooking, water from a spring. I always loved it and when I was a kid. We'd come up to visit for a week or two in the summer, and a few times I stayed on with Sy and Claire for a month or so.

But it really wasn't their style any more. So they said yes, happy to be a part, if only tangentially, of their niece's bold experiment. They didn't have any kids, and had been wondering what to do with the place.

The big question for us had been relevance. "How does running away to the country help end the war? What the fuck does growing vegetables have to do with the revolution?" Howie, the oldest member of our group, and the most doctrinaire Marxist, was incensed at the suggestion.

"We're not running away," I told him. "We're building something new, a model for after the revolution. And we'll be a base for the movement. We can help folks across the border, be a place where people can get away when they get too stressed, and we can grow food for the Panthers' and the Young Lords' free lunch programs. We'll live off the land in solidarity with the peasants of Vietnam, China, Cuba, Africa…the revolution isn't just about politics— we've got to change everything!"

Howie had never come around, but some of the others did. More people would be joining us in a couple of days, and then a few more. We expected the numbers to grow after word got around. Lots of people were looking for a way out of the system, and this was it.

But now that we were here, I was having some doubts. I hadn't remembered the house being in such rough shape, or how far off the paved road it was. And who expected snow in April?"

I looked around the old farmhouse and sighed. In the growing darkness the place looked dingy and sad, everything covered in dust and smelling of mold. Not like I remembered it in the summer. I went to stand by the wood stove that was slowly spreading its warmth to the far corners of the house. I glanced back at David, who looked alarmed, his thin face drawn tight by a grimace that brought deep furrows to his forehead "Looks like we've got our work cut out for us."

"I guess, but I don't want to think about it now. I'm tired, and hungry, too. Let's eat." He was always hungry.

"All we've got is some bread and cheese."

"Then let's go out."

"Out where? It's not New York, the nearest restaurant is about twenty miles away, and it's snowing again, if you hadn't noticed. We'll have to go shopping tomorrow. I guess it's gonna to be bread and cheese tonight."

"Can we at least have grilled cheese sandwiches?"

"Sure, if you want to make a fire in the cook stove."

WE SPENT THE NIGHT huddled together under a quilt in the largest of the upstairs bedrooms, and woke to a cold house, the fire having gone out at some point in the night. I pulled on my jeans and a flannel shirt and went about rebuilding it while Jill lay in bed, her feelings of doubt reinforced when she rose and saw her breath fog the mirror over her dresser. She put on a robe and made her way downstairs where I was still struggling to get the fire lit. I finally got some kindling to catch and stepped back.

"There must be some trick to it, I mean they lived like this for hundreds of years, right?"

"Don't worry Dave, practice makes perfect."

"Yeah, and I guess we're gonna get plenty of practice." We laughed. "So what's up today?"

"Well," Jill consulted a piece of paper on which she had been writing, "Lots of cleaning. We've got to go into town for supplies. I've been making a shopping list for groceries."

"Cool, what's first?"

"Cleaning up here will go a lot easier if we can heat things up a little. Let's build up the fire and go out shopping. Maybe it'll be warm when we get back."

"How much wood? Should I chop more?"

"Split more? Let's just fill the stove. We'll deal with it when we come back."

"Okay."

I looked at Jill. Her wavy hair, parted in the middle, hung just past her shoulders. She had full lips and hazel eyes with long lashes, which gave her a kind of languid sensuality, counterbalanced by the serious cast of her brow. I had been struck by her beauty when I had first seen her at a meeting, freshman year. She was tall and slim, graceful, even as she crossed the room toward me with an armful of firewood.

"Here, this ought to do it."

It was mid-afternoon by the time we returned from town. We had purchased a sled of our own, on sale at the hardware store in Newport, and loaded it up with bags of cleaning supplies and groceries. When we opened the mudroom door and entered the kitchen, it was warm. I checked the stove and added another armload of wood, and looked around the house, seeing it for the first time in warmth and full daylight, taking in details that had escaped me. I noted the centuries-old beams that had been exposed in the ceilings, and the supporting posts that bisected the plaster walls. Another post sat in the middle of the room, evidence of where the wall had been torn down to open up the space. The old pine floor, scarred, gouged, and darkened with age, was made of boards that must have been fourteen or fifteen inches wide. The windows, which shuddered every time the wind blew, were double hung with twelve individual wavy panes of glass in each sash. The place was really ancient.

What kind of stories could it tell? How many births and deaths had it contained? How many peals of laughter? How many dark secrets? The possibilities washed over me—Thanksgivings, Christmases, birthdays, comings and goings. I stood for a moment, taking it all in.

"I'm going to start on the kitchen." Jill's voice brought me back to reality. "Why don't you see what you can do out here?"

Everything, coffee table, windowsills, floors, was covered by a thick layer of dust. That seemed to be the logical starting point. I took a rag and began by wiping down the hard surfaces with Pine-Sol and water that I mixed together in a tin pail which I used later to mop the floor. Then I removed the cushions from the couch, took them onto the porch, and beat them without mercy until the dust stopped billowing out.

LATER THAT DAY I returned the sled to the trailer's woodshed and when I turned back to the road an old man with a gray beard was standing there. "You must be Jill's friend." He was thin, wearing overalls, an unbuttoned tan barn coat, and sported a John Deere cap.

"You must be Leland." I held out my hand. "I'm Dave."

The old man shook my hand with a grip like a vice. "Pleased to meet you." He had big ears, his brow was creased and his shoulders stooped, but his blue eyes shone bright and clear. "Wife says you're movin' in. Gonna farm the place."

"That's the plan. Start with a garden, some chickens, maybe a milk cow or some goats."

"Goats?" He squinted a little and cocked his head.

"I don't know, maybe."

"Well, my family farmed this hill almost two hundred years, and I don't believe we ever raised any goats. Some sheep way back before the war, but no goats."

"Sheep? I thought Vermont was a dairy state."

"That'd be the Civil War."

I chuckled.

"Well, I wish you luck anyway; place sent me to the poorhouse, maybe you can do better with it. You need any help, I'm right here down the road."

"Thanks, I appreciate it." I thought for a moment. "You know," I hesitated, "I hate to ask, but have you got a snow shovel I could borrow?"

"Got a shovel up to the barn you can use."

The barn was a large three-story structure sided with weathered gray boards and a slate roof that sagged in the middle, looming over the trailer from the side of the road. Leland had sold the farm but he kept some acreage, and had planted the trailer on the site of his great-great-grandfather's original log cabin, long abandoned and collapsed under the weight of neglect and years of heavy snow, near the still standing but slightly listing barn.

When I first entered, trailing behind Leland in search of the snow shovel, I couldn't take it all in. Thin paths wound their way through a chaotic jumble of countless piles, even towers, of what at first glance looked like junk. Closer examination revealed both order of a sort, and substance to the piles that, in spots, literally filled the barn to its rafters.

Hundreds of items, some recognizable, others obscure: cast iron wood stoves, porcelain cook stoves, stove pipes, thimbles, andirons, screens, bellows, fire pokers, chains, axes of all types, chainsaws, and that was just the pile devoted to getting and burning firewood. Others contained ox yokes, wagons, sleds, buckets, hand tools, chairs, bureaus, tables, desks, pots and pans, snow shoes, tanks, casks and barrels, even an old Model T Ford, rusted and piled high with boxes overflowing with dishes and kitchenware; a packrat's heaven.

"Wow! Don't you ever throw anything out?" I asked, as I carefully picked my way through the seemingly precarious piles.

"Not if I can help it." There was pride in Leland's voice. "Waste not, want not. Never know when something's gonna come in handy."

"Yeah, but some of this stuff looks like it's been sitting here for fifty years."

"Well, I guess it's a little longer than that. Bunch of this is my great-great-grandpa's things. Real antiques, you know. He brought some of this up from Connecticut when he settled the place."

Looking again at the piles, I began to pick things out. My initial perception of chaos gave way. I spotted a spinning wheel off in a corner, and recognized a piece of horse-drawn farm equipment. "You know, I bet some of this stuff is really valuable."

"Suppose it is. Had a fellow come up here from Boston one time, some kind of antiques dealer. Wanted to buy the whole barn full. I wasn't interested though. Not back then, not now."

"Why not?"

"Mary didn't want to let it go neither. Told him no. He went away pretty disappointed."

"But, couldn't you have sold him something? I mean, you've got so much stuff in here..."

"Well, these are my family things, two hundred years of family history, right here."

I was silent for a moment, staring around.

Leland pulled the shovel out of a pile and handed it to me. "Here you go, that ought to do you pretty well."

Two hundred years in the same place. I was impressed, my grandparents had come over from Russia, or Lithuania, some place over there, I wasn't even sure where.

THE OTHERS STARTED ARRIVING two days later; struggling up the muddy hill in Brian's old green Beetle and a VW van covered with bumper stickers. They whooped and hollered when they saw us, as they poured out of the vehicles.

We settled into the farmhouse, still smelling of Pine-Sol, the mold mostly banished to the background. Jason and Suze, probably our closest friends from the New York collective, took the back bedroom; Brian, who dropped out of grad school at Harvard to join us had the small room upstairs, Nancy and Bill, also from New York got the other room upstairs when they arrived. Max, from the collective, was crashing on the couch for the time being, and Becca and Tom, old SDS buddies, claimed the downstairs bedroom. The house felt full.

We were convinced we could make a difference and get it right, sure we knew better. We were kids, really, the oldest only a couple of years out of college, but we felt like veterans, like we had been through a war together—and we had. A war against a war. And it had taken a toll; plenty of knocks on the head, bruises and broken bones; for some, time in jail, others, exile in Canada. For all of us plans put on hold or forgotten altogether in the urgency of resistance, the righteous anger of revolt.

I remembered the time we had marched across the quad, hundreds, with a detachment of campus cops standing on the steps between us and the admin building. The warm air hummed with suppressed violence, waiting only for a word, a step in the wrong direction, a taunt, or an order from above to call it into being.

We joined arms and walked toward the building, hunching our

shoulders, against the billy clubs still hanging harmlessly at the cops' sides. I thought briefly about a butterfly that had landed on my arm that morning when I left the dorm, then looked up and saw the line of cops drawing closer.

"NO MORE WAR RESEARCH", "END ROTC", "BOOKS, NOT BOMBS", "HELL NO, WE WON'T GO"; signs bobbed above the sea of people like buoys.

"What do we want?" Sam, the bearded guy at the front of the march, shouted into a bullhorn.

"Peace!" the crowd responded.

"When do we want it?"

"Now!"

The cops drew their batons and lowered the face shields on their helmets.

"What do we want?"

"Peace!" I roared along with the rest of the crowd.

"When do we want it?"

"Now!"

The cops were hitting their nightsticks into their open palms. We kept walking.

"What do we want?"

"Peace!"

"When do we want it?"

"Now!"

The cops moved down the steps in formation to meet us as we surged forward.

"What do we want?"

"Peace!" I saw the cops break into a trot.

"When do we want it?"

"Now!"

Jill and I were in the front line of marchers that came up hard against the cops' billy clubs. The crowd fractured, with people running for cover; me, Jill, and others ducking, dodging, and grappling as best we could to break through the line of cops to the steps and the offices beyond. The cops were clubbing, kicking, and punching; grabbing anyone they could out of the crowd and cuffing them on the ground.

WHEN WE FIRST ARRIVED, and I saw what a different world it was, I came to understand that Vermont counted as a time out; so far away from the boiling pot we had been immersed in that it constituted an alternative universe, one where we could step back and really think things through.

That was what I wanted, a way out that could help me figure a way in. I had so many questions, things I needed to know, so much ambivalence about the right path. Time to read and think; I was looking forward to that. Contemplation, reflection, introspection—things I had given up to wade into the frothy mix of organizing and direct action. No time for anything but the movement, the feeling of being connected to millions of others around the world. I was hoping to get some writing done, to try and make sense of things.

We lived like a family; caring for each other as we would our own kin. We were on the cusp of a new world. We were immersed in it, there and then, with each other. Was it Marx who talked about a "festival of the oppressed"? A time without consequences, fueled by desire, a suspension of disbelief that made anything possible. Those moments sustained me, gave me a glimpse of what could be, and I found them intoxicating; hard to come down from. So I spent my life pursuing them, trying to create them by any means I could, ferreting out brief moments. At a demonstration, smoking a joint with friends, or dancing to Aretha, I would taste it briefly—a rush of euphoria or utopia, or whatever it was. I had times like that in bed with Jill, too.

But to really feel it, to lose oneself in it, to live it, you had to be part of a group, a community, people united by a purpose, or a belief, or a dream. I knew it could happen because I had experienced it, and so had lots of others.

How to sustain it? That was the challenge. "The world turned upside down." The American, or the English revolution? Diggers, Levelers, the Brotherhood of Love forever lurking in the background; Gnostics, Anabaptists, Utopians, Anarchists, Revolutionaries, on and on…all part of something bigger, ever present and never complete, like individual flakes of snow disappearing into the heart of a blizzard.

So why not pursue it? I knew that the world was slowly turning toward the place I wanted to live, and if we all shoved together, it would get there sooner rather than later.

And for me, deep down that was what the farm and Vermont was really about. I could see all the important work we would do, but ultimately it was about something more, transcending the given! It just made sense. We had been together ever since college, part of an SDS chapter that had become something else; sharing a house, organizing off-campus; caught up in the whirlwind together. It was time to take it to a new level.

THE SNOW STILL HUNG on in the field, but every day there was less of it until the sun finally melted it back to the edge of the forest and, finally, only deep in the woods.

The land too wet to work, we kept busy in and around the house, and out and about. Seeds, potting soil and flats to buy, starts for the garden, chicken wire and cedar posts, meetings about housework and cleaning, political education. We drove the rutted back roads with mud up to our axles.

Then one day spring arrived. Even the deep woods were clear. There was a new warmth in the air, the willows down by the creek were heavy with buds, the grass had started to turn green, the old flowerbeds surrounding the farmhouse were alive with shoots, spring bulbs straining to put forth blooms, daffodils and narcissus planted long ago by Leland and Mary. And that night the little pond at the edge of the field exploded in sound—wood frogs, newly hatched, croaking so loudly that at first we thought a flock of ducks must have taken up residence. They were joined the next day by spring peepers, adding their higher-pitched song to the chorus.

We were anxious to get going. The field had been free of snow for a while and days of sunshine had dried out the ground. "What do you think?" Suze was sitting at the kitchen table sipping a mug of chamomile tea. "Time to start clearing for the garden?"

"Yeah, it ought to be fine. Who's down for bustin' some sod?" Jason looked around the table.

"Sure," Tom looked like he was still half asleep, rubbing his eyes and yawning. "but how, exactly are we gonna do that? I mean, like hoe, or use a shovel?"

"It's a big project. I figure we need to open up at least an acre or so, two would be better." I had been reading a Rodale book on organic gardening. "And we need manure and compost, too."

"Where do we get that?" Nancy was at the stove, cooking a pot of oatmeal.

"Don't know," Jill had just come downstairs, "but I bet Leland can tell us."

"It's gonna be a huge job." Max sounded apprehensive.

"Yeah, it'll take some work." Jill poured herself some coffee. "But that's what we moved up here for, right?"

"Well," Bill hesitated, "that's part of it. But I'm no farmer, I'm all about the revolution."

"What, you're not gonna help?" I was taken aback.

"No, I'll help—it's just…"

"Just that Bill doesn't like to get his hands dirty." Nancy laughed and the rest of us joined her.

As we were clearing the table, getting ready to attack the garden, the stillness of the morning was punctured by the steady popping of a diesel engine.

We left the kitchen, walked in the direction of the sound, and discovered Leland seated on his ancient John Deere in the middle of the field. He was dragging a tiller behind.

"Where'd you want that garden?" He peered out from under the bill of his cap with a grin on his face.

With his help we turned about an acre in the middle of the field to grow vegetables. Jason and I, at Leland's suggestion, asked a neighbor down the hill who still kept a dairy herd if he had any manure to spare and he directed us to a half-collapsed barn, which had a bottom story full of well-rotted cow poop, rich with the smell of decomposition. We threw a tarp in the back of the Volvo wagon and piled it high.

"You know, we should really think about getting a truck." I said as I shoveled the last of twenty loads onto the garden. Suze, Brian, Bill, Max, and Jill had been working it into the freshly tilled ground with shovels and hoes. "It would have been a lot less work with a truck."

"Yeah, good idea," Jason agreed, "and the car wouldn't stink of cow shit."

"That's the smell of success when you live in the country." Jill rested on her shovel. We all laughed.

After dinner that night we gathered around the wood stove. "What a great day." Jill was sitting on the couch.

"Yeah, I know what you mean. It's far out!" Jason beamed as he looked out into the fading light at the forest, just starting to leaf out, surrounding the house on three sides.

"It's like we're living on the edge of the wilderness. I mean, I've been hiking up at Bear Mountain and stuff like that, but I never..." I stopped short, "Yo, check it out!" I looked out the window as a deer stepped out of the woods and picked its way down the path into the open field.

"Wow!" Jill was in a good mood. I had rarely seen her so lit up. "I can't wait! Of course the place needs some work. Nobody's even been up here for a couple of years. But isn't it great? What a place!" She took a deep breath. "I mean, even the air. Different up here, sweeter or something."

"If a New York winter was rough, what do you guys think it's gonna be like up here?" Suze rose to throw another piece of wood into the stove.

"Don't worry, I'll keep you warm." Jason put his arm around her.

The next day we bought a rusty Ford pickup for $125 from an old guy down in the village.

A week or so later Ted and Simon rolled in from the West Coast. Former members of our SDS chapter, Jill didn't recognize them at first, as both had grown their hair long and were sporting full beards. Cindy and her sister, Liz, followed them a few days later.

It was still May and there were already over a dozen of us, the newcomers crashing on the floor in sleeping bags. The farmhouse was filled to overflowing, with folks lining up some mornings to use the single bathroom.

We were together for an ecstatic moment; sharing, loving, ready to bring on the new world. Sometimes we just looked at each other and started laughing. And sometimes we got on each other's nerves.

But everything was an adventure. One day, while we were having a picnic down at the creek, swarms of tiny black flies surrounded us, getting in our eyes, ears, even our noses. Swatting at them did no good, and we discovered over the next few weeks that they didn't so much sting, as take a bite out of you, which itched unbearably. By the end of the month we looked like victims of a measles epidemic.

One night we built a huge bonfire from scrap lumber that we piled at the edge of the field. We passed a joint and sat around talking.

"It's like we're brothers and sisters, but ones we got to choose, not just some accident of birth! How cool is that?" Jill was really sold on the communal thing, and, though almost terminally ambivalent about most things, I had to agree. I grew up a single child and it was the closest I had ever come to having siblings.

Now that the land had dried out and the days were getting warmer, the pace of life quickened. For me the garden was the center of activity. My life began to revolve around cycles of planting, mulching, weeding, fertilizing, and generally worrying over the young plants. Would there be a late frost? Were the tomatoes getting enough water? What was eating the strawberries? I knew nothing, and depended on Rodale, and Leland and Mary for advice.

We went to town one day and bought twenty chicks. When we got back we built a coop for them out of a pile of lumber found in one of the sheds and attached a large run fenced with chicken wire, looking forward to fresh eggs. One morning a couple of weeks after the chicks had been installed Becca went to feed and water them and found the run littered with their feathers.

"Fox, coyote, fisher cat, weasel, raccoon, who knows? All kinds of varmints kill chickens." Leland stroked his beard. "Maybe you need a farm dog."

We rebuilt the chicken coop, patched holes where a varmint might enter and planted the chicken wire in the dirt so they couldn't dig their way into the run. The feed store in Newport provided more chicks, and we tried again.

I SAW THE SIGN on the bulletin board at the general store down in the village and went to see the puppies on a whim. The father was a black Lab retriever and the mother a Great Dane, a harlequin; white with black markings. The puppies were sprawled in a tangled mass under the front porch of a dilapidated farmhouse. There were seven of them, three black, like their father, three white with black markings like their mother, and one gray, with white blaze and chest, black mask, and black spots.

I knelt and the puppies swarmed around me, vying for my attention. I reached out and scooped up the gray pup. It was love at first sight. The pup, barely eight weeks old, went home with me that afternoon.

The helpless creature sat shivering on my lap as I drove the orange and white VW van up the rutted road, offering reassurances as we went. "It's okay, pup. Good puppy, good boy. Don't be scared."

I was half way up the hill when I felt a spreading warmth on my thighs. "Oh, fuck!" I said, then I looked down at the tiny mass of gray, white and black huddled in my lap, and started to laugh. "Off to a great start there, buddy."

When I walked into the farmhouse with the pup cradled in my arms everyone gathered around. "Wow! What a cutie!" Jill stroked his fur. "So soft."

"What kind of dog did you say he was?" Suze came closer to get a better look. "Great Dane? He's gonna be big."

"Take a look at the size of those paws!" Jason loomed over the puppy, "He's not just gonna be big, he's gonna be huge."

"What are you going to name him?" Jill stroked the pup's belly.

"Haven't really given it any thought. I'm open to suggestions."

"How about Che?" Suze offered. "Or Zapata? Zappa for short, or for Frank?"

Jason chimed in. "You could call him Fidel."

"I don't know, I can't see it yet. The dog's only been here five minutes. Maybe it's gonna have to wait till I know him better."

"How about Ranger?" Jill looked at him.

"What, like the Green Berets? Kinda militaristic."

"No, like the Lone Ranger, those black markings around his eyes look like a mask."

"Not bad! I kind of like it." Nancy was standing by the stove.

"Come here, Ranger." I snapped my fingers and the puppy waddled towards me.

The dog quickly became a house favorite, always there and, more often than not, being held or petted. At the same time, it was apparent that he was very much my dog. He followed me wherever I went and developed an almost slavish devotion. If I strayed from his sight he searched until he found me, would wait patiently outside any door I entered, and was only truly happy when in my presence. The pup would sit at my feet and stare at me while I read, insisted on sharing the bed with Jill and me and, even when walking in the woods made sure that I remained in his realm of perception. I was the leader of his pack.

Longer days meant more time outside, gardening, building, exploring, being together on the land. We went swimming at the town beach on the lake. The old farmstead echoed with the sound of work; hammers banging nails, mauls driving fence posts, saws at work in the woods, shrieks of delight and shouts of encouragement coming from the garden and kitchen. The land was awakening and we were awakening to the land, something none of us had ever really experienced before. Oh, a few came from the suburbs, and Nancy's parents even had a small vegetable garden. Brian, Becca and Jason had all gone to summer camp in the country where they had learned simple skills, like how to start a fire. But overall, the depth of our ignorance was astounding. So much to learn.

I was walking in the woods one afternoon taking in the calls of a half-dozen different birds and realized I couldn't identify one of them. How many more birds than people lived on the hill? A hundred times, a thousand? I didn't have a clue. How ignorant, how impossibly ignorant. In fact, I realized I knew nothing and I could do nothing. I was helpless.

Here my knowledge of history, philosophy, politics was all worthless. Leland, who had left Vermont only once in his life to go to Boston to see the Red Sox at Fenway, knew every inch of the home place; every bit of the woods, every mower busting rock in the hayfield, every patch in the barn roof, and every ledge outcropping on Hardwood Mountain. He knew every creature in the forest; could fix a roof or a rebuild a tractor, birth a calf, build a barn, prune an apple tree, and much more. That, I thought, was knowledge worth having.

But, despite our ignorance, things were getting done. The garden was coming in, early crops like peas and spinach would be ready in few weeks. The pantry had been gutted and new shelving built, we had dug a line from the spring to the garden, and the house had taken on a certain order. We'd been working on our group process too, long meetings, making lists and setting priorities, and, of course, continuing political education.

Every day we worked so hard, and I fell into bed exhausted every night. But it felt good, it really did. I loved waking up early and getting outside before the sun melted away the valley fog that hung between our hill and the next ridge. The dew-covered grass and the green tones of the garden plants coming to life in the flat light of early morning made me feel like I was witnessing something miraculous; a new world, a new chance.

"It's hard work, but it feels good." I was getting ready for bed, taking off my jeans and pulling on a flannel nightgown. "Like things are starting to come together."

David was lying under the covers. "Yeah, it's been groovy, but there's so much to do. I don't know how…"

He was such a worry wart. "In another month or so we'll have more help than we can handle. Everybody from the city will be up here," I reassured him.

"But there's stuff that just can't wait. We've got to finish the planting now, or we'll be too late."

Sometimes his negativity really pisses me off.

THE BIG ROOM DOWNSTAIRS, the one where the wall between the kitchen and parlor had been torn out, was the center of our lives. The sink was full of dishes and the rhythmic chopping of a knife evinced Nancy's presence. More often than not she took charge of the evening meal that brought us all to the table when she rang the old school bell hanging from a rafter on the porch.

We all straggled in from one corner of the property or another, where we might have been working in the garden, stacking wood, feeding chickens, gathering herbs, or daydreaming in the upper pasture. Everyone grabbed a bowl from the counter and lined up to fill it with rice and beans topped with cheddar cheese—grated ends and leavings from the local creamery.

We sprawled out in the room, some seated around the kitchen table, others on the couch and in chairs, the fire in the kitchen stove cutting the chill that came with the evening. The room grew silent as we tucked into our bowls.

"Hits the spot!" Brian rose from the table for another serving.

"Yeah? I'm getting a little tired of it." Jason stared into his bowl. "What is this? Rice and beans the fourth night in a row?"

"Fuck you!" Nancy exploded. "If you don't like it, you cook for a dozen people! What is it you're doing all day, anyway? You know, it's not like I've got a lot to work with. You want to be in solidarity with the Third World? Well here you go!" She shoved his bowl of rice toward Jason.

"You get to play outside. I'm stuck here in the fucking kitchen all day and it's not fair. You think I can't pound a few nails? Or dig a fucking ditch? Not exactly skilled labor. I'm sick of this crap!"

"But…" Jason began to protest.

"But what?" Jill was at the counter. "Nancy's right, this is a bunch of sexist bullshit! How come it's always the girls in the kitchen?? If we're really trying to become new men and women, we should switch things up. Let the guys cook and clean, we'll work in the woods and do the building."

"Jill," my voice was tentative. "Do you really think you're strong enough to…?"

"Oh, fuck you, David!" Jill flushed with anger. "We're done. If you want dinner tomorrow, cook it yourselves!"

Jill was all about challenging the status quo, questioning the way things were. It was one of the things I loved about her. She moved through life with a level of self-confidence that allowed her to never question herself, something I found truly remarkable. She had a level of self-assurance I could only imagine, at ease anywhere.

The one time my father met her he said, "Dave, my boy, you're batting way out of your league." And he was right. Private school? The best. Top of the class? Of course. Prettiest girl at school? Sure. Star athlete? Tennis. Editor of the school paper? Duh!

But it didn't end there. She was left-wing royalty. She grew up on Central Park West in a nine-room apartment in a pre-war building, her father a crusading lawyer, defending anti-war activists and Black Panthers, standing up to the man, friends with Leonard Bernstein and Ossie Davis. It seemed like she belonged anywhere she went, and charmed anyone who met her. I honestly couldn't figure out why she was with me.

I had seen her face down the campus cops at the Dean's Office, and speak out trying to organize a union for the maintenance staff. She was fearless and passionate, able to fully commit to a cause.

I envied her ability to make an unreserved commitment. I was more ambivalent. I held back, often felt conflicted. I was slow to decide and slower still to act. Oh, I could get caught up in the moment, but my enthusiasm usually faded to questioning, while she could fully enter into things.

I knew there was no point in further discussion, her ire was up, and she wouldn't back down, so I resigned myself to a day of cooking and cleaning. And, I had to admit she was right. The old ways had been so easy to fall into. We had to become different people if this was going to work. That was the whole idea. We had to break out.

And it was also true that some people worked more than others. We identified priorities together, but it seemed like everybody ended up doing, or not doing, what they thought was important. I was sure we could have gotten a lot more done if we worked in a more coordinated way. But what the hell, things were happening—lots of projects, and part of it was not wanting to have a boss, or be a boss. Everyone was their own boss. That was the way it should be. Do your own thing.

The garden was mostly my project. We were totally screwed if the garden didn't come through. We were depending on it so we would have something other than rice and beans to eat, and we were counting on it to provide food for the city. It was one of our reasons for being here. But I worried that no one else took it seriously, and it felt as if, after an initial burst of enthusiasm, we were falling behind, like others had lost interest. Yeah, we needed other things too. But a treehouse in the woods? A flower garden?? I worried about it at night, and put in long days, all too often alone, working to prove my fears unfounded.

The euphoria of the first few weeks was wearing thin, and the same kind of conflicts that had led to the breakup of our group in the city had started to surface. Living collectively was hard, and everyone living on top of one another in the farmhouse made it tougher.

Now that it was getting warmer, folks were thinking about private spaces. Bill went to Cambridge and came back with a canvas teepee he and Nancy planned to raise at the edge of the creek. Brian decided to build a cabin out of logs he would cut himself. Becca and Tom had brought up an old army surplus tent they wanted to put up out in the field.

LIFE IN VERMONT WAS different, no doubt about that. I woke up every morning to the sound of birds chattering away outside our small bedroom window. I started to take note, really take note of the weather. I scoured the sky for signs of what was blowing in over the next ridgeline, delighted in the chevrons of geese flying back north as the days grew longer. I waited impatiently for the last vestiges of snow hanging on deep in the woods to finally melt away.

One day Jill and I took a walk down the remnants of an old road leading to a high pasture where Leland and the other local farmers used to drive their heifers in the spring, leaving them there till fall to grow fat on the sweet grass. The field was filling up now with juniper and poplar, natural succession gradually returning field to forest—the story of Vermont.

It was a peaceful spot, perched high on a hillside, looking out over the ancient river, twisting its way through the valley it had cut three million years ago when the rugged hills were young. We sat together on a large rock, a glacial deposit. To our west, the granite cliff up Hardwood Mountain glinted in the sun. Overhead a red-tailed hawk circled, riding the thermals, much to the chagrin of a chipmunk chattering away under our rock.

"Beautiful," Jill sighed as she rested her head on my shoulder.

"Yeah, it's gorgeous, like being on an acid trip or something. I never knew it was like this."

"What's like this?"

"The world, like this, full of trees, and birds, and mountains. I mean I knew in the abstract, but…"

"That's nature," she touched my cheek, "the real world."

I turned toward her. "Yeah, I know. It's just…"

She brushed my hair off my forehead. "You sure know how to kill a romantic moment."

"I'm sorry, I can't help it. It's…"

"Shut up." She looked over and kissed me.

We found a spot in the grass. The wind gusted through the old pasture and the poplars swayed in its wake. She took off her shirt while I undressed. With my help she removed her jeans. We embraced and then lay down together on the grass, warm in the sun and out of the steady breeze that washed the hillside. We made love in the grass with the sun at its zenith.

We lay in each other's arms for a long time, and the sun was on its way toward Hardwood Mountain before we rose and dressed.

She squeezed my arm.

"Yeah, I know." We never really talked about our feelings for each other, we didn't have to.

I LOVE DAVID, I think I have ever since I saw him the first time: tall and thin, with his curly mass of hair, he called it his "Jewfro." He was so serious and smart. That's why it's so annoying. Sometimes I feel like we don't communicate at all. He's always off in his own head somewhere. I feel like I can't really reach him. I mean we're so connected in some ways, but I can't ever get him to talk about his feelings.

It's so frustrating. It seems like everything is an abstraction to him; something to turn over, poke at, measure; not experience. I'm used to it, and it usually doesn't bother me, but sometimes, like today, after we made love. He's so deep in his own head.

UNBEKNOWNST TO US, WE were big news in town, the biggest news in a long time, and our every move was scrutinized and debated over coffee at Johnson's general store, and at the church suppers that enlivened the life of the little town.

The general store was the throbbing heart of the village where neighbors met while pumping gas or buying groceries. Mac Johnson, the store's proprietor, was a gruff man, purveyor of a little bit of everything; canned goods, dairy products, woolen jackets, pack boots, plumbing and electrical supplies, nails, tools, fishing tackle, guns and ammo, and from outdoor pumps, gasoline and kerosene. There was a constant conversation at the lunch counter fronted by a half-dozen stools filled with townsfolk, mostly men, and it always stopped cold when one of us came into the store to make a purchase. I noted two signs in the store's front window the first time I entered. One read "Forget the Dog, Beware of Owner", and the other, "This Property Protected by Smith and Wesson".

The village itself consisted of little more than the store, a small post office, a white clapboard church, and a dozen houses arrayed on either side of the state highway, which cut through what had once been the town green, bisecting the village on its way north to the Canadian border. The majority of the town's three hundred residents lived up in the hills above the river valley where the village was nestled.

Most in town were curious at first, but curiosity soon mixed with hostility and outrage. Leland, however, was our staunch defender in his own taciturn way. He had come to like us, and even respect us. Oh, as far as he could tell we befuddled city youth had no idea what we were doing, but our hearts were in the right place. At first our clumsy attempt at gardening had provided endless amusement for him and Mary, but we had stuck with it.

"At least they're tryin' to work that old hill farm." Leland told them down at the store. "Don't see nobody else round here give a tinker's damn about them old places. Maybe a little foolish, but they're doin' somethin' with the land, 'stead of lettin' it go back to poppels and scrub, and they're not scared to get their hands dirty and put their backs into it either. Wish I could say the same about our own young folks—can't wait to move down country and get away from the old home places. No, they're alright in my book."

His, however, was a minority opinion. For the most part folks were all too ready to gossip and spread rumors. "They're up there runnin' around naked, havin' group sex, and takin' drugs." "The only thing they're growin' up there is a big plot of marijuana." "Bunch of communists, anarchists, radicals, subversives, hippies and foreigners."

After Jill and Suze were spotted skinny dipping in the pond on the first hot day in June by Bobby LeTourneau, as far as the town was concerned, the rumors were confirmed and a steady stream of pickups began to cruise up the hill hoping to catch a glimpse of a naked hippy.

In fact, we *were* running around naked. The privacy afforded by our hundred and twenty acres emboldened us, and on sunny days it was not uncommon for some of us to walk around outside with nothing on but our shoes. We reveled in the freedom and even I began to lose my self-consciousness.

"We're getting in touch with nature, and our own nature too." Jill was never embarrassed by her nakedness. "We're new people, a tribe of lovers, not hung up on all that bourgeois crap; pioneers creating a new world."

And as far as group sex, well, not quite, but we did have a smash monogamy campaign. We worked on it in criticism/self-criticism sessions, understanding how it limited us, and that it was a form of petite bourgeois individualism. Eventually we drew names and posted a list of partners on the refrigerator in order to break the old patterns of codependence.

"I'm not sure how I feel about it. And me and Jason paired up for tonight?" I told Jill the next morning.

"I thought it was groovy, super cool. It felt like we were finally all together. I mean really together."

"Yeah, I guess, I just don't…"

"Oh, don't be like that, Dave. It was beautiful; an expression of solidarity."

"Yeah, but…"

"Fuck! What is wrong with you? You are so uptight!" scolded Jill.

"It's just not my thing."

"You've got to purge yourself of all that individualistic crap. It's just sex, the most natural thing in the world. How are you ever going to make a revolution if you can't handle this. I think you're homophobic! You didn't have any problem sleeping with Suze."

I thought about my experience the previous night.

"What's wrong Dave, don't I turn you on? Is there anything I can do to help?" Suze had had been naked under the sheet. "I'm sorry."

"No," I had told her. "It's not you, it's me. I just, I don't know, maybe I'm just not ready for this level of communal life. I mean I'm into sharing, but…I don't know it's just that I haven't been with anybody but Jill for a long time and I can't help thinking about her and Bill. It's tough for me. I mean you're really attractive and sexy and all, but I can't get the two of them out of my mind."

"It's okay, Dave. We agreed to sleep together. We didn't say we had to have sex. If you don't feel like it, you don't feel like it. I won't tell anyone. Don't worry about it. It feels a little weird for me too."

"Maybe I am uptight," I told Jill. "It just doesn't feel right. I'm not going to do it."

I realized that I wasn't alone in my discomfort when I walked into the kitchen and saw a kind of shyness in the group I had never seen before, a tension that we talked about that evening after dinner, and decided maybe switching partners wasn't the solution after all.

WHY IS DAVID SO fucking uptight? He's just not as open to experimentation as I thought he was. He really has some bourgeois tendencies he has to work on.

MONEY WAS GETTING TIGHT too. "We're running out of cash," Jason said. He was seated at the kitchen table for our regular weekly meeting. "What's up with that?" We had all kicked in whatever savings we had when we arrived in Vermont. From each according to their ability, share and share alike, that was the ethos. We kept our living expenses low; rice, beans, coffee, gas for the cars, a few groceries. But it cost money to start a farm: tools, seeds, fencing, pipe, the truck. The cash had gone fast, out in a river, and only a trickle was coming in.

"It's the smokers." Suze spoke up. "You guys spend more on cigarettes than we do on groceries."

Brian groaned. "What, you want us to quit? It's not that easy!"

"No, but maybe you should roll your own. It's a lot cheaper that way."

"But I like my Camels! What about that fancy tea you buy?"

"Everybody drinks tea." Suze looked disgusted. "There's only four of you who smoke. Besides, that tea is healthy, maybe the only reason we haven't got sick."

"Yeah," Nancy interjected, "the way you guys clean, it's amazing we haven't all got bubonic plague or something."

"Can we get back to the money?" I was concerned. "What are we gonna do?"

"Get jobs?" Tom's voice was tentative.

"Fuck that. We came up here to get out of the system, live off the land, all that. Remember?" Jill was adamant.

"Yeah, but…"

"No, no buts, we really just need to hold out a few more weeks. The garden'll start to come in and we'll have a lot more folks coming up to put cash in the kitty…"

"A lot more mouths to feed."

"I'll get a loan from my parents to tide us over."

"Yeah, that's really living off of the land." Bill laughed.

"Hey, I bet some of us could get food stamps. Lots of the other communes get 'em." Nancy offered.

"But they have kids." Brian sounded skeptical.

"That has nothing to do with it." Jill shook her head. "They're income based, and we don't have any income."

"So now we're going from living off the land to depending on the government?" I was incredulous. "Look, if we put more work into the garden maybe—"

"Food stamps are the least the government should be doing!" Jill was angry. "In a country as wealthy as this…I mean with an equitable distribution of wealth…"

"Yeah! Yeah!" Bill jumped up from his seat. "You're right. We should get food stamps, just to tide us over a rough spot. We're not gonna get dependent on the government. We hate the fucking government, and this will help us subvert it. I love it, the State funding the revolution! Pretty far out, huh?"

"I really don't agree!"

"Oh, get over it, Davey, we're scamming the system!"

"It's unprincipled, it's a total contradiction of what we set out to do."

"Hey, brother," Jason looked at me. "You're right. It is a contradiction, and I don't like it either, but what choice do we have?"

"We can start our own business," suggested Brian.

"Like become capitalists?" Jason snorted.

"No," protested Brian. "A collective."

"Selling what?" Jason asked.

"Our labor," Brian replied. "Odd jobs. There must be folks around here who need help with stuff; cleaning out barns, mowing lawns, raking leaves, painting houses…"

"Hmm…" Jill mused. "Not bad; it might work. I mean it's at least worth a try."

"Yeah!" Suze was enthusiastic. "It's a great idea, that way nobody goes to work for the man. We could do that."

"We can put signs up on the bulletin board down at the post office and the store," I suggested. "Maybe Leland and Mary would take messages on their phone."

In the end we agreed to both offer our services and apply for food stamps.

The odd jobs idea turned out to be brilliant. We started getting calls right away, mostly from old people who needed help with little things around the house; an old widow down in the village who needed her lawn mowed, Calvin, the farmer down the hill, who had us haul rotted manure out of his dairy barn. We got a house painting job that lasted a couple of weeks, then someone hired us to stack firewood.

We usually sent out a crew of two or three on a job, so there were still plenty of us left to work around our own place. We weren't highly skilled, but we were hard workers, and folks got to see that we weren't the drug addled monsters they might have initially imagined us to be. We worked for minimum wage, which was a big help since our expenses were so low, and it helped us make connections with our neighbors. There weren't so many hostile stares and blank looks when we went downtown.

However, when we started using food stamps to purchase milk and butter, that hammered the last nail in our coffin as far as the crowd at the store was concerned. Mac sneered and slid the government coupons across the counter like they were made of human feces. He never really said a word to any of us after that.

Summer 1968

As the summer deepened, more kids arrived at the farm, folks we knew from SDS, friends and comrades, but also people we didn't know, friends of friends, and even some street kids from the Lower East Side who had heard about us. Our original group felt at times like we were under assault; an invasion that set our fragile community spinning into chaos.

"Who the fuck are these people?" I walked downstairs into the kitchen full of the usual suspects, and about a half-dozen others who had rolled in the night before.

"Friends of Bobby's," Jill offered. "They're cool."

"Who's Bobby?" I was not happy.

"You know, the guy who Bill met in jail."

"Oh yeah, Bobby. So now we're feeding his friends too?"

"Well, they just arrived."

"Shit, we can barely feed ourselves!"

"Dave, don't be so uptight. It'll work out. It's all about freedom, and sharing and love, remember?"

"Yeah, I know, I just feel…I don't know, displaced. I mean we worked so hard getting shit together, and now—fuck, I don't even know the names of half the people here. Kind of tough to build a community when there's so much coming and going. And then there's the money thing…"

"You worry too much." Jill touched my arm. "It's cool, you'll see. Just go with the flow. Besides we've got a solid core group, and you know when summer's over most of the others will be gone. This is what we wanted, remember? A refuge, a place people could come to spend time out of the city and get their heads together."

"I guess," I looked around the crowded room. "I just wish they'd, like wash the dishes and clean up after themselves a little."

The farmhouse was overflowing and the desire for personal space took on a new sense of urgency. The commune spread out over the land. The field now sprouted a dozen tents of varying configuration, pup tents, army tents. Doug's teepee had a prime spot near the creek, or at least it had seemed like a prime spot till it was flooded out by a heavy rain at the end of June that left all of his and Betsy's belongings soaked. The tree-house was finally finished. Ezra and Kristen, a young couple from New York with a three-month old baby girl, the collective's first child, took up residence twenty feet off the ground in the welcoming branches of a hundred-year-old maple.

Carly, an old high school friend of Suze's, decided to build a stone house using a technique for forming the walls she had read about in a book by Scott and Helen Nearing. She scoured the land for suitable stones and enlisted a crew to help her haul them to her building site. Brian's half-built cabin in the woods was joined by a couple of lean-tos and a shack made from scrap wood with the hoods from several old cars pieced together to serve as a roof.

I was all about the work. In addition to my time in the garden, where I had a constant struggle trying to recruit helpers, I knew a little about tools from hours spent working in my parents' hardware store back in the Bronx after school and Saturdays when I was a kid. I had always loved sitting behind the counter, weighing nails, restocking shelves, whatever. I was no expert. In fact, I knew almost nothing, but it was more than anyone else, and, much to my surprise, I quickly became the go-to guy for all things building related.

I secretly took pride in my role, but it was a great relief to have Leland nearby. Leland had done nearly everything at one time or another— building, plumbing, wiring, auto mechanics. He was my guru, always there with support, and advice. His barn could be counted on as a repository of the right tool for the job, no matter how specialized or obscure, and it remained a source of wonder for me.

Despite feeling there was never enough time to do everything that needed doing, I was still trying to get to know the land. I took occasional walks with Leland, always accompanied by Ranger. The pup loved running ahead and pursuing the scents that wafted his way, but checked back regularly to make sure I was still there.

"He's gainin'," Leland stroked the dog's gray fur. "Must be fifty pounds or so already."

"Uh huh, and he's only five months old." I looked at the dog's broad chest and smooth flanks. "I'll bet he gets up over a hundred."

"No doubt." Leland scratched behind the dog's ears.

We were walking down an old road, more of a path really, an old logging road kept open by constant use over the years as the route over Hardwood Mountain to the lakeshore and Canada beyond. It cut through a thick grove of maples. Their crowns reaching for the sky made it feel almost like a tunnel and there was something calm, grand, and mysterious about it.

"You know this path was part of the Underground Railroad back before the Civil War." Leland stepped over a tree that blocked the trail. "Hmm, have to do a little clearing, I guess."

"You're kidding!" I looked at him wide eyed. "I didn't even know there was an Underground Railroad in Vermont."

"Oh, Mr. Man, are you foolin' me? More abolitionists in Vermont than anywhere. Why, we were the first state to ban slavery, right in the state constitution, from the very start. Not to say there weren't some who opposed the idea though. Always some folks too nasty or stupid to see what's right. They had to be careful. It took some courage to stand up.

"Why over to Canaan, just across the river in New Hampshire, abolitionists started a school. Taught white students right alongside the Black ones, and oh Mr. Man, they didn't care for it at all. Them that were against it came one day with ten teams of oxen, pulled the school right off its foundation, dragged it down Main Street and left it lying in the middle of a field. The Noyes School, it was called.

"And that's not all. Why they'd break up meetings if there was talk of abolition, contact slave catchers if they got a whiff of any Black folks in the area. Made life pretty tough for the anti-slavery folks. Took a lot of gumption to stand up to 'em, I'll tell you that.

"And my grandparents, well, that house where you live, that old farmhouse was the last station on the road north—we're only couple miles from the border here. One of the trunk lines out of Hardwick. They came across the Connecticut from Lyme, New Hampshire over to Newbury, then to Hardwick, Craftsbury, Albany, and then up here. Ought to have a plaque or something. You can bet my Grandpa and Grandma was anti-slavery, and it wasn't just talk with them. They helped dozens of people down this path.

"It's all recorded in the family bible. And there were slave catchers who'd come up here looking for them, after the Fugitive Slave Act especially. The stories I heard growing up…why you wouldn't believe what those people endured. Grandma told us about the scars she saw on folk's backs, from the whipping. And the fear, right up until they crossed that border into Canada, that somebody was gonna come and take 'em back."

"Far out! I had no idea!"

"Oh yes, sometime I'll show you the little secret room in the basement where they'd hide 'em, and the tunnel that came out behind where the barn used to be.

"Path has been there a lot longer than that though." Leland stopped and looked as Ranger came bounding out of the woods towards us. "Been there forever, old Abenaki path. They were real active around here. Had a big village down the other end of the lake. And after that, smugglers, always been a lot of them around here, from way back in the olden times right through prohibition. Still a bit today too, I'd imagine." Leland's eyes twinkled under the brim of his John Deere cap.

"Bootleggers, huh?"

Ranger's nose twitched and he ran off into the woods again. We watched him go.

"Oh yes! Mister, but that's a whole other story. Lots of action up and down this little trail over the years." Leland chuckled.

Ranger, somewhere down the path, barked, a high pitched, excited bark, like none I had ever heard from him before.

"Sounds like he's onto something." Leland turned in the direction of the noise. "Let's go see what he's got."

We followed the sound of the dog into the woods, and after several minutes found him circling the base of a large hemlock, howling. I looked up and saw nothing.

"Treed him a big one!" Leland was staring up into the tree. "Didn't know you trained him to hunt 'coon."

"What?"

"Up there" Leland pointed about twenty feet up into the crotch of tree.

I called Ranger to me. "It's okay boy. Calm down, it's all right." The dog danced away from me and resumed barking.

"Good thing he didn't run into him down by the pond."

"Why is that?" I looked at Leland.

"Nothin a 'coon likes better than to get a dog to chase him into the water. Gets him in deep enough, then the 'coon'll turn on him, get right on top of the dog and drown him. I've seen it happen, even with a trained 'coon hound, get so excited by the chase."

"Come, Ranger! Here, boy!" When he came, I took him by the collar and began leading him away from the treed raccoon. Ranger strained toward the hemlock, but I was insistent, and the dog finally accepted his fate and followed us back to the path.

The next day I asked Leland to show me the hidden room. He led me down the steps to the basement of the old farmhouse. It had a dirt floor and a low ceiling. A single light bulb hung swinging from one of the central beams gave little illumination and cast ghostly shadows. The foundation was made from dry-laid fieldstone. Along one end there was a row of wooden shelving filled with old canning jars and wooden crates. There was a large ceramic crock sitting in front of the end section of shelving.

"Salt pork," said Leland, nodding towards the crock. "I used to love my salt pork and milk gravy when I was a boy."

He moved the crock away from the shelf, and then swung the last section of shelving out from the wall, revealing a small room, maybe six-by-six hollowed out and lined with fieldstone. At the far end of the little room was a doorway that opened into darkness. There's the tunnel," he said. "Runs about forty feet to the bank the far side of that stand of popples. Used to be a barn out there, but it collapsed back in the thirties. We played in that tunnel when I was just a boy. Shored up by posts and beams, probably collapsed by now, don't know for sure. Haven't been in there since…well I don't really remember when I was last in there."

"But if they heard of slave catchers in the area, they'd sneak 'em out through the tunnel and help 'em down the path, over Hardwood, and across the lake to Canada. Stories I heard from my Grandma, anyway. Got no reason to doubt it."

I walked into the little room and tried to imagine what it was like in those days. I even stooped down and entered the tunnel, feeling the cool earthen walls and walking down as far as the light from the room penetrated. I thought of the courage it must have taken to make the journey into freedom.

NOT LONG AFTER, I had occasion to walk the path again. We made trips across the border with draft resisters on a fairly regular basis, connecting them, via Montreal, with a community we worked with in Toronto. But in June, the Canadians started turning away anyone AWOL. Shortly after the change in policy a guy named Jimmy arrived at our door. He was a skinny kid from Brookline, home from 'Nam to attend his mom's funeral, when he decided he couldn't go back. He was nineteen, but he looked about fifteen, with sandy hair just starting to grow out from his military buzz cut.

He hung out in Harvard Square, and found out about us from a guy we knew from SDS He showed up on a gentle evening in June, with a backpack and a scared look on his face.

"No way I'm goin' back! I don't want to kill nobody. And I don't want to get killed. I saw too many of my buddies go down. No way I'm goin' back there, and I sure as hell ain't goin' to Leavenworth, so I figured why not Canada?"

We made contact with our friends in Canada, and then a few nights later, set out down the path. A sliver of moon was high in the night sky as I led Jimmy to the edge of the woods, where the path became a dark tunnel through the trees. I clicked on a flashlight. "Stay close, we can use the light in the woods, but once we get to the lake, we're going to have to be careful. There's people staying in those cabins this time of year, mostly on the weekends, but you never know. They'll come get you in a canoe, less visible, no noise. You'll be just fine."

Jason, Jill, and Suze had accompanied us to the edge of the woods.

"Good luck!"

"Be careful!"

"Bon voyage!"

Their voices were full of good cheer, but I swallowed hard as we entered the path. Who knew what waited on the other end? It was just me and Jimmy, who stumbled over a root and grabbed my shoulder to steady himself.

"Take it easy," I turned to him. "We've got a couple of miles to go and it would be pretty tough with a sprained ankle."

I was concentrating on the path ahead, trying not to think too much about the crossing. It was unusual, but we had seen a launch from the Customs Service out on the lake once, and Fish and Game was sometimes out there checking fishing licenses. It was unlikely at night.

We walked on in silence. A pine bough whipped Jimmy in the face after I brushed it on my way past. The path steepened as it climbed Hardwood Mountain, switching back and forth, following a ridge when it reached the steepest section. Then the woods fell away and we scrambled across a field of scree and boulders that guarded the upper reaches of the slope. I felt a breeze cool my brow as we emerged into the open, and then paused to rest on a ledge of rock where we had a clear view of the lake beneath us.

We were both breathing hard at that point and Jimmy removed his backpack.

"It's not too far now, just over there." I pointed to the lake. "Another hour, maybe less. And then you've got to paddle across. Ever do any canoeing?"

"Hell no, I was on one of those Swan Boats in Boston Garden once, but that's about it as far as me and boats go."

"No big deal, the guy picking you up knows what he's doing, besides the worst that can happen is you'd capsize, and the lake's not that cold this time of year."

"Yeah, except I can't swim. Never learned how."

"Don't worry, he won't let you drown."

We sat there for a few minutes, contemplating the crossing and catching our breath.

"Ready?" I stood up first.

"I guess." Jimmy rose and we crossed the narrow ridge, then plunged down through the dark forest that framed the path, snaking steeply toward the lake. After the upper portion, the track leveled out and we walked with measured steps, accompanied only by the sound of our own breath.

A fluttering of wings overhead made me duck, then look up in time to see a huge bird flapping down the path six feet over our heads.

"What the fuck?" Jimmy was startled.

"An owl. How out of sight is that?" I laughed. "They hunt at night."

"Cool, who knew?" We walked on.

"So, you got plans for when you get to Toronto?"

"Not really. Not yet. Get a job, I guess, I don't know. But there's no way I'm pickin' up a gun again for Uncle Sam. Fuck that! I figure anything's better than that. I ain't gonna die, and I ain't gonna kill no more either."

"Right on brother! I hear you loud and clear."

We walked on through the night, the path running straight now, crossing a creek on a makeshift bridge made of logs and planks, then following alongside until it emptied out into a small bay on the southern shore. I stopped and surveyed the lake, an empty expanse about a mile wide at that point. On the far shore I saw an occasional light flicker from the little colony of cabins lining that section of the lakefront. I looked farther up the shore, and checked my watch. "They ought to be there." Jimmy just stared out at the lake.

I pointed the flashlight toward the lake and turned it on and off twice. Almost instantly we both saw a flash of headlights from the boat launch in response.

"Guess they made it." Jimmy sounded shaky.

"Guess so." I lit the light and placed it down on the shore. "Don't worry, they'll take good care of you. They're really great people. They'll hook you up; job, house…the works."

"Yeah, I just…I don't know…heavy changes."

"I get it, but you're doing the right thing, I mean what you're doing is important."

We stood there, silent under the sky full of stars while a sliver of moon steadily traversed west. I didn't know what else to say, and Jimmy was working it all out in his own head. A loon called from somewhere out on the lake, and another answered with an other-worldly cackle.

The canoe cut silently through the calm water, and I scanned the lake for a sign of its passage. They were not far off when I first saw them silhouetted against the dome of the sky. The water looked like black velvet, unruffled by the wind, and strewn with the diamond-like reflection of the stars. I shone the flashlight on the little craft and the canoe made straight for us.

The paddler beached the canoe on a gravel spit, got out and walked towards us.

"What's up Jed? You got here, man!" I was relieved. "This is Jimmy."

"Hey." Jimmy stuck out his hand.

"Hey, yourself." They shook. "Grab your stuff and let's get going. The longer we spend out here the more likely somebody'll spot us. Plus we've got a long drive."

Jimmy threw his backpack into the bottom of the canoe, and then I helped to steady it as he lowered himself onto the cane seat at the boats bow. "Wish me luck!"

"Good luck." Jed had positioned himself in the stern, and I pushed them off the gravel back out onto the lake.

"Thanks, man, thanks for everything, and them back at the farm too, everybody."

"Ain't no biggie. Good travels! Thanks, Jed." I stood there watching until the shadow of the boat merged into the velvet lake, and then I turned back home.

Zion Farm, that's what we call ourselves, make a point of saying that we're a collective, not a commune, in order to make sure were not lumped in with all of the other back-to-the-landers who moved up to Vermont in the last few years, mostly a bunch of hippies.

We're not just up here to grow a few carrots and milk some goats, is the way I put it. We're an island in a sea of oppression—personal space to be free and create a communal utopia, modeling how everything will be after the revolution, sure. But that's not enough. The way I see it we have to be the vanguard of the revolution, the pointed end of the spear, plugged in, putting it all on the line. Otherwise the whole country thing is, like, really, on a certain level, a cop out, petite bourgeois individualism.

I constantly remind us that we're here to serve the movement: R&R for burned out activists, getting draft resisters to Canada, veggies for peace, whatever we can do. The farming thing is cool too, though some of the others shy away.

"You are what you eat!" We can't let the system define us. Food is a basic right. If they control it, we're screwed.

We're building a new world on the corpse of the old, hollowing it out; one more way to bring the change we know is coming. It just makes sense.

I WAS TOTALLY CAUGHT up in the community, despite my innate ambivalence. Being together on the land was incredible. No confining grid or cookie cutter houses, nothing but open space, trees and fields, views like a postcard, the night sky filled with more stars than I'd ever imagined. And my friends—family really, brothers and sisters—beautiful, giving, sharing, loving.

I know it sounds sappy, but it really was about love. That's what it came down to—loving each other. I really felt it on the land, sharing a joint down by the brook in a circle standing naked, passing the weed like it was some kind of ancient sacrament.

Jill woke up on the Fourth of July excited. "Get up!" she shook me. "The parade starts at ten, and we don't want to miss it!"

"Parade?" You mean you want us to buy into that yankee-doodley bullshit? Sorry, but I don't do flag worship."

"No, it's not like that. It's different up here. I used to go sometimes when I was a kid. Small town; fire engines, kids on bikes. Nothing militaristic or anything. Really cute, kinda cool."

I groaned. "I don't think so."

"Oh, come on, you'll love it."

I turned to my side in bed. "You're serious about this?"

"Totally! Honest, you've got to see it. It's great."

"Oh, what the hell. If you insist." I rose, pulled on a pair of jeans and we headed down to the kitchen together, where Suze was standing at the cook stove folding an omelet in a large cast iron frying pan. Jason, Brian, Mia and a kid who called himself Sunshine were seated around the table drinking coffee.

"Are you all coming to the parade?" Jill poured herself a cup from the pot that sat on the counter.

"What parade?" Brian looked up, from a months-old copy of *Rolling Stone*.

"It's the Fourth of July! Downtown, in the village. It's really far out, like nothing you've ever seen." Jill's enthusiasm was unrelenting. "Me and Dave are going."

"Why not?" Suze flipped the omelet. "Count me in."

"Sure, I could use a break." Jason looked around the table. "What the hell, let's go." The others at the table agreed. Suze served the eggs and after wolfing down breakfast we loaded into the Volvo wagon and drove down the hill.

The state highway was already lined with parked cars and a sheriff's deputy directed us to the ball field at the edge of the village where we left ours.

"Shit, I didn't know the town was this big. There must be a couple thousand people here." Jason surveyed the crowd lining the highway along the parade route that ran from the fire station at one end to the ball field at the other.

"Folks come from all over for this. It's a big deal." Jill spotted Leland and Mary, seated in folding chairs across from the post office. "Let's go over there." As we made our way through the crowd we were followed by silence, curious looks and hostile stares. There was a group seated on the porch of the general store, gathered around Mac, the store owner, that glared at us with particular intensity, and then began talking among themselves.

"Hi, Leland! Hi, Mary!" Jill shouted and waived, trying to appear oblivious to the attention directed at us.

"Well, hello neighbors!" Mary called out, and embraced Jill when she drew close enough. "Don't mind them." She waived her hand at the crowd. "You're just something new and different, and they don't see a lot of that around here."

The parade began with a ragtag marching band dressed in blue jeans and plaid shirts. "The Hobo Band," Jill explained to the others. "They practice all year in the fire station for this."

The band was blaring out some Souza tune as they marched. Three ancient men dressed in antique military uniforms followed them. The one in the middle carried a flag and the other two shouldered rifles. Half way down the route they stopped, raised their guns, and fired into the air. The crowd burst into applause.

"I thought you said they weren't into military crap." I glared at Jill.

"Oh, come on, those guys must be ninety years old; practically Civil War vets." Jill laughed.

"Actually, Spanish American War." Leland had been listening.

"Yeah," Jill looked triumphantly at me. "And besides, that's the last of it."

She was right. A dozen kids riding bikes decorated with red, white, and blue bunting followed the veterans' contingent. There were little ones, two- or three-year-olds on tricycles with their parents beside them and older kids riding in circles as they made their way towards the ball field. A line of antique tractors came next: John Deere, International, Massey Fergusson. The drivers of the tractors were throwing pieces of penny candy as they popped and clattered down the road, and kids were rushing to see how many pieces they could gather up.

The local 4-H club followed on a float pulled by a tractor—a hay wagon full of fresh bales and overflowing with kids tending baby calves, piglets, chicks, and bunnies. "Now you've got to admit, that is cute!" Jill's eyes sparkled as she elbowed me in the ribs.

Then came the politicians, marching with banners identifying themselves and waving to the crowd; state senator, local representative, county attorney.

"Holy shit! That's the governor." I recognized him from news photos. "What's he doing here?"

"Vermont politics is up close and personal," Leland frowned. "He's just puttin' in an appearance to remind us he's still around. Easy to forget, so little gettin' done in Montpelier these days. Damn Republicans!"

Then came the antique cars, mostly Fords; Model A's and Model T's, chugging down the line, their drivers also dispensing candy to the waiting kids, whose attempts to gather it up were increasingly frenzied.

The creamery, based one town over, and the mainstay of the few surviving dairy farmers, had one of its milk trucks, polished stainless steel tank shining in the morning sun, creeping along the parade route. The driver was tossing out small, pre-wrapped pieces of the white cheddar that was their main product as he made his way through the crowd.

A group of riders on horseback followed, some of the horses a bit skittish as they pranced down the road.

The rear was brought up by a half-dozen fire trucks from the volunteer fire departments of the surrounding towns, the end of the parade signaled by a sustained blast from our town pumper.

"That's it?" I was disappointed "That's the whole parade?"

"What did you expect? I told you it was cute and small town." Jill glanced over at me.

"Yeah, but...I guess I just figured there'd be a little more."

"I think it's great!" Suze was enthusiastic, as usual.

"Yeah, it was great. I just thought, you know, the Fourth is such a big deal…"

"It is a big deal! This what a big deal looks like up here." Jill brushed her hair back.

The crowd that had lined the highway was breaking up now, slowly moving in the direction of the ball field, where the parade had ended. The volunteer fire department was holding a chicken barbeque there as a fund raiser. The Hobo Band had regrouped and was working its way through a medley of Beatles songs; the tunes were barely recognizable. Tables were set up on the field's perimeter where folks were selling crafts and produce.

Mary and Leland folded up their chairs. "You comin' to the barbeque?" Mary looked at Jill.

"I don't think so. We've got lots to do at home." Jill looked at the others who nodded in agreement. "Guess we'll just head back up the hill. Good to see you though."

"Good seeing you too." Leland took Mary's arm, and they turned toward the ball field.

We walked with them as far as the Volvo, then piled in and drove off, slowly making our way through the crowds still on their way to the field until we reached our turn.

With July, the summer began in earnest; mostly sunny days, blue skies punctuated by fluffy cumulus clouds that offered brief respites of shade as they floated past the sun. The coming and going was constant, as a new group of backpack-bearing pilgrims arrived almost every day to replace those who left. Word was out, and Vermont was the place to be that summer; so they came, most just passing through, but a few really looking to sink roots. The floor of the farmhouse was full of sleeping bags every night, to the increasing discomfort of those of us who were actually living there.

"Shit," I muttered under my breath as I picked my way across the room with mincing steps till I reached the kitchen. I poured myself a cup of coffee. "This sucks! I can't even walk to my own fucking kitchen." I was addressing no one in particular, though the table was already full of early risers drinking their morning java.

"Be cool, man," I was advised by a Black kid with a bushy Afro whom I had never seen before.

"Easy for you to say, I actually live here!"

"Me too, man. I arrived last night." He offered his hand. "Lonny,". I shook it.

"I heard there was a groovy scene happening here. What are you all uptight about? Go with the flow brother, this is beautiful, so far as I can tell. I mean we're all brothers and sisters, right?"

"Yeah, right." I turned my attention to my coffee. "What brought you up here?"

"You mean, like, what's a Black man doing up here?

"No…well, maybe, yeah. I mean this whole state is lily-white."

"Uh huh, I noticed. But, you know, it's a long hot summer in the city. And, like the Chambers Brothers say, 'My soul has been psyche-delicized'. So why not, man, I dig this country shit, I really do. And the hippy chicks are alright too."

"Well, welcome to Zion Farm."

"Thanks. So what did you say your name was?"

"David, I'm one of the folks who started this place, back in the spring."

"Far out! An originator." Lonny ran his fingers through his Afro. "So what needs doing?"

"Doing? Everything!"

"Cool, I came here to work, you know. I'm no freeloader, so point me in the right direction."

"No shit? Right on! I've been waiting for you to show up all summer!" I laughed. "Want to help out in the garden? There's a shitload of work to do."

"Hell yeah! I'm down! Bring it on!"

"Let me finish my coffee and we can head out there." I sipped at my cup.

Lonny and I worked together, weeding all that day and the next as well, creating a few rows of order amidst the growing chaos of the garden.

"I just can't keep up with the weeds," I wiped sweat from my forehead. "They're winning, and nobody besides you and me seems to care."

"We need a new approach." Lonny was leaning on his hoe. "Turn it into a party or something."

"Yeah, right, a weeding party. That will go over real big."

"Why not, man? Get some music out here, make it fun. Everybody'll turn out. Have a picnic lunch, make it like one of those old time barn raisings, you know."

"Well, nothing else has worked. It might be worth a try. I'm feeling desperate. If we don't get on top of this soon, we might as well give up."

At dinner that night I announced a weeding party for the next day.

"Sounds cool!" "Count me in!" "I'll be there." "Me too!"

The next morning Lonny and I stood alone in the garden looking at the long rows, carrots, peppers, tomatoes, and brassicas, choked with witch grass.

"What a fucking mess!" I was discouraged. "Where is everybody?"

"Yo bro, don't get upset." Lonny put a tape in the portable cassette player he had brought out from the house. Wilson Pickett's "Mustang Sally" blasted through the still morning air. We picked up our tools and started weeding.

Suze and Jill were the first to arrive, and we put them to work among the rows of cabbage, poor stunted things just starting to head-up and overshadowed by weeds. Brian was the next to wander over.

"Ready to go?" I offered him a hoe.

"Sure," Brian took it, laughed and waded into the sea of weeds.

As the sun rose higher, others joined us. Lonny played DJ, following Wilson Pickett with a set by Marvin Gaye. Suze and Jill started to dance to the beat, and the vegetables were emerging from the weed filled rows. Others caught the spirit and soon the garden was full of gyrating workers. At noon we took a break and feasted on fresh-picked salad, homemade bread, and hunks of cheddar cheese. Maia brought out a huge Ball jar full of iced tea.

After lunch, as the sun grew hot, our energy began to peter out. Folks drifted off to rest in the shade or take a dip in the pond. But when I surveyed the garden I was pleased to see that we had made substantial progress, and for the first time in weeks I could look at it without feeling panic or frustration.

"Hey, man," I turned to Lonny, "you were right! It worked, we actually got something done out here today."

"Yo, what did I tell you? You got to have a little faith in your fellow man. You know what I'm talkin' about?" He raised his palm.

"Right on!" I slapped him a high five.

Building on the energy that we had marshaled through the garden party, folks got on board and we managed to keep the weeds mostly at bay for the rest of the summer.

LELAND AND I WERE walking through the woods. Ranger ran up and down the logging road, chasing scents borne by the wind that cut across the ridge, blowing north toward Canada.

"You ever think about leaving here?" I looked toward Hardwood Mountain.

"Crossed the line to Canada a bunch." Leland scratched his nose. "Like it well enough, but it always felt mighty good to get home."

No, I mean moving away; really away, like a city, New York, San Francisco…"

"Went to Boston once, saw a Red Sox game at Fenway. That was something; Ted Williams hit a home run. Didn't much care for the city though. This is my place, in my blood. Don't think I could ever really live somewhere else."

"Must be nice."

"What's that?"

"Feeling like you belong somewhere." I stared off into the woods.

"Everybody belongs somewhere." Leland paused. "But sometimes it takes a while to find out where."

The more I talked to Leland the more I discovered what we had to do, and do soon. I was seduced by the run of dry, sunny days that had begun in late August, but Leland, in his laconic way, kept reminding me that a change was not only coming, but soon. Over the course of several days he handed me these nuggets: "Most years we've had a killing frost first full moon in September, but sometimes it comes sooner." "Usually cut my firewood the winter before I burn it so it can dry out." "Last time we lived in that house, we'd burn through ten, twelve cords depending on the winter."

I realized there wasn't all that much time left. We had to start harvesting, even though it wasn't yet September. Leland said we were due for a frost soon. Warm sunny days kept coming, and it was easy to believe they would go on forever, or at least another month or two. I knew better intellectually, but I couldn't bring myself to pick the tomatoes just yet, with so many still green on the vine. And the good weather hung on.

The garden was my pride and joy. Despite our ignorance we had managed to make it work. We not only fed ourselves on fresh beans, peas, carrots, broccoli, onions, squash, and potatoes, we managed to send a couple of vans full of produce down to New York for the Panther's free-lunch program over the course of the summer. Now we needed to bring in the rest of the crop—tomatoes, peppers, cabbage, brussels sprouts, winter squash, and more. We had been canning all along and the pantry shelves were full of Ball jars waiting to be joined by tomato sauce, apple sauce, and other seasonal delights. Our root cellar was full of potatoes, carrots, and onions, but no doubt about it, there was plenty of work left to do in the garden. That was my priority, and I recruited whoever I could to bring in the harvest.

"What now?" Lonny asked over breakfast, He looked around, drumming his fingers on the tabletop. The guy was like a coiled spring, always ready to go.

Nobody else responded, so I spoke up. "Well, there's still plenty to harvest and lots of canning and stuff like that. And we better start thinking about firewood, and cleaning the stoves and chimney."

"Firewood?" Brian looked alarmed. "How much firewood?"

"Well, Leland said we should figure on twelve cords or so. A pile four feet high by four feet wide by eight feet long. Twelve of 'em."

"Twelve cords! That's a fucking mountain of firewood. What an operation."

"Yeah, that's why I was saying we need to get started soon."

"I don't even know where to start." Jason chimed in.

"Leland said he'd help us mark trees, then it's just us and a chainsaw, I guess. How hard can it be?"

"Those saws scare the shit out of me." Suze stepped out from behind the stove.

"Hey, I'll give it a try!" offered Jill. I glanced her way, but decided not to say anything after she narrowed her eyes at me; her "don't you dare" expression.

The firewood was really daunting. I hated to admit it but I shared Brian's apprehension. It was a lot of wood to cut, and not just cut; it had to be split and stacked as well. The cold nights were coming soon and all we had was a little pile of small sticks, good for the cook stove, but not for heating the house. This became clear at the end of the second week in September when we woke up shivering in a cold house and saw frost on the ground.

People started leaving. The thought of winter was enough to send most of the folks who had drifted up for the summer scurrying back to easier berths in the city. Over the course of a few weeks we lost half of our population. I saw it as both a blessing and a curse. We were getting back down to the hardcore, the ten or so folks who were really committed, or had no other place to go. It seemed like a more manageable number to me, and a chance to regain some of the intimacy that we had lost with the crush of visitors and transients who had crowded the place over the summer. Then Nancy and Bill announced they were leaving, splitting up and she was going back to the city.

But on the other hand, between the garden and the firewood we could have used the extra workers. I was frustrated that they had bailed at the first hint that winter was coming, and felt kind of used. Like we had supported a crew of freeloaders all summer long, and now that it was time to get serious, they all left. But there was nothing to do but get to work, so that's what we did.

We had an old McCullough chainsaw that Leland had dug out of his barn. It was big and unwieldy, I thought of it as the yellow monster. None of us had any idea how to work it.

In this, as in so many things, Leland was my teacher. The damn saw was half his size, but with his wiry strength he had no problem wrestling it into submission. He taught me how to change and gap the plug, get the oil/gas mix right, how to tighten the chain, and how to keep it sharp. "Never fight the saw," he told me with a serious tone of voice. "If you're fighting it, it's time to stop and sharpen your blade. Why a good running saw with a sharp blade will cut through rock maple like it was butter."

We spent two days bushwhacking through the woods with a can of blue paint, marking trees to cut. Even though he was in his seventies I had a hard time keeping up with him on the uneven terrain. He was what you would call spry. He tried to explain to me how he knew which trees to cut, but I have to admit I never really got it. Even after two days with him I still couldn't tell the difference between a red maple, a silver maple, and a sugar maple.

"It's not just the type of tree that tells you what to cut, you've got to look at the whole forest; where it needs thinning, what kind of damage is the tree gonna do when it comes down; is the tree sick or healthy? Gets easier over the years. Why I've known a lot of these trees since they were saplings. These woods are like another room in my house, got a real familiar feel to them." When we walked through the woods together, he didn't miss a thing. It was like he actually did know every single tree.

He taught me so much, and not just about the woods. I never met anybody like him. He had a gentle way about him, an almost ethereal sweetness, but he was tough as the granite outcropping that hung above us on Hardwood Mountain. Even at his age he could outwork most men half as old, and most definitely me. And when he spoke about the forest, the surrounding hills and the little village nestled in the river valley it was with a kind of wonder, like he lived in an enchanted world. He saw the life in everything; the grass, the trees; the wind itself was almost an animate being for Leland. He took pleasure in it all, and watching the seasons change through his eyes was like watching a great drama unfold.

The second day we were out marking the trees he told me more about the path that gave us access to the woodlot. "Who knows how old it is. Was here when my folks came up from Connecticut. Abenaki used it to get over Hardwood so's they could get to the river. They had a big village over on the lake, used to hunt and fish this whole area. I found a bunch of arrowheads when I was a kid, though they were mostly growing crops when my people first came up. Took quite a beating in the French and Indian War I heard, Mohawks, Roger's Rangers and all that. But they're still here you know, certain last names, a dark cast to the eyes. Oh, they blended in pretty good; had to in order to survive. But you go down the rec field Fourth of July; Vincent, that old man selling the baskets he made. Why you'll see the same thing in the museum up to the University, exact same thing. They know who they are, though you or me might be hard pressed to tell. I've got some Abenaki blood myself. I could show you in the family bible if you come up the house.

"And speakin' of the French and Indian War, why we had French troops use that path on their way to go raid down country. Some colonel or other under orders from Montcalm himself, marching right on this patch of earth we're standing on. Jeezum Crow, gives me the shivers just thinkin' about it. They were through here during the Revolution too, they'd go down and connect to the Bayley Hazen Military Road."

Leland's world was infused with wonder; history lived for him. It was like he could still hear those Abenaki footfalls, and the boots marching to war. It was almost tangible when he talked about it. All of that was a part of who he was and what this place was to him; a seamless tapestry of history and nature that he embraced in a completely unselfconscious way. I really did envy him.

He bent to examine a shelf mushroom growing out of a blown down trunk. "Think I'll bring that home to Mary, might be gone by, but could be there's still some good eating in there. She'll know for sure. Got a good eye for that sort of thing." He pulled a folding knife out and cut the mushroom free from the trunk, smiling as he slipped it into his pocket Leland took great pleasure in the quotidian.

"Smugglers path after that, anything with a tax or a duty on it, anybody wantin' to get in or out, either side of the border. Started as soon as they set a border. Been going on for a couple hundred years. In that embargo in 1808, why without the Canadian market folks around here would've gone broke. Pot ash, pearl ash, pork, cheese, butter—why they used to bring cattle from Craftsbury, pick up cows all the way north till they had a big herd, drive 'em across the border. Right under the nose of customs.

"And people going both ways as well. Chinese wanting to go down to New York, and escaped slaves…I told you about the Underground Railroad. Folks looking to escape from somethin' or to somewhere always made use of this path. Still do, I imagine." He gave me a knowing look.

When you first met Leland you might think him a little slow, his movements, his speech; he only graduated high school, but he was one of the smartest people I ever met.

I changed the subject. "What about prohibition?"

"Holy Christmas! It was like a war zone all up and down this border! Boats with machine guns patrolling the lake, armed guards at road crossings. Wasn't much they could do about it though, the liquor just poured in like a flood. Too much money to be made to stop it. Pretty much everyone up here at least stuck a toe in. Lots of fellas with farms on the border built line houses, barns that straddled both sides. Booze come in on the Canadian side, came out in the US. Folks packed it through the woods, or drove wagon loads over paths like this one." He smiled, "one fella had a broke down old horse that he'd lead over to Canada, load him up and then turn him loose and let him find his own way home.

"Can't blame anybody. Hard times, though it's always pretty much hard times around here. But this was real bad. Milk prices in the toilet. Couldn't make a nickel farming. No jobs anywhere. Cash money was mighty short. Hell, even I took a job off the farm."

"Doing what?" I asked.

"Might've done a little bootlegging myself back then."

I was genuinely surprised to hear that. Not shocked, or disapproving or anything, but surprised. I guess I thought of Leland as some sort of saint. He seemed so far removed from the dirty reality that most of us experienced. A man in nature, a Rousseauian ideal that I had built up in my head. But reality and people have a way of being more complex than we imagine them to be. "Really?" was all I managed in response.

"Well, like I said, hard times, and there were fellows over to St. Albans, and down to Barre who paid good money for all the whiskey you could bring 'em. The booze that came down Lake Champlain ended up in St. Albans. The whole town was run by gangsters. Why they had the highest murder rate in the whole damn country back then. Worse than Chicago. They were some hard characters.

"But Barre…let me tell you Mr. Man. Everything that didn't come down Champlain, came to Barre. It was a hub. Why any given day there you might see a real big-time, big-city mobster, like Legs Diamond or Lucky Luciano. We brought it in from Canada. Not just me, but lots of folks from up on the border. Then they took the stuff down to Boston or New York.

"Oh Mister, Barre was hopping in those days. Plenty of places to have a drink, or buy a bottle. Not that I went in for that sort of thing much, but I was a younger man then, and I hadn't spent a lot of time in a city like Barre before."

Ranger came tearing down the path toward us with his tail wagging wildly from side to side. He ran past Leland at full speed and nearly bowled him over, then slid to a stop in front of me. "Hey Ranger! How's my boy? How's my good dog?"

Leland gave a low whistle and Ranger swung his head toward him. "Gettin' to be a big fellow. How old is he now?"

"About eight months." Leland was right, Ranger was huge, still skinny and awkward; but big boned and already around ninety pounds. When I looked at him I could clearly see the Great Dane, but the Lab part was just emerging, hinted at by his broad chest. He roamed freely around the farm and in the woods, but didn't normally like to get too far away from me, and this was one of his frequent check-ins.

His fur was gleaming, and his white and black markings stood out sharply against the predominant gray of his coat. His eyes shone and energy seemed to surge through him; he shuddered with delight while I petted him and ruffed the fur behind his ears.

"Handsome animal," Leland observed admiringly. "I like a dog."

"Me too." I responded. And it was true, Ranger was a better friend to me than most people. It was like he could read my moods. If something was bothering me, he sensed it and came over to nuzzle me or lick my face to try to make me feel better. He was always ready to go out with me on a walk or drive. He was loyal and patient. He would sit out on the stoop of Leland and Mary's trailer for hours waiting for me if I was visiting them. He was protective, didn't let any of the other dogs that showed up over the course of the summer near me, or even in the house, almost like he was jealous. He waited every morning at the foot of my and Jill's bed, until I woke to feed him.

I know it sounds weird, like I'm anthropomorphizing him or something, but he was my nearly constant companion, and I swear he did love me. I saw it in his adoring gaze, and the way he came alive when I walked into a room.

And I had a deep and abiding love of him too. I confided in him, complained to him, and all in all probably talked to him more than I did anyone else, except Jill. In a way he was like my therapist or something.

He turned his head and raised his muzzle in the air to catch a scent, and then flew down the path again. I watched him go, admiring his speed and his agility as he suddenly veered off into the woods.

Fall 1968

THE COLORS SEEMED TO COME OVERNIGHT; heather tones, a pallet of pastel pinks, soft ocher, muted yellow; a fluorescence of orange, flaming red, chartreuse, and purple followed a few days later, and suddenly the green landscape was transformed into something else. An endless sea of color unfurled at every roadside, like a living thing expanding with altitude and almost a sense of purpose, to disenfranchise the shades of green that ruled spring and summer and reduce them to a smattering of evergreen; hemlock, spruce and pine that soldiered through the long winter, holding out long after the bright colors had given way to gray.

I had never seen anything like it; the hills vibrating with intensity. Climbing Hardwood one day and looking out, I felt like I was tripping. The pattern of colors unfolding before me was psychedelic,like a page torn from a high-gloss travel magazine, but real. I had seen leaves change color before, but had never imagined a spectacle of this magnitude.

The beauty of fall even brought a few visitors to our quiet corner of the world. Traffic was notably heavier on the state highway, and the cars had out-of-state plates. "Leaf Peepers", the radio called them. Leland referred to them as "Swivel Heads".

The fall was sudden and beautiful, but bittersweet. With the colors came the realization that in a few weeks the leaves would be gone altogether, the trees bare, the fields brown and the woods gray. And our first snow would come not long after that.

It was definitely time to get in the firewood. It was mostly me and, in the beginning, Jason who wrestled with the yellow monster, and we made quite a mess. It took us a while to learn how to fell a tree without hanging it up or dropping it on top of one we had just cut. In fact, we never really figured it out. The saw continued to scare us both, and that was probably a good thing, because it kept us cautious. You had to be constantly aware of what was going on around you or you could get badly hurt. Cecil, an old guy who lived down the hill from us in a falling-down farmhouse, had a hook instead of a hand from a logging accident. The work was hard too, I mean, physically demanding, and I was exhausted at the end of every day.

Typically, I would get up early, eat a big breakfast and try to get out into the woods before eight. The mornings were cold and, more often than not, I would wake up to see frost creeping out from the edges of the panes of glass in our bedroom window. Suze would usually have a big pot of coffee going by the time I got downstairs. Eggs, toast, pancakes, I would shovel down whatever was available, and then make myself a peanut butter sandwich or something to eat on a break. Jason just sat there and drank coffee. I could never understand it, but he said, "I'm not a breakfast person."

Our plan was to drop a bunch of trees, block them up into stove size chunks, split them and then get Leland to bring in a wagon and, after we loaded it all up, haul it back out to the house where we would stack it up to dry, covering it with pieces of corrugated metal roofing that we scrounged from the collapsed barn down the road.

It was easier said than done. Twelve cords is a lot of firewood. It seemed like an insurmountable task, but we kept at it steadily. We took turns dropping the trees, by far the scariest part of the job, though the potential for killing, or at least maiming, yourself was present at every stage of the work. We were both city boys, and, like I said, we never fully got the hang of it.

Then, while one of us ran the saw, trimming limbs and bucking up the logs, the other used the cast iron maul to split the wood. I brought a jug of water out, and we drank a gallon between us every morning. Even on the coldest days we stripped down to T-shirts after the first half hour or so of work. We usually took a break mid-morning, and I ate my peanut butter sandwich.

One morning, about a week into the project, after the break, Jason was running the saw, trimming a limb away from the trunk of a good-sized ash tree we had just felled. He was halfway through when he hit a knot, or something, and the saw kicked back. I heard his scream over the howl of the chainsaw, and when I looked, saw blood coming out of a rip in his jeans. I dropped the maul and ran over to him. "Shit!" He grimaced, tearing away the denim to reveal a gash oozing blood.

"Take it easy, Jason. Let me see." I leaned over to get a better look at the cut. I took a bandanna from my pocket and wiped away the blood. "It's deep, but it doesn't look like you cut an artery or anything."

"Well, it hurts like hell!" His teeth were clenched.

"Let's get you to the house and clean it up." I tied my bandanna around the wound and supported him while he got up. Then he leaned on my shoulder and hobbled back to the farmhouse kitchen. Jill and Suze were sitting there drinking coffee.

"What the fuck??" Jill exclaimed when she saw Jason.

"Chainsaw." I said.

Jill ran to the sink and soaked a clean dishtowel with water. When I pulled the bandanna away and Suze got a look at the bloody gash; she turned kind of green, and sat down. Jill wiped away the blood and examined the wound. "We better get you to the doctor, you need stitches, and probably a tetanus shot too." She bandaged the cut with a clean rag.

The three of us helped Jason while he limped down to the end of the drive and we got in the Volvo wagon and drove him to the ER at the little hospital in Newport. It took sixteen stitches to sew him back together.

The next morning I was back in the woods on my own. What had seemed like a nearly insurmountable task before now took on almost Sisyphean dimensions. I am sure for someone like Leland, who knew what he was doing, it wasn't such a big job, but for me, well, let's just say it was daunting. Twelve cords—a veritable mountain of firewood. I had hoped that Brian would help pick up the slack, but after he saw Jason's leg, he begged off. "I'll help stack it when you get it to the house." He offered.

There was really nothing for me to do but pick up where Jason left off, so I grabbed the yellow saw, that lay where he had dropped it, started it up and finished trimming off the limb that had been his downfall. I worked all morning, slowly and carefully, but steadily, and was depressed by how little I managed to accomplish. At the rate I was working, winter would be over by the time I got in all the wood.

I went back to the house for lunch. "How's it going?" Jill asked when I walked into the kitchen.

"Shitty." I told her. "It's going to take forever if it's just me." I looked past her to where Brian was washing dishes. "I could really use some help."

"Dave, I told you, I'm no good with machinery. I'd just be in your way out there." Brian shrugged. "Sorry."

"I'll be back out as soon as I can." Jason piped in from the couch, where he sat with his leg up.

My frustration was building, but I finished my coffee. "Guess I'll head back out to the woods."

"Why not wait till Jason gets better?" Jill asked.

"We really can't wait. Winter'll be here before you know it."

"But I worry about you, out there all alone with that saw."

"Yeah, me too," Suze chimed in.

"Well, somebody's got to do it, or we're gonna freeze our asses off." I was tempted to give in to their arguments, I don't know if it was a sense of urgency or pure stubbornness that sent me back out, but I left the warmth of the kitchen behind me and walked back down the path.

I had only been working for about fifteen minutes, using the maul to split the blocks I had bucked up earlier, when Jill showed up, wearing one of my flannel shirts and a down vest.

"I came to help." She said. "I don't think I can run the saw, but I can split wood." She walked over to the large piece of rock maple I was using as a chopping block, and reached out for the cast iron maul. "At least let me give it a try."

With some trepidation I handed it over to her and she pulled it back and let fly on a piece of the ash I had cut that morning. The head of the maul bit into it and it split cleanly down the straight grain. "Not so tough!" she smiled over at me.

"Great!" I said. "But, Leland told me to hold it out in front, don't bring it back over your head. Maybe you don't get quite as much power, but it's more accurate that way. Less chance of hitting your foot."

"Okay." She made the adjustment and split another piece.

Though I had my doubts, I was glad to see her. She was game, ready for anything, and not afraid of hard work—one of the things I loved about her. And as the afternoon wore on she proved her worth, working steadily, first taking off the down vest and then stripping down to her T-shirt. She was thin, but solid and I was surprised to see that she was able to more than keep up with me, actually splitting faster than I could saw out the blocks.

"You're better than Jason!" I said when we took a break after the first hour or so.

"I told you I could do it." She smiled over at me. "We're a good team."

I looked at her as a shaft of afternoon light, soft and filtered through the remaining leaves of a maple, illuminated her face and made a halo glow around her wavy auburn hair.

I walked over to where she was seated on a half rotten log, bent over and kissed her forehead, damp with sweat.

She laughed. "What was that for?"

"You really are amazing," I told her. I couldn't be sure, but I think she might have blushed. It was one of those moments when I felt my love for her course through my body like a physical thing. I mean here we were, like a couple of pioneers on the edge of the wilderness, well, except for the chainsaw; just us, up against nature. There was something almost primal about it. I shivered. In those days it felt like we really were pioneers, pushing boundaries, mapping uncharted terrain; doing something old, basic, organic; but brand new at the same time.

I KNOW DAVID DOUBTED I could handle getting in the firewood. But it wasn't as tough as he made it seem. I wish he didn't always assume I was incompetent. He seemed surprised I could do it. I really didn't have any problem with the maul. And splitting wood was kind of fun. I mean it was hard work and all, but also really satisfying. He ran the saw and I split. I kind of got a rhythm going.

We worked together like that for the rest of the day, and when we went home my whole upper body; arms, shoulders, back, was aching. There was still a ton of wood to get in, but somehow, it didn't seem as hopeless as David had made it sound that morning. And I stuck with it the next day, and the next, and the ones after that until Jason's leg healed and he replaced me in the woodlot, and the work was almost done by then.

I wish he wouldn't always assume I'm helpless. I know he means well, but I really hate it.

By the end of October we had most of the firewood in. Leland helped by hauling wagon loads to the house where he showed us how to stack the wood in neat rows that we covered with the old metal roofing we had scrounged. We filled the porch as well, with kindling and some of the more seasoned wood we brought in. The harvest was long over, the root cellar was full, and the shelves of the pantry were packed with cans of tomato sauce, applesauce, broccoli, peas, beans, pickles, and whatever else from the garden. All the foliage was gone, and trees were great gray sticks that revealed the true contours of the forest.

The folks who had come up over the summer trickled away; California, New York, even Lonny left to go back to Boston. I missed him, though I have to admit it was kind of a relief to see some of the others go. They had never really pulled their weight as far as I was concerned.

We still had to get in a couple of more cords to be on the safe side. The *Farmers' Almanac* said it was going to be a cold winter, and, more importantly, Leland concurred. It didn't feel like such a big deal though; Jason and I had a pretty good routine going by then, at least for us, and I figured that in a few more days we would be done.

Snow fell the first weekend in November, not much, just a dusting, but then the trickle of departing folks turned into a hemorrhage. Anybody still living in a tent, a shack, or a cabin in the woods came to the kitchen the next morning to say their goodbyes. Suddenly we were down to just five; me and Jill, Jason and Suze, and Brian. It felt like we were ready for winter, or at least as ready as we could be considering how little we knew of what was really in store for us.

It kept snowing every couple of days all through November. No huge storms, just a steady accumulation; an inch here, two inches there, until there was almost a foot on the ground by Thanksgiving. The days were below freezing, and the nights sometimes went down into the low teens. We had a minimum/maximum thermometer nailed to the post on the porch, and I checked it every morning.

The house stayed pretty warm, but I was amazed by how quickly we were running through the firewood. It was quiet, like we were just waiting. We started playing Scrabble after dinner, just to kill time. I kept thinking I should use the time more productively, reading or writing, but I couldn't tear myself away from the game.

Thanksgiving was like nothing I had ever experienced before. The snow-covered landscape brought alive postcard images, a neighbor down closer to the village even brought out an old horse drawn sleigh. I almost expected a pilgrim to walk out of the woods.

Pine boughs hung heavy with snow, and we huddled around our wood stove and bustled about the kitchen. The cook stove was cranked up and by mid-afternoon we, well really mostly Suze and Jill, cooked a real feast. Occasionally one of us guys would cook a meal, but, despite their protests it was still the women who did almost all of the cooking, and that was the case for Thanksgiving.

We had a fresh turkey from a farm across the valley, mashed potatoes, and creamed onions from our own garden, plus canned broccoli and string beans cooked with slivered almonds, not to mention the pies. We had apple, with apples from our trees, pumpkin, made from one we grew ourselves, and Brian made a pecan pie that was truly over the top.

When we sat down for dinner Jill spoke up: "Before we eat I want us to go around the table and say what we're thankful for."

Brian groaned, "What is this, some kind of a religious ceremony? I'm Jewish, I don't go in for this shit."

"I'm Jewish too," replied Jill, "but this really doesn't have anything to do with religion, it's just about being thankful. Don't you want to give thanks for something?"

"Yeah, I guess." Brian relented, then paused for a moment. "I'm really thankful I'm not having Thanksgiving at home with my family. Uncle Morty would be passed out drunk in the corner by now, and I'd be in the middle of a fight with my father about politics."

We all laughed, then Jill responded. "But you are having dinner with your family. Me too, and that's what I'm thankful for, my family. My real family, brothers and sisters who I chose."

Jason went next. "Yeah, I guess that's what I'm thankful for too, you guys."

We continued around the table and Suze spoke next. "Thanks for the food, fresh, homegrown, local, well mostly. I guess not the pecans," she glanced at Brian, " but we used maple sugar. You guys have been so supportive and great. I really love you."

It was my turn next. "I give thanks for all of you of course, but also for this place. . . just being here. It feels like maybe what America was like a hundred years ago, and that's a good thing. But mostly, I'm thankful for the chance to try to make things better, and to make a difference."

"Yeah, yeah, all that too," said Brian. "Can we eat now?" After that there was a long silence as we tucked into our meal.

After dinner Jill could barely contain her excitement. "I got us a special treat, Suze and I checked out the ski and skate sale down at the school last week, and we picked up some sets of used cross-country skis. Check it out!" The skis had been stored in the basement, and she brought them upstairs to show us.

"Who wants to go out?" She was excited.

Suze was enthusiastic and Jason was down with it, but Brian, as usual when any physical exertion was required, held back.

"I'm ready." I said, "but I've got to warn you, I've never been on skis before."

"Oh, it's easy. You'll do fine." Jill held out a flimsy looking pair of black shoes to me. "Put these on."

I laced up the ski shoes and followed Jill's lead, pulling my calf high wool socks up over my jeans. She led me, Suze, and Jason to the path outside our door, then showed us how to clamp down into the three pin bindings that held our shoes to the skinny skis.

"It's simple really," she demonstrated. "Kick, glide, kick, glide."

At first it felt incredibly awkward. I must have fallen four or five times in the first hundred yards, but after not too long we were all kicking and gliding our way down the path. It was fun, a great way to get out and play in the snow, and good exercise as well, as it didn't take too long for us to all start huffing and puffing. Then we approached our first hill, Jill showed us how to herringbone up, making a V shape, with the tips of our skis pointing outward. Climbing left us all completely exhausted. We stopped just below the crest to catch our breath, and Jason, who was just above us on the trail, started slipping backwards, lost his balance, and knocked Suze into me. All three of us fell down in a tangle of arms, legs, skis, and ski poles. We laughed as we extricated ourselves from the pile, and climbed back up to the hilltop. Jill used a neat kick turn to reverse her direction, but the rest of us shuffled around until we were facing back down the hill.

We looked towards the farmhouse and the rows of snow-covered ridges and peaks that rolled off into the distance. Then Jill launched herself back down the hill with a whoop. Jason followed and almost immediately fell, Suze crouched low on her skis and made it down to bottom.

I swallowed hard and pushed forward, the speed built quickly and I felt like I was flying by the time I made it halfway down, then something happened, I'm not sure what it was, but I lost my balance and tumbled, head over heels into the snow. When I looked up, they were all in hysterics.

"Are you alright?" Jill finally managed through her laughter.

"I guess," I said, "Thanks for asking. Nothing seems to be hurt. Fun!" I said as I picked myself up and dusted off the snow that covered me. "Let's go again."

We spent a couple of hours sliding down the hill, and gliding around on the path and in the field. By the time we got back to the house the afternoon light was fading, but I was feeling a lot more confident and was sold on skiing. It was really great, a whole new way to be outside in the snow.

That night, seated around the table with the others waiting my turn to play Scrabble, I looked around the old farmhouse and realized how much I really had to be thankful for.

IT WAS REALLY A *hoot getting David out on skis, he isn't what I would call a natural athlete; he fell a lot, but he was a good sport about it, and by the end of the day he seemed to get the hang of it. We've really settled in. It feels like family here. Cozy. Maybe too cozy. We're not doing much political work these days. I feel a little guilty about that.*

Winter 1968-69

As THE WINTER UNFOLDED, the pace of our lives grew slower. Patterns developed: feed the stove, clean the house, prepare meals, go skiing, read, play Scrabble. We didn't have any visitors at all, except for Mary and Leland, and not much work either, except for shoveling walks and drives, and, once, after a really big snow, shoveling roofs for a few old-timers down in the village. We made weekly trips to St. Johnsbury, shopping with food stamps at the health food store. The weather started getting colder and in mid-December we had our first below zero night. The house was freezing that morning, with a thin skim of ice in the kitchen sink. The wind was blowing from the north, rattling our thin windowpanes. An Alberta Clipper, Leland called it when he came by to check on us.

"Gettin' chilly out there. Stay warm last night?"

"No," Jill replied, huddled under a blanket on the couch.

"Not surprised," Leland said. "Lots of leaks in here."

"What do you mean?" I asked.

"Air leaks. You never banked the foundation, and these windows of yours could do with a sheet of plastic over them, maybe seal up the bottom your doors too. Make it a lot easier to warm things up in here, save some firewood too."

"How do we bank the foundation?" I asked.

"Well, most folks nowadays use hay bales, but always seemed like a waste of good hay to me. In the olden times we used to use pine boughs, or spruce boughs. Just pile 'em up pretty thick where the foundation is exposed, snow'll do the rest."

Most people would have been shaking their heads by then, amazed by our ignorance, but Leland was endlessly patient with us, though I imagine he and Mary had a good laugh about it when he got home.

His comment about saving firewood had particular resonance with me. I couldn't believe how quickly our woodpile was diminishing, and it seemed like anything we could do to conserve heat should be done. So that afternoon I was back out in the woods again with a saw, trimming off low hanging spruce branches, and hauling them back to the house on the toboggan to pile up against the foundation.

The next day we went to the hardware store in Newport and bought a roll of heavy-gauge plastic to stretch over the inside of the windows, and secure with felt strips we tacked to the frames. It was a milky color, translucent rather than transparent, and when it went up the house got noticeably darker, but a lot less drafty.

I went out skiing almost every day, sometimes with Jill, or Suze and Jason, but often on my own, well, not really on my own because Ranger always came along. He loved being in the snow-filled woods and I liked to take long skis, sometimes up and over Hardwood, all the way to the lake, so he had more scents and tracks to explore. I had picked up a pair of skins for my skis that made climbing easier.

Ranger seemed like he could go on forever. He was in constant motion, disappearing into the woods for ten or fifteen minutes, and then rushing back to make sure I was still there. He must have covered five miles for every one I skied.

It took me the better part of an afternoon to ski to the lakeshore and back, a real workout. But I loved it—the feel of the skis on the snow, the silence of the woods, the fresh taste of the air, the views from the ridge on Hardwood. I even came to look forward to the burning in my legs and the straining in my lungs. The physicality of living in Vermont continued to amaze me. I felt my muscles, my whole body, in a way I never had before.

ONE NIGHT AFTER DINNER we were sitting around the table talking and playing Scrabble. It was about a week before Christmas and it had been snowing steadily for a few days. The moon had just risen, almost full, and bright enough that at least some of its luminescence made it through the cloudy plastic that covered our windows. We had grown used to silence when the night surrounded us, punctuated by the slight hum when the refrigerator turned on, the crackle of a burning log, or sometimes the distant grunt of a truck shifting down to climb the hill north of the village, the night sounds muffled by the snow that covered everything. It seemed to me that we even spoke in voices softer than those we used in the city, evoking the subtle shifts in pitch and intensity of the constant wind that stirred the tree branches and occasionally rattled our thin windowpanes. The quiet was a comfort, not oppressive: it lent solemnity to our daily rituals, gave emphasis to what was said when words were spoken, and helped us to listen, really listen, to each other.

It was still relatively early, though the days were so short now that it was hard for it not to feel much later; by seven, it had already been dark for a couple of hours. The peace of the night was disturbed by a discordant note heard at first from down the hill, but moving towards us. It sounded like the buzzing of angry bees, getting louder as it approached until it took on the high-pitched whine of a two-stroke engine. In fact, it was a half-dozen two-stroke engines.

We looked at each other around the table, puzzled, but no one provided an answer. I stepped out onto the porch, and as I stood there for a minute the whine built to a shriek, and I saw a row of single headlights turn off the road onto the path that ran along the edge of our field. As I stood there I was joined by the others and we all watched as a half-dozen snowmobiles roared past us, leaving the smell of burning oil in their wake.

"What the fuck??" Jason had to yell to be heard. "What are they doing here? Fucking assholes!"

We watched them head up the path, past the house, into the woods, and saw their lights reappear as they went up Hardwood Mountain. Our ears rang from the noise, and the smoke from their exhaust hung thickly in the air. When the last taillight disappeared, we went back inside.

"Wow," said Suze, "that was a bummer."

"Can they just do that?" asked Brian, "I mean it's our property, nobody asked permission or anything."

"Leland said local folks have been using that trail forever." I offered.

"Yeah but we could stop them. Post 'No Trespassing' signs or something." Jason was pissed.

"Let's talk to Leland and Mary about it," suggested Jill. "Maybe we can work something out. I mean, we want to keep good relations with our neighbors, right?"

"Well, I sure as hell don't want to live with that!" Brian was worked up. "I didn't move up here to breathe exhaust fumes. I could've stayed in the city for that."

"I know how to stop them." We all looked at Jason. "String some wire across the path at head height, that'll slow them down."

"Sick! You're a fucking idiot sometimes." Suze glared at him.

"Hey, it was only a joke," Jason insisted.

"Jill's right," I said. "We should ask Leland and Mary the best way to handle it. This could turn into a big mess if we're not careful."

Everyone agreed to seek council before we decided how to deal with it.

We went back to the game; after the last letter was played, folks began to turn in. I was the last one up, and I went out onto the porch to bring in firewood. I surveyed the night, taking in the stars sparkling in the clear heavens, and something else, something new; up on Hardwood's granite ridge a fierce orange glow danced into the sky. A bonfire, no doubt built by the snowmobilers. I stood there and watched for a while, imagining the heat those flames must throw. Then I gathered a load of wood, and left the night and the bonfire for the comfort of the house and my bed.

Later that night I was awakened by the pack of snowmobiles when they passed by again on their way back down the hill. I listened while the scream of their engines receded into the distance, and then I went back to sleep and dreamed of a fire rising into the sky.

The next morning Jill and I walked over to Leland and Mary's trailer. She knocked on the door and Mary invited us in.

"How are you kids doing over there?" She asked. "You staying warm? Can I get you a cup of tea?"

"Oh, no thanks," Jill replied. "We just had breakfast."

We sat down at the small table where Leland was thumbing through a magazine. "Well how's David? How's Jill this morning?" He asked.

"No major complaints," I said. "But did you hear those snowmobiles last night?"

"I guess we did," Mary frowned. "So much for quiet winter nights. They'll be up here making a racket from now till the snow's gone."

"What's up with that?" I asked. "Can't we keep them off our property or something? I mean that noise…"

"Well," Leland thought for a moment. "I guess legally, you could post your land. But I'd advise against it."

"Why?" I asked.

"Be stirring up a hornet's nest," Leland offered. "Wouldn't be seen as neighborly, and I think Mac and his buddies wouldn't be real happy about it."

"Mac, the storekeeper?" Jill raised her eyebrows.

"Yup, that was him and a bunch of the fellas he runs with." Leland explained. "Most every night all winter they ride up and over Hardwood. They go on into Canada, buy some of that Newfoundland Skreech, build themselves a big fire up on the ridge over by the cave and drink themselves silly."

"Newfoundland Skreech?" I'd never heard of it.

"That overproof rum, 151 proof. Illegal over here. Why a bottle of that stuff'll blow up if you put a match too it." Leland rubbed his chin. "I believe they'd be quite upset if they couldn't use that trail. Like I told you, local folks been using it forever. I wouldn't cross 'em, not over something like this. They can get pretty nasty, even when they're sober."

"But it's our land," I protested.

"Yes it is." Leland acknowledged. "But is it worth going to war over?"

"We never cared much for it, any of it, the noise, or those people," Mary frowned. "But we put up with it. We try to be good neighbors. I've got to agree with Leland. I think it'd be a mistake to post, create a lot of ill will in town, and not just with them. It's sort of the principle of the thing. Folks around here don't like it when flatlanders come in and start denying access to their land. Open land is sort of a tradition."

I was frustrated with their response. It really wasn't what I wanted to hear. But, I had to admit that, as usual, their advice made sense. No point in going out of our way to piss people off. We seemed to being doing enough of that without even trying.

CHRISTMAS CAME AND WENT, hardly a blip on our screen. As a household of Jewish nonbelievers, Pagans, and atheists, we studiously avoided making any kind of a fuss. The "Holidays" had always felt so phony to me anyway, so blown up and full of unmet expectations, so fraught with anxiety and guilt; caught up in a false heartiness, and an extreme expression of the commercialism and commodity culture that I abhorred; in short, everything I rejected. Still, there was a part of me that succumbed, and we cut a bough of white pine to stand at the center of the kitchen table as a Christmas tree/Chanukah bush. Suze led us in a ritual on the solstice calling for the return of the sun, and that was about as far as our observance went.

Probably Suze, our resident Pagan, was the most religious person at the farm. Me? Well I had a bar mitzvah, to please my grandparents, but that was the last time I set foot in a synagogue. After my mom died, we stopped eating special meals at Passover and Chanukah. No, I wasn't religious, but I was discovering a kind of spirituality; a hearkening to the wind, the woods, the weather. Not nature worship, but a new appreciation for what was, and a kind of awe for the vastness, the fecundity, the power, and the randomness of it all. I started to understand nature not as some set of external objects; mountains, trees, grass, birds...but rather as an ongoing process, one that I was also part of. I found myself responding physically and emotionally to changes in weather, aware of the quality of light, governed by the length of the day and the direction of the wind. It felt good.

Anyway, Christmas, Chanukah, all that formal, institutionalized crap just seemed false to me, and more alienating than integrating. I was happy to let it all pass by without the fuss. I did call my dad collect from the payphone down in the village to wish him a happy New Year. It had been a while since we had talked. He sounded lonely to me, sitting home watching TV. I felt a moment of guilt when he told me how empty the house felt without me or mom there.

The snowmobilers kept coming, most clear nights and every sunny weekend. Their passage no longer elicited any comments. Sometimes when we were out skiing, they came by. We always made a point of standing off of the trail as they flew past, and occasionally we would get a wave or a nod of the head in acknowledgment. The fumes hung in the air long after the sleds passed. They really were obnoxious, but we came to accept them as just another aspect of rural life.

They didn't all seem to accept us though, once when a pack of them passed instead of a wave or a nod one guy raised his middle finger in salute. It was impossible to tell who it was given the hats, scarves, and goggles, but I thought I recognized those particular sleds as the ones sometimes parked by Mac's store.

"I'M GOING STIR-CRAZY," BRIAN declared.

"You've always been crazy," I laughed. "And besides you're not locked up, you've just got a case of cabin fever." That's what Leland had called it the other day. "You need to get out more."

"Out where? There's nowhere to go."

"You should come out skiing with us," said Jill. "It feels great! Get those endorphins going."

"That's why I smoke pot," Brian said, "gets the endorphins going. Right Jason?"

"Right on, brother!" Jason shot a fist in the air.

"I'm just saying," Jill was unrelenting, "that if you went outside, got some fresh air and some sunlight, you'd feel better. Winter's long here, you've got to get motivated."

"Yeah," said Brian, "I'm getting motivated, motivated to head down to

New York, or Boston; somewhere I can see a stop light, go to a decent book-store, or a movie without it being an all-day outing. I mean, not to suggest that you guys are boring, but how many games of Scrabble can we play?"

"You know, I sort of miss the city too," Suze chimed in.

"So how about a road trip?" said Jason.

"Hell yeah! I'm down. When do we leave?" Jill was excited.

"And where do we go?" asked Suze. "Boston or New York?"

"How about Montreal? It's closest, only about two hours," suggested Jason.

"Cool!" Now Jill was really fired up. "It'll be like going to Europe, they all speak French. Do we know somebody there we can crash with? How about that guy Jed, who helped with the kid this summer?"

"Yeah, Jed's there. I don't know how much room he has, but..." I looked at Jill. "I won't be going. Somebody has to stay and feed the fire."

"And take care of the chickens?" said Suze.

"Shit, that's right," said Jason.

"Hey, I don't mind. It'll be nice to have some time alone."

"I'll bring you back a croissant," promised Jill.

"Won't you get lonely?" asked Suze.

"No. I won't be alone anyway, Ranger will be here with me." The big dog, who had been sitting at my feet, looked up at the mention of his name and began thumping his tail on the floor.

"Well, all right then! Montreal it is!" Brian was elated.

"It'll only be for the weekend." Jill looked at me.

Truth is, I was looking forward to having some time to myself. I loved them all, but sometimes the house did seem really small. There was always someone there. It was different in the fall, before it got so cold. People would hang out on the porch, or around the campfire at the top of the field, but it was mid-February and the temperature hadn't gone above zero for almost two weeks. The piles of snow cleared from the roof stood almost to the eaves, and most of the household only ventured out long enough to bring in a load of firewood. I still went for a ski whenever the weather allowed, but the Alberta Clipper, still blowing down from Canada made it a challenge too many days.

I had seen winter, cold, and snow before, but never anything like this, never anything that even came close. Let them go. At this point the thought of some solitude appealed to me more than the promise of bright lights and big city, even with a French accent.

I DON'T KNOW WHY David didn't come to Montreal with us. It's like he always holds back. Leland and Mary could've fed the chickens. Well, the hell with him!

THE NEXT MORNING, after coffee and eggs they left, laughing and singing "Frère Jacques". I washed the breakfast dishes, loaded the stove, then sat on the couch and savored the silence that filled the house. It made me aware of how full of people my life was. There was always an undercurrent, a constant presence that had abruptly disappeared, and as I took a deep breath I felt its absence, more than I had been aware of its presence. It was as though a sudden vacuum had descended, leaving things strangely still. I was aware of my aloneness in a way I hadn't experienced in the house before.

The emptiness was strange; not unpleasant, but different in a qualitative way: no chatter, no banging pots and pans or running water, no music from the radio, no laughter or drama, nothing but me breathing in and out, aware of the heat radiating from the wood stove, and the sense of calm that settled over me. I picked up *Ecology and Revolutionary Thought*, a pamphlet I had been meaning to read, but I put it down after a few minutes and just sat there, soaking up the solitude and wondering what it had been like for Leland, growing up in this house.

He never mentioned it, but it must feel strange to him, having a bunch of longhairs in his ancestral home. It surprised me that he didn't resent us, and seemed not only accepting, but welcoming. From the stories he told, I gathered it was a different world when he was a kid; a working farm was a busy place. But no electricity, not even a single paved road in town back then, more like the nineteenth century than the twentieth. As isolated as we often felt, we were way more connected to the outside world than he was, but I never got the sense that he or Mary were aware of any deprivation, they had just lived their lives, and that was the way things were. They took pleasure in the little things; simple things like feeding the birds and walking in the woods. They reveled in each other's company, an occasional chat with a neighbor their only relief. Self-reliant in so many ways, including emotionally, they depended on no one but each other.

I contrasted their reality with ours, our constant need for distraction, companionship, action, for a sense of engagement with something bigger than ourselves. Maybe it was generational, I'm sure that was a part of it, but the difference was also situational; they only knew the life they had lived in Vermont, on this hill, with each other. Not that we were so sophisticated, or cosmopolitan, but we had seen so much more; been made aware of larger concerns, had our noses rubbed in modernity in a way they never had. It enabled Leland and Mary to be grounded and secure in a way we weren't, and probably never could be.

Interesting to think about, how really being of a place made such a difference. Compared to them, we were transients. Thinking back, I realized that this was the sixth place I'd lived since graduating from high school. No wonder I had never felt a sense of place before, a connection to a natural community. It was largely a function of time, but also commitment, I found it took a conscious effort for me to tune in to the eternal world; the forest, birds and animals that constituted the overwhelming reality of Vermont. I was so conditioned by the built environment, the constant distraction provided by the city, the selective inattention required for urban survival, that it took a while for those habits to fall away and allow me to really become aware of what was going on around me.

The solitude settled on me like a fog creeping in on a sultry summer evening, soft and comforting; something about it seemed inevitable, natural, like a visitor I had been waiting for my whole life. Ranger noticed it too. He sighed deeply and rested his head on my knee.

The few days they were gone passed quickly. I kept the fire going, fed the chickens, cleaned the house, read, and finally got some writing done, an essay about Marcuse. One day I made a peanut butter sandwich, loaded a thermos full of hot tea into my daypack and bundled up to brave the frigid weather and venture over Hardwood. Ranger was thrilled and his whole body quivered in anticipation as I laced my boots and stepped into my skis.

It was one of those gorgeous mid-winter days I had come to love, hovering around zero, but the Clipper had fallen off and the sun was bright in a pure blue sky, free of clouds all the way to the horizon. With Mansfield and Camel's Hump visible, snow-capped and shimmering off in the distance to the southwest, and the Presidentials floating in the sky above the hills rolling off to the southeast, the view from Hardwood's granite ridge was spectacular, and well worth the climb. I sat in the sun, eating my sandwich and taking it all in.

Right behind me, near the entrance to a shallow cave, I could see the circle of stones that served to contain the bonfire built by the snowmo-bilers on their regular visits to the ridge. The area was littered with empty liquor bottles. It bothered me to see the bottles lying in the pristine snow. I picked one up and looked it over. *Newfoundland Skreech* it declared, a yellow label on a green glass bottle smelling more of turpentine than any rum I had ever drunk. *151 PROOF*. There were at least a dozen empties scattered around the fire pit.

Ranger was off in the woods higher up the mountain. I could see his trail in the snow where he had entered the forest. When I finished eating, I called out to him, packed up my garbage and a few of the empty bottles of Skreech, all that I could fit into my daypack, and headed back down the mountain.

Not far from home I heard the whine of an approaching snowmo-bile, and as it grew louder, I skied over to the side of the trail to allow whoever it was to pass.

It was a big yellow Ski-Doo, like the one that had given me the finger that other time. As it approached, it seemed to me the driver steered towards me and gunned the engine. I had to throw myself off of the trail into the woods to avoid being hit. He sped away, and as I dusted the snow off I imagined I heard laughter above the snow machine's roar.

When the sled disappeared down the trail Ranger loped out of the woods. He sniffed the air and gave me a look of concern, cocking his head to one side. "It's alright, boy," I reassured him as I brushed the last snow from my plaid wool jacket. "Just some jerk." It was easy enough for me to dismiss the incident to the dog, but I kept thinking about it for the rest of the day. It pissed me off. I could have been hurt. Were they sending some kind of message? Who would do that?

Jill and the others got back from Montreal the next day around noon.

"How was it?" I asked.

"Ooh la la!" Jill laughed. "It was great! Really cool! We went to the museum, saw a Renoir exhibit. Ate a lot of pea soup and poutine. Jed introduced us to some really cool people up there. They publish a magazine, *Our Generation*, anti-war activists. It was almost like being in Paris. I mean, everybody speaks French…the signs, the shops. And I did bring you back a croissant, but also we found these really delicious bagels up there, not like New York bagels, wood-fired, completely different. It was so cool, I mean really dynamite! You should have come." Jill was lit up.

"Maybe next time," I said.

"Yeah man, we missed you," offered Jason. "How were things here? Chickens still alive?"

"Things were cool, in fact downright cold."

"It was cold up there too, windy as hell on the St. Lawrence," Brian chimed in.

Then I told them about the snowmobile.

"What the fuck!" Jason responded. "I told you we should have stopped them! Strung up that wire, or at least put up 'No Trespassing' signs! Those assholes!"

"It was only one guy," I said. "One asshole."

"Maybe it was his idea of joke," said Suze.

"Yeah, very funny!" Jill brushed her hair off of her cheek. "I'm sure he thought so, anyway."

"Well, what do we do about it?" Brian asked.

"It was just one guy," I said. "Most of them have been pretty decent, and they do make the trail good for skiing. Maybe he didn't see me, I'm not sure. It seems kind of harsh to shut them all out, and Leland said it would create a lot of bad feeling in the neighborhood."

"Well, we've got to do something," Jason insisted. "We can't just let whoever it was get away with it."

"Maybe a sign 'Share the Trail' with a skier drawn on it or something," said Suze.

"Cool," Jill replied. "Good idea, nothing harsh, just a reminder."

"Sounds pretty lame to me," Jason was not happy.

"Hey, we can try it," said Brian. "If there are more problems we can deal with them then. I see Leland's point though. I don't think we want to piss off our neighbors."

Suze used a red magic marker to make a sign on a piece of a cardboard box that we posted on a fencepost at the top of the field where the path began.

WE READ IN THE *local paper that Nixon's daughter, Julie, was going to visit our state capital, Montpelier. I was outraged. "We've got to protest, at least go with some signs or something! Show them what we think of her daddy's war!"*

David was all for it, and so was everybody else; down and ready.

"It's about time, I was wondering when we'd get around to doing something political; starting to think that maybe we really were only here to raise vegetables." Brian looked at me.

We were pissed. It had become Nixon's war now, he and Kissinger replacing Johnson and McNamara as the objects of our rage. Same shit, new package. The war seemed a bit more distant now, easier to ignore from our peaceful vantage in the woods, but all we had to do was read the news or hear a radio report to bring it back.

And I think we all shared a bit of Brian's unease at our lack of activity, and maybe I felt a twinge of guilt on top of that. Could our Black brothers in the ghetto forget the war? Or the latest round of draftees, or the Vietnamese on the receiving end of our latest escalation? No. The truth was that the war was everywhere, it infected everything and there really was no getting away from it, even in Vermont.

The next Wednesday we drove over to Route 14 and then took Route 2 straight into downtown Montpelier. I had never been there before, and my image of a state capital was shaped by Albany, an image that Montpelier most definitely did not fit. There was a gold-domed capitol building that backed up against a wooded hillside, two or three other smaller official looking government buildings and two banks, three churches, and two business blocks of four-story brick buildings housing store fronts, with apartments and offices above. On a few surrounding blocks stood an assortment of Greek revival and Victorian houses. A very neat and tidy little town, oozing New England charm.

"There's only about four thousand people living in the whole town," said Brian, who always loved to supply little known facts.

The article had said that Julie was going to a fundraising lunch at the hotel, so we parked the car at a meter, piled out with our signs, and walked that way. When we pulled into town we saw a small group already there, standing on the sidewalk behind a banner that said "PEACE NOW!" We hadn't expected anybody else, and we joined them across the street from the hotel entrance, which had a State Police cruiser parked nearby.

There were eight people there, men and women, most young, like us, plus a couple of old women I knew right away were Quaker ladies.

A girl with long blonde hair approached. "Hey, far out, we didn't know anybody else was coming. I'm Ella from Cold Mountain Farm, over near Franklin. You guys from around here?"

"Wow," I said, "Cold Mountain, isn't that a commune? We're from Zion Farm, up on the border."

"You guys have a commune too?"

"Well, sort of," I replied. "We're a political collective."

"Cool! Anyway, glad you made it. We couldn't believe it when we heard

Julie was coming to Montpelier. What an opportunity!"

"Is she inside the hotel?" Jason asked.

"Yeah, that's her limo, just pulled up to the entrance, so we figure she's coming out soon." A bearded guy answered Jason, and introduced himself. "I'm Jess."

"Hey, there's somebody in the limo." Brian called out.

He was right, we could clearly see a girl around our age sitting in the backseat.

"I bet it's Dabney Hibbert," said Brian.

"Who?" I asked.

"Dabney Hibbert, I read this article in 'Life' about Nixon's daughters that said Julie's best friend, Dabney Hibbert, traveled with her sometimes."

"No shit." I said, and then I had an idea. I put down my sign, walked down the block, crossed the street and then approached the hotel like I was walking past. When I reached the limo, I leaned in to the open rear window.

The girl sitting in back was wearing makeup, a camel colored coat, and a knit beret that made her look like she had just stepped out of "Ozzie and Harriet".

"Hi Dabney," I said. "I know in your heart you're against the war. You and Julie have got to tell her dad to end it now." She had a look of shock on her face, and just when I finished talking, two burly guys in dark suits, who came from the hotel lobby, grabbed me by the shoulders and pulled me away from the window. Cheers rose from across the street.

The big guys shoved me down the sidewalk, and I crossed back to rejoin my friends.

A few minutes later Julie came out and we started chanting anti-war slogans. She was hustled into the limo by the guys in dark suits, and they drove off toward Burlington with a State Police escort.

We hung around on the sidewalk for a while, waving our signs at passing cars, and talking among ourselves. The people from Cold Mountain were cool; it was nice to discover that not all of the communes in Vermont were a bunch of hippy dippies. They invited us to come over and visit, and we did the same.

All in all, not a bad day, and we headed home feeling like we had made a statement, at least, and happy that so many cars had honked or given us a thumbs up when they passed our signs. Vermont continued to surprise me. The hostility I had expected hadn't happened. Something about civility, or tolerance, I don't know what it was, but Vermont was different.

THE SNOW KEPT COMING, but finally, toward mid-February, the bitter cold broke and when I was out for a ski one afternoon I met Leland coming out of the woods on a pair of snowshoes. He carried a bow saw.

"Hi neighbor!" Leland greeted me.

"Hi Leland! How are you? What are you doing out here?"

"Oh, just doin' a little work out in the sugarbush. Time to get ready for the sweet season." He ruffled Ranger's fur when the dog came running up to him. "How's the big fella today?"

"Sweet season?" I asked.

"Sugaring…maple time, you know. Won't be long now before we get our first run of sap. Truth be known, it's my favorite time of year."

"Really? You make maple syrup?"

"Much as we can, that's how we pay the taxes." His eyes twinkled.

"Wow, I'd love to learn how." I said. "That would be cool!"

"Well, come around when we start boiling and I'll show you how we do it."

"We can help," I offered.

"Well, I guess I could use some help. I'm not getting any younger and neither is the old lady. Used to be we'd hang a thousand buckets, but now…well, like I said, we've slowed down a little. Forty gallons of sap for every gallon of syrup, that's a lot of buckets to haul."

"Hey, I'm down for it. I mean, let me know whenever you're ready. I bet Jill and the others would help too. It's not like we're super busy these days."

"Thanks," Leland said. "Some help would be much appreciated, maybe we could hang more buckets this year." Ranger caught the scent of something and took off into the woods. "He knows spring is coming, things starting to come alive again." Leland took in a deep breath.

You could have fooled me. The woods were still deep in snow. The days were getting a little longer, though daylight was still a pretty rare commodity. Maybe it wasn't below zero any more, but it still felt damn cold. It seemed incredibly optimistic to announce the coming of spring.

"Stop by for a cup of tea sometime," Leland offered. "I'll show you the whole operation."

"I will." I replied. I kicked off down the path and called back over my shoulder. "See you soon!"

A couple of days later I knocked on the door of the blue trailer, and Mary answered.

"Well, hi, neighbor! Come on in. How's David?" She was smiling.

Mary had a way of really making you feel welcome, a genuine concern for other people and their wellbeing that shone through.

"Can I get you a cup of tea?" She turned toward the tiny kitchen. "I was just about to make a fresh pot."

"Thanks Mary," I answered, as I stamped the snow from my boots on the front porch. I walked into the trailer and took a seat at the blue Formica kitchen table. "Leland said I should stop by and he'd show me the maple syrup operation."

"Oh my goodness, was he ever enthused the other day when you offered to help. Talking about cleaning all of those old firkins and spouts, hanging buckets like in the old days!"

"Really? Leland got enthused?" It was hard to imagine Leland actually getting excited.

"Well, Mister, I guess so. Had a hard time calming him down, he wanted to go out to the barn and get started right away."

"Is he around?" I was surprised he hadn't joined us.

"Took the truck into St. J to see his doctor."

"Nothing serious I hope?"

"Just a check-up." Her kettle whistled and she poured the steaming water into a ceramic teapot. "They like to keep an eye on him. Good thing they gave him that Medicare."

"No kidding? You like that program? I thought all you Vermonters were Republicans. That's socialism." I couldn't help teasing her.

"Oh, that's not socialism," she replied, laughing. "I know all about socialism. I'm from Barre."

It was the second time she had made a reference to Barre, and this time I rose to the bait. "So what's up with Barre? Lots of socialists there?" It seemed unlikely. I knew enough about Vermont to know that they had rejected the New Deal and voted Republican from before the Civil War until forever.

"Socialists, anarchists…real revolutionaries too. You name it. Used to be, at least, when I was growing up. My father was an anarchist you know, a lot of them were."

"Anarchists in Barre? Come on!" I couldn't believe what I was hearing.

"You've got to be kidding!"

"He came from Carrera. They had a saying there, 'even the stones are anarchists'."

"Carrera? Like Italy?"

She nodded and continued. "He, and a lot of others, came over to work the granite."

"I had you figured for a tenth generation Vermonter or something."

"Been living with Leland long enough, guess some of it rubbed off. But truth be told, I'm an Italian girl from Barre. My Dad, Salvatore, he was a sculptor, he worked in a studio, not down in the quarry. Would have been better off in a way, out of the dust; that's what killed him. Still a young man, forty-seven years old."

"Your father was an anarchist?" I had to hear more.

"Well they were all anarchists pretty much, or socialists, the Italian colony. Three thousand or so of us, off in the east end of town. Most didn't even speak English. Why I'll tell you, they were quite a bunch, my Dad and his comrades. Guisseppi Squallini, named his twin daughters Dyna and Mita; they were my best friends growing up.

"Oh, they were a pair of pistols, let me tell you. They'd come runnin' down the street, four braids flying in the wind. Sometimes I couldn't even tell 'em apart. They were the smartest girls at school. I figured both of them for great things. Then their daddy, Guisseppi, got deported, sent back to Italy in '21, and things kind of fell apart for them after that."

"Deported?"

"Yup, there were a couple of them. He'd gone down to Mexico to fight with Pancho Villa, and when the Secret Service found out, well, they didn't think too fondly of that, so they sent him back."

Mary glanced at the counter. "Oh, I bet it's ready now." She poured the tea from the pot into two cups and handed one to me.

"Anarchists in Barre! Jill won't believe this."

"They weren't playing around, either. The socialists, they ran candidates, but the anarchists were real militant. Guns, bombs. They figured that's what it was gonna take to make a revolution, bring down the bourgeoisie. They didn't have any illusions. Been through it back in Carrera. Couple of uprisings there, real rebellions, smashed by the army. That's why a bunch of them came over here, get away from the repression."

"Wow!" I sipped my tea. "Sounds like Barre was quite a place."

"Oh, that it was. I loved it there. We would ride the streetcar downtown, buy penny candy and walk up and down main street looking in the fancy shop windows. In the summer we would go swim in the Jail Branch, behind the opera house, to cool off. Sometimes I'd go down Granite Street to where my dad worked and watch while he carved the stone. He specialized in lettering, but he could carve anything. It was so loud down there, with the sawing and coring, and polishing machines. It amazed me that he could concentrate in the middle of all that. Belts humming overhead, and the dust, that terrible granite dust, filling the whole building. You could see it floating in the beams of sunlight that came through the upper story windows. That's what killed him, the dust; silicosis, gray lung disease. Oh, now they got dust collectors, filters, ventilation. But there wasn't any of that back then. I guess they didn't know any better, or they didn't care.

"The natives, they didn't think much about us. We hardly existed for them. I remember one time, a horse pulling a cart ran amuck downtown. There was a big story about it in the *Barre Times*: 'Mr. Smith's horse Alice ran wild, knocked over a vegetable stand at the Star Market, broke a window at Nelson's Hardware, scared Millie Jones who was on her way to visit Pastor Carter at the Congregational Church', on and on like that, and then, the very last sentence: 'The wagon also killed an Italian man.' Didn't even name him. That's how much we mattered to them."

There was more than a trace of bitterness in her voice, and I stared at my tea.

"There was a man named Luigi Galliani, published a magazine called *Chronica Subersiva*. Ever heard of it?"

"No, but I like the name." I knew next to nothing about anarchism.

"Well, it was famous. Italians all over the world read it. Ever hear of Sacco and Vanzetti?"

"Yeah, of course."

"They were friends of Galliani. But he lived over there in Barre. Folks there took care of him. He was a fugitive, wanted on some fake murder charge in New Jersey.

"It was really something, where we lived. Could have been a town in Italy. We had a winery, a bakery, a food co-op. All based out of the Labor Hall, over to Granite Street. Socialist Labor Party, but the anarchists helped build it too. Emma Goldman talked there, for the workers. She also gave speeches at the Opera House. I remember when she debated some minister there, made him look silly. Mother Jones, Big Bill Haywood, all the main Wobblies came to town, IWW, you know, International Workers of the World."

"Sounds pretty wild. I had no idea."

"Was pretty wild; strikes, meetings, arson, gun play, you name it. Why, they shot the sheriff, somebody burned down the Anarchist Library, and then there was poor Elia Corti, shot dead on the steps of the Labor Hall."

"Who was he?"

"Another sculptor, an anarchist. You can go over to Hope Cemetery, see his monument. What a shame that was. Sweetest person you'd ever want to meet."

"What happened?"

"Well, the anarchists and the socialists, they pretty much got along, cooperated on some things, like the Labor Hall and all that. But there was this fellow Ceratti, edited a paper down in New York, and he started writing against the anarchists, Galliani in particular. So they got into a big debate, in their papers, name-calling and all. Ceratti was coming to town to give a speech, and the anarchists didn't much care for that. Big crowd gathered down to the Labor Hall. Somebody went to the train depot to warn Ceratti, and when word came he was on his way a big argument started. Then there was a scuffle. Somebody pulled a pistol, not clear why. Some folks said the anarchists wanted to assassinate Ceratti, but I don't believe that was the case, most likely just some hothead. There was plenty of them around.

"Anyway, Corti, he was on of my father's best friends, he saw the gun, went over to try to calm the fellow down, and the pistol went off. Dropped him dead right there on the steps. A real tragedy. Everybody loved Elia Corti, and his comrades carved him that beautiful statue, best piece of sculpture in the whole cemetery, and there's some fine monuments there too. Lots of the sculptors made their own before they passed; everybody knew a life in the sheds meant an early death. My dad finished his a year before he died. It's down there in Hope Cemetery with lots of others. You can tell the anarchists, they wore black bowties, the socialists favored red cravats, though you can't tell the colors in the memorials."

"Wow! I had no idea...I'll have to go down and check it out some time." I looked at Mary and shook my head. It was quite mind-blowing. This old farmer's wife I had made so many assumptions about...

goes to show, you never can tell until you sit down and talk to someone what they're really about. She and Leland both continually amazed me. It made me realize again how little I knew about the world.

I sipped my tea and stared out the window at Mary's bird feeder, under assault by a ravenous flock of yellow grosbeaks. I had been studying an Audubon guide that had wound up on the kitchen table one day, and was now capable of identifying a dozen or so of the most common species we saw around the house and back in the woods. The birds fluttered around the feeder and pecked at the snow-covered ground beneath it where some sunflower seeds had fallen.

"You know when Leland is getting home?"

"I imagine a couple hours. He didn't leave all that long ago and sometimes they keep him waiting."

The sun broke through some high clouds, suddenly washing the small trailer's interior in sunlight. I finished my tea and carried the cup to the kitchen sink.

"I'll come back a little later then. Tell him I talked it over with the others and we're down for helping any way we can. Might as well make ourselves useful, and learn something in the process."

"Well no doubt he'll be mighty happy to hear that. He loves sugaring better than just about anything. Gets like a little kid."

I was ready to say goodbye and leave, but before I could get to the door she spoke again.

"You folks goin' to Town Meeting? You really should. Be nice to hear some new voices there, some young voices."

We had received a notice in our PO Box, but I hadn't really thought about it and we never discussed it as a group. "I don't know. What's it all about?"

Mary looked startled. "Why it's about the business of the town. It's the way we make decisions. Taxes, roads, the school, fire department, town officers…everything. Folks around here take it pretty seriously."

"I get the feeling we're not too popular with most folks around here." I thought about the snowmobilers.

"Popular's got nothin' to do with it. You're citizens, you live here. It's your right— no," she looked me firmly in the eye, "I'd say it's your duty. You've got as much say as anyone else. You're affected by it, so you've got a say in it. That's democracy!"

"I'll bring it up with Jill and the others, I guess we hadn't considered it before."

"Kind of important, if you ask me."

"Okay; thanks for the tea Mary. See you later."

"First Tuesday morning in March. Nine o'clock in the Town Hall."

THAT NIGHT OVER DINNER I raised the issue of Town Meeting.

"I don't get it." Jason reached for another serving of brown rice. "Everybody in town goes to this thing?"

"Everybody who wants to. You have to be a registered voter in the town to have a say." I had read up about it in a book about Vermont history, and took a look at the actual warning that had come in the mail, making me the expert.

Brian proclaimed. "The New England Town Meeting tradition. Goes back to pre-Revolutionary War days. I can't believe they still do it up here."

"How cool is that?" Suze responded. "I want to go check it out."

"Me too," said Jill.

"Then you better get down to the town clerk's tomorrow and take the Freeman's Oath."

"Freeman's Oath? What the fuck?" Jason raised his eyebrows. "I don't do that pledge allegiance shit."

"Well it's to the town, and the state. It actually struck me as pretty cool. Wait…I'll find it." I walked to the coffee table and picked up the book, thumbed through it a bit. Then I read:

"You solemnly swear or affirm that whenever you give your vote or suffrage touching any matter that concerns the state of Vermont, you will do so as in your conscience you shall judge will most conduce to the best good of the same, as established by the constitution without fear or favor of any person."

Jason furrowed his brow. "That is kind of cool. I mean I guess I could live with that."

Jill Laughed. "I love the language 'You shall judge will most conduce to'. What a kick."

"Direct democracy," Brian added, "like the participatory democracy in SDS. I can dig that. Sign me up."

"I don't know," Jason hesitated. "How's that gonna work in a town full of reactionaries? It sounds to me like it might not go so well."

"You're just assuming the town's full of reactionaries. It's not. Look at Leland and Mary, and the folks we've worked for." I felt I had to defend the town—I didn't know why. "I'm sure not everyone is a right-winger. Anyway, even if they are, they should hear what we've got to say. I mean all of this affects us pretty directly, and I really want to see how this whole thing works. I am definitely going."

In the end we all took the oath and decided to attend the meeting. In fact, in reading over the warning Brian discovered a clause that allowed for issues to be raised from the floor that hadn't been previously warned, and we had drafted a resolution.

When our VW van hit the state highway there was a line of cars parked all along the right of way that ran through the center of the village.

We pulled in and joined a dozen or so others walking briskly toward the white clapboard Town Hall. A few folks nodded in recognition.

When we entered the hall, our names were checked against a list of registered voters, and we were handed nametags to fill out. There were fifteen or so rows of folding wooden chairs filling the large meeting hall. In front there were three chairs arrayed before a table that looked out on the rapidly filling room, and a lectern with a microphone standing in front of that. I was surprised to see Leland sitting in one of the three chairs, the others were occupied by a man I didn't know, and a woman I recognized as the postmistress.

Mary was seated towards the back of the room. She waved her town warning at us and we found seats next to her.

The hall was buzzing; "Hey, how you doin'?" "How was winter up your way?" "Long time, no see." "Heard your Missus had a tough winter." "How about them milk prices?" as friends exchanged greetings, gossiped, and found their seats.

There were a couple of tables pushed up against the back wall. One with coffee and donuts sold by the Northern Star Grange, another was full of literature from the State Extension Service. The 4-H had their banner draped over a table that offered cookies, brownies, and slices of homemade cake. All very Norman Rockwell, I thought.

A tall, thin man with a gaunt face walked to the lectern and banged a gavel on its wooden top. The buzzing stopped and people found their seats.

"I hereby call this Town Meeting to order. We've got a bunch of business to get to, but before we start, I want to take a minute to remember Thomas Lyford, who we lost back in September. Everybody knows how much he did for this town. We owe him a debt of gratitude and we will miss him." There was a silent moment.

"Just one more thing before we get down to business. Tinker

McAndrews, our state rep, wants to give a report. Now he's not from here, so legally we don't have to let him talk." A chuckle rumbled through the crowd. "But if nobody objects, we could give him a few minutes." There were no objections raised, and a heavy-set fellow in his fifties, wearing a blue blazer over a plaid shirt and blue jeans walked to the podium.

"No campaign speeches, now Tinker!" The moderator teased, and the crowd chuckled again.

Tinker began. "Thanks, Liam. It's true, I'm not from here. I was born and raised two towns over, but you voted me in to represent you at the State House, at least some of you did." Some of the crowd chortled at that. "So I figured I'd tell you what we've been doin' down to Montpelier, then I can get back to milking my cows.

"Well it's been quite a year. Big changes afoot, probably most of you followed the billboard law. I'm kinda proud of that one. We're the first state to ban 'em, and I'm bettin' it's gonna help us attract the tourists up here to enjoy our unspoiled landscape. That's a big step ahead for us. One thing I could agree with the governor on.

"You know I sit on the education committee, and I'm not too pleased with what happened to the schools, but we had to do something to cut costs, make 'em more efficient, keep the taxes down. I know a lot of us got our schoolin' in the old one-room schoolhouses, and it worked fine for us. But like they say, 'the times they are a changing'. Union district schools work better for the kids, and it's a lot cheaper.

"We made some progress on the roads, and the state highway out here is scheduled for repaving next year, so just slow down when you hit those frost heaves for a little bit longer. Help is on the way.

"We did what we could about milk prices, but to get what we need is really gonna take action by the Federal Government. So when you see Bob Stafford or George Aiken give 'em an earful. I guess that's about all

I've got to say. Any questions?" He scanned the crowd, but no one raised a hand.

Liam, the moderator, took the podium. "Thanks, Tinker. Alright then, let's turn to item one, 'Shall the town of Zion elect town officers?'"

"So moved." "Seconded." Voices rang out from the crowd.

"Okay then. The floor is open for nominations. First, town moderator."

"Nominate Liam Martin," someone called out.

"Second," a woman sitting in front of me said. "Any other nominations?" He paused for a moment. No one else spoke. "All in favor of Liam Martin for moderator say aye."

The room filled with "ayes".

"All opposed say nay."

Silence.

"You have elected Liam Martin to serve as your town moderator."

"Next, the position of town clerk for a term of one year."

"I nominate Catherine Merrill," a voice spoke from the second row. I couldn't see who it was, but it was quickly followed by a woman sitting near us. "Second."

Liam scanned the room for a moment, and then spoke. "Catherine Merrill has been nominated and seconded for town clerk. Any other nominations?" He was greeted by silence. "No other nominations? Then let's vote. All in favor of Catherine Merrill for town clerk say 'aye'."

The room filled with an echoing "aye!"

"All opposed say 'nay'."

There was no opposition. "Catherine Merrill is hereby elected to a one-year term as town clerk. Next order of business is to elect a member of the select board for a three-year term. Any nominations?"

Our neighbor Calvin, the one with the collapsing barn who lived down the hill from us, stood. "Nominate Leland Smith." Several voices rose to say "second".

"Any other nominations?"

A guy who I had seen hanging out down at the store rose. "Nominate Mac Johnson." His nomination was seconded by a skinny fellow sitting next to him.

"Any other nominations?" Liam queried the room. "No, well then we have Leland Smith and Mac Johnson nominated for a three-year term on the select board. Let's hear a little something from each of them. Leland?"

Leland rose from his chair at the table in the front of the room, which I now realized was where the select board sat. I hadn't known he was a member. "Well, I been here a couple terms, always did my best to serve the town. Wouldn't mind staying on board to finish up some of the things we been workin' on, but if folks want somebody new, that's okay too." He sat.

"Mac?" Liam stepped aside as the storekeeper stepped up to the podium.

"I want to straighten things out around here. Taxes keep goin' up and I don't see we're getting much out of it. We got some problems. Freeloaders from down country comin' up here and goin' on welfare." He made a point of staring at us. "We're spendin' too much on the library and the school. The 'three R's' were good enough for me. And we're losin' taxes; sell off the town forest and the pasture. That's what I say."

"Alright, thank you, gentlemen. Any questions for either candidate?" No one raised a hand. "Okay then, let's vote. I'll call for a voice vote, but if it's close, we'll divide the house. All in favor of Leland Smith say 'aye'." The 'ayes' resounded around the room.

"All in favor of Mac Johnson say 'aye'." The response seemed almost as loud, but concentrated in just the few rows near where the storekeeper was seated.

"Too close to call," said the moderator. "Let's divide the house. All in favor of Leland stand to my right, those for Mac to my left." People rose from their seats and walked either right or left. After a few minutes it was clear that a large majority supported Leland, only about thirty people stood on Mac's side of the room.

"The people have chosen Leland Smith for another term on the select board," Liam announced.

There was some chit-chat as people reclaimed their seats. We then elected two school board members, the town constable, the auditor, a lister, the collector of delinquent taxes, a budget committee member, a library trustee, town juror, town agent, health officer, fire warden, cemetery sexton, pound keeper, dog officer, three fence viewers, tree warden, inspector of lumber, shingles, and wood, and a weigher of coal. Most of the votes were by affirmation, since there was only one candidate.

I leaned over towards Mary. "Who pays all these people? Seems like an awful big bureaucracy for such a small town."

She laughed. "Paid? Why all of 'em's volunteers, except the clerk and the road crew. Just bein' responsible members of the town, good neighbors, that's all. Why, you could have had most any of those positions you wanted. Some years we can't even fill 'em all."

"What does a fence viewer do anyway?"

Mary had a laugh that lit up her face, and her cheeks got even redder.

"Not much these days, most of the boundary disputes were settled years ago. But you never know."

We heard reports from all the town officers. There was a lot that went into running the town I had never thought about; schools, maintaining the roads, buying equipment, running the library. There had been two fires that past year, and some flooding in the village last spring. A rabid fox had been found. The town forest had a lottery for taking out firewood. They had installed a new culvert on Creamery Street, and the school needed a new roof. We had discussions about all that and more. Then we broke for lunch.

The Sisterhood of the Northern Star brought out chafing dishes full of chicken pot pie swimming in creamy gravy. For $1.25 you got a tray holding chicken and a biscuit, a small salad of iceberg lettuce, and a brownie for dessert. It was good too.

I ate mine as we traded impressions over lunch. "Pretty cool!" said Jill. "It's amazing," Brian looked excited. "Democracy in action. I've never seen anything like it."

"These old Yankees really get down to it," offered Suze.

"We should have gone on one of the boards or something," I suggested.

"Yeah, right. Jason for weigher of coal," laughed Suze.

"No, seriously. If we want to be part of the town," I insisted.

"Question is, does the town want us to be part of them?" Jason asked. "I'm not feeling a lot of love here."

It was true. Besides Mary, Leland and Calvin, our neighbor down the road, and some of the folks we had done odd jobs for, nobody had really done more than nod to us, and there had been more than a few hostile glances.

"Maybe next year, when we're not so new," suggested Jill. "Besides, there's still half the meeting to go. Let's see what happens then."

Liam called the meeting to order after lunch. "Let's thank the Sisterhood for a delicious lunch," he began. "And let's thank the high school kids for taking care of the little ones." He nodded toward the lobby where a group of teens had been playing with the smaller children all morning.

"Now it's time to talk about money. You've all had a chance to look over the town budget, what's your pleasure?" A women up front raised her hand.

"Seems to me we're spending a lot more on the roads than we need to. Why not cut that budget? Better we keep the roads, the faster folks go. Let the snow pile up some, leave those ruts and heaves from mud season, slow 'em down a little. That's what I say."

A half-dozen hands went up. Liam called on a burly guy with a beard. "Seth, you next."

Seth rose. "That's just silly. The road crew does a good job, and we need them to keep it up. Some of us have to drive those roads every day to go to work. School bus needs to get up there too. That's about the last thing I would cut."

Ron Carter, the road commissioner, spoke next. "We got over a hundred fifteen miles of town roads we maintain, all of 'em dirt. We don't dare fall behind on maintenance, or they'll be impassible before you know it. Broken axles, mud over your hubcaps…do you really want to go back to the bad old days, when there were weeks out of the year the farmers couldn't even get a wagon out over those roads?" The crowd appeared to nod in affirmation, and the issue seemed resolved.

We discussed the allocation for the library, the senior program, and the fire department. Then we voted on the budget. It passed by a large majority.

The next question was a proposal to create a town planning commission, apparently a controversial item, because before he opened the discussion the moderator spoke. "I know there's some disagreement over this issue, but I want to remind you that we were all neighbors when we came to this meeting, we're all neighbors while we're here, and we'll all be neighbors when we leave. Now we'll make sure everybody gets their say."

The debate was heated. Mac, the storekeeper, began. "Nobody's got the right to tell me what to do with my land. You start out with a planning commission and pretty soon you got zoning and codes and all kind of other restrictions. This is a free country and we don't need none of this down-country horse crap up here in the Kingdom. You can pass all the laws you want, but I still got the right to my private property. We been takin' care of ourselves up here for a long time, and I'm not gonna let anybody else tell me what I can and can't do. I got my rights, guaranteed by the constitution, by Jesus, anybody tries to take 'em away, well, I ain't gonna say what I'll do, but use your imagination!" There was laughter, and part of the audience applauded.

A woman named Doris spoke next. "Well, I can appreciate what Mac said, but I've lived here a long time, and seen lots change over the years. This is about taking control of our future, deciding what we want our town to be like. What if they decided to build a ski area over on Hardwood Mountain? Or run a pipeline through Calvin's cow pasture? Put some kind of big factory in off the state highway? Way things stand now we got no say over it. If we had a plan, we could have some control. Nobody's tryin' to take away anybody's private property, but don't the community have somethin' to say about it if it's gonna affect all of us?"

Hands went up all over the room after that; all of the speakers expressed one sentiment or the other, pro or con. It seemed to revolve around the question of individual property rights versus the right of the community to have some say over their collective fate. It was a tough question, made more difficult for us when someone talked about how planning could help "Keep out more of those communes." Discussion went on for almost an hour, and the same points were repeated a dozen times each. Finally, Liam called for a vote. It was close, but after a count of the divided house, the question passed. The select board was empowered to appoint a five-person commission from a group of volunteers. It was the last item on the official agenda, and, as Liam asked if there was any additional business to be raised from the floor, people began to gather their papers and reach for their coats.

Brian raised his hand and was acknowledged by the moderator. "I have an item." He cleared his throat and read from a piece of paper we had prepared the night before. "The town of Zion resolves that the war in Vietnam is an immoral action bringing great suffering to the people of Vietnam and the people of the United States, and it should be brought to an end immediately."

The crowd froze. Liam hesitated a moment, looked at the select board, and then spoke. "Well, I don't know if we can even consider this motion. Town Meeting's supposed to be about town business."

"That's right!" Mac shouted out. "You damn hippies got nothin' to say about it anyway!"

"Hold on Mac," admonished Liam. "Wait till you're recognized before you speak." He looked back at the table behind him. "I'm not quite sure about this. I'd like to hear what the select board has to say, maybe hear from Lawyer Blachly as well." He nodded to the select board.

"Well," said the postmistress, "it would have been nice to get a petition on this. That's the proper way to bring an item to the floor, give folks a chance to think on it a little. But it's sure not illegal. That's why we list other business on the warning."

"Not the point," said the other selectman. "Mac's right, Town Meetings are for town affairs, this has got nothing to do with the town."

"Now I don't know about that." Leland spoke in his usual quiet manner. "Seems to me we've got several boys fighting over there, and isn't Mrs. Brown a Gold Star Mother? Lost her boy a couple years ago, so you can't rightly say it doesn't concern the town. Also, I believe that back before the Civil War towns in Vermont passed lots of resolutions against slavery. And I remember back when I was younger we passed a resolution against Roosevelt, opposing the New Deal. So I guess there's precedent."

"Lawyer Blachly?" asked Liam.

A bearded guy in his thirties wearing an argyle sweater rose. "Well, it's certainly not going to be binding, but if the voters want to consider the question, I see no legal reason not to take it up. Really though, I think this would be something to ask the secretary of state about."

"Well, that helps clarify things," said the moderator. "What's the pleasure of the voters? All in favor of considering this item say 'aye'."

The 'ayes' echoed throughout the house.

"All opposed say 'nay'."

There was a smattering of 'nays', most concentrated in the seats around Mac.

"The ayes have it," declared Liam. "The floor is open for discussion."

Brian's hand shot into the air.

"Yes, young man."

"I raised the resolution because I am appalled by the illegal war our country is waging against the innocent people of Vietnam. We're wasting millions of dollars a day to kill women and children in a country thousands of miles away where we have no real strategic interest. Thousands of our own soldiers are dying there. And for what? What have the Vietnamese ever done to us?" He sat down and I clapped him on the back.

Liam pointed to a young woman. "My cousin is over there and he's fighting to protect our freedom! They're communists, and if we don't stop 'em over there, they'll be over here before you know it. In fact, maybe they're already here." She stared at Brian. "If you think it's so great why don't you move to Russia instead of here?"

It would have been funny, except for the hate in her voice and the grumbles of affirmation from some in the crowd.

An older woman standing back at the Sisterhood's food table was recognized next. "I hate war, all war. Lost my son in World War II, and that one I could understand. His name's on that memorial plaque right out in the lobby, don't make it any easier, but I could understand it.

"This war don't make no sense to me. Don't want to see any more mothers lose their sons, hardest thing there is, so I support this resolution, and I'm glad it was brought to the floor. 'Bout time we said somethin' about this."

By now the moderator had a list of people waiting to speak, and he began making his way through it. The debate continued for the better part of an hour. Most people who spoke evoked familiar themes: patriotism, freedom, support our boys. And for the most part discussion was civil, but there were exceptions.

When Mac finally got the floor, he rose, red in the face, and practically shouting. "How can you people sit here and let these draft dodgers get away with it? This is still America, the land of the free and the home of the brave! I'll be damned if I'm gonna let these cowards," he glared at us, "tell my town what to do. They start with somethin' like this, then they tell us what to do with our private property, pretty soon they'll be tryin' to take away our guns!

"Well, I won't stand for it, and you shouldn't either! They're a bunch of dirty hippies, they're not from here, and as far as I'm concerned, they got no right to be here, no right at all! If you vote for this, you'll be playin' into their hands. Bad enough we got the damn senators against the war, now this. Let's show 'em how real Vermonters feel!"

The debate finally subsided and the moderator called for a vote. The resolution failed on a separation of the house, but it was close. Then the meeting was adjourned. On our way out the door the woman who had spoken earlier about losing her son in World War II stopped us.

"Thank you," she said. "My name's Lillian. I been against this damn war from the start. Don't make no sense, boys dyin' over there for no good reason. None of our business. Been wantin' to say somethin' about it, but it took you young people. Makes me so mad, I want to have a protest or somethin', march around with a sign."

"Well, we could do that," said Jill with that sparkle in her eye she got when she was excited about something. "We could hold a vigil out in front of the post office. With signs and banners, show everyone driving by how we feel about the war."

"Raise a ruckus, huh?" said Lillian. "Well, I like that. Bet there's other folks would come out too. I know how they feel, and there's some Quakers in town too. Some of the others might not like it much, but I feel it's time to do somethin'. Jeezum Crow, how many more have to die?" We decided to meet at the post office at noon on Friday.

On our way back to the car we caught up with Leland and Mary. "Now what did you make of that?" she asked us, her white hair barely visible from under a dark blue wool cap. "Wasn't that something? Now don't mind that fellow Mac. He's a big bag of wind, there's not many who side with him, you must have seen for yourselves."

"It was pretty amazing!" I said. "I mean, the whole town making decisions like that? Wow, very cool."

"Well, that's how it is up here," said Leland. "Always has been, and I like it well enough. Glad you got a taste of it." He opened the door of the truck for Mary. "You know, Town Meeting Day's usually when we get our starts goin'. Planting season be here before you know it." He shut her in and walked around to get in the cab himself. "You need some flats, let me know, I'm pretty sure I got some extra out to the barn."

TOWN MEETING WAS SOMETHING of a turning point. It still snowed regularly, but the days were getting noticeably longer, and the growing daylight seemed to buoy everyone's spirits. I felt some of the weight that had seemed to accumulate over the depth of the winter begin to drop away, and as we started to plan the garden and plant the flats of seeds I could begin to imagine that winter really would come to an end.

We had poured over seed catalogs starting back in January and had decided to concentrate on heirloom varieties. The colorful seed packets covered the kitchen table now: purple runner beans, rainbow chard, I drew a rectangle on a sheet of paper and divided it into rows. We planned to plant two acres.

Those of us who had spent the winter in the farmhouse had really come to appreciate the jars of tomato sauce, dilly beans, slaw, pickles, and other produce we had canned in the fall, and we were still eating potatoes, winter squash, onions, and carrots that had come from last year's garden. Before, it had been an abstract concept for us, but now the importance of the garden was clear to everyone, even Brian, and I felt a new level of commitment from the group that raised my spirits and my level of confidence about trying to grow more.

The garden had a real hold over me. Just thinking about it made it easier to take the winter that remained. I dreamt about sinking my hands into the dark soil, and sought out books to supplement Rodale, which I began to think of as my bible. It amazed me, and Jill too.

"You're quite the country boy," she teased. "Man, I never would have imagined it a year ago. You are deep into this organic shit, it's like some kind of spiritual connection."

And she was right, it was. "You are what you eat," I said. I felt transported preparing the flats, pressing the seeds lightly into the soil, and placing the trays in front of our south-facing windows.

We talked about expanding our farming to include animals besides chickens, decided on a milk cow, and some pigs for meat. It meant we had to build a pen and a shed. I was excited by the prospect.

"Great, we can use the manure for the garden. And we won't have to worry about chemicals, nitrates, and all that crap in our meat either," I said.

It was also time to get out in the woods and help Leland with sugaring. True to his word, he had cleaned almost a thousand buckets and spigots and had already started hanging them along the road and close to his trailer. I went to see him the day after Town Meeting and he was ready to go.

"Figure we can head up to the sugarbush this afternoon," he said in his usual laconic fashion. But the twinkle in his eye revealed his excitement.

"Things are startin' a little late this year, but I figure we're due for a run any time now, maybe later this week. We'd best get the buckets hung. Sap waits for no man. Got to warm up over freezing in the day and cool down overnight, then we'll see those buckets start fillin'. Yes, we will Mr. Man, you betcha."

Leland had a pile of slabs and scrap wood ready, stacked in the shed beside the sugarhouse, and he had spent the previous weeks working on the equipment, cleaning firkins (the wooden buckets he hung from the trees), spouts, and his five-hundred-gallon wooden collector tank. He had washed the cobwebs out of his stainless steel evaporator pan, and made sure his arch was ready to fire up. All that remained, and where he "reckoned our help might come in handy," was to pound in the spouts, hang the thousand or so buckets, gather the sap, and boil it down.

It sounded easy, but our first day trailing after the sledge that Leland dragged behind his old John Deere—drilling holes with a bit and brace, hammering the metal spouts into the sugar maples in his "maple orchard", and hanging the wooden buckets on the spouts—left us bone weary with our muscles aching. Jill, Jason and I were on skis, Brian and Suze favored snow shoes. We used an assortment of hammers to pound the metal spigots through the holes we had drilled into the tree bark and the inner flesh of the maples so the sap could bleed out into the wooden buckets.

On our third day of work the sun shone brightly, penetrating deep into the woods with no leaves to impede its rays, and the sap began to run, dripping into the firkins with a steady rhythmic plop that served as a counterpoint to our heavy breathing, and the sound of our hammers. It was hard to believe that the two gallon buckets would ever fill at that rate, but as the day warmed the flow of sap grew heavier, and when we returned the next day to the first buckets we had hung it was time to empty them into the five-hundred-gallon wooden gathering tank sitting in the middle of Leland's sledge. We didn't fill the tank, but there must have been at least a couple of hundred gallons of sap.

"Oh Mister, we'll be boiling down tonight," Leland said, with an edge of excitement in his voice I had never heard before.

As the sun sank we followed the sledge back to the sugarhouse while the sap sloshed around in the big tank. Mary was waiting with a big pot of steaming chili and a platter of corn bread. We tucked into our plates without a word, ravenous after a full day of work in the woods.

"Now the real fun begins," announced Leland after we had finished our meal. He had a big ladle with a long handle that he used to transfer the sap to his evaporator, basically a large stainless steel pan with baffles in it. When it was full he lit a fire under it in his cast iron sugaring arch, feeding it from the pile of scrap wood.

"Stuff's not fit for burning in a stove, but it works just fine for sugarin'," he said as the chimney began to draw and gray smoke poured from the metal stove pipe. It didn't take long before the sap in the evaporator began to boil and he opened a vent in the roof of the sugarhouse. Steam billowed out the vent and from outside it looked like the whole sugar shack was enveloped in smoke and steam.

As the evening went on, we continued to feed the fire while Leland monitored the progress of the sap, which was foaming in the evaporator. He tossed in a bit of lard to stop the foaming. Every now and then he pulled out a ladle full and examined it, slowly pouring it back into the pan, until, finally, he pronounced it done. Then we drained the golden syrup off through a lamb's wool filter into a milk can.

We filled the evaporator, fed the stove and began the process all over again with a new batch. While Leland minded the pan of boiling sap Mary dipped into the milk can and spread a ribbon of hot syrup onto a pine board covered with snow. It turned into a taffy.

"Try some of this," she offered. Jill took a scoop of snow with the syrup on top.

"Sugar on snow," said Mary, with a hint of pride in her voice. "First of the season. Oh, that's some Grade A Fancy syrup alright, no doubt about that!"

From then on for the next several weeks we emptied buckets almost every day, and boiled down every night, sometimes all night long depending on how heavy the run was. Most nights Leland and I worked alone, me feeding the arch, him keeping an eye on the syrup.

He taught me what to look for, how to add a little butter or lard when it boiled over the edge of the shallow evaporator pan to reduce the foam, and how to tell by the way it poured out of the ladle when the sap was syrup.

Ranger loved sugaring season, following us into the woods each morning and orbiting around us all day long, pursuing scents of the new life that was pulsing all around us. He had been gaining size and weight all winter long and probably weighed over a hundred pounds already. He was truly magnificent and completely in his element in the woods. He bounded through even the deepest snow, his muscles rippling under his smooth gray coat.

One day out in the woods we were surprised when a deer charged past us, not more than a dozen feet away. It was a big buck with a ten-point rack and a panicked look in his eye, followed a few seconds later by Ranger in full pursuit.

"Wow!" Suze was wide-eyed. "Groovy! The call of the wild and all that."

"Not good," said Leland. "It's not a pretty thing when a dog takes down a deer." He wiped his nose. "Drags him down by his hind quarters, tears him up, don't even eat him most of the time. Don't worry though. That dog, big and strong as he is, will never catch that deer, not this time of year with the deep snow slowing him down. Real problem comes in a few weeks, when the snow crusts up at night. The deer break through and the dog runs on top, easy for him to get the deer then, especially if he runs with a pack. Better keep an eye on Ranger. If the warden sees him runnin' deer he'll shoot him on sight."

I heard what Leland said, but I didn't have the heart to keep the dog on a chain. He had always run free, and this was the first hint I had that it could cause problems. It worried me a little, but not too much. I hadn't ever seen Ranger chase a deer before, and I hadn't ever seen a game warden on our hill, or a cop, or hardly anybody who wasn't there to see us. It seemed like our private slice of paradise, especially private in the winter, when visitors were few and far between.

Forty to one, the five-hundred-gallon tank full we poured off into the evaporator yielded about twelve gallons of golden liquid that we strained into milk cans and then tin containers with a picture of a sugarhouse, or into glass jugs sealed with screw-on tops of black plastic. Pints, quarts, half-gallons, and gallons, the containers were stacked in a corner of the sugar house and Mary proudly affixed labels to them so all the world would know they came from Rocky Hill Farm, and that the golden liquid inside was "Made in Vermont."

Early in the season all the syrup was labeled Grade A Fancy, but as the sap continued to run, the labels read Grade B, and as the syrup darkened further, finally Grade C.

"That's my favorite," Leland proclaimed. "Grade C, can't beat it, don't bring as much money, but it's got that strong maple flavor, and oh Mr. Man, that's the one I'd take on my pancakes every time, I tell you."

I had to agree with him. As the sugaring season came to an end, Leland let the last batch we poured into the evaporator boil down, getting darker and thicker, past the point of syrup. He ladled off the gooey mass into a large pot and used a wooden paddle to stir it, until the thick liquid, in a moment of alchemy, was transformed to its crystalline essence, and we ended up with a pot full of granular maple sugar.

"Sugaring down." Leland explained. "Pure sweetness, better than anything you can buy at a store."

By the time the syrup was Grade C we were into our fifth week of vigils out in front of the post office. It was usually just us, Lillian, our new friend from town meeting, and an older Quaker couple, Sam and Dotty, but sometimes Leland came down and joined us.

That day we stood there displaying signs drawn on poster board with magic markers; "END THE WAR NOW!", "HOW MANY MORE MUST DIE?", "BRING HOME THE TROOPS!" Pretty mild stuff, but we still managed to attract plenty of angry shouts and insults from passing cars. Others, however, waived and honked, affirming our message.

It was cold and blustery, spitting snow in a casual way. Not too bad a day, as winter went in the Northeast Kingdom. The bitter cold had left, and the days were getting longer. It still got chilly standing out by the side of the road for an hour, but it was bearable, and we thought it was important to be out there every Friday at lunchtime.

We had the usual hostile stares directed our way from Mac's general store, but overall things were going pretty well. We had been standing there for about a half an hour when a battered Chevy pickup rolled into the post office parking lot. A skinny kid, wearing an olive green field jacket got out and walked toward us.

"Hi," he said. "My name's Steve. Mind if I join you?"

"Hell no! I mean welcome!" I said.

"Been drivin' by, past couple of weeks," he said, looking at the ground. "Figured it was time I stopped. I was there, you know, Vietnam. They drafted me right out of high school. You got no idea how bad it was." He stared off into the distance. "I still have nightmares. Nobody should have to go over there. Ain't no reason for us bein' there. They all hate us. The things we did…" His voice trailed off. He pulled up the collar on his jacket and joined us at the roadside. He smelled of cow manure and alcohol.

"You a farmer?" I asked.

"Well, my folks are. We milk forty or so Jerseys over on New Jerusalem Road. That's where I am, for the time being anyway."

"How long have you been back?" Jill joined the conversation, looking into his eyes that were staring at something a million miles away. She placed a gloved hand on the sleeve of his jacket.

"Almost a year," he said. "Don't know which was harder, bein' over there, or being back here." He had bags under his eyes and his look was spooky, haunted. "Nobody gets it. They all act like I'm some kind of hero or something. I know what we did, what I did…it's not like I had a lot of choice, but still…I mean there's always right and wrong, ain't there? I guess you know it's wrong. Most people don't know, but we gotta tell 'em. Even the kids I went to school with—it pisses me off." He furrowed his brow. "Nobody wants to hear the truth."

"Hey, it's cool," said Jill. She gave his arm a squeeze. "Anytime you want to talk about it, come see us."

"You're from that hippy commune, right?"

"Yeah, I guess that's us. I mean we don't really think of ourselves as hippies, but…whatever. Come up and talk whenever you feel like it."

He smiled at Jill. "Yeah, maybe I'll do that sometime."

She had a quality about her, empathy…I don't know what to call it. She cared about people, and they sensed it and responded to her. It was one of the things I loved about her, but it was also a problem. She felt other people's pain, and she took it on. She fretted after we met Steve.

"He really got messed up by the war," she declared the next day. "You can see it in his eyes. I wish there was something we could do for him, but I don't know what, maybe just be here to listen if he ever wants to talk."

A few nights later, as we were getting ready to turn in, there was a knock on our door and Steve came stumbling into our kitchen, very drunk, covered with snow. "Comin' down pretty good out there! Brought some wine! Anybody want some?" He held out a half-empty bottle of Boone's Farm.

"You said come up whenever." He staggered towards Jill. "Got sick of talkin' to the cows, figured I'd try you." He plopped down on the old couch. Ranger stared at him with his head cocked, not quite sure what to make of him.

"Good puppy," Steve reached out to pet Ranger, who drew back. "Nice dog—hey, have some wine." He held the wine bottle aloft again, but there were no takers. "What? Too good to drink with me? C'mon," he insisted, extending the bottle to me.

"No, thanks, I'm cool, really man. Maybe you ought to take it easy yourself. You drive here?"

"Hell yes, know these roads blindfolded, don't worry 'bout me, I'm just fine. Just fine..." he trailed off and got that distant look in his eye again. "Just an old woodchuck, drivin' around, drinkin' a little wine, figured to stop by and see what you're about. Heard a lot of stories..."

"Well, don't believe everything you hear," I said.

"I don't believe nothin' I hear these days. Used to, before...but they were all lies, all lies..." He was staring off again, nodding his head, then he started shaking.

"Hey man, you okay? What's going on?" Jill was alarmed. We all were.

Steve put his head down on the arm of the couch. "I just can't get rid of the people in my head. They won't go away, they won't leave me alone...even when I try to sleep..."

We looked at each other, helpless. Brian shrugged his shoulders. Jill reached out and stroked his head.

"It's okay," she tried to reassure him. "It's okay."

"No, not okay, nothin's okay, nothin', nothin'." He was sobbing now.

"Take it easy, calm down. It's alright, really. Relax. You want some coffee?" Jill kept stroking his head.

He threw up his arms. "No, no coffee. We're fucked! We're screwed! We're completely fucked! Coffee won't help! Nothing will help!" He was flailing around on the couch now, really agitated. Ranger began to bark.

"Listen, Steve, be cool, man. Calm down. You're here with friends, it's alright, nobody here is going to fuck with you. Honest. We're your friends." Jill seemed to be getting through to him. He stopped waving his arms around.

"You don't know me! You don't! Not at all. Nobody knows me!" His tears were flowing, we all felt pretty helpless, and it freaked us out.

Jill kept trying to calm him down, soothing him the way you would a scared puppy, and soon he buried his head in his arm and just sat there sobbing softly. We let him sit. Didn't really know what else to do for him.

After ten minutes or so he picked up his head and looked around the room. He looked deflated, like everything had drained away and left him empty, like all he had inside was pain and anger, and when that dissipated there was nothing left. He retrieved his bottle of wine from the coffee table, and held it out again, an offering we all refused, at which point he shrugged his shoulders and took another swig.

"Don't know what you're missing," he said, wiping his mouth with the back of his hand.

"Yeah," said Brian. "It's done wonders for you."

"Go fuck yourself," Steve muttered, and his head rolled to one side. "Fuck you, Fuck all of you!"

"Don't get belligerent!" said Jason. "We're just trying to help."

"Can't help. Nobody can help. Don't need no help." He drank what remained of the wine, and slammed the bottle down on the coffee table. "Don't need no help!" He slumped back into the couch and closed his eyes. Soon he was snoring.

"Great," said Brian. "What do we do with him now?"

"Let him sleep," replied Jill. "Poor guy."

"What, all night long?" Brian asked.

"Well we can't send him home; he can't drive like this. Let him sleep it off on the couch." I agreed with Jill.

"Just what we need, a crazy drunk vet crashing on our couch. I hope he doesn't have a gun," Brian looked nervous. "Kill us all in our sleep."

"He seems harmless," said Jill. "I'm more worried about what he'll do to himself. He is one tormented dude. A lot of them come back from 'Nam like that. War destroys their souls. Shit! I hate it, I fucking hate it!"

Jill unlaced his boots and pulled them off his feet. He tossed around a little but he didn't wake up. I threw an old green blanket over him, filled the stove with wood, and then we all went off to bed, leaving Steve to toss and turn, battling his demons all night long.

When we got up the next morning he was gone, the only reminder of his presence, the empty bottle of Boone's Farm lying on the floor in front of the couch.

Steve started coming by quite a bit after that, two or three nights a week. He almost always showed up drunk, or partly drunk at least. He liked to hang out and smoke pot with Jason.

"Man, you wouldn't believe the weed we got over in 'Nam," he bragged one night. "Thai stick, man that shit was killer! Three tokes, I swear to god, and you wanted to take a nap. Everybody over there got stoned, even the officers. You know, a lot of that 'hurry up and wait'. Lots of sitting around, until they sent you out on patrol, then the shit really hit the fan." He was absently twisting a magazine while he spoke and the thing was starting to fall apart. He looked down suddenly and stopped, as if surprised to discover the destruction that had occurred by his hands.

"I'll tell you man, weed was the least of it. Lots of guys came home strung out on smack. I don't blame 'em. I mean the shit we saw, the shit we did…like who wouldn't want to block that out? Forget it, even for a little while? Fuckin' nightmare."

He always brought a bottle of Boone's Farm with him, and he was usually the only one who drank it. He told us some stories about the war, mostly about crazy stuff he and buddies did when they were on R&R, but he never talked about the fighting and killing, never anything specific, though he alluded to it all the time. We could tell it was bugging him though, always there, lurking in the background. Sometimes he'd get really drunk and go off like he did that first night. It freaked all of us out a little, but we came to accept him, and some mornings we would wake to find him passed out on the couch.

He liked to hang out and listen to music. Sometimes, when Suze pulled out her guitar he would sing along. He had a high voice that wasn't half bad, and he knew the words to every pop song from about 1955 on.

He would bring us raw milk from the farm, or fresh butter from his mom. He tried to be helpful in his own way, but he was clearly damaged goods, living every day with demons we could only imagine.

For some reason he felt more comfortable hanging out with us than spending time with his high school friends who still lived in town. "They got no idea. At least you guys know what we're doin' over there is wrong. They don't want to hear it from me."

Steve started to confide in Jason, telling him about his nightmares, and how sometimes he felt like he was back there in some firefight in the middle of the jungle. One night he had another flashback while he was sitting with us, and started shaking and screaming.

Jason grabbed him by his shoulders and looked him in the eye. "Come back Steve, it's okay man, you're home. You're with friends, it's cool."

Steve snapped out of it. "Sorry man, I'm startin' to lose my shit. Happens sometimes, can't shake it loose. I don't know…I mean what the fuck…you know?"

"Yeah man, I can dig it…with all you've been through." Jason tugged at his beard. "You ever think about getting some help? Talkin' to some-body?" We were all staring at him as Jason spoke.

"Help? Like a shrink?" Steve looked shocked. "Are you kidding? You think I'm crazy?"

"No," replied Jason, "not crazy, just…upset. You know, I mean, it would get to anybody, what you saw and what you had to do…"

"Well, it did get to me I guess, but I can deal with it. Don't worry about me."

"But I do worry about you Steve, we all do." Jason looked around the room for affirmation.

Spring 1969

SPRING SLOWLY CAME OUR way, like a man walking north at a leisurely pace, fourteen or so miles a day. Longer days gave way to milder nights, and by mid-April the maple trees began to bud out.

It was an in-between time, too late to collect sap and boil down, and way too soon to get out and work the garden. It was hard to believe a year had passed since we arrived. When I thought back to those first uncertain days, I hardly recognized myself, or Jill. We knew then we were beginning an adventure, but we could have never imagined all that had happened.

I felt like everything had changed: my whole sensibility, what I valued, what mattered to me, what I thought about day to day. My life had taken on a kind of immediacy I had never experienced before. Every task had a real purpose, every action an impact on my surroundings. Nothing was abstract anymore.

And I had changed physically too. I had lost any trace of the softness I had brought from the city. I reveled in my newfound strength, was aware of my body in new ways. It was a good feeling.

Things made a kind of sense to me that they never had before. I had a connection to this place that surprised me, a fierce attachment that seemed almost inappropriate considering the short time I had lived here. But it really did feel like our place, home, something we had created ourselves, not just somewhere we had moved into.

Jill felt the same way. "Kind of amazing," she said one night when we were lying in bed staring out the window at the full moon rising huge and orange over Hardwood Mountain. "This place really gets to you, you know? I mean it's really kind of magical. Sometimes I feel like we're living on the frontier, or something."

We had grown up with Davy Crockett and Daniel Boone on TV, John Wayne and cowboy movies. The restless western migration that made America was imprinted on our brains, and as much as we consciously knew it was a colonial enterprise, that archetype of the frontier remained. The desire for a fresh start, the sense that something new, something better, was just around the corner— that was part of what motivated us.

We felt like we were on the cusp of some huge change. Call it a sense of history, or call it delusion, but we were certain, more than ever; we knew we were changing the world, and changing ourselves in the process. We were new men and women, committed not just to a political revolution, but to transforming everything; turning it all on its head—ourselves, our relationships, our way of being in the world, every facet of our lives. We challenged all the old attitudes and institutions—family, sex, music, language, gender roles, economics, politics, drugs…you name it.

And we were convinced of our own righteousness. Look at what a mess our parents' generation had made: repression, oppression, imperialism, war, the environment. We knew better. And we weren't just talking about change, we were living it, making our lives an example of how things could be, how they should be, goddamnit!

This sense of purpose pervaded all that we did. We had fun, but we were earnest; every action had meaning and every action had consequence. We took ourselves seriously. We weren't fucking around.

The war gave it all a sense of urgency and import, but it was bigger than just that; the old world was crumbling, anybody could see that, at least anybody under thirty. We were part of a movement that was sweeping the world; surfing in on a tidal wave of change; caught up in one of those rare, cathartic moments where nothing is given and everything is possible.

That elusive feeling of connection I always hoped for swept over me as I lay in bed with Jill looking out at the rising moon. I hugged her close; she felt it too. We just stayed there, holding each other, and the feeling grew and swelled; it was like sex, orgasmic, but all we were doing was lying in each other's arms. We didn't talk, we were lost like that in each other, until we fell asleep.

When we woke early the next morning there was a dusting of fresh snow and the sun was shining. Ranger was at the foot of our bed waiting to go outside. Jill looked out the window.

"Let's pack a lunch and ski over to the lake. It's a beautiful day, and who knows how much longer the snow will last? We should get out and take advantage of it."

No one else was up yet, and I didn't need much convincing, so while I brewed coffee and scrambled us a few eggs for breakfast Jill made sandwiches and filled a thermos with hot tea.

By the time we pulled on our jackets, Ranger was tap dancing by the door, anxious to be out and away. We stepped into our skis and glided away down the trail, packed solid by the snowmobiles. There was an overlay of an inch or so of fresh powder. Ranger ran ahead. The rhythm of skis on snow was hypnotic, and the world seemed to be rotating under our feet, kick glide, kick glide…a gentle fugue through the woods and beyond, climbing skins on and then up the steep pitch to Hardwood's shoulder, hearts beating like tympani building to a crescendo as we topped the rise and pulled in to catch our breath and take in the valley unfolding at our feet.

We sat at the fire circle, sipping tea from the thermos, silently scanning the view that extended from New Hampshire's White Mountains in the east, Mansfield and Camel's Hump to the west, and ridge after ridge of Canada's Eastern Townships rising across the lake that sat snow covered, sparkling in the sun beneath us.

Ranger joined us and sat at my feet, panting, and wagging his tail, admonishing us for resting, anxious to return to his manic investigation of the surrounding countryside. I reached down and roughed his fur. "Take it easy boy, we'll be with you soon."

I thought often about Leland's warning when Ranger disappeared into the forest, but I didn't have the heart to leash him or leave him home. He came alive in the woods, tapped into something primal, all his senses amped up to another level. To deny him that would be cruel; would condemn him to half a life, and I couldn't do it.

We sat basking in the sun on the ridge, drank another cup of tea, took in the view for a while, then plunged back into the woods to follow the switchback trail that dove down toward the lake. Ranger led us, but at one point stopped, put his nose in the air, and tested the breeze. He suddenly veered off, and I noticed that when he left the trail to head into the woods, he was running on top of a crust that had formed on the snow last night.

Jill and I continued down, forced to snowplow in order to control our speed on the steeper sections. The snow was fast. Trees flew by us and the wind whistled in our ears. Adrenaline coursed through me and I let out a whoop.

The track flattened as the trail approached the lake, and we took our time through the last section, arriving lakeside as the sun approached its zenith. We took off our skis, and cleared the snow from a big rock on the shoreline, which we used as a bench.

Jill made a snowball and threw it at me, hitting me square in the face. "Sneak attack!"

"No fair!" I protested. "I wasn't ready."

"That's the whole point of sneak attack," she laughed.

She looked so beautiful there, standing in the sun, her cheeks red from the cold and the exertion, the highlights in her hair sparkling where it tumbled out from beneath her wool cap.

"You're gorgeous," I told her. "And I love you, and I can't believe how lucky I am to be with you."

Her cheeks seemed to glow a deeper red and she looked away for a moment. "You are the biggest goofball I know," she said, and she threw another snowball.

She took off her pack and took out the sandwiches—cheddar from our local creamery on whole wheat bread that Suze had baked the night before. I uncapped the tea and poured the remainder into the top of the thermos for us to share. We ate our lunch in silence, looking out at the lake and the row of hills beyond. The sun had begun to warm things up and drops of water started to drip from the thawing branches of the trees.

I looked back towards the woods and saw Ranger loping towards us down the path with what looked like a big stick clamped between his jaws. As he drew closer, I saw that the object in his mouth was not a stick, but rather, the leg of a deer, covered in hair and skin and bloody flesh. The dog pranced proudly up to us and deposited his prize at our feet.

"Holy shit!" I said, shocked.

"What the fuck?" Jill asked. "What is that thing?"

"He must have run down a deer," I answered.

"He killed a deer and tore its leg off?" She asked in disbelief.

I looked down at the bloody limb on the ground before us. "Probably chewed it off," I suggested.

"He killed a deer by himself? How could he do that?"

"Well, Leland says it happens when there's a crust on the snow. Ranger's a big, strong animal…"

"It's disgusting! How cruel!"

I looked at Ranger who sat there wagging his tail, staring up at me like he expected to be praised. "It's nature, no cruelty involved. He's just following his instinct. I mean it's kind of awful to think of a deer dying like that, but…"

"No buts," Jill insisted. "It's horrible, and it's not natural, he's a domesticated animal, he should know better. We need to train him."

"Yeah, he's domesticated, but he's still an animal; there's a part of him that's still wild. I don't know about training him. Leland says once they get a taste for it there's not much you can do," I looked at Ranger and noticed his muzzle was covered in blood. "Keep him chained up, I guess, but that's about it."

"Well, then chain him up!"

"Jill," I protested. "That's being cruel to him. Maybe just the next couple of weeks, till the snow goes away, even then though…" My words trailed off, and I thought of him whining on a chain all day long.

"Well, a leash then, keep him on a leash, and we'll take him out on walks."

"Like in the city?" I asked.

"We can't let him kill more deer, it's not cool. It's for his own good."

"Uh huh." The thought disturbed me, but I knew she was right.

We clamped back into our bindings and turned toward home. The sun was still shining, but my mood had turned sour. As we kicked off, Ranger retrieved the leg.

"No! Goddamnit! No!" I shouted at him. "Drop it!"

He let it fall from his mouth, cocked his head and stared at me uncomprehendingly, but trotted after us as we glided down the path heading back towards Hardwood.

When we got back to the house the others were sitting around the kitchen table looking morose. Suze's eyes were rimmed with red.

"Hey, what's going on?" asked Jill.

"We got some bad news today," said Brian. "Saw Leland down at the post office and he told us that Steve died."

"Oh, shit!" I said. "Car accident?" I thought about how drunk he usually was when he drove over to visit us.

"No," answered Brian. "They found him hanging in his folks' dairy barn."

"No!" cried Jill. "I knew it, I knew something had gone wrong with him. Fuck! This fucking war! Why didn't he talk to us? We could've helped him!"

"Uh uh," I said. "There was nothing we could have done for him. Nothing anybody could have done. He was haunted."

We attended his funeral at the small clapboard church in the village the following Sunday. Pretty much everyone in town was there, and for once we felt like we were part of the community, bonded together, at least for a moment, by grief. It's amazing how a tragedy can blur divisions and bring people together.

The preacher stood at the altar going on about Jesus and the joys of heaven while Steve's mother and father sat in the front pew holding hands and looking shell-shocked. The actual burial would have to wait a few weeks until the ground thawed in the little town graveyard that stood halfway on our hill.

We passed it every time we headed down to the highway. The "Granite Orchard", as Leland referred to it, was surrounded by a white picket fence. Once, on a walk, Jill and I had opened the gate that hung on rusty hinges and surveyed the dozens of simple markers that stood in tidy rows within. There were three or four surnames that represented the bulk of those buried there; the founding families of our little town.

The oldest marker dated back to 1793, a four-year-old girl, according to the dates on her stone. She rested between her parents, among her uncles, aunts, sisters, brothers, cousins, and their progeny. The grass in the cemetery was neatly mowed, and a few of the graves had bunches of fresh wild flowers adorning them.

I thought of Steve lying there and hoped that he found the peace and forgiveness he had been unable, or unwilling, to grant himself. It was a sad ceremony on a gray April day, and as we left the church all we could do was nod to the familiar faces that had gathered there, and tell his parents how sorry we were, how very sorry.

I HATE THIS FUCKING WAR! I can't believe Steve is dead. I know he was hurting, but to hang himself like that? He's another victim, just like the countless Vietnamese. His poor parents. We've got to do something! I don't know what, but something!

THE SEEDS WE HAD started in March were seedlings now, little plants gaining strength daily as they struggled toward the sun. They lined our windowsills and brought traces of green into a world that had been gray and white for almost six months. The roads turned to mud again and the woods began to return to life; the trees putting out tender pink buds, swelling until they burst into leaf.

I was anxious to get started out in the garden, tempted by the warm winds that began to occasionally blow from the south. But memories of last year's late snowstorms helped me contain my enthusiasm, so I waited impatiently for mud season to pass and spring to truly arrive.

The days were pregnant, promising new life, and more…I didn't know what, but I felt like something momentous was coming towards us, ready to engulf us, swallow us whole. Maybe it was just spring fever—we had been locked in the jaws of winter for half a year and it was in the process of spitting us out.

I took long walks with Ranger, marking the egress of the snow that had defined our world for so long until it existed only in memory and small patches that hung on deep in the woods. He could run free again, no longer constrained by the leash that kept him close to my side for the rest of the winter after he had killed the deer.

Then one evening the pond at the edge of the field again exploded with sound. A symphony; the lower register of wood frogs, joined a few warm evenings later by countless peepers, convinced me that spring had arrived. We could see the Vs of the returning geese in the sky, and hear their honking as they passed on their way north. The brown grass turned green, the muddy ruts congealed into hard ridges. Passage up the hill no longer risked a broken axle, and our communal energy began to rally to the tasks at hand.

We went to St. J and picked up fifty chicks, some layers, other for meat. We fenced an area at the edge of the field and built an open shed for the tiny brown and black Tamworth hogs we bought from a farmer a few towns over, and Bessy, our newly purchased pregnant milk cow, was a source of delight as we anticipated her freshening and the coming of her calf.

The habits of country life were becoming ingrained. We woke with the sun and spent most of our days outside. I was in the garden any day the weather allowed, prepping the soil for planting. Jason and Brian were busy expanding the chicken coop and then building a shed for the cow. Jill and Suze were caught up in a frenzy of spring cleaning, tearing the gray plastic off the windows, washing the glass with vinegar and water until sunlight once again streamed into the kitchen. They enlisted my aid at lunch one day to hang the large rag rug out, and beat the dust out of it.

I hadn't realized how much the winter had constrained us, how small our world had become, until we were liberated by the spring. Suddenly we were free to roam the woods, to move beyond the snowmobile path and sugaring roads that had defined our boundaries for so long.

Suze, who had spent the winter studying Euell Gibbons' *Stalking the Wild Asparagus*, began foraging, and soon our dinner table was enriched by ramp, wild ginger and fiddleheads. She roamed the hill, top to bottom, relying on Mary for advice when Gibbons failed her.

Hoping to keep out at least some of the pests that had bedeviled us last year, I built a chicken wire fence around the garden, using cedar posts I cut in a wet portion of the woods. The peas I planted early in May soon set tendrils climbing the fence closest to the road.

We were poised on the edge of summer, and I felt like we were about to plunge into the green depths of another adventure. It was just a matter of time until the wave began. We had already heard from old friends planning to return, and who knew what other flotsam might blow up on our shore? It made me nervous.

I thought back to the chaos and overcrowding last year, the resentment I felt toward those who didn't contribute. I remembered how we had spread over the land without regard to protecting it from abuse, and realized it was something we needed to talk about.

"We need to set some guidelines for visitors," I announced at dinner one night. "Summer's coming and you know we're going to get hammered. We've got to get ready."

"What do you mean? Like rules?" asked Brian, skeptically.

"Well, something. I mean we've got to look out for the land, and basic hygiene…and we can't afford to support a bunch of freeloaders. Folks staying need to help out, to pitch in, and we should be working toward a goal. We need a plan or at least a set of priorities, projects to channel their energy. This 'do your own thing' shit only goes so far, and I'm sick of cleaning up messes made by people I hardly know."

"Whoa, that's harsh, dude!" Brian grimaced.

"Maybe, but that's how I feel. Think about it, man, we've been busting our asses getting this place together. I don't mind sharing, that's the whole point of this, right? But I want some reciprocity, 'from each according to their ability, to each according to their need', okay? That's all I'm asking for. I can't stand this 'what's yours is mine, and what's mine is mine' attitude. It's got to go both ways."

"I see your point," said Suze. "I mean we want to be welcoming, but sometimes last year I felt like I was cooking and cleaning for a bunch of spoiled brats instead of working for the revolution. Not everybody, a bunch of people really tried to help, but we were so disorganized."

"Yeah," said Jill, "there was a lot of wasted effort last summer. I can see the point of getting more organized, but guidelines...I don't know, sounds a little fascistic."

"Oh, now I'm a fascist?" I flushed red. "You know that's not what I mean. Let's just lay things out a little more clearly. Can you handle that?"

"Yeah, of course," Jill said, and the others agreed.

We ended up creating a chart that broke down different projects and jobs; meals, cleanup, garden, firewood, animals, housing, building, odd job crew, and we agreed to be responsible for coordinating the areas. We decided to ask each new arrival to commit to work twenty-five hours a week.

DAVID IS SO UPTIGHT! But he might be right about a little more structure being a good thing. If we get organized, we should be able to get a lot more done. I just wish he would cool out a little. We didn't come up here to be slavedrivers.

I WAS UNLOADING MANURE into the garden one Saturday morning in early June when the first car of returnees arrived. I leaned on my shovel and watched as the VW van disgorged its passengers, a woman with long red hair wearing a long skirt and a tie-dyed shirt and holding a child on her hip, followed by a skinny guy with a wispy beard, and then, a familiar lanky shape emerged from the back door: Lonny.

"Yo, brother, what's shakin'?" he called out. "Am I late?"

"Late? You're a sight for sore eyes! Groovy man, I wasn't expecting you." It was great to see him.

"Yeah, I figured you could use a little help. I mean, now that winter's over, the garden and all. Damn, Bro, you turned me into some kind of farmer or somethin' I guess, and besides—summer in the city? I mean, that shit is not cool, not at all cool, so I figured you dudes wouldn't mind...yo, these are my friends, Cassie and little Sebastian, and this is John." He indicated the skinny guy.

"They know the deal, I explained everything to them. Good people, man. They're gonna stay in their van—it's a camper. Check it out, John's a great carpenter, he built it himself. Handy guy to have around."

"Cool," I said, and then hesitated. "But you know, we made some changes since last summer. Anybody staying more than a few days has to sign up for twenty-five hours of work a week. We've got a chart up in the kitchen."

"That's cool, man," said John. "We're not afraid of a little work, sounds fair. We're just lookin' to get out of the city, back to the land, you know?"

I left my hoe in the garden and they followed me back up to the farmhouse, where Suze was making a pot of black bean soup and a salad for lunch. She gave Lonny a big hug and he introduced her to Cassie, John and Sebastian.

Cassie put the little boy down, and he started to run around the kitchen, chasing after Ranger, who had followed us in from the garden.

"He's adorable," said Suze. "How old?"

"Almost three," replied Cassie. "He loves dogs, I hope it's cool."

"Oh, yeah," I told her. "Ranger's good with kids, we had a baby crawling around here last summer."

The little boy was chasing after the dog, who didn't know quite what to make of the situation. Sebastian stood as high as Ranger's back, and couldn't have weighed more than thirty pounds, but he was fearless in his pursuit, calling out delightedly: "doggy, doggy!"

The boy wore a pair of Oshkosh overalls, and a red and white plaid shirt. He had long curly dark hair that framed his face, with its bright brown eyes. He finally caught up with Ranger, who looked at me with confusion.

"It's okay, Ranger, good boy!" I reassured him. "Sebastian won't hurt you. He wants to be friends."

He hugged the big dog, and patted him on top of his head. "Nice doggy," the little boy said in a sweet voice. "Nice doggy."

I kneeled down to join them. "His name is Ranger," I said.

"Wanga," the little boy intoned. "Good doggy, Wanga."

He was awfully cute.

The others came in for lunch. Everyone was glad to see Lonny, and after introductions we all shared a meal of soup, salad, and homemade bread.

After lunch the newcomers checked out our chart, and each signed up. Cassie took an assignment in the kitchen, John signed on to the carpentry crew, and as I hoped, Lonny agreed to work with me in the garden. So far so good.

Little Sebastian kept us entertained after lunch as he acted both parts in a battle between a teddy bear and a stuffed dinosaur, complete with growls and a spirited dialogue, that no one but his mother could understand. I realized it might be fun to have a little kid around.

After the break Lonny and I headed back out to the garden. There was a still a lot to do get the soil ready for the last of our starts, tender stuff like peppers, tomatoes and eggplant, that I had been hardening off in a cold frame made from old window sash, a design I had seen in the *Whole Earth Catalog*.

"So, man, what have you been up to? How was the winter up here? We got a lot of catching up to do." Lonny was talking a mile a minute, as usual.

"I was out on the coast, man, diggin' that warm California sun, you know what I mean? Oh, I got into that scene out there. It was a groove, beautiful really. All those blonde chicks, and the beach…it was really cool. Can you dig it?"

"So why'd you come back," I had to ask. "I mean, it sounds like paradise."

"I don't know man, I got tired of it. One beautiful day after another, it gets boring. Not my thing, you know? I guess I need a little adversity in my life, so here I am," he laughed.

"Besides, Cassie and John were drivin' back east, so…" he laughed again. "I couldn't stand the thought of you out here planting shit without me. I wanted to see how it was goin' back here. Last summer, you know, you really made me feel welcome. I mean, you're all right for a white boy."

We saw folks trickle in from that day on, every week two or three showed up, either returning from last summer, or new arrivals. The word was still out, Vermont was a cool place to be—New Mexico, California, Vermont; all hot spots for back-to-the-landers, and as the urban scenes got more chaotic, more people wanted out.

Our little family expanded. I don't know if things were really more organized, or if I was just more laid back, less uptight, but it felt better to me; like we were pulling together more and really getting stuff accomplished. Lonny and I got everything planted out by mid-June and it looked to me like we were headed for a bumper crop, especially with later arrivals signing up to help and enough hoes and cultivators available to put them to work weeding.

Lonny's friend John turned out to be a real carpenter, much more knowledgeable than I was, and he organized a crew that built a small barn for the cow, expanded and improved the chicken coop, and made a better shelter for the piglets. Then they dug a pit and built another outhouse that stood about fifty feet away from the farmhouse, so we wouldn't overflow our cesspool, which seemed like a good idea with all the new folks taking up residence.

DAVID, JASON, SUZE AND I took off for few days to drive out to Chicago for the SDS National Convention. The convention had always been a high; the people, the rush of energy and ideas; the excitement that came from being with thousands of like–minded folks; realizing that you were part of something bigger than yourself. It was great to see old friends, and we always ended up meeting lots of cool new people too. Even David seemed so relaxed, so comfortable with everybody.

This one was a disaster, though. In a way, it's where things really started to turn to shit. Progressive Labor had bussed in their cadres to take over SDS. They elected the national leadership, and forced a split in the organization. Huge bummer. Just when other things had begun happening. The more they escalated the war, the faster we'd grown; three hundred thousand members in over three hundred chapters on campuses all over the country, and the Economic Research and Action Project too, organizing off campus in poor neighborhoods in a dozen cities. Really cool shit. We were starting to make progress. Then the sectarian assholes fucked everything up.

There was a big fight—PL versus everybody else, and then everybody else split; Revolutionary Youth Movement I (RYM I) versus RYM II, and then Weatherman split from everyone else and took over the national office in Chicago, and New Left Notes, *the newspaper. SDS was torn apart. What a waste. We went back to Vermont thoroughly disgusted.*

Summer 1969

By LATE JUNE, THINGS were feeling kind of settled, as a routine of work, meals, meetings, and partying set in. The schedule seemed to be working out. Oh, there were a few slackers, mostly young guys who always seemed to have time for a dip in the pond, or to smoke a joint, but even they did a little work, and, what the hell, the farm wasn't a factory, and what was the point of living in the country if you couldn't enjoy it? I felt more confident about our prospects for survival, having made it through the last winter.

Money was still a concern. Most of the newcomers kicked in a little to the communal kitty, but even with food stamps, and the cash we generated from odd jobs, we were living pretty close to the bone. Jason took a job helping Calvin, the dairy farmer down the road, milk his cows, and brought in a little money for us that way. He also convinced us to plant a bunch of pot in a clearing back in the woods, with the hope that it could bring in enough cash to get us through the next winter.

Most afternoons, after we tired of working, if the weather was nice, Jill and I would meet at the pond. Leland told us his great-grandfather had dug it, using a team of draft horses to dredge out a wet spot in the field where a spring surfaced.

It covered a half an acre or so, mostly shallow with a muddy bottom, but John and his crew built a floating dock supported by empty fifty-five-gallon drums, that extended far enough out that we could dive in.

The water was a deep green that turned brown after a rain. Cattails grew at one end, and it was home to the thousands of frogs that serenaded us nightly from early spring on. The underground spring that constantly replenished it ensured that the water was always cold, and after a day sweating in the garden I looked forward to plunging into its welcoming darkness, and emerging refreshed and renewed.

Jill and I were lounging on the dock one afternoon, soaking in the late afternoon sun. Ranger was hunting frogs among the cattails at the other end when he suddenly stiffened. A figure emerged from the woods across the field. I could see he was carrying a rifle. I threw a towel over Jill, who was naked, pulled on a pair of shorts, and then rose to see who it was, and what he was doing.

As I walked toward the man across the field Ranger loped up to join me.

I checked him out as I drew closer. He was an old guy with long hair that fell to his shoulders from under a battered fedora. Despite the warmth of the day he wore a long-sleeve shirt, corduroy trousers and a tattered woolen hunting vest in red and black plaid. As I drew near, I saw he had something slung over his shoulder that had attracted Ranger's attention. When I approached closer still, I saw that it was a string of five or six squirrels. He carried a single-shot .22 that looked more like a toy than a real rifle.

"Hi," I said, squinting a little into the sun. "How's it goin'?"

"Not too bad," he responded. He was creased and wrinkled; his face looked like a piece of dried out leather. "Got some squirrels."

"I see," I couldn't help staring, he was such an odd-looking old man, like someone out of another era. "What are you going to do with them?"

"Well. Take 'em home and stew em' up, maybe can a couple."

"You eat squirrel?"

"Good eatin', not many who still do, but ain't no huntin' season on squirrels. Takes a couple to make a meal, but no shortage of 'em around here. No sir, nothin' wrong with a squirrel. Squirrels are alright by me."

"You live around here?"

"Well, I guess I do, all my life. And my people's been around here forever."

"Oh, early settlers?"

"You could say so, I'm Abenaki."

"Abenaki?"

"The original settlers, 'bout five thousand years ago. People of the Dawn. My names Vincent, Vincent St. Francis." He held out a leathery hand, which I shook.

"I'm David, and that's Jill," I saw she had managed to get dressed while I talked with Vincent. "And that's Ranger." The dog was staring up at the dead squirrels, whining.

"I know," he said. "Seen you around. Skiing back in the woods, sug-aring with Leland."

It seemed odd to me, because I had never seen him, I was sure of that.

"What, have you been spying on us?" I asked, only half joking.

"Nope, just livin' my life; huntin', fishin', trappin'. Seen you in the forest."

"Where did you say you live?" I asked.

"Oh, I got a little cabin back in the woods, not far from here, other side of Hardwood, near the lake. You're my nearest neighbor so I figured it was time to introduce myself."

"We've been here for over a year," I said. "Why now?"

"I been watchin'. You're all right. You respect Mother Earth. I stay away from most people. Got to be careful," he said, looking around. "Especially with white people. I know they call me a hermit around here, but that's not it. I'm just selective, real selective, 'bout who I associate with."

"Well, I'm honored," I responded.

"Don't be," he said. "I'm not associating with you. I just came to warn you."

"Warn me about what?"

"Game warden was up in the woods today. Found your pot garden. Probably be back with the State Police. Hate to see anybody get in trouble. They arrested me for poachin' a couple times. I told 'em I had aboriginal rights, but they didn't care. If I was you, I'd pull them plants before they come back."

"Holy shit!" I said. "Thanks for the warning. I'll get right on it."

He turned away from me to head back into the forest.

"Nice to meet you," I said to him as he retreated into the woods.

He didn't look back at me, but I heard him say, "good luck."

Jill and I returned to the house and rallied a crew to go back into the woods and pull the plants. We brought them back to the house and threw them on a bonfire.

Sure enough, when Lonny and I were out in the garden the next morning a State Police cruiser pulled up behind a Fish and Wildlife truck.

A trooper got out, complete with Smokey the Bear hat, and he and a game warden, dressed in a brown uniform, started to walk up the path to the house.

"Can I help you?" I walked over to intercept them.

"Yeah," the cop said. "I received a report of marijuana being cultivated on your property. When I investigated the site, while there were no plants present, there were signs of recent activity. What do you know about that?"

"Nothing officer, nothing. We grow vegetables here. You're welcome to look in the garden, we have nothing to hide."

Lonny was leaning on his hoe with a smirk on his face. The cop gave him a hard look.

"Must have been some local kids or something," I said. "We'll keep our eyes open."

"Uh huh," he said, clearly unconvinced.

"Who's up at the house?" he asked suspiciously.

"Just some friends," I said.

"Uh huh," he said. "Mind if I go up and look around?"

"Well, that's our private space, you know. Maybe better if you stay down here."

"You're telling me I can't go up to the house?"

"Do you have a search warrant?" I asked.

"No, but I thought you had nothing to hide. Why can't I go up there?" he demanded.

"It's a matter of principle. You know, civil liberties and all that. Freedom from arbitrary search and seizure; the constitution, stuff like that."

"Smart-ass, huh?"

"No officer, I just know my rights"

"Oh yeah, what's your name?"

"David," I said.

"Well, David, maybe I'll come back with a search warrant."

"If you do, then you can come up to the house."

"We'll see smart-ass, we'll just see. You and your associates better watch yourselves."

"I don't have any 'associates', just friends."

He turned and walked away, back towards his cruiser with the game warden trailing after him.

I have to admit I was shaken up by the encounter. So far, we had managed to minimize our contact with the authorities, and I wanted it to stay that way. The last thing we needed were the cops poking around. I was thankful that Vincent's warning had given us time to pull the plants.

At lunch back in the farmhouse I told the others what had happened.

"Fuck!" said Jason. "You think he'll come back with a warrant?"

"Don't know, but it's probably a good idea to prepare for the worst, clean the place out. Have everybody stash their weed out in the woods or something, just in case," I suggested.

"Don't get all paranoid," said Jill. "I doubt if he can get a warrant." Her father was a lawyer.

"Maybe," I responded. "But it wouldn't hurt to take some precautions just in case."

"I guess not," she conceded. "I just hate giving them that kind of power over us. It feels like a violation, or something. I mean, we're doing our thing and we're not hurting anyone. Why should they harass us?"

"Well, marijuana is illegal," I said tentatively.

"What, are you defending them?" Jill's voice held an edge of anger. She'd been getting pissed off at me a lot lately.

"No, of course not, I'm just saying we should be careful, that's all. Better safe than sorry. We've got important shit to do here, and I'd hate to see it get fucked up because of a little weed."

"Groovy," interjected Lonny. "It's cool. Dave's right. We don't need no bullshit busts. Shit, I hate to think of what would happen to my Black ass in jail up here. Let's just take a little care these next few days, ain't no big thing."

"Thanks for the vote of confidence; be a little careful, that's all I'm saying." I glared at Jill.

We did clear the drugs out of the house, and hid them in a plastic bag under a log about a hundred yards back in the woods. But after a week or so, with no further sign of the cops, we relaxed and things went back to normal.

I RAN INTO LELAND a few days after my encounter with the trooper and told him about meeting Vincent.

"Oh yeah, old Injun Vince, quite the character. Known him ever since I was a boy. Surprised he put in an appearance, mostly he avoids people. Got a little cabin way back in the woods, not far from the lakeshore. Grows himself a garden, runs a trap line, hunts and fishes, makes baskets, and keeps pretty much to himself these days. Claims to be pure-blooded Abenaki.

"We got quite a few of 'em lives around here. St. Francis, Lapan, couple other family names. Mostly they blend in pretty good, but old Injun Vince, he keeps to the old ways and he keeps his own company. Used to be he'd come to town pretty regular, shop at the store and all that. But after they got ahold of his wife back in the twenties, he stopped coming around, except once or twice a year, when he'd come in to sell his furs and buy matches, flour, stuff like that."

"What do you mean they got ahold of his wife?" I asked.

"Well, I'll tell you, it always seemed wrong to me, damn cruel, I didn't care for it at all, but it was the State of Vermont. Got the idea from some professor up to the University in Burlington. Eugenics, they called it. Build up the breeding stock by makin' it so's the mentally deficient couldn't have babies. 'Cept it was anybody a little different or troubled they picked."

"What do you mean? They sterilized them?"

"Yup, took those parts right out of 'em. They went after any women in the State Hospital, took women off of the poor farms, and particularly anybody they thought had Abenaki blood in 'em. That's when a lot of 'em started tryin' to blend in more. But not old Vincent, and they came and took his wife up to the hospital and gave her the operation, cut her womb right out. She was never the same after she came home. That's when he stopped comin' around, and started keeping to himself. Kind of a hermit."

"It's like Nazi Germany or something! Wow, what a story, I had no idea. Poor guy."

"Well, it was a long time ago and she's been dead a good thirty years at least. You'd think they would've let him be after that, but they arrested him a couple times for takin' deer out of season. That just made him more determined to have as little to do with 'em as possible."

The more I learned from Leland and Mary about our little town, and Vermont in general, the more surprised I was. Bucolic Vermont had a dark side, a seam of evil and prejudice that mostly stayed underground, but surfaced occasionally in ways that were pretty shocking. I should have realized that once you dig beneath the surface of most places you will discover some dirty little secrets; our town was no different.

THE GARDEN WAS FINALLY in, and my attention turned to an ongoing battle against the weeds that began to assert their presence in an aggressive fashion. Lonny and I, with the help of a couple of more recent arrivals, were able to stay on top of things with two or three hours a day of weeding. As June approached July, the rains that had made everything so lush and green through the spring gave way to an extended dry period. And the water line we had run from the spring box in the creek turned out to be a blessing, saving us the work of hauling cans all the way to the garden. It still took some effort to make sure the growing plants got the water they needed, but we were able to manage it. I'd be damned if, after all the work we had put into the garden, I would allow the young growth to succumb to drought.

We decided to have a float in the Fourth of July parade that year. I talked about the idea with Leland, and he agreed to help. We filled his hay wagon with bales, and draped the sides with signs that read "Zion Farm, Farmers for Peace". Our milk cow, Bessie, had recently given birth, and the calf was to ride in the wagon with Suze, Jill, Maia, Cassie and little Sebastian. Leland would pull the wagon with his tractor and the rest of us planned to march along behind, with placards and a banner made from an old bed sheet. Not real elaborate, but a way for us to make a statement; to amplify the message of our weekly vigils at the post office.

The day of the parade dawned hot and muggy, the sun a hazy presence trying to burn through a thick cloud cover that finally gave way by the time we headed down the hill in the hay wagon. The parade assembled down at the ball field, and we joined the line—marchers, horses, fire trucks, antique tractors, old cars, and bicycles festooned with bunting waiting to make their way down the state highway through the village.

We arrived early, but the road was already lined with spectators and their ranks continued to fill out.

"Looks like it's gonna be a real corker this year," Leland observed as the Hobo Band began to tune up.

I hadn't been sure what kind of a reception we would receive, but people were friendly enough, offering greetings and comments on how cute our calf was. Sebastian attracted a fair amount of attention as well. Cassie had dressed him in Oshkosh overalls with a plaid shirt and a John Deere cap, like a real little farmer, and he was adorable. It seemed to me that people were a lot friendlier than they had been last year. Baby animals and little kids, I guess that was the path to social acceptance.

The parade moved out, and Leland started his old Deere, the two cylinders popping as we made our way along the parade route.

For the most part people waved and applauded as we slowly rolled down the highway. There were a few folks who looked confused as we passed, and a handful who booed and made angry gestures, but Jill and the others ignored them and waved to the crowd from the float.

I was marching along with Jason and Lonny behind the hay wagon carrying a banner that read "End the War Now!" When we passed the general store, Mac and his cronies were sitting on the porch. They looked at us and started shouting. "If you don't like it here, go back to Russia!" "You fucking cowards!" They rose from the chairs they had been sitting in and started waving their fists. I thought they might come off of the porch and attack us, but just then Donna and Ronald, Steve's parents, joined in to walk behind our banner, and so did Lillian. That seemed to give them pause, though they continued to shout and jeer at us.

The parade only lasted about a half an hour, but by the time we were done I was soaked in sweat. It was incredibly hot and muggy and it looked like there was a storm blowing in. The wind picked up and dark clouds threatened on the horizon. I could hear thunder in the distance. It seemed as though the barbeque was going to get rained out.

Soon the rain started to fall; big lazy drops at first, but as the towering dark clouds drew closer the pace quickened, thunder started booming and flashes of lightning illuminated the interior of the cloud, and at that point people started to abandon the rec field and head for cover. Most ran for their cars, but we had ridden down on Leland's hay wagon, and had nowhere to go to escape the storm

It didn't take too long for all of us to get thoroughly soaked. Then, the sun came out. A rainbow appeared in the sky above, and hailstones began to pelt us. They soon grew to the size of peas, and everyone left on the field scrambled for whatever cover we could find. Jill, Suze, and the others crouched under the hay wagon, the rest of us ran for the little league dugouts on either side of the field. The hail bounced off of the corrugated metal roof, sounding like a barrage of gunshots.

"Holy shit!" exclaimed Brian. "What next? Is it gonna start raining frogs?"

The hail continued for a while, hard to say exactly how long, but long enough for the hailstones to begin to accumulate, turning the green grass of the ball field a frosty white.

The storm passed as suddenly as it had arisen, the sun shone brightly, the hail began to melt, people left their cars and the festivities resumed. I hung around a set of risers where the Hobo Band was performing a horrible medley of patriotic tunes, when Leland sidled up to me.

"Hope the hail didn't hurt your garden," he said. "Corn crop won't benefit much."

I thought of the tender plants sitting unprotected from the onslaught that had just passed over. "You think so?" I asked anxiously.

"Don't know," he replied. "Storms can be awful local, hail here don't necessarily mean we got it up to the hill. Guess we'll see."

My concern about the garden took the fun out of the rest of the afternoon for me. But I ate a piece of barbeque chicken, and went through the motions of visiting with neighbors. I saw Vincent selling baskets at the far end of the field and went over to say hi and thank him again for the tip. Leland had told me where the old Indian's cabin was, and I had been meaning to go check it out, but hadn't got around to it yet. Despite the distractions, mostly I worried about the garden.

When we arrived home later that afternoon, I rushed to check on the plants. At first glance everything looked all right, but a closer examination revealed that almost half of our little tomato and pepper plants had their spindly stems snapped off.

"Oh shit!" I exclaimed to Lonny, who had accompanied me to the garden. "Fuck! What do we do now?"

"Plant some more. It's still early. We can get some starts, it's not too late."

"Yeah, I guess." I looked around at the damage. "It's just...I don't know, they're like my babies."

Lonny laughed. "Oh, come on man, they're just some little plants. Completely replaceable. Don't be freakin' out on me over this shit. Ain't no big thing. Really Dave, we can deal."

"I know, I know. I've just been growing them since March, all different heirloom varieties, all organic..."

"Hey bro, like I said, ain't no biggie."

I was surprised at the intensity of my reaction, but like I said, I had a lot invested in the garden. Luckily, most of the lower-growing stuff had survived with just a few damaged leaves. Anyway, Lonny was right, we could put in some new tomatoes and peppers, and besides there was nothing to be done about it except replace the damaged plants. I learned something that day about gardening, though it was a bitter lesson.

THE FOURTH SEEMED TO signal a shift. Summer went into high gear; long, languid days, blue skies and hot sun. I started taking walks with Ranger in the afternoons, after a morning of work in the garden. We explored the woods and rambled down old paths and game trails. I thought about going to find Vincent's cabin, but I never did till later in the summer, though I found traces of old farms—stone walls that ran in straight lines through the forest, foundations of long deserted houses and barns, and what looked like an old stone tower, half collapsed, but still impressive. When I next saw Leland I asked him about it.

"Why that's the old potash furnace. Goes way back to the early days. They burned up this whole forest to make potash, shipped it up to Montreal, down to Boston, all over. Number one cash crop back in those times. Hardly a tree to be seen around here back then."

I gazed around at the thickly forested hills and ridges that surrounded us. "Hard to believe, the way things look now."

"Exactly the opposite in those days," Leland explained. "Eighty percent open, twenty percent forested, just the reverse today. Folks see these woods, think they're lookin' at virgin forest or some kind of untouched wilderness. But that's not the case. All this land's been worked, hand of man touched pretty much every inch. One exception round here, upper reaches of the east face of Hardwood Mountain. 'Bout fifty acres up there," he pointed up above the granite outcropping that shone in the sun. "Practically the biggest parcel of virgin trees in the whole state. Not many that know about it. Awful steep, pretty much impossible to log, and back when my folks owned all this," he swept his arm across the horizon, "Great-grandpa saw what was comin', put a covenant right in the deed sayin' those trees should be saved."

"Wow, far out!" I replied. "I'd love to get a look at it sometime."

"Well, I guess it is kinda special—big trees up there. State forester come by a few years back, made some measurements, put some markers on some of those trees, said they're the biggest in the state; maple, birch, tamarack. Yep, some pretty nice trees up there. We can scramble up and take a look sometime."

"That would be very cool!"

"Sure thing. I like a big tree," he looked wistfully up above the ridge. "I took Mary up there, first time she came by to see the place."

"Back in the twenties?" I asked.

"Yep," he replied. "It was a long ways from Barre, but I wanted her to get a feel of the home place, asking her to move all the ways up here to the middle of nowhere. Though, of course we had more neighbors then, all those abandoned farms were still milking cows."

"How did you two meet, anyway? I mean I know she was from Barre, that's down near Montpelier, right?"

"Down near Montpelier, alright, but a whole different world, 'specially back then. It was a wild place. I told you a little 'bout prohibition—Barre was a center. Big time bootleggers, speakeasies, lots of radicals still around, though things got tough for them. But the liquor business was booming. Anything didn't come down Lake Champlain to St. Albans, funneled through Barre.

"That was what brought me down there when I first met Mary. Now, you realize I was a much younger man then. I had just rode in on a truck-load of Canadian whiskey, and you'd think I could have wet my whistle whenever I wanted. But I didn't.

"You see, when I first came there, a buddy of mine got me a drink of something called grappa, some sort of brandy. The Italian folks made it. Well really the Italian widows made it. They had no other way to earn a living. Strong drink all right! So when I hit town I went lookin' for some.

"Well, you'd go right to the house. They'd sell it to you and some of 'em let you sit in the parlor and drink it. They had tables set up like a little tavern or something. Now, I asked at the Quality Market, and they told me that a lady named Lydia made the best grappa, and she had a house down Granite Street, right near the sheds.

"I went over down street and knocked on her door. Prettiest girl I ever saw answered. That was Mary, only she went by Maria back then. Just out of high school and helping her mama out with the youngest kids and her grappa business. I was dumbstruck, couldn't say a word to her, but she showed me in and I got a glass of brandy, sat there for an hour drinkin' it and hopin' to get another look at her.

"Came back next trip, sat there again. Finally, third time around I screwed up my courage, talked to her a little, and pretty soon I was signin' on for every load goin' down there I could find. Makin' good money and payin' court to Mary.

"Her mama wasn't crazy about the idea either. Didn't know quite what to make of me. Guess she figured Mary'd end up with an Italian – though she had no love for the granite, neither the quarries nor the sheds. She'd seen 'em kill plenty of men.

"Wasn't no shortage of other young fellows wantin' to be with Maria either. She was a beauty, and just about the sweetest person you'd ever want to meet. Still is," he beamed, like he had won a prize. "It took a while, but I finally won her mama over as well. Whenever I'd come, I'd bring her a little something from the farm: some maple syrup, an apple pie, or fresh raw milk that she'd make into mozzarella cheese. Got to be she actually looked forwards to me comin' round. Religion was never an issue—she hated the church, called the priests bloodsuckers. Didn't even seem to mind so much I wasn't Italian after a bit. After all, in a way we were in the same business.

"They were used to all kinds of people in Barre at that time. Folks from all over came there to work the granite; mostly Italians, but Scots, Spanish, Lebanese, Quebecers, you name it. Was a regular United Nations. Everybody got along pretty good too.

"I'll never forget the first time I brought Mary up here. We drove in a Model T pickup. Took the better part of a morning to get here, roads weren't what they are today. When she first saw the place…well, let's just say it was love at first sight. Barre back then, it was dusty, dirty, kind of raw. And livin' on Granite Street like she did, right near the sheds, it was loud; heavy machines, saws, compressors, all that.

"Took her up Hardwood with a picnic lunch, then we went up top among those big trees I told you about. She said it was like a cathedral. Sometimes I think she married me as much for the place, the peace and quiet…" His voice trailed off.

"Whatever the reason, I'm mighty glad she did. We're a good team, we worked this place together pretty hard, I'll tell you. Went at it as long as we could till it just didn't make sense anymore." Leland stared into the distance. "Damn bulk tanks! Why we didn't even have electricity back then, even if we could have afforded one. Stupidest thing I ever heard of. We did just fine before that."

It was the first time I ever heard a trace of bitterness in Leland's voice.

"We even made it through the depression, and those were real hard times, let me tell you, Mr. Man. We had our chickens, milked some cows, grew a big garden. We got on alright, better than a lot of 'em, I figure.

"Well, we had a good long run anyways, milkin' cows, and boilin' syrup. Only disappointment was we never had any kids. Wish we had, coulda used some help around the farm. Mary never complained, but I could tell she would've liked some. That's why she took such a shine to Jill when she used to come up summers. Awful nice to have a young one runnin' around.

"Yep, time sure goes by fast, almost fifty years the two of us been together. Hard to believe." He gave a little laugh. "and we ain't done yet, not quite. Least I hope not."

"Me too," I said. I had really come to admire Leland, and to depend on him. He taught me so much that first year. In his own unassuming way, he had become my guide, or my guru, or something.

THINGS SEEMED MORE SETTLED that summer. There was still a lot of coming and going, a steady flow of visitors, but we had achieved a kind of order; tasks were apportioned, most of what we wanted to do got done. Though far from being universally accepted, we felt more at home in the little town. Our work doing odd jobs had made us some friends. For the most part we were acknowledged. We got fewer hostile stares and blank looks when we checked our box at the post office, and a few folks stopped by to talk to us at our weekly peace vigils, which we continued to hold every Friday.

Lonny was right. We replaced the damaged tomatoes and peppers with new starts, and the garden recovered from the hail damage. It was getting harder to keep up with the weeds as the summer progressed, pretty much an ongoing battle.

I came to realize that was just the normal state of a garden; a constant process of growth, flowering, fruiting, death, and decay, for crops and weeds alike. In fact, sometimes it was hard to distinguish between the two. We ate dandelion greens in our salad, and Suze made wine from the flowers, not half bad either. We rid the garden of chamomile, but dried it for tea. I was beginning to learn that a lot of what we assumed to be pests had a use. That went for everything in nature; insects, birds, even varmints. They all had a place, and when we tried to eliminate them, we did so at our own peril. Rodale taught me that, but so did Leland and Mary, and my own experience as well.

Though by no means an expert, I was beginning to feel more comfortable in the garden, more at ease and trusting of myself and what I knew. It was good to have Lonny to count on and others to help. The long winter seemed distant and we were living in the green moment, soaking up the sun to nourish us for the inevitable return of the cold and snow.

Our collective had lived through a full cycle of the seasons, and we were all stronger for it. Things were still awful in the larger world; the war raged on, injustice was all around us, but I felt a kind of confidence, almost optimism welling up, not complacency, but a sense of connectedness I had never felt before—to other people, to the land, and the larger place.

We read about the gathering on the bulletin board of the health food store in St. Johnsbury where we bought our supplies of brown rice and beans. "A Gathering of the Tribes," the poster proclaimed, "An inter-communal mid-summer meeting to build a statewide network."

"A commune of communes." I was all for it. "That has some possibilities."

"Sounds kinda hippy dippy to me." Brian sat in the shady part of the circle.

"No, it's like how can we share more—tools, food, maybe a co-op garage, or a free school, health care, you know? Sounds kinda cool to me!" Suze was fired up. "I'm going whether anybody else does or not."

We talked about it that night for almost an hour, and in the end decided that those who wanted to would go check it out, see if there was any common ground for building alliances.

We took the VW van that day, packed to the gills with an almost giddy crowd. Suze, me, Jill, Jason, Bobby, Maia, Janna, even Brian, plus a couple of others who had just arrived the day before. We felt like we were off on a holiday. It took over an hour to get there, another old hill farm long dormant and now inhabited by a group that, according to the sign on the side of the drive leading in, called themselves the Cold Mountain Community. We had met some of the members before at the anti-war demonstration in Montpelier where we had gathered to protest the visit of Tricia Nixon to the state capital.

We parked at the top of a large hayfield, joining twenty or so other vehicles; a mixed bag of VWs, battered pickup trucks, and rusting sedans. Jill, who had been sitting up front, was the first out of the van.

"Wow! Far out!" She surveyed a sprawling encampment. "What a scene! It looks like a gypsy camp or something." Tents had been pitched in the dooryard of the old farmhouse, festooned with colorful banners filled by the wind and hand-painted flags flapping in the breeze: "Love", "Peace", "Be Here Now", "Good Food", and variety of flowers and plants.

Off to one side of the tents was a long table made of planks on saw horses and covered with bowls full of rice, beans, salad, loaves of homemade bread, platters heaped with carrots, a large wheel of cheese, and a huge pot of boiled potatoes. Behind the table someone had dug a pit, and there was a pig roasting over glowing coals.

I was greeted by a girl with long blonde hair as I walked toward the spot where a group of people had gathered. "Hey, glad you made it. David, Zion Farm, right? I remember you from the demo. I'm Sarah."

"Yeah, good to see you. What's happening? This is Jill, Suze," I pointed out the others, "Jason, Bobby, Brian, Janna, and Maia…"

"Cool, well, folks are still arriving, but, you know, we've already sort of gotten started. I mean, we've been talking about shit, kinda informal, but like, there's guys talking about farming and food over there," she pointed to a group of a dozen people seated in a circle on the ground to their left. "There's an herb walk gonna start soon, they're gathering under the thistle banner. Ernie's got a couple people interested in draft horses up in the barn. We've got a bunch of workshops happening this afternoon, Karl has a schedule somewhere, but you know, like grab a bite to eat and wander around, get to meet people, if you're not into the program, or start your own workshop. Like do your thing, you know? We're gonna get everybody back together tonight for a feast and get reports back from the different groups. Oh yeah, we've got a little work project too we could use some help with, a new garden we want to open up."

"Sounds cool! Thanks, I guess we can figure it out from here." I turned to the others. "I want to check out this farming thing. Should we split up, cover more ground that way? Meet back here?"

"Groovy! I always wanted to learn about herbs." Jill looked around for the banner with a thistle.

"We ought to try and find the schedule," Jason glanced at Sarah. "You know where I can find this guy Karl?"

"He's hard to miss. He's got long red hair and a big beard, plus he's wearing a white jumpsuit." She surveyed the yard. "Actually, he's right over there." She pointed toward the food.

"I'll check with him. I want to see what's happening so we don't miss anything important."

"Yeah, right on! Me too." Brian joined Jason and they walked over toward a group gathered by the food table, where Karl, his flaming red hair in a long braid hanging down his back, was standing.

Jill and Suze meandered toward the thistle banner and I joined the circle on the ground, eager to learn whatever I could.

When the ag workshop broke up around noon, I got on a line that had formed at the food table, grabbed a plate and filled it with salad and veggies. I was standing next to a girl with short black hair.

"We grew it all ourselves!" She turned to me. "I'm Marcy."

"Hi, I'm David. You live here?"

"Uh huh, this is gonna be our third winter here. Well, not mine, I arrived last summer, but Karl, Sarah, Bear, a couple of others."

"Far out, how was the winter?"

"Kinda rough, a bunch of folks left, went down to Boston to earn some money, but a few of us hung in here. Fuckin' cold, that's for sure. But most everybody came back, and, you know, summertime we always get a big influx."

"Yeah, us too."

"Where are you from?"

"Zion Farm, we're about an hour north, right up on the border."

"Oh yeah, I heard about you. You guys are political, right?"

"Yeah. I mean, we're into farming and stuff too, but..."

"You're with SDS, aren't you?"

"Well, sort of. I mean we used to be, down in the city."

"New York?"

"Uh huh."

"Cool! Little different up here, huh? How are you guys doing?"

"Good, great really. It's totally out of sight. We put in a huge garden. We're gonna donate the extra food to the Panthers for their free lunch program."

"Groovy!"

I spotted Jill, Suze, and Jason seated under a maple tree. "Hey, nice meeting you." I turned to join them.

"Yeah, see you around."

I sat down between Jill and Suze. "How was the herb walk?"

"Far out!" Jill was lit up. "I had no idea, I mean the woods around here; it's like nature's medicine cabinet. I can't wait to get home and start putting together an herb shelf"

"Hey, speaking of herbs, man, they are growing some serious pot up here. That guy Ernie pulled out a joint of homegrown after the draft horse workshop...wow! It was totally unreal! I mean that shit was dynamite!"

"Damn, Jason! I haven't seen you this enthusiastic since we moved up here." Suze laughed.

"Well, I'm gonna see if I can get some seeds from him."

"I got the schedule for the afternoon. No pot-growing workshop, though." Brian took a piece of paper from his shirt pocket and unfolded it. "There's some pretty cool stuff goin' on." He passed the sheet around the circle.

"Free School, Co-op Garage, Peoples Health and Wellness, How To Start a Food Co-op, Women's Health, Self-Defense, Co-op Bank... damn!" I read aloud from the list. "Wow, some of this stuff looks really good. Who wants to go to what?"

As the day warmed, more people kept arriving. While we were contemplating our options a group of a half-dozen motorcycles roared into the dooryard. I recognized the distinctive blat of Harley Davidsons. The riders dismounted and parked their bikes. They were all big men, rough looking, with long tangled hair, wearing denim vests with distinctive patches on the back.

"Bikers." I did a double take. "What are they doing here?"

"Well, it's a gathering of the tribes right?" Jill was looking them over. "I mean they're outlaws, they've been sticking it to the man for years."

"Yeah, but aren't they, like reactionaries?" Suze was skeptical.

"Not necessarily. Don't be so judgmental." Jill rose to their defense.

"They're a bunch of thugs, lumpenproletariat." I was dismissive. "They're criminals."

"Hey, 'we are all outlaws in the eyes of America.'" Jill quoted the Jefferson Airplane. "Don't be so harsh, give them a chance. Besides, the revolution could use some thugs." She looked pointedly at me.

"Oh yeah, that's all we need!"

"Come on Dave, we've got to build alliances. Isn't that what you always say?" I had no response.

Suze gave the group of bikers a wary look. "Didn't the Hell's Angels attack an anti-war march in Oakland last year?"

Jill was conceding nothing. "So? You don't know anything about these guys. We'll find out where they're at."

We finished our lunch and I got up. "I'm going to the food co-op workshop."

"Women's health." Suze tossed her hair to one side.

"I'm checking out the co-op garage idea, we could definitely use some mechanical help."

"Yeah, Jason, far out! We need all the help we can get." Jill laughed.

"I'm all about self-defense. The revolution's coming, and who knows what kind of shit's coming down. We better be ready!" She was emphatic.

The workshops were held in the open air, with groups of anywhere from six to a couple of dozen seated in circles on the grass, or under the shade of the big maples that dotted the front lawn of the farmhouse. Late in the afternoon clouds started rolling in from the west, and a breeze picked up. When the sessions broke up, we regrouped at the food table, which now had a whole roasted pig as its centerpiece.

"Well, how did it go?" I asked as we stood in line to load our plates.

"Cool!" Suze was glowing with excitement. "I mean, I learned so much! There are people here with some real skills too. This girl Rachel used to be a nurse, there were a couple of women who are midwives. Man, we're going to start a network of all the communes, set up a traveling clinic. It was so great! I'm really glad we came!"

"This co-op garage, I don't know. They want everybody to drive like, '53 Chevys or something so they can get parts from junkyards and keep 'em rolling. Not really practical, if you ask me."

"The self-defense workshop was far out!" Jill was tapping her fingers on her plate as she waited. "These people are serious. I didn't know what to expect, you know? I thought they might go all hippy dippy on me, but some of them...this guy Mark, very cool. He was a Green Beret in 'Nam, got out and saw the light. Oh, and by the way, he's one of the bikers. I invited him to the farm. He's gonna teach us how to shoot!"

"Far out!" Jason sounded excited.

I rolled my eyes. "What are we going to shoot at?"

Jill turned to me. "You know David, sometimes you are just so full of shit!"

"What do you mean? Why do you want to learn to shoot? We're nonviolent, right?" I looked to the others for affirmation.

There was a moment of awkward silence, then Jason spoke. "Well, what the fuck, it wouldn't be bad to learn how to defend ourselves, would it?"

"What are you talking about? Defend ourselves from who? This is crazy!"

"Well, you never know what's gonna come down. The pigs...who knows? It couldn't hurt to learn, that's all I'm sayin'." Jason looked at the ground.

"Well, count me out! I think it's a really bad idea." I spooned a load of potatoes onto my plate, and followed it up with a healthy portion of roasted pig.

After dinner we all gathered in the dooryard, over a hundred people at that point. The sun was sinking lower and the flat light of early evening shone through a cloud bank, tinting the edges a rosy pink and illuminating the hayfield in a golden glow. Each workshop gave a report, and then anyone who wanted to speak was passed a carved stick.

We just listened, and then, when the meeting broke up and people started pulling out guitars, drums, flutes and fiddles, we headed back toward our van.

"You sure we don't want to stay overnight? I mean, we didn't help with the garden or anything. I feel a little bad about leaving." Suze sounded wistful.

"We didn't bring a tent," Jason said, as he drove out of the field back onto the rutted road that had brought us to the gathering.

"And," I said, "we've got plenty of work to do in our own garden." I was already worrying about getting the tomatoes weeded and another batch of lettuce planted. "We've really got to get our asses in gear if we're going to have anything for the Panthers."'

"You know, I don't get it, Dave. You support the Panthers, but you're against us learning to defend ourselves. Kind of a contradiction." Jill was still pissed at me.

"We don't have cops kicking in the door and trying to kill us."

"Not yet, but it's coming, and we better be ready."

"Look, I just don't think we can ever achieve the kind of world we want through violence. If it comes to self-defense, I guess, maybe, under certain circumstances, I can see it. But guns at the farm? Sounds to me like asking for trouble." I clenched my jaw. "But what the fuck, go ahead and do whatever you want!"

WHAT AN ASSHOLE DAVID can be! I can't believe he doesn't get it after everything that's happened. The war, the Panthers, he still doesn't see. If he thinks sit-ins are gonna change anything he's blind!

JILL AND I LAY in bed that night under a thin blanket that kept us from the chill that still hung in the air, despite the fact that we were well into the summer. We were silent, each lost in our own thoughts, and feeling a little bruised. We fought occasionally, but had never had a real political disagreement before.

I dreamed that night of guns and flames and the farmhouse falling down around us while bullets whined overhead. It was like a bad movie, but disturbing nonetheless. I woke shaking, covered in sweat, and reached over to hug Jill. She was my anchor; her warmth and the steady rising and falling of her breath calmed me down until I returned to sleep.

I woke early the next morning, before the sun was fully up, and as I walked down to the garden, a pinkish glow infused the eastern sky over the high peaks of the Presidentials, and the sun rose, glowing red over Mount Washington. Birds called back and forth, singing to welcome the morning. The dream began to fade as I walked through the dew-covered grass and put my hands in the cool earth of the garden, weeding between the rows of carrots that marched on to the garden's edge.

I usually loved this time of morning, cherished the silence and the coolness, looked out over the fog that had gathered in the valley overnight, and was now quickly burning off as the heat of the day began to assert itself. But that day I felt almost vaporous myself, as if I could be consumed by the sun's rays too, dissipated by the heat and light, fleeting as the morning mist.

Something in me had been shaken, disturbed at an elemental level. I was hyperaware of the impermanence of it all, of everything we had built and grown on the farm; the structures, the garden, and the relationships we held dear; they all suddenly had assumed a kind of fragility that had escaped me. Funny, how in that moment I was near panic at the thought that we could lose it all, that *I* could lose it all.

It had only been an argument, and it had only been a dream, but the rest of that day the feeling stayed with me. It wasn't anything I could talk about. I would have seemed foolish. It was just a premonition, but it hung over me like a threatening cloud.

THE SUMMER REACHED ITS zenith and began to slowly turn toward the change we all knew was coming. The day to day, the quotidian, was my concern. My daily cycles grew out of the cycles of nature. At first glance it had all seemed random, but the order of things became clearer to me as one day turned into another and the summer advanced, defining a steady rhythm.

We found our way through the days and nights. Our lives became almost routine, or as routine as any anarchic group of twenty people's lives could be. We grew more introspective, paying even closer attention to our comings and goings, coupling and splintering, finding new ways to be together and apart.

Where it was all headed, I had no idea. I tried to stop worrying about the future, as was my nature, and live in the day. But I found that to "be here now", a mantra of the counterculture, was easier said than done. A lifetime spent defining and pursuing goals was hard to leave behind, and I found myself, despite my best intentions and Jill's admonitions, falling into old patterns of worry and constraint.

Maybe I was too damaged by my middle-class upbringing, too scarred by my Jewish guilt to be truly liberated. I tried to free myself, I really did, but the old neurosis of achievement and anticipation were deeply rooted, and the total liberation of self that seemed to come so easily to others continued to elude me.

In some ways I did feel brand new, but I couldn't shake off my need to orient myself toward some kind of external measure, some assurance that I was on the right track, while it seemed to me that everyone else on the farm was content to be off-track. It wasn't ambition, or ego, at least I hoped not, but something kept me driven to achieve success, even if it was only a successful garden.

These feelings continued to haunt me through the summer. I could never quite bring myself to relax or relent. Others noticed it too.

"You're wound pretty tight these days," Jill observed. "Relax, give yourself a break. It's really okay if you take a day off."

"No, it's really not," I responded. "If we're gonna have enough to eat this winter, now's the time to pour it on. We've still got a long way to go till harvest, and a lot can happen between now and then."

"Come on," she said. "Cool out. Lonny and the others can handle things. You need a break. Look, I saw a poster for a big music festival over in New York State, Woodstock. It looks really cool: Hendrix, Janis, The Grateful Dead, lots of other bands. We should go, take a couple days off. What could it hurt?"

"Oh, I don't think so. I mean it sounds like fun, but I've got to stay on top of things here or it'll all turn to shit."

"Come on! You're not the only one here who knows how to pull weeds, get over yourself!" Jill was exasperated, and she almost swayed me.

"Just seems like a bad time to be away." I replied.

"Well then, the hell with you!" Jill's nostrils flared. "I'll find somebody else to come with me."

And she did, in fact a half-dozen people loaded into the VW bus with her, and were joined by John, Cassie, and little Sebastian in their camper. The farm was half-empty that weekend, and I can't say that it bothered me. I spent my time in the garden, with only Ranger to share the bed.

That summer the garden took on new meaning for me. I explored a part of the world I had only become aware of after moving to Vermont. I had started out viewing it as a battleground—man (or, rather, me) against nature. It had seemed to me that all of the forces of the natural world were conspiring to kill off the young plants we had tended indoors since March. Cold, frost, birds, deer; too much rain, too little rain, hail, weeds, moles, woodchucks, dozens of insects, you name it, it was a threat. And I fought back with almost every force at my disposal short of chemicals and poisons. I was engaged in a constant struggle to keep things alive and growing.

But slowly my perception shifted and I came to understand gardening not as a battle between people and the natural world, but rather as a collaboration—the greatest collaboration in the whole of our history on the planet, a coming together of culture and nature in a dynamic partnership that had allowed for our sustenance, growth, and development as a species. The garden was the matrix of our being. We made gardens and gardens made us. It seemed so obvious once I understood it. And while the knowledge lent a new appreciation to my undertaking, it did not mean that I could relent or slack off, but that I had to work harder, and smarter to insure that this particular collaboration prospered.

The philosophy of organic gardening finally became real to me. I was working in concert with nature's forces, totally dependent on them, not in conflict, and it was incumbent on me to find ways to enhance and mitigate, not overcome and obliterate those forces. A subtle shift in perception, perhaps, but an important one. And when I approached my tasks with this new sensibility, I found myself in awe of the whole process.

As I mentioned, I'm not a religious person, but I found a bond, a kind of spiritual connection with the rest of nature when I worked in the garden. I felt myself both an extension of the earth, the rest of nature, and an active agent helping to give it shape and form. I was engaged in a dance of give and take; of acceptance and transformation. The boundaries were defined by the larger cycles of sun and rain; I was constrained by the seasons and the requirements of the plants themselves, but within this frame, on a canvas stretched tight by longitude, latitude, and altitude, I was granted incredible freedom to create.

Sometimes, when I was working under the hot sun, my hands in the damp earth, I could sense the immensity of life contained in the soil under my fingers, a whole universe, complex and complimentary, the basis for everything. At those moments everything else fell away, and some elemental truth was revealed. I know it sounds clichéd, but we really are what we eat, made of the same stuff, the same cosmic detritus that feeds the soil feeds us, allows for all life on the planet, and we are all one.

I also used the weekend to look for Vincent's cabin. On Sunday I packed a lunch and hiked over Hardwood Mountain, with Ranger loping along ahead of me, running off into the woods every now and then. When I got to the lake, I found a narrow path that ran parallel to the shore, just as Leland had described it.

I walked through the woods, following the path for about half a mile until I reached a clearing that contained a small log cabin with a stone chimney sticking up from the roof. A row of furs was hanging from the rail of the front porch, and a large cast iron cauldron was steaming, suspended from a tripod over an open fire in the front yard. The whole scene looked right out of the eighteenth century, and that impression was only reinforced when Vincent walked out onto the front porch.

"I guess you found me," he said by way of greeting.

"I told you on the Fourth that I'd come visit."

"Don't get many visitors," he said. "Don't much care for 'em."

"Sorry! I can leave, didn't mean to intrude. I thought you might like some company."

"Well, you're here now, might as well stay. Come in and have some tea." He waved me onto the porch and then ushered me into the cabin. Ranger waited by the front door.

It was only one room, with a rough-hewn table on one wall, a cast iron cook stove, on another. A couple of handmade cedar chairs sat in front of the stone fireplace that filled another wall. There was a loft with a thin mattress, reached by a rustic ladder. The place was surprisingly neat. The only modern touch was a battery-powered radio sitting on a shelf.

Vincent wore the same tattered hunting vest he was wearing when I'd first seen him. He went to the stove, removed an enameled teapot, poured a reddish liquid into a chipped mug, and held it out to me.

"Sumac," he said.

"Really?" I sipped the hot liquid. "Not bad."

"Healthy," he said. "Good for you. Been drinkin' it my whole life."

"Where do you get it?"

"Same place I get everything, Mother Nature. It grows everywhere. Likes wet spots. Just dry out the red pods in the fall."

"You get all your food from nature?"

"Not all, just most. Most everything, not just food. Mother Nature provides."

"Everything? You mean like hunting and gathering?"

"I grow a garden too. But between the lake and the woods and the garden I get pretty much what I need—trout, pike, bass, perch, deer, moose, bear, squirrel, ramp, fiddleheads, mushrooms—and then I got my garden. All the medicine I need grows in the woods. I steam willow for my baskets over the cauldron. Baskets and my trap line for cash, but I don't need much—matches, flour, kerosene, bullets for my rifles. I live simple, close to the earth, like my people used to. It's better that way. Much better."

"Aren't you lonely all by yourself out here?"

"I'm not alone. I keep company with the birds and the animals."

"But don't you miss people?"

"Only my wife, and she's been gone a long time."

"I'm sorry…Leland told me what happened."

"That's what they do, white people, they destroy what they don't understand. Why would I want anything to do with them?"

I was blown away. My first impression of him had been that he was half-crazy, but seeing him at home, and knowing a little about his story, I could understand his choices.

I finished my tea, and then Vincent took me outside and showed me how he steamed the thin strips of willow that he had shaved and wove together into a small basket. It was fascinating to watch how quickly his gnarled fingers were able to weave the intricate pattern. After he was done, he handed me the final product.

"For you," he proclaimed.

"It's beautiful!" I said. "But I can't take it. You could sell it for cash."

"No, I want you to have it. Keep it. And when you use it remember me and all the people who still live from Mother Earth." Then he turned and went back into his cabin.

I didn't go on the trip to Woodstock, and Jill and the others made sure I knew all that I missed. But I wasn't sorry. I had found solace in the garden, the woods, and my visit with Vincent. Honestly, it sounded like a muddy mess to me. I don't doubt it was groovy, and history has proven it a seminal event, the apex of the whole hippy era, but I was happy to have stayed home. I was struck again by what an interesting feeling that was, a sense of home, of being someplace I wanted to be.

The summer rolled on, and the days felt like they went on forever. At one point it stayed light until past nine, and we greeted the moon most nights, at least when it wasn't raining, from around a campfire that we burned at the edge of the field closest to the house. The fire was hypnotic; someone usually pulled out a guitar, and we sang, watching the sparks from the fire rise into the night sky full of stars.

It was like living in a novel, or a movie, something majestic and suggestive, a drama moving inexorably through the season toward a climactic moment—not preordained, or carefully plotted, but a climax of some sort. What? I couldn't guess; but my sense was that all of our struggles, all of our labor would amount to something and that we all had a role to play.

No ONE WAS QUITE sure how it happened. Lonny, as usual, was full of energy. In his spare time, when he wasn't gardening, he enlisted

John's help and built a little cabin, more of a shack really, at the edge of the field just past the pond. He had framed it with posts he cut from a stand of cedar that edged a swampy area near the creek, and scrounged the siding from a stack of old boards lying in one of the sheds. The roofing was some rusty corrugated metal picked up from a collapsed barn down the hill. Nothing fancy, but it gave him a little privacy, shelter from the rain, and a place to sleep. Mostly life on the commune was lived outdoors and in the public spaces anyway, like the farmhouse.

That was where we were, at one of our interminable community meetings, seated in the kitchen/parlor debating the morality of eating meat for the fifth or sixth time in a month, when Ranger, who had been lying at my feet, rose, barked, growled, and ran to the door. Brian opened it and the dog went running out. A few minutes later Suze noticed the red glow in the sky.

"What's that?" She pointed out the window.

"Fuck, looks like a fire!" I was on my feet.

The twenty or so people ran out to the porch for a better view and then followed the red glow, now throwing visible sparks into the air, toward the site of the blaze.

Lonny let out a wail. "Shit, it's my cabin! All my stuff, my backpack! My sleeping bag!"

We reached the fire in time to see the roof collapse in on what remained of the walls, sending a fountain of sparks into the night sky. "Bummer!" Jason put his arm around Lonny's shoulder.

"Sorry man, it's gone. You must have left a candle burning, it doesn't take much," Jill offered.

"No, no candle, and how could it burn so fast?" Lonny protested.

"Well, could have been a cigarette, or, I don't know..."

"I don't smoke cigarettes."

"Then a joint?"

"Maybe," Lonny conceded, but he still sounded unconvinced.

"Does anyone else smell gasoline?" I was downwind of the flames.

"What the hell!" Jason's nostrils flared. "You think somebody torched it? That's fucked up!"

By then we had been joined by Leland and Mary. "Saw the flames from our place, guess it's too late to bother callin' it in at this point." Leland had his hands in the pockets of his overalls. "Shame. Somebody got careless I guess."

"Maybe not," I was watching the flames consume the last of the shack. "I thought I smelled gas. Did anybody see anything weird?"

"Well, come to mention it, me and Mary thought we heard a car come up here a little earlier. I looked out, but didn't see no lights or anything. Don't know."

"Who would do something like that?" Jill was outraged.

"We don't really know if anybody did it. Don't get all freaked out. Odds are it was an accident." Brian didn't sound very convincing.

"I bet it was those guys from the general store. I get a very hostile vibe from them." Suze was hugging herself.

"Maybe," I drew a deep breath. "Who knows?"

"Well, I'm not sure," Suze said, shaking her head. "But did you see the looks those guys were giving us down at the parade? They freaked me out."

"Kind of suspicious that it's the cabin of the only Black guy in two counties," Lonny added. "I been getting dirty looks from those guys ever since I arrived. Motherfuckers." He shook his head in disgust.

"What can we do?" Brian was pacing in front of the smoldering fire. "We can't prove anything. Shit, we don't even know for sure what happened."

"Something happened," my brow furrowed. "This sure as hell wasn't spontaneous combustion. Lucky nobody got hurt."

"Yeah, this time." Jill' sounded serious. "See," she turned to me, "this is why we need to learn to defend ourselves."

"What, you're gonna shoot whoever did this? Believe me, guns would just make it worse."

"Fuck you! Should we just sit here and take it while they burn the farm down around us?" Jill's face was red. Maybe it was just the fire. She looked at the group gathered around the burning shack. There were murmurs of affirmation.

Later that night there was a thunderstorm, the sky lit by flashes of lightning, with thunder pealing almost continuously for a half an hour of fury, leaving us huddled together back in the farmhouse.

"It sounds like the end of the world." Mia said, staring out the kitchen window as the wind driven rain lashed the side of the house.

The next morning, I saw Lonny looking through the charred ruins of his shack, poking around in the rain-soaked ashes searching for anything that might have escaped the destruction. He found his army surplus canteen, the canvas cover burned off it, but the metal canister itself still intact. That was about it. He was clearly bummed out.

"Man, this really sucks!" he looked at the ground. "I had a sweet little scene happenin' here, but I guess these honky bastards got it in for Black folks, just like everybody else. I thought maybe it was different up here..."

"I'm so sorry, Lonny. Listen, I'll help you rebuild, or we'll make room for you in the farmhouse. Don't worry man, it's cool. You're family, I mean we'll take care of it."

"Yeah, right," he snorted. "We gonna hunt the fuckers down who did this, Dave? How are we gonna take care of it? Huh?"

"I don't know. I'll talk to Leland, maybe he's got an idea who did it. We can go to the cops."

"The cops?" Lonny looked surprised. "Nah, don't be callin' the cops. They ain't gonna do shit for us, 'specially not for me. Forget it. I'll be okay."

"Well I'm gonna talk to Leland anyway. I want to know who did this. We can't just sit back and take it. I mean Jill has a point—are they gonna come burn down the farmhouse next time?"

"I'm thinkin' they were sending a message, and I got it loud and clear: 'No Black folks welcome.' I can tell, I been hearin' it my whole life. Fuckin' racist pigs. They're everywhere Dave, everywhere."

Lonny, ever a source of positive energy, was deflated. It killed me to see him like that. I reached out and put my arm around his shoulder. "I know man, I know."

That afternoon I went to see Leland. I found him in the barn piling items in a box. "Thought maybe your friend could use some things, figured he must of lost about everything in that fire." He said by way of greeting.

"Thanks, Leland," I replied. "He did lose everything. He's completely bummed out. Feels like he was singled out 'cause he's Black."

"Could well be right," Leland said. "I've got no proof, but I got my suspicions 'bout who did it." He scratched his ear. "Wouldn't put it past him."

"Who, Leland? Who do you think did it?"

"Well," he said, "apple don't fall far from the tree."

"What do you mean?"

"You know the Klan used to be real active up here."

"The Ku Klux Klan? In Vermont? You've got to be kidding."

I was astounded at the thought.

"Oh no, they were here all right, had a chapter in town. Ugly business. All through the twenties and thirties."

"But there weren't even any Black people up here then, were there?"

"No sir, hardly a one. But that didn't stop 'em." Leland narrowed his eyes. "They went after anybody a little different; French, Italians, Catholics, Abenaki. We had a Jewish family in town back in '33-'34, depression times. They came up from New York, bought the general store. Klan organized a boycott, bankrupted 'em, and then put 'em on a train back to the city. That's when Mac's family got the store. His daddy was the preacher at the church here in town, that's why we stopped going. He was the main Klan recruiter around here.

"Lot of folks signed up. Oh, for most it was like a social club, but it fed their ignorance and hate. Mac's dad, he was pretty good at gettin' 'em all fired up. He carried on quite a bit. Had big rallies and cross burnings. State Klan marched with a thousand people down to Montpelier. He had 'em burn a cross one Fourth of July at the ball field here in town after the parade. They had a funeral for him down to the church when he died. Full regalia, had on their cloaks and hoods, the whole thing. Nasty business, real nasty.

"So anyway, like I said, I got no proof, but my money'd be on Mac. Chip off the old block, just as mean and stupid as his old man was. Wouldn't surprise me at all."

"Unbelievable! I never, I mean…" I was dumbstruck. "What can we do about it? Should we call the cops?"

"Don't know what can be done about it. Unless you want to take on Mac and his buddies," said Leland. "No evidence, just my suspicion. Doubt callin' the police would help. State cop for this district's a good buddy of Mac's, hangs around down to the store. Might have been in on it himself. Wouldn't put it past him."

"Holy shit!" It was even worse than I'd feared. Much worse. "So there's nothing we can do?"

"Well, I guess you know who you've got to watch out for, at least," Leland offered.

I was still having a hard time getting my head around it. "How can he get away with this?"

"He's a bully, always has been. Intimidates a lot of folks. Oh, he's got some friends, a few folks who think the way he does, but there's a lot more in town who won't have anything to do with him. This sure won't make him any more popular when word gets out."

"To be honest, Leland, that's not real reassuring." I was upset. "I'm not worried about his popularity. Is he gonna come back and try to burn us out?"

Leland thought for a moment. "Don't know. Doubt it. He could, but probably not. Try to scare you out, that's more his style."

"Well he's made a good start," I said.

The fire freaked me out, all of us, in fact. We spent the next night talking about it, seated around our kitchen table.

"What are we gonna do?" asked Jason. "Are we gonna let him get away with it?"

"How about an arson investigator? The state 'cops' must have an arson unit," Brian suggested.

"Yeah," Suze brushed her bangs back from her forehead. "There must be somebody we can go to."

"Don't expect anything from the cops," I said. "If Leland is right, one of them probably helped set the fire. They protect their own."

"Right on," said Lonny. "Those fuckers just as soon burn my ass as help us. They won't do shit, and probably turn it around to find some way to hurt us. Remember when that cracker statey wanted to bust us for growing pot? I say stay the fuck away from them."

"Yeah, I'm with you." Jill was seated next to me, and she gave me a meaningful glance. "The system is totally corrupt. We've got to handle this ourselves. I told you we needed to be ready for this shit."

"What? Guns again?" I turned toward her. "How would it have helped? Get real!"

"I don't feel safe sleeping in our camper." Cassie had her kid on her lap. "I can't take any chances with Sebastian. John and I are thinking about leaving. I mean, it's been really cool here, and you guys are great, but if there's gonna be violence…"

"Fuck!" I said. "That's what they want, to scare us off. It's harassment. They're cowards, they sneak around in the night. We can't give in to this."

"Well, what do we do then?" asked Jill. "If you're not willing for us to defend ourselves…" She looked at me. They all did.

"There are ways to defend ourselves without guns," I responded.

"Yeah? How?" Jason's question hung in the air.

"I don't know, we'll set up a night watch or something." My answer sounded pretty lame.

"Or something?" Jill wasn't letting up.

"We'll take turns standing watch, get a whistle; or one of those foghorn things."

Nobody seemed to be buying it. I didn't know what else to suggest and looked around the table in desperation.

"Well…maybe," Jason finally spoke. "It's something, anyway. Better than just waiting for somebody to sneak up and burn down the house."

"I hate this shit," said Suze. "Just when things were starting to come together a little."

"I know," I said. "I feel the same way. All the more reason not to let them run us off." I turned to Cassie. "I wish you and John would reconsider. We'd miss you, and Sebastian too."

"We'll see," offered John. "We're just talking about it. But you know, with Sebastian and all. If it was just us…"

"Yeah, I know. I get it," I responded.

We set a schedule for guard duty and began that night with three-hour shifts that started at ten and lasted till dawn. I spent my first shift patrolling between the house and the road with Ranger by my side.

I tried not to wake Jill when I crawled into bed that night, but she turned to greet me.

"How did it go?"

"Uneventful," I replied. "As I expected."

"You don't think they'll come back?"

"I doubt it. I think they were just trying to scare us."

"Well, I'm scared," she said, reaching over and hugging me. "Those fucking assholes! Why can't they leave us alone?"

"We threaten them. We're different, we're radical, we're pushing for change, and they're a bunch of ignorant right-wingers, and yes, assholes. They see the revolution coming too, only they don't like it. In fact, they hate us, and they think if they get rid of us, they can stop things from changing. But they're wrong, wrong on both counts. They can't get rid of us, and they can't stop the changes."

"You're so rational about it all," she observed. "I don't know how you keep your cool. It makes me want to scream!"

"Me too," I said. "Only I don't think screaming will help. We've just got to deal with it. I doubt if they'll come back, not with someone standing guard. Anyway, we'll see."

"I guess we will." She squeezed me tightly, and then we both fell into a deep sleep.

We continued to post a watch for the next several weeks, but when nothing happened, slowly, a sense of normality returned, and we stopped the patrols at the end of August.

Fall 1969

I COULD DETECT THE coming change of seasons, as summer slowly faded and fall began to assert itself. Milkweed pods opened, their silky contents floating on the breeze, sumac and maple showed tinges of red; the nights grew chillier, and the days began to grow shorter. The signs were everywhere.

And then it was harvest time, days spent gathering the fruits and vegetables of our labor—the glory of vine-ripened tomatoes, the sweet taste of red peppers, and the wonders of fresh corn, unpicked until the water in the cast iron kettle was boiling and ready to receive it.

I was in my glory, my dreams of bounty came to fruition and I relished every meal, every fresh taste, each morsel a result of that greatest human achievement, the highest collaboration of people and nature, the garden—my garden, and I did take pride in it. While I readily acknowledged the contributions of others, I saw my role as central, the garden largely a product of my planning and my labor.

The kitchen filled with the smell of tomatoes boiling down into thick sauce, sweet and faintly acidic. Broccoli was blanched and canned in glass quart jars, crocks full of briny pickles filled the shelves, winter squash, potatoes, carrots, parsnips, beets, and turnips lay in the root cellar under the basement steps. Our harvest began to accumulate, take on weight and fill our depleted larder—next winter's food, a product of our own labor. I felt a growing satisfaction with each jar, each bushel, each braid of garlic hung from the kitchen rafters.

Radio reception sucked, but occasionally we could pick up the English language broadcast of the CBC out of Montreal. The war raged on, the casualties mounted; Nixon and Kissinger promised victory by Christmas. The more we listened, the greater our outrage grew. It was easy to feel isolated and insulated living on our hill. But the visitors who kept arriving through the late summer filled in the blanks with stories of demonstrations and actions, ever more militant in direct proportion to the ratcheting up of the war.

"Fuck this! We've got to stop them!"

"Right on! But what can we do up here?"

"There's the senators. We could sit in."

"They're already against the war."

"There's that factory over in Burlington. Gatling guns." Brian suggested.

"What?"

"They make machine guns for helicopters."

"In Burlington?"

"Yeah, a GE plant."

"Fuck, let's do an action there!"

"Hell yeah!"

Organizing is basically the same everywhere: meetings, mailings, posters, press releases, more meetings, and more meetings. We used the network of communes established earlier in the summer as our base, connecting with like-minded activists and spreading the word as best we could. There was a small Quaker community up in Burlington that offered their meetinghouse as headquarters. They hooked us up with some organizers at the university, and we planned an action for when the students returned, first week in September, hoping they would swell our numbers. We felt good, like we were back in our element; unlike the gardening and building, this was something we knew how to do.

Jill was adamant. "It can't just be another march. We've got to shut them down, make a real statement."

Boundaries had to be crossed—transgression, revolt, revolution, a need to act strong enough to consider possibilities previously unthinkable, a free ride for imagination, a fuckin' free-for-all. There was no way of knowing where it would go.

The GE demo took on a life of its own. We planned a symbolic direct action intended to immobilize, or at least slow down production at the plant.

I had no fucking idea what to expect. I thought the best thing to do would be a mass action, blockading the plant. Most sitting down linked together, with some of us chained to the gate. But there was no way to get everybody to agree, so in the end each group decided to do their own thing.

We did all agree to rally in the park near City Hall; from there we would march to the plant near the lakefront. After that our ways would part. Most folks would just rally at the entrance while the workers arrived before nine, but some of us were determined to stop business as usual, even if it meant getting arrested.

When we woke up the morning of the demonstration it was still dark. I had a hard time getting out of bed. I'd spent the night tossing and turning and finally got to sleep about an hour before wake up.

There were already a half-dozen people gathered when Jill and I made it downstairs for breakfast. Suze, as usual was standing at the stove, dishing out runny scrambled eggs to Ben, Brian, Mia, and Lonny.

"All right!" Lonny and I exchanged a high five. "Ready to rock and roll?" Lonny was practically vibrating with excitement.

"Sure thing!" I was getting kind of excited myself, anticipating the visceral release I almost always felt at a demonstration. "Yeah man, I been out of action for too long. Time to make them see they can't get away with this shit."

We had to get on the road early to be there in time to meet the workers. Burlington was over an hour away. Jill drove the Volvo wagon with me, Lonny, Ben, and Brian, and everyone else crammed into the VW van with Jason driving. The sun was coming up as we rolled down the hill into the fog that filled the valley. We followed the river south, then cut west. The sunrise was spectacular, but I think Jill and I were the only ones who actually saw it. The others were sleeping as best they could.

We picked up Route 15 in Johnson and rolled through Jeffersonville and Underhill. It promised to be a hot one as the sun made its way higher into the cloudless sky. It was about seven in the monring when we pulled into downtown Burlington and found a parking spot in front of City Hall. We all piled out and headed to the park. There were about twenty people there when we arrived, and I touched base with Dana, an organizer from UVM, a guy with curly black hair and a scruffy beard.

"What's up, man?"

"Just waiting for more folks to show up."

"How many are you expecting?"

"Don't really know. I'm hoping for a hundred or so, but, shit, at this point I'd be happy if fifty turned out."

"Fuck, don't they know there's a war going on?"

"Yeah, but it's the first week of school, we're just starting to organize. A lot of the freshmen are kind of clueless."

An older Quaker woman named Carol walked over, smiling, carrying a sign that said, "END THE WAR NOW!"

"We should start the march soon if we want to meet the first shift." She squinted. "The latecomers will have to join us en route."

I nodded my head in agreement and surveyed the crowd, which had grown to about thirty as we stood talking, mostly Quakers and community activists. Not as many as we had planned on, but it would have to do.

Hopefully our numbers would grow by the time we reached the plant. Where the fuck were the UVM students? Or the other communes? I thought we could at least count on the Cold Mountain group—they had seemed pretty hardcore. I took a deep breath and joined Jill and the others.

"I guess we'll get started now."

I felt pretty deflated as Jill looked around, then looked back at me with raised eyebrows. She didn't say anything, but I knew what she was thinking. Carol, the Quaker lady, led us out onto the street that ran down to the lake. Once we left the park and reached South Champlain Street we were surrounded by rundown industrial buildings, most of which seemed to be abandoned. The GE factory was about a mile down the lakefront, and as the crowd began to march, we thinned out into a line that made it look like there were even fewer of us than there actually were.

About three blocks before we got to the factory gates, a group of UVM kids joined up, marching behind a bright red and blue banner, not exactly swelling our ranks, but adding enough to make the protest a little more respectable, and more importantly, in contrast to the Quakers' silent witness, much louder. They were chanting the usual slogans and carrying signs. It raised my spirits anyway, and then, when we reached the plant, I saw the group from Cold Mountain, about a dozen familiar faces including Bear, Karl, and Sarah. They were standing across the street from the factory gates, holding signs and some of the banners that had been flying in the wind at the gathering earlier in the summer. They looked relieved to see us.

I was feeling better; there must have been over a hundred of us by then, a decent sized protest for a town like Burlington. We gathered together across from the chain link gate. Behind the gate was a large, two-story brick building that looked like it was built in the nineteenth century. A sign above the gate said "General Electric Corporation-Gatling Gun Division". This was the place where they manufactured the machine guns mounted on helicopter gunships that regularly and indiscriminately strafed Vietnamese peasants and Viet Cong fighters—a tangible manifestation of the war machine we hated. We had come to protest, but also to stop production, at least for a day.

I looked around at the others and saw a mixture of determination and apprehension in their expressions. I glanced at the watch on Carol's wrist and saw it was about ten minutes before the eight o'clock opening of the plant. There were two security guards glaring at us from behind the gate, but so far, they were the only people there besides us.

"So, what now?" Dana sidled up to me.

"I guess it's time to get it on. Everybody who's gonna sit in should get in place." I turned to Jason, Jill, and the other folks I had come with but raised my voice to address the whole crowd. "We're gonna block the gates now! Anybody who doesn't want to get arrested should stay on the sidewalk, everybody else, lock arms." A group of about thirty people, mostly communards and UVM kids walked into the roadway in front of the plant, linked arms and sat down on the tarmac.

The security guys on the other side freaked out, and one them started talking into a walkie-talkie or something. The first car, a Ford sedan, arrived at the gate, slowing and honking his horn as he approached, but seeming to head directly into the crowd of protesters. We were seated three deep. I was in the first row, and I held my breath as the car kept moving toward us. I could feel the tension in the crowd and saw a look of fear cross the face of a girl in the SDS contingent sitting next to me. "Don't panic," I called out, "hold your ground." The car finally stopped, about a foot away from our front line, blowing its horn madly. I could see the guy inside shouting, cursing at us, but I couldn't hear his voice over the chants coming from the street and the sidewalk. "HELL NO, WE WON'T GO!" "END THE WAR NOW!"

Folks were chanting and shouting; more workers' cars arrived, backed up behind the Ford and honking their horns in frustration. It was getting loud now, really loud, and it took a while before I heard the sound of approaching sirens. "Here we go." I looked over at Jill, and she, Jason, Suze, and Brian rose and joined me wading through the seated crowd of protesters to the gates. By then there was a long line of cars and trucks backed up waiting to get into the plant. Some of the Quakers were walking along the line of vehicles trying to hand out pamphlets and flyers. A few workers rolled down their windows and took the literature, but most ignored them and a few made a point of shouting at the mostly old ladies. "Fuckin' commies!"

Our group made it to the gate and we each pulled out army surplus handcuffs we had purchased for the occasion. We cuffed ourselves to each other, and Jason and I, who were at either end of the line, were each cuffed to opposite sides of the gate. We stood there, facing out toward our chanting resisters, and the increasingly angry line of workers.

That was when the cops arrived. Two cruisers, sirens blaring, slowly made their way past the line of cars to the front. Two cops got out and walked to the edge of the protest. Only two! Apparently, we'd caught them off guard.

"You are illegally blocking traffic here," one of them shouted, trying to be heard over the chanting and honking horns, "Clear the intersection and let this traffic through." No one moved.

Jill was elated. "No way two cops can handle this!" She was right. The cops realized it too. They looked at each other, not sure of what to do, and then retreated to their cars, one of them standing and writing in a notebook while the other was talking on his cruiser's radio. It looked like we'd at least bought a little time.

By now the sun was warming things up and a little breeze picked up out on Lake Champlain. I figured it was just a matter of time before more cops arrived and we were dragged off, but we had managed to disrupt production. The way I saw it every hour lost on the assembly line meant fewer Vietnamese would fall victim to the machine guns. And we weren't done yet. Who knew how long it would take reinforcements to get there?

A few minutes later two more Burlington police cars arrived, each holding four more cops. One of them had a bullhorn, and wore a white shirt under his blue jacket. He was a big man, with an air of command. He spotted Carol, the Quaker lady, who was standing on the sidewalk with a sign that read simply "END THE WAR". He approached her like he knew her and she lowered her sign while they talked. I couldn't hear what was said, but after a few minutes he turned red in the face, threw up his arms in frustration, and walked away.

By then, some of the workers waiting to go into the plant had left their cars and gathered in an angry knot behind the cops. They were shouting and waving their fists. The cop in charge told them to back off. Then he spoke into the bullhorn. "This is an illegal protest. You are blocking the intersection. If you do not clear the street and return to the sidewalk you are subject to arrest."

People looked around, nervously. The chanting died down for a moment, but then Jill started singing, loudly. *"We shall not, we shall not be moved. We shall not, we shall not be moved."* We all joined in. *"Just like a tree that's standing by the water, we shall not be moved!"* The song swelled, drowning out the angry shouts and raising our spirits while the bright late-summer sun shone on the line of cops standing uncertainly before us. It was one of those moments for me. I looked around at the singing kids seated on the ground in front of the gate and my chest swelled. I glanced over at Jill, who was singing out with a look of joyful defiance on her face. It seemed to me I had never seen her look so beautiful. Tears welled up in my eyes, and I felt an electrical connection to the others; we were all together, righteous and strong.

Then the press arrived, TV cameras and everything. I guess we were big news for Burlington. The cops were still waiting there, they seemed kind of uncertain, and then the state troopers showed up. A half dozen cruisers rolled up and a dozen guys in Mountie hats joined the city cops. One of the staties took control with the bullhorn. "You have two minutes to clear this area or you will be subject to arrest"

A blue bus had pulled in up the street. We kept singing while the cops started dragging us off, two burly troopers to each protester, one on each side picking them up under the arms and then dragging them, heels trailing, over to the bus for processing. We kept on singing, but nobody resisted arrest: folks just went limp and let themselves be dragged away. They worked steadily for a half an hour clearing the intersection.

Traffic was being rerouted down Pine Street by then, but the workers were still backed up waiting to get into the plant. Now those of us chained to the gate were the only thing standing between them and work. I looked out over the heads of the advancing cops, and I saw the crowd waiting to get in, really saw them for the first time. Almost all men, mostly middle-aged, but a few my age. Some of them carried tin lunch pails, they were wearing T-shirts and jeans. I figured they were all union guys. How could they support the war? Couldn't they see what they were doing, what horror they were supporting by working in the plant? It was so clear to me, so simple.

The state cop who had made the announcement approached us. "It'll be a lot easier if you just unlock the cuffs."

Jill stared at him. "We're here to shut down production of these machine guns. Don't you know they're being used to kill innocent women and children in Vietnam?" Her eyes flashed. We all shouted our agreement.

"You're gonna have to drag us out of here with the gate attached!" Jason was in his element; he had always loved confronting authority.

"Have it your way." The cop turned away and walked back to his cruiser. He called another trooper over. We waited to see what their next move would be. The other cop left, and in a few minutes returned with a bolt cutter. They walked up to where my handcuff was attached to the fence, and clipped the chain that held the bracelet to my wrist, then clipped me free of Jill, and so on until we were all unattached. We just sat there, and went limp while they dragged us away.

Someone struck a microphone in Jill's face as she was being trundled onto the blue bus. "What did your protest accomplish today?"

"We slowed down the war machine. The guns built in this plant kill dozens of innocent Vietnamese people every day, so by shutting down production, even for just a couple of hours, we're saving lives." And that was the sound bite that made the news that night.

I felt pretty good about the way it went. We had slowed things down, and made a point. Jill and I, and the others chained to the fence, got a criminal trespass charge and a court date out of it, but the folks who just sat in the street were given citations for blocking an intersection and let go. It felt great to have done something to express our outrage. The whole thing—the arrest, the lock up, the arraignment—all very civilized. Vermont! What a trip.

The Quakers posted our bail, and by late afternoon we were driving back over the mountains, heading home, basking in our righteousness. "We fucking did it!" Jill's eyes were shining.

"About time!" Brian fired up a joint he had stashed in the Volvo.

"I was starting to wonder what the hell we were doing up here. I mean, gardening and all is fine, but we're supposed to be about change, right?" He took another toke and passed the weed.

I inhaled deeply, and it felt good, one of those rare moments when I actually let myself relax, and admit that things had gone well.

THE ONE AREA WE had neglected was firewood. Winter was fast approaching and once again our woodshed was bare, except for some smaller chunks to fire up the cook stove. Jason and I turned our attention to replenishing our wood supply.

We knew it was going to take a shitload of work, but we were a year stronger and more experienced, and Jill said she would work with us again. I helped Leland mark trees, and he offered to haul out wagonloads of split wood for us to stack near the house. It felt like a few weeks of concerted effort would be enough to see us through, and I was relieved at the thought.

We had been in the woods for three days, and we had a rhythm going, taking turns dropping trees, blocking them up with the chainsaw, and hefting the maul to split them into usable chunks. It was hard work and my muscles ached the first couple of days as I adjusted. We were cutting mostly standing dead wood, dry and straight-grained. It usually split with a satisfying pop at the first swing of the maul, but sometimes I would come up against a knotted piece, and no amount of effort with the maul could get it to split. Leland had lent us a set of iron wedges for those hard to split blocks, and occasionally the sound of metal striking metal resounded through the woods, offering a counterpoint to the usual symphony of grunts and pops.

We were making good progress, the pile of split firewood getting bigger by the hour. It was hard work, but satisfying; the evidence of our labor lay before us on the growing pile of wood. Nothing abstract, or cerebral about getting in the firewood—it offered both instant gratification and the knowledge that our efforts would warm us through the coming winter. I felt like I was accomplishing something important, something directly related to our survival.

Jason was running the saw and I had been splitting for about an hour when we took a break. It was almost noon, and, though my ears still buzzed with the sound of the saw, silence settled over the clearing where we had been working.

I listened to the bird song rise in the forest, heard a blue jay call from somewhere nearby, and a crow cawed, off in the distance. Ranger had been orbiting around the clearing all morning, checking in occasionally to make sure all was well, and I was surprised when I heard him bark, then I heard a low rumble in the distance. We were just finishing up for the morning and were heading back to the farmhouse for lunch when the biker showed up. The blat of his Harley filled the air as he pulled into the drive.

I'D NEVER LIKED THE guy, from the first minute I saw him swaggering up the path to the farmhouse. He was wearing his colors, a death's head with wings in a large patch on the back of a sleeveless denim jacket with his gang's name spelled out in an arc of letters above. He had a look of constant amusement on his face, as though he had just finished chuckling about some private joke, and he wasn't going to let anyone else in on it.

He came onto the porch and walked into the farmhouse like he owned it. Jill looked up from the table, and smiled when she saw him. "Mark!" she said. "You made it!"

"I told you I'd come," he replied.

Jill rose, walked over to him and gave him a big hug. "Hey everybody, this is Mark. We met at the gathering of the tribes, at Cold Mountain. I told you about him, remember?" She was clearly excited.

He stood there with his arm still around her waist, like he didn't want to let go. He was a big man, at least six foot two and solidly built. He seemed to fill the room as he loomed over Jill, who was still smiling.

Brian nodded. "Hey man, what's up?"

"Good to meet you," said Jason.

"Hi, I'm David," I walked over to shake his hand, which he finally removed from Jill's waist. "Jill's boyfriend."

He grinned at me and nearly crushed my hand when he shook it. "Groovy," he said, "what's goin' on?"

"We're just finishing up in the garden and cutting some firewood, trying to get ready for winter." I told him. "What brings you here?"

"Oh, I promised the little lady," he grinned at Jill, "that I'd come visit. Didn't want to disappoint her." He flashed another smile in her direction. "Thought maybe I could help you all out a little."

He spoke with a trace of a southern accent and shifted his weight, checking out the room. I didn't like the way he was looking at Jill at all, as though he were a cat contemplating a tasty morsel.

"Cool!" said Suze, who had emerged from behind the stove. "We can use all the help we can get."

"Mark was in 'Nam, Special Forces," Jill explained. "But he gets it, he really gets it. He's a real revolutionary now."

"Fuck the war, fuck the man, fuck the system!" he exclaimed. "We got to bring the war home, take this whole motherfucker down! No doubt about it." He gave Jill a high five.

"All right, brother, right on!" said Jason. "That's what we're all about. Welcome to Zion Farm."

"Oh yeah! So what kind of shit are you guys into? I mean for the revolution and all." He raised an eyebrow.

"Well, we grew vegetables for the Panthers' summer lunch program," offered Suze.

"Vegetables?" Mark snorted.

"And we help draft resisters get to Canada," Jason added. "We just organized a big demo up in Burlington last week, at the Gatling gun factory. And, you know, like R&R for folks from the city."

It all sounded pretty lame and ineffectual to me as I heard our exploits recounted, and Mark looked singularly unimpressed.

"We've put a lot into this place," I explained, "creating something new here, a model for how we can live after the revolution, and minimize our contradictions until we get there." I resented having to justify our lives to him.

"Minimize your contradiction, huh?" Mark snorted again.

"David's our philosopher," Jill said, almost apologetically. Then she took his arm and smiled. "Let me show you around the place." She led him towards the door.

I suppose he had a certain charisma, though he didn't appeal to me at all. Jill was clearly taken with him, and Jason listened attentively at dinner while Mark told stories about 'Nam. He had a booming laugh that grated on me, but he kept talking and laughing, captivating all the others around the table, and after, when we shared a joint in a circle outside around the fire.

My discomfort was growing by the minute as I watched Jill hang on his every word. The crowd started to thin out as the moon rose higher, but I stayed until the bitter end when even Jill had had enough, stretched, yawned and announced she was ready for bed. I was hoping that was it, and he would ride off into the full moon, but he had brought a tent rolled up on the back of his Harley, and he pitched it in the dooryard. He was sitting in the kitchen drinking coffee and telling stories when I came down in the morning.

"Hey!" Jason said when I sat down at the table. "You know how we wanted to dig out the spring to increase the flow?"

"Yeah," I answered. "We've been talking about it all summer, but I'm not ready to take on another big job till we get in the firewood."

"Well, Mark said he'd help us blast it. He was a demolitions expert in the army, says all it would take is a few sticks of dynamite." Jason was excited. "Maybe an afternoon's work. Cool, huh?"

I looked at Mark who gave me that Cheshire Cat grin of his that I already found infuriating. "Cool, I guess, I mean I don't know where we'd get explosives, but it sounds a lot easier than digging."

"Mark says we can get it over in New Hampshire, it's legal there, for construction," Brian chimed in.

"Great," I offered, without much enthusiasm. "Just don't blow yourselves up."

"Oh, don't you worry about that," said Mark, grinning. "I took out half of the Viet Cong's tunnel system. I guess I can handle a little job like this, okay."

"We're gonna drive over there this morning and pick some up. What a groove! I always liked playing with firecrackers," Jason laughed.

"Well, be careful, I don't want to be out there looking for body parts."

Mark guffawed, his laugh echoing off the plaster walls. He leaned back in his chair, and spread his arms wide. "Where's the little lady this morning? I promised I'd teach her how to shoot today, but I guess it's gonna have to wait."

"You brought a gun?" I asked.

"Sure," he replied. "A couple. I've got an AR-15 broke down out in my tent, and this one." He raised his denim vest to reveal an automatic pistol of some sort stuck into his waistband. "Never leave home without one," he laughed. "That's why she invited me here. To teach you all to shoot. We met at that self-defense workshop. And from what she told me yesterday, sounds like it's none too soon."

I thought of the fire that burned Lonny out, and wondered if being armed would have made a difference. It made me really uptight, but before I could say anything, Jason responded.

"I'm ready!" he said. "There's been a couple times we could have used some self-defense."

"Hell yeah, armed love!" said Mark flashing me his grin and laughing.

"Makes me uncomfortable. I don't like guns," I said. "I believe in nonviolence."

"You are so uptight!" Jill came down the stairs and into the room, still rubbing sleep from her eyes. "I would have thought by now you'd have gotten it. 'Political power comes out of the barrel of a gun.' That was Mao, right?"

"That's right, babe. You got it!" Mark grinned at her. "I never heard of a revolution that didn't involve violence."

"Right on! That's why we're learning to shoot." Jill looked pointedly at me.

"Hey, I'm sorry," Mark apologized to Jill, "but the shooting lessons are gonna have to wait. We're gonna get some dynamite this morning."

"Dynamite?" Jill sounded excited.

"To blast the spring," Jason explained.

"How cool!" Jill smiled at Mark.

"Shooting lessons tomorrow then?" Mark grinned back at her. "Is it a date?"

"It's a date!" she replied.

Jason and Mark got up to go, and on his way out the door, Mark looked back over his shoulder at me, grinned, pointed his index finger, cocked his thumb, like it was a pistol, and left me with a parting shot.

I SPENT THE MORNING back out in the woods, working on the firewood myself. As I split the blocks of maple I imagined they were Mark's grinning face. I had to admit he had gotten to me. I began to understand the appeal of violence.

The rhythm of the maul rising and falling usually led me to an almost meditative state. But as the morning progressed all I could think about was Mark leering at Jill and the way she lit up when she saw him. It made me wonder what I had missed. I realized that after four years together, I had been taking for granted that Jill loved me as much as I loved her. We had been fighting a little more lately, but I'd assumed it was just the normal stuff that comes up in a relationship, not some existential crisis that threatened our being together.

For the first time, I began to question how solid we really were, and it freaked me out. I couldn't get rid of the image of her taking his arm and smiling the other night. My stomach flip-flopped as waves of anxiety washed over me. What the hell was going on? Was there really something between them?

I couldn't figure out the attraction. I mean what did she see in him? He was a thug. Give me a break! I agonized all morning, but ultimately decided there was nothing I could do. Whatever was happening would just have to play itself out. If I raised my concerns with Jill it would just confirm that I was uptight, and make me look like a jealous fool on top of that. Besides we always agreed that monogamy was a petite bourgeois institution, and people should only be together if they really cared for each other. I would look like a hypocrite as well!

When I took a break to sit on a log and drink from the plastic water jug I'd brought, Ranger came over and sat facing me, with his head cocked to one side as if to ask what was wrong. "It's okay, boy," I said to him, ruffling the fur behind his ears. "It's all gonna be okay." I was reassuring myself more than him, but it helped a little. He wagged his tail.

I worked in the woods for the rest of the morning and when I returned to the farmhouse for lunch, Jill was nowhere to be found.

"Oh she's down at the spring, helping them with the blasting," Suze said nonchalantly. "They got back about a half an hour ago."

I was going to go over and check it out, but the thought of Mark swaggering and smirking while he showed off his expertise with dynamite was too much for me, and I opted to stay and have some lunch.

While I was eating, I heard the sound of an explosion. It was loud, and close enough that the dishes shook in the old cupboard. Ranger gave a deep growl. I looked out the window in the direction of the spring and saw a cloud of smoke, or dust, rising into the clear blue sky.

"Wow!" said Suze. "Groovy! I guess they did it. Maybe now we'll have enough water so we can do the dishes and water the garden at the same time. I could dig that!"

It was true that we needed more flow from the spring, but the fact that Mark was responsible for it made me feel less enthusiastic. "Yeah, cool, great."

I decided to head back into the woods before the conquering hero returned to the farmhouse. I refilled my water jug and walked out the door. "See you at dinner," I said to Suze.

Change was in the air. Traces of fall were painting the leaves, turning the woods into an impressionist palette of heather tones just hinting at the color to come. The first frost had hit the week before, as we salvaged the last remnants of the garden. Birds had begun to gather, and flock together in a steady stream flowing south. The farm had pretty much emptied of our fair-weather friends, and only a hearty handful remained, digging in for the long haul, getting ready to brave another season locked tight in winter's grasp, while smaller creatures burrowed and furrowed, sought warmth and food to see them through.

Knowing what to expect should have made it easier, but it also was a reminder of the uncertainty, the fragility of our situation, the tenuous nature of our tenure in this place and our relation to it, and then, for me, the tenuous nature of our relationships to each other.

I was obsessing about Jill and Mark. His arrival had me questioning all my assumptions, and the thought of losing Jill had me near panic. Of course it was all in my head, I told myself, nothing had really happened between them, but then I thought about his arm around her waist, and the way she looked at him.

Even the glory of autumn building all around me couldn't jar my thoughts free. I passed the afternoon steadily working my way through the blocks of wood, and thinking about Mark and Jill. I realized that I had never really been jealous before, never had a reason to doubt Jill's devotion, or question our bond. Why now? What was so threatening about the biker? And what was it about him that appealed to her?

It only got worse over dinner. While we sat around the old farm table, I looked at him closely. He was dark, almost olive-skinned, with thick brown, wavy hair that flowed to his shoulders, and a scruffy black beard. His brown eyes shone brightly in a face that looked constantly amused. He was a big man, built like he lifted weights. Handsome, I guess, in a rough kind of way. Not what I would have thought of as Jill's type. There was a raw energy about him, a domineering affect that filled the room. He laughed too loudly and too often, but I was the only one who seemed to notice—the others were enthralled by him.

He held court throughout the meal. We started talking about the war, and the anti-war movement. I mentioned our protest up in Burlington.

"It was a start. We've got to build some kind of a statewide network."

"Fuck that pussy shit!" Mark exploded. "There's Vietnamese dying everyday, Panthers being killed in their beds. We better be able to come up with something stronger than another fuckin' protest rally! It's time to act, put the motherfuckers up against the wall!

"We've got to make them pay for all their bullshit, hurt them, really hurt them! Fuck protest! Bring this motherfuckin' empire to its knees. Set an example, show our Black brothers they're not all alone in their struggle!"

"I'm with you, bro! Down and ready." Jason pumped his fist in the air. "Right on!"

I glanced over at Jill and saw her hanging on his every word, eyes shining. My stomach did a flip-flop. I snorted and turned away, but there was no stopping Mark.

"It's so easy for you college kids," he continued. "It's time to get serious. See what you're made of." He gave me a withering look. "No more time for bullshitting. We've got to get down to it. Me, I want to throw a monkey wrench in the war machine, bring it grinding to a halt, make 'em think twice before they drop another bomb. I don't know about you," he looked at Jill, "but I'm tired of sittin' on my hands while people are dying because of US imperialism."

Everyone around the table was nodding in agreement. He was giving voice to the outrage we all felt. The war had been dragging on for years. How many protest marches had we organized? And what had really changed? His outrage seemed like the antidote to the impotence we all felt to a greater or lesser degree.

"So what do we do?" asked Jason. "What the fuck can we do?"

"Time to pick up the gun," said Mark. "Isn't it obvious? We've got to make the fuckers pay for what they're doing." He glared around the table. "We've got to bring the war home."

"Fuck, yeah!" said Jason.

"You know, it's like when I first got back from 'Nam, I was really fucked up, going kind of crazy. It was like all my nerves were raw, over-stimulated. I mean there was so much going on over there, and then all of sudden I was back to nothing. I felt empty."

I noticed Jill staring at him like she was sharing his pain.

"Man, I was a mess. I tried filling the space up…drugs, sex, motor-cycles, whatever. But nothing worked, and it felt like nobody else got it. That's when I started riding with the club; a lot of the guys had been over there, too. That helped—at least I didn't feel all alone. And we got into some crazy shit, that helped too, a little action. But it wasn't enough.

"Then one day I was going through a town upstate and I passed a recruiting billboard. You know, 'I want you!' I thought about all of my buddies who had died over there. And I started asking myself what the fuck they died for.

"I mean," he continued, "all that time in the jungle, I thought I was doing something righteous, serving my country, all that bullshit, and then one afternoon I realized that they'd just been using me, using us all. I rode back to the billboard that night with a Molotov cocktail. That made me feel a little better. It just made sense."

No one said anything, but I could sense a shift, a recalibration around the table. Mark had made his point, and it was sinking in. I had to admit, there was something compelling about him, an intensity that drew you in.

Finally, Jason spoke. "A blow against the empire."

"Yeah, that's what it felt like, like I was finally really doing something that mattered."

That night in bed I turned to Jill and voiced my discomfort. "Something about that guy Mark, I mean he's pretty cool and all, but I just don't trust. I mean coming in here and preaching violence, putting down everything we've been working on for all these years."

"Oh, come on David!" said Jill. "Who are you to question him? After all he's been through, all he's done? I think he's amazing! He's the real deal, and he's talking sense. Think about it. Our marching and organizing, what have we really accomplished?"

"But Molotov cocktails?" I argued. "What's that going to accomplish? How can guns and bombs bring peace? There's a basic contradiction…"

"You've always got a theory, don't you? Maybe we don't need peace, maybe we need a revolution!"

"Yeah, I agree. We need a revolution, a non-violent revolution that embodies our ideals, that mimics the kind of society we want after the revolution. I thought that's what we were trying to do here."

"Oh, you have all the answers, don't you?" She pulled at the covers.

"No, I just think—"

"David, shut up! Just shut the fuck up/"

THE MORNING WAS PERFECT; bright sun, blue sky with high, puffy cumulus clouds floating by. Birds were singing outside our window and the fall colors seemed to have intensified overnight, now almost fluorescent. I turned to hug Jill and found the bed empty.

Downstairs a group had gathered at the kitchen table around Mark, who was sipping coffee and telling more war stories. Jill was seated next to him. No one looked up as I walked to the counter and helped myself to a cup. When I sat Mark noticed me.

"Hey, Davey boy, how's it hangin'?" he said. "We're gonna get some target practice this morning. You gonna join us?"

All eyes turned to me. "I don't think so. We've still got firewood to cut. Besides, I'm not into guns."

"Oh, that's right, a non-violent warrior. I forgot," Mark laughed, and the others joined him. Then he resumed his stories.

I sat there drinking coffee and pushing a couple of scrambled eggs around my plate. To be honest I didn't have much of an appetite. After five minutes or so feeling really uncomfortable at the table, I slipped away to gather up what I needed out in the woods. Ranger followed me out the door and up the path to the woodlot.

A couple of hours spent blocking and splitting firewood left me with aching muscles. The roar of the chainsaw and the pop of the maple under the maul was punctuated by the sharp crack of shots being fired. When I stopped to take a long pull of water from a gallon jug, I heard rapid fire that sounded like a string of firecrackers exploding.

Ranger, sitting at my feet, cocked his head and whined. "It's okay, boy," I reassured him. "This too shall pass." How many rounds had they fired? I wondered. Must be hundreds by now. I dreaded going in for lunch. I returned to the woodpile and worked a few more hours, then headed back to the house for something to eat.

I heard renewed gunfire as I walked out of the woods, and when I neared the house, I saw them at the impromptu firing range they had set up at the edge of the field. They were standing with their backs to me, aiming at a group of cans that sat on a sawhorse about thirty feet away. As I approached them, I could see Mark standing beside Jill, with his arms around her to steady the rifle, his cheek pressed against hers, speaking in her ear.

There was a crack, and a can went flying off of the sawhorse.

"Yes!" She shouted, flushed with excitement and turned to embrace him.

"Feels good, huh?" he said. "Now imagine the feeling if it was a pig in your sights, and not just a can."

"You're insane!" I said, coming up behind them.

"Davey boy!" Mark responded. "You want a turn?"

"Come on Dave, try it. It's a pretty cool feeling." Jill was amped. "Powerful!"

"No thanks," I said. She turned back to Mark and I made my way to the house.

That evening the moon rose nearly full and the air was crisp. After dinner we gathered out around the fire. Mark produced a bottle of Jack Daniels that he passed around the circle. Jill was sitting next to him on the ground. I was surprised when she took a sip—I'd never seen her drink whiskey before.

The stars shifted in the sky, evening turned to night, a wind rose up, and I saw Jill shiver, and Mark put his arm around her. She snuggled close to him.

I was sitting directly across the fire from her. The flames were dying to embers, and Jason threw on another log. Suze had out her guitar and was strumming the chords from a Joan Baez tune. Jill didn't even glance over the flames at me, so she never saw the crestfallen look that crossed my face.

How could she be so cruel? So hurtful? Maybe I was overreacting, reading in more than was really there. I couldn't believe the despair that washed over me as I sat there.

Suze started singing in a sweet, quiet voice. "Where have all the flowers gone? Long time passing. Where have all the flowers gone? Long time ago." Then Jason joined in, singing harmony. They sang low and sweet, the sound incredibly sad—a lament. And by the time they ended, with the line about the soldiers in the graveyards, I was overcome.

I found myself quietly crying, and not quite sure why. The song? The night? The situation with Jill? I turned away hoping no one would notice.

But Suze did. "Are you okay, Dave?" She asked.

"Yeah, I'm fine. It's nothing. Some smoke blew in my face, that's all." I couldn't take it anymore. "I'm gonna turn in. Another big day of firewood tomorrow." I rose from the circle, said 'goodnight,'" and walked back toward the house.

A chorus of goodnights, including Jill's, followed me up the path. Ranger loped up to me and nuzzled my side, offering comfort. I rubbed his ears. "Good boy. Good dog."

I lay awake in bed for what seemed like hours before Jill came in, pulled on a flannel nightgown and crawled under the covers. Feigning sleep, I never said a word, nor did she.

The next day I escaped to the woodlot early, before anyone was awake. I had hoped that physical labor would banish the thoughts racing through my head, but my unease only increased as the day wore on.

That night after supper Jill and Mark strolled out to the fire circle, arm in arm. We all shared a joint as the flames of our campfire sent sparks in to the sky.

When the moon came up Jill and Mark rose from the circle. "We're going for a walk," she announced, and they headed down the path toward the road.

My heart sunk as they disappeared from sight. We hung out around the fire for an hour or so and then people started drifting toward the farmhouse. I waited, silently staring into the flames, waited until the flames died back to embers and I was the only one left, waited as the embers turned to ashes, hoping for Jill's return, and then finally gave up and went back to our bedroom.

I lay awake in bed, consumed by anxiety. As the first hint of dawn made its way through the window, I finally fell asleep, alone. Later I awoke to an empty spot on Jill's side of the bed. I lay there, with sunshine pouring through the window, but felt like my arms and legs had been encased in concrete. I didn't want to move, didn't want to get out of bed, or go downstairs to face the pitying looks I was sure to get from my friends. I couldn't stand the thought of seeing Mark's smirking face at the table, and had no idea what I would say to Jill. I was devastated, my whole world turned upside down.

I WAS STILL LYING under the covers, with my head buried in the pillow when Jill came into the bedroom.

"Hey, sleepyhead, what are you still doing in bed?" She sounded cheerful.

"I don't feel so good this morning, my stomach." I said. "What happened to you last night?" I couldn't stop myself from asking, even though I didn't want to hear her answer.

"Oh, I was hanging out with Mark." She offered no further explanation.

"Mark?" I asked.

"We had lots to talk about."

"Talk?"

"Back off, David!" her eyes flashed. "I can spend my time with whoever I want. I'm a free woman!"

"Yeah, of course you are. It's just that I thought—"

"I don't want to talk about it," she cut me off. "Besides, he's gone, he went back down to the city."

"Glad to hear it," I said.

"You can be such an asshole sometimes!" she said to me as she undressed and took her robe from a hanger in the closet. "I don't know about you, but I've got things to do today. I'm going to grab a quick shower and head into St. J." She put together a pile of clean clothes and was on her way out the door when she turned to me over her shoulder. "Can I get anything for you before I go?" she asked.

"Get anything for me?"

"Your stomach. You want some tea or something?

"No, thanks." I heard her footsteps on the stairs, waited ten minutes or so for her to be gone, and then went down myself to a thankfully empty kitchen.

WHAT CAN I SAY to David? I feel bad, know he must be hurting, but he doesn't own me. I mean, I love him and all that, but I'm a free woman, and I always made that clear to him. We both agreed, monogamy was a bunch of petite bourgeois bullshit, and we experimented; we've both been with other people. It was just never really an issue before. I don't know why he's so uptight about Mark. Okay, well maybe I do.

Mark is different. I mean I am really attracted to him. He's almost the exact opposite of David. David's so predictable; we've been together so long, been through so much, I know him so well. He's like a comfortable old shoe, a perfect fit, broken in, like an extension of me.

Mark's been through hell and back, and it really got to him. I know he comes across super-confident, but he's carrying a lot of pain—the things he's done, the things he's seen. Behind that smile he's haunted. He really opened up to me last night on our walk.

He was an orphan, dropped out of high school. Joined the army to get a fresh start, and it didn't work out like he hoped. I can only imagine what it was like for him, growing up like that, and then the war. And he came out of it all a revolutionary. He's incredible, spontaneous! He's like nobody I ever met before—a real risk taker, ready to take things as far as he can. He constantly challenges me. And it doesn't hurt that he's absolutely gorgeous. No, gorgeous isn't the right word. He's too masculine for that.

You could say he's a little macho, but he's the real deal. He's earned the right. I mean, he's put his life on the line. Maybe he doesn't have the most sophisticated analysis, but he lived this war from the inside, and he hates it, he really does, probably even more than I do. And he's ready to do something about it. Really do something.

I honestly don't have anything to apologize for. So how come I feel so shitty?

IT WAS WEIRD, THAT day and the next nobody mentioned Mark at all, at least not in my presence. It was like we were all trying to pretend nothing had happened. But something had, and I could feel it—a growing distance from the others, a tension in the air. And, despite both of our efforts to ignore the situation and the fact that we still shared a bed, it felt like Jill and I were just going through the motions. Something was lost. Trust, intimacy, love? I don't know, but there was a palpable change.

I felt constantly off balance; uncomfortable, somehow an object of pity. Maybe I was imagining it, maybe not. Maybe I was just heartbroken, but I felt wounded in a way I never had before. I began to question whether I could keep living this way, feeling this ache. I told myself I was being stupid. This was my home; they were my family. Of course I would stay, I had to, things would get better.

Then the fall was truly upon us. We woke one morning to frost covering the long grass in the field, and a cold snap in the air despite the bright sun. Whole hillsides seemed to suddenly burst forth into bright reds, oranges, yellows, purples—a psychedelic pallet.

Those fall days often left me gasping for breath. On a drive to St. J, every turn in the road revealed a new vista, an extraordinary view unfolding to the horizon that looked like an impressionist painting; luminous, and richly textured, almost fantastical in its grandeur. I was amazed again for the few short weeks that the color, like my hopes for a return to normality, hung on.

It was a Thursday, late morning. Jill and Suze had gone to the health food store and the others had formed a work crew and headed out to rake the lawn of an old lady down in the village. I was on kitchen duty, and was washing dishes in the old soapstone sink when I heard a knock on the door.

I looked out the kitchen window and saw a pair of strangers wearing suits and ties standing on the porch. I walked over and opened the door.

"Yes?" I asked. Ranger stood behind me with a low growl in his throat.

"Agents Axton and Terwilliger, FBI," the taller one said, flashing a billfold with his ID. "We're here to see Jason Weintraub." They looked incongruous in their formal attire.

"Jason's not here," I said. The shorter one, Terwilliger, was trying to peer around me, looking into the house. What the hell did the feds want with Jason?

"When will he be home?" Axton asked.

"I'm not sure," I hesitated. "What do you want to talk to him about?"

"We just have a few questions for him," Terwilliger replied.

"About what?"

"I can't comment on that, it's part of an ongoing investigation."

"Do you have a warrant?"

"We just want to talk to him," Terwilliger insisted. "But if he doesn't cooperate, we'll be back with a subpoena."

"How many people live here, anyway?" asked Axton.

"It varies," I said.

Axton handed me a card and said, "Tell him we'll be back about this time tomorrow."

"I'll give him the message," I replied, and I stood in the doorway watching as they walked back toward the road and then stopped while Axton took a notebook out of his coat pocket and wrote down the Volvo's license number.

I turned back to the dishes and finished scrubbing a skillet. I kept busy tidying and cleaning the rest of the morning, but I couldn't help thinking about the FBI. What the hell did they want? Was it about the demo at the GE plant? That's all I could think of that might interest them. Maybe it was just part of the general harassment of the movement that we had been hearing about. The repression was getting really bad, especially for the Panthers. Maybe that's what it was about, us giving food to the Panthers.

Around lunchtime the kitchen door burst open and Jill and Suze came in, followed by Jason and Brian.

"Dave, you should have come with us!" Jill enthused. "We saw a moose on our way up the hill. A fucking moose! The thing was huge, unbelievable!"

"The FBI stopped by while you were away," I announced.

"What?" asked Brian.

"The feds," I answered. "They wanted to talk to Jason. Wouldn't tell me about what, said it was 'an ongoing investigation' and they'd be back tomorrow morning. They said they'd get a subpoena if he wouldn't talk to them."

"What the fuck?" Jason exploded. "I've got nothing to say to them. What do they want with me?"

"What should we do?" Suze looked nervous.

"Lawyer up," said Jill. "I'll call my Dad." Her father was a big-time civil liberties specialist.

"I don't need a lawyer. I didn't do anything," Jason insisted.

"Never talk to the FBI." Jill was adamant.

"They wanted to know who lived here. They were looking around, I didn't let them in, but I saw them writing down the Volvo's license number."

"I bet they want to know all about us." Brian's forehead had a deep furrow.

"Well they won't get anything they can use from me," Jason insisted. "But if I don't meet with them and they start with the subpoenas and all that shit…" His voice trailed off. "Let 'em come. I've got nothing to hide."

"Bad idea. Never talk to the cops," Jill was insistent. "You don't know what they're looking for. How can you be sure you won't say something they can use?"

"But if they subpoena me and I don't talk, I could go to jail," said Jason. "Fuck that! I mean, I'm ready to go to jail for doing something, but not for something I didn't do. You can dig that, can't you?"

"Well, it's your choice," said Jill. "But I think it's a stupid move."

"I'm telling you, they won't get anything they can use from me, and we can find out what they're looking for."

We all thought about it for a moment, and then Suze, who was heating up some leftover rice and beans for lunch, spoke. "Well, if they're coming, we ought to prepare a welcome for them."

WE SLEPT UNDER A down comforter that night, and when we woke, there was still a chill in the air. Everyone gathered around the kitchen table and we went over our plan for the FBI's visit. When the knock on the door came, Brian answered.

"Commune Patrol, here." He greeted them wearing a baseball cap with a red star cut from cardboard on the front lettered "CP". "Identification?" he held out his hand.

Axton stared at him and said "What?"

"I just need to check your credentials," Brian said, blocking the doorway.

Axton looked at Terwilliger and then shrugged. They showed him their wallets, open to their FBI ID cards and shields.

Brian brushed his hair out of his eyes, stared at the IDs, made a show of examining each one closely, and then, taking a pen out of his pocket, wrote the badge numbers down in a spiral notebook.

He handed them back their wallets and said, "Alright, looks okay, you can come in now. Mr. Weintraub is expecting you."

Brian led the way as the men stepped into the room. Ranger, standing next to the door, began to growl.

"Here, boy," I called, and he came to my side. "Sit," I said.

Ranger sat on the floor next to me. His lip was curled. He growled and never took his eyes from the two agents as they warily walked past him, following Brian into the kitchen.

The sounds of music suddenly blasted through the still air of the old farmhouse, "We are all outlaws in the eyes of America," the Jefferson Airplane's latest anthem was at full volume. At the same time, I pulled out a camera and snapped a picture of the two feebies. Ranger bolted to his feet, but I ordered him down again.

"Just documenting your visit," I told the agents as I continued to click away. "Jason's in the back room."

They crossed the kitchen and entered the main room, where, at the far end, Suze stood naked, posing for Jill who was sketching her in charcoal. Terwilliger stopped short, and Axton stumbled into him, blushing visibly at the sight of a naked woman.

Suze looked over at them. "Real men," she purred and licked her lips. "What a treat after all these hippies."

"Right this way," Brian guided them toward the parlor door with a flourish of his arm. "Mr. Weintraub is waiting."

I let the camera hang from a strap around my neck and picked up a cassette recorder and followed them.

"What's that for?" asked Axton.

"I'm going to record the interview. We want a complete record of everything, on advice of our lawyer," I told them.

The two agents exchanged panicked looks. "I don't think we can allow that," Axton finally said. "This is a confidential investigation."

"Oh, that's okay," I said. "Mr. Weintraub waives his right to confidentiality. His lawyer couldn't be here, but he wants a complete record of the interview."

"We're only going to ask him a few questions," Axton was annoyed.

"Well, then he'll need his lawyer present." I was improvising at this point. "He has a right to counsel. This is still America, isn't it?"

"He's not under arrest." Terwilliger chimed in.

"What is he being investigated for?" I asked.

"Listen, wise guy!" Axton took a step toward me. "This is a confidential investigation. He can talk to us now, alone, or we come back with a subpoena and force his testimony before a grand jury, and he won't have any lawyer there, just the prosecutor. His choice. Now turn off the recorder."

"Hey, this is our home, you don't have a warrant. We don't have to let you in at all." Sometimes I don't know when to keep my mouth shut.

"You people are crazy! We're the FBI! I'll come back with a warrant!" Terwilliger threatened. "Or you can let us talk to him and then we'll leave."

I looked at Jill and she shrugged. "Well," I said, "I don't know. Let me check with Jason."

I went into the parlor, and closed the door behind me. I consulted with Jason for a moment, then ushered them in. Jason sat in an old blue wing chair waiting for them. I stepped back out of the room and Axton closed the door.

After twenty minutes or so the agents came back out, pocketing their notebooks in their overcoats. I resumed snapping pictures and Frank Zappa blasted from the stereo. Ranger, sitting on the couch, stared at them growling and baring his teeth as they made their exit.

When the kitchen door closed, we looked at each other and burst out laughing. Jason emerged from the parlor and joined us.

"Well?" asked Jill. "What did they want?"

We all looked at Jason expectantly. He hesitated.

"Come on Jason! What are they investigating?" Jill demanded.

"I don't really know," he said. "It was weird."

"Well what did they ask you?"

"They wanted to know about the dynamite."

"The dynamite?" Jill's brow furrowed.

"Yeah, that we used to blast the spring. Why did we buy it? What was it used for? Stuff like that."

"And?"

"That was it. So I told them."

"You told them what, exactly?" Jill was concerned.

"The truth, that we used it to blast the spring to get a better flow. That was all I told them."

"No other questions?" Jill asked.

"Oh yeah, they wanted to know if I knew anybody in Baltimore."

"Baltimore?" I asked. "Why Baltimore?"

"I don't know," answered Jason. "I told them no, and that was it."

"Did they say what this grand jury's all about?" Jill wondered.

"No, I asked them, but they wouldn't say. But they mentioned that every batch of dynamite has some kind of chemical identification code, or something. So it has to do with dynamite. I don't know, maybe a bomb or something."

"You didn't tell them about Mark, did you? That he detonated it?" Jill seemed concerned.

"No, of course not," answered Jason. "I didn't give anybody's name. I told them I bought it and I set the charge. They seemed satisfied, but they did say it was an ongoing investigation and they might be back in touch if they had any more questions."

"Shit!" I exclaimed. "I hate this. The last thing we need is the fucking feds breathing down our neck."

"Well, at least they're not busting down our doors and shooting us in our beds, like they are with the Panthers," said Jill.

Their visit made me really on edge. I obsessed about it for a couple of days, and that was on top of my uncertainty about Jill.

THEN CAME DESOLATION—THE GRAY time of bare trees, cold rain, and ever-shortening days that left us feeling trapped inside the farmhouse. Time to bank the house with spruce boughs and cover the windows with milky plastic to keep out the growing chill borne by the Canadian wind.

It was mid-November. Thanksgiving was approaching. Brian was planning a trip home to New York. I had toyed with the idea of joining him for the drive and spending a little time with my Dad, but decided against it. I was starting to feel a little better about things with Jill, and I thought maybe the holidays would help.

It was snowing that night, a steady fall that promised to cover the bare ground with a couple of inches by morning. We were sitting at the table, just finishing up dinner, when the door opened and Mark walked in, brushing snow from his leather jacket. I felt my stomach drop.

"Mark!" Jill rose and greeted him with a big hug. He grinned and kissed her.

"Hey babe! What's shakin'? I told you I'd be back." He looked around the table. "Jason! How you doing, brother? Suze," he nodded to her. "Brian, my man!" Then he flashed me his fucking Cheshire Cat smile, "Davey boy, what's up? How's the revolution?"

I could hardly look at him. Jill was standing at his side, beaming. He left her to walk to the table, where he took a chair, spun it backwards and straddled it.

"I missed you." He looked at Jill. "Did you miss me?" He laughed. "No, really, I been thinking about you guys."

"Where have you been?" asked Jason.

"After I left here, I checked back in with the club. Everybody was getting ready to pull out of Norton, winter comin' on and all. Tough to ride a Harley in the snow, brought a car up this time. We went back to the city. Then I took a little road trip, down to Baltimore."

"Baltimore?" Jason was concerned. "What were you doing down there?"

"Oh, visiting some friends. I got into some shit too," Mark said coyly. "Nothing that would interest a bunch of stone revolutionaries like yourselves."

"The FBI were here, asking about the dynamite," I said. "So we're interested."

"The fuckin' feds were here?" It was the first time I ever saw Mark look rattled. "You didn't tell 'em nothin', did you?"

"Jason talked to them," said Jill. "Against my advice, but he didn't give them anything they didn't already know."

238

"Like what?" Mark gave Jason a cold look.

"I just confirmed that I bought some dynamite and that I used it to blast the spring. They said something about chemical markers or something. Then they asked if I knew anybody in Baltimore, and I said I didn't. That's all."

"Fuck! My name never came up?"

"No, never," confirmed Jason.

Mark regained his composure. "Then they got nothin'. Just a little test of a timer anyway, nothin' heavy. I'm surprised they even picked up on it."

"You put us all at risk," I said. "We're on their radar now."

"Oh, come on, David!" said Jill, "You think we weren't before? Besides, it's for the revolution. Whatever we can do to help, remember?"

"You're kidding, right?" I said. "He put all of us, all of our work, everything we've built up in jeopardy, brought down the heat on us without even consulting us, and you're defending him? I don't believe it!"

"Fuck you, David!" she shouted. "You're so fucking high and mighty! All-knowing, all-seeing David! Well, fuck you!"

That was all I could handle. I went up to our room, closed the door and waited for Jill, but she never came. I decided that night to leave with Brian for New York the next day.

THE FOLLOWING MORNING, I packed a backpack and took my stuff downstairs to the kitchen, where Suze, Jason, and Brian were seated around the table. The air was thick. As I was pouring myself a cup of coffee, Mark and Jill came in together from the back parlor. He had his arm around her. She wouldn't look me in the eye.

"I'm leaving after breakfast with Brian," I announced.

"I thought you'd decided not to go," said Suze.

"I changed my mind."

"For how long?" Jason asked.

"I don't know," I said, "through Thanksgiving, I guess, at least. I'm taking Ranger with me." The dog's tail began to thump at the mention of his name.

"Well, have fun," said Suze, without much enthusiasm.

I sat there sipping my coffee in awkward silence as the conversation picked up around the table.

"Heavy weather out there, and I don't mean the snowstorm." Mark stretched his arms out above his head and yawned. "You guys heard about the Weathermen? I mean, who are these guys? They sound like they're ready to get down. Bring the war home, Days of Rage, Off the Pigs. I can dig their shit! Finally, somebody lookin' to make it real!"

"They're the old Action Faction from Columbia, and some midwesterners out of Chicago," said Brian.

"A bunch of adventurists," I grunted.

Jill glared at me. "Don't be so condescending, David. At least they're doing something."

"Yeah," said Mark. "Sounds like they're ready to get heavy. I thought of you when I heard about them, figured you'd know them, and know what's up. I'd like to hook up with them, can you dig it?"

"They're calling themselves the Weather Organization now," said Jason.

"Where'd they get 'Weatherman' from?" queried Mark.

"You know," Jason replied. "'You don't need a weatherman to know which way the wind blows'? Dylan?"

"Yeah, right." Mark smiled.

Jill disappeared with Mark after breakfast, and I left without saying goodbye to her. Brian and I headed down on a brand new stretch of interstate. As we drove farther south the snow-covered landscape gave way to bare ground, and the snow changed over to a steady rain that followed us all the way to New York.

BRIAN DROPPED ME AND Ranger off at my father's brick cottage in the Bronx.

I felt like I was returning to my childhood—everything was so familiar; unchanged since the day almost ten years ago my mother had died. I found the key where Dad always left it, under the doormat, and let myself in. He would be surprised to see me when he walked in that evening.

My dad and I were never that close. He was always busy at the store, working long hours, and too tired when he got home to have much energy for me. Plus, something about men of his generation—he had been in the war, and had this stoic attitude. He never complained, in fact he never said much at all, at least not to me. My mom was the glue that held the family together.

I remember coming home from school one afternoon when I was twelve. My father was sitting at the kitchen table with his head in his hands. I knew something momentous was going on—he never left the store early. It was cancer, he told me. Mom would need an operation, but there was nothing to worry about—a short hospital stay, and then she would be back home, good as new. But I saw a shadow of fear hovering over my father, and despite his assurances, I felt it too. It unsettled my stomach, and kept me from sleep at night; it followed me to school every morning, and even if I could escape it for a few hours at my desk, or playing stickball with friends, it was there waiting on the stoop when I came home.

She went into the hospital for a week the first time. I remember the antiseptic smell in the halls, and the tiny TV mounted on the wall where we watched reruns of "I Love Lucy" together. Then they sent her home and said they thought they got it all.

But six months later she went back in and they cut some more. They wouldn't let me visit that time. She said she didn't want me to see her like that.

She came home again, a different person from the mom I used to know. When I hugged her, I felt her ribs, and her spine, and I involuntarily shuddered. She held me tight and told me it would all be fine, but when she finally released me, I saw that she was crying, and it scared me even more.

Then they tried chemo; her hair fell out and she was sick all the time. She grew even thinner and she barely had the energy to lift her fork as we sat in silence around the dinner table. It was as though she was disappearing before my eyes.

The final time she went into the hospital she hugged me and stroked my head, told me she loved me, and that I should be a good boy. My father helped her out the door, and that was the last time I ever saw her.

And it was like my father died too. Never very talkative, now he brooded silently every night when he came home from the hardware store. Sometimes I tried to tell him about school, or talk about sports, but nothing reached him. He seemed diminished—like he was disappearing too. I didn't know what to do, or who to turn to. It was like I had lost them both.

So home was not a place of happy memories for me. Like I said, Dad worked all the time and after Mom's death he tried to find refuge at his store a few blocks away. I started going in to help after school and on Saturdays; stocking shelves and helping customers find what they needed. But it was always like we were there in separate worlds. He was distracted, off somewhere in his head with my mom.

The trouble at home fed into a growing feeling I had that things were just not right, despite all the Yankee Doodle bullshit and flag worship they tried to feed me at school. Their version of the American dream was contradicted by everything I saw around me: my father and mother, exhausted from working twelve hours a day, constantly worrying about meeting their payroll and paying their rent. The homeless people panhandling at the subway stop. I saw the lie of America in the defeated faces of the young Black men standing on the corner a few blocks south of me.

The house brought back memories of the palpable fear when my parents talked in whispers about Joe McCarthy and his witch-hunt and their friends who couldn't find work.

I remembered mom's urgent warning to my father. "Cancel the subscription to the *Nation*, buy it on the news stand so they can't trace you."

All of this and more washed over me as if I reentered my childhood. The duck and cover drills, cowering under my desk, shaking with fear at the thought of a Russian A-bomb landing on top of the school or our house. I imagined it with a red bullseye painted on the roof, visible only from high above, with a missile heading straight for it.

I remember going home and urging my parents to stockpile food and water, just in case, and the sad look in my mother's eyes as she hugged me and told me not to worry.

Ozzie and Harriet, smiling through their perfect suburban lives were as distant from me as the pogroms that my grandparents talked about escaping when we gathered for Passover dinner.

Growing up in the Bronx was not like growing up in America. And not quite like growing up in New York either. The neighborhood was its own world, and had nothing to do with the bright lights, glamorous people, theaters, and museums I saw in the movies and glossy magazines.

As I got older, I explored that other New York, and, as much as I loved it, I never really felt connected to it.

I had a few friends, and on Sundays we would go into the city and hang out in Washington Square. The park was filled with kids and dozens of people playing guitars and banjos. It was a scene, and I always wished that I could really be part of it.

Ranger was wagging his tail and sniffing out every corner of the small house. What can it be like for him? This blaze of reality rushing through him, overwhelming him. Scents and sounds. Not just the new place, but the cacophonous background he had never experienced before.

I sat in the kitchen. The table had the same red checked covering. I looked in a cupboard and discovered my father was still subsisting on the same Rice-a-Roni and Hamburger Helper that had been staples for us after Mom died. Nothing changed here—it was why I had to leave.

DAVID TOOK OFF WITHOUT even saying goodbye! I don't believe what a jerk he's being! I mean he never even talked to me about anything. I guess he's really pissed at me. Well too bad! Mark came back 'cause he wants to work with us. Yes, there's a spark between us, but if David can't handle that, tough shit. You'd think after all our time together he could give me a little space, that he'd trust the strength of our relationship to survive a little fling. Well, we'll get it straightened out when he gets back from Thanksgiving.

A COUPLE OF HOURS later I heard my father at the front door. "Dad!" I called out. "I'm here, in the kitchen." Ranger thumped his tail on the linoleum floor.

"Dave? What are you doing here? Everything alright?"

I rose to greet him as he walked into the kitchen. "Everything's fine. I just figured I'd come home for a visit. Holidays and all that." We hugged.

"Well, nice to see you." He stepped back. "You look good. Hair's too long, but you look good. Healthy. How's everything up at the commune? How's that girl of yours?"

He saw my face fall. "Oh, I'm sorry...I liked her."

"Well, I thought I'd take a break and come see you. Hope it's okay."

"Yeah, sure, of course. Don't know that there's much to keep you occupied here..."

"I thought I could work at the store for a few weeks, make a couple of bucks. I know the holidays are your busy time."

"Great! Good idea, I can definitely use the help. Alright then..." Ranger had come over and was sniffing his crotch. "Who's this?"

"Oh, that's Ranger. He's a good boy. Aren't you, boy? Yes, you are." The big dog shook with pleasure.

"Big boy."

"Part Lab, part Great Dane."

"He'll make a good watchdog down at the store." My father grinned, ruffling his fur.

"Cool," I replied.

My days were spent at Dad's store, mostly behind the counter or stocking shelves. Then home to a meal of Rice-a-Roni, a little TV after dinner, and then to bed. I took Ranger for long walks, and even let him off the leash in the park, but I could tell he was missing Vermont, and so was I.

I called Brian one night and he picked me and Ranger up and drove into the city to visit a friend on the Lower East Side. I had been back in the Bronx for about two weeks at that point. Thanksgiving had come and gone—turkey breast from a neighborhood deli and mashed potatoes from a box. I needed to see friends, Dad was driving me nuts, I couldn't engage him. He was so deep in his grief that I couldn't pull him out, same as always.

On our way downtown Brian seemed a little uneasy. "I decided to go back to grad school," he said. "I'm starting up again spring term. I'm driving up to Vermont before Christmas to pick up my stuff, then to Cambridge, back to the place I used to live."

"You're shitting me, man!" I was surprised. "I thought you were in it for the long haul. I mean—"

"I thought you were too," he interrupted me.

"Yeah, well, Jill and me...you know."

"That's bullshit, Dave! That's a lot of bourgeois bullshit. I thought you were up there for the revolution," Brian insisted.

"Well, I was, or, maybe I am...I'm trying to figure shit out. Just this thing with Jill. I mean, we were together a long time."

"I know. It's tough, and it sucks. But you were really the one holding it together up there. I don't think I'll be missed that much."

"That's not true," I countered. "Everybody up there loves you."

"And I love them too," he said. "I didn't mean I wouldn't be missed, but in terms of what I contributed to the group. You though, you're the glue. I doubt the place will hang together without you."

I felt a pang of...I don't know, guilt, or longing? Something tugging at me.

We went up to Jeffrey's fifth-floor walkup. He was sitting on a mattress on the floor in the living room just about to fire up a joint when we came in.

"Hey, look who's here. Back from the mountains, huh? What's shakin' guys? What brings you back to civilization?" He laughed. "Good to see you, brothers. And I see you brought reinforcements." He pointed at Ranger. "Cool."

"He's very devoted," I said. "I couldn't leave him back at my dad's."

"So how are things? How's everybody doin' up there?" Jeff had been part of our collective in college, but he elected to stay in the city when we made the move.

"Things are good," I lied. "I mean nothing good comes without struggle, right?"

"Uh oh! Do I detect a hint of trouble in paradise?"

"Come on, Jeff." Brian interjected. "You know how it is. It's hard to live with a group. We're trying to become new people, but there's a lot of old shit to work through to get there."

"Amen to that, brother!" replied Jeff. "That's why I live alone. Anyway, have a toke and relax. Everything's cool here. Lot's happenin' in the Lower East Side—I mean a whole lot. We got Abbie, Jerry, and the Yippies running around. We got the Panthers and the Young Lords. These hippies from California, call themselves Diggers, anarchists or something hit town a couple summers ago, started a free store, just giving shit away! Crazy artists, into 'armed love', called Up Against the Wall Motherfucker. Free concerts in the park all summer. Demo's going all the time. Crazy, and very cool!"

"Wow, sounds like the revolution's about to break out!" I was impressed.

"'Course things have slowed down a little now that the colder weather is coming."

"Don't talk to me about cold weather," said Brian. "I almost froze to death up there last winter. I'm not gonna take another one."

"What a wimp!" I teased. "It only went down to thirty below a couple of times."

"Thirty below! Holy shit! You're kidding." Jeff was amazed.

The joint made its way around and I was starting to relax. Jeff put on the new Dylan album and we listened intently to both sides.

"I can't believe he's gone country, what a cop-out." I gave vent to my disappointment. "He was a really important voice, almost prophetic, and now he's singing about moon and June and that crap! What a drag."

"Oh, I don't know, there's some good songs on there. What the fuck, he's an artist, not everything has to be political," argued Brian.

"Everything is political," I responded.

"Hey, anybody for a beer?" asked Jeffrey.

"Sure," said Brian.

Jeff rose and opened the fridge. "Shit, all out. Guess I'll go down to the bodega. Anybody got a few bucks?"

I pulled a couple of dollars out of my jeans. "Here you go."

"Hey, can I take your dog down with me?"

"I guess, why not?" I said

Jeffrey attached the leash to Ranger and headed down the five flights.

He came back fifteen minutes later with a six-pack of Budweiser and no dog. He looked shaken.

"What the fuck! Where's Ranger?" I asked.

"Sorry man," said Jeff. "I tied him to a newspaper machine out front of the bodega. While I was inside a truck went by and backfired. Must've freaked him out 'cause he took off down Avenue A dragging the fucking thing. I ran after him, called him, but he just kept on goin'. Fuckin' bodega owner was yellin' at me in Spanish and—sorry man, really sorry."

"Oh, shit! You're kidding, lost? Fuck—we've got to find him!"

"Let's go look for him," offered Brian, trying to calm me down. "We'll take the car. He's probably right around here. He can't have got too far dragging a paper machine."

"Right on, brother," offered Jeffrey, rather lamely. "We'll find him."

We spent the next two hours fruitlessly driving up and down the avenues and cross streets of the Lower East Side. I called his name until I was hoarse. No luck. My stomach was flip-flopping the whole time. I couldn't believe it. Ranger was gone.

We went back up to Jeff's and I spent the next hour on the phone, getting the runaround from the cops, animal enforcement, the ASPCA, and the city animal shelter. I was frantic, sick to my stomach as I tried to locate him.

I finally gave up, and Brian drove me back to my dad's. We were both silent the entire trip, as I tried to resign myself to the fact that the big dog was gone forever.

It was past midnight by the time I entered the silent living room. I entered the living room and sat on the couch. It was all too much; the loss of Jill, the commune, now Ranger. I felt an overwhelming sadness wash over me. Why had I let Jeff take him out? How could I have been so stupid?

I thought about Ranger running through the woods while I skied. I remembered how he looked when I first brought him home, a clumsy puppy snuggling with me and Jill in our bed. Then I started to sob. He was gone, and a big part of my life was gone with him.

I sat there for a long time, head in hand. As I edged toward sleep, I thought I heard a whine at the door, which I ignored as a figment of my guilt. Then I heard a scratch, a distinct scratch.

I got up, went to the front door, turned on the porch light, and there was Ranger, sitting on the stoop. He had lost his collar somewhere, he was soaking wet, and he was panting, but there he was.

I couldn't believe it. "Ranger! Ranger!" I ruffled his fur. "How the hell…?" I couldn't imagine how he found his way back to me, miles of unknown territory through the mass confusion of the metropolis. It was unbelievable, but there he was! I couldn't understand how he did it then, nor do I understand it now.

He came inside and I threw my arms around him as he wagged his tail wildly, sending a cut glass candy dish flying off the coffee table. He licked my face and nuzzled me in delight.

He slept close to me on the bed that night, a reassuring presence at my side.

MY DAD AND I rarely spoke, not out of any animosity, but because neither had anything to say to the other. Our days were spent largely in silence, both at work where discussion was limited to his telling me what to do, and at home where conversation was usually on the level of "Pass the salt".

Yet somehow I knew what he was thinking. He was still brooding over Mom's death these ten years later, and now, in addition, worrying about me.

I knew I was a disappointment to him—not that he ever mentioned it. But he had such high hopes for me. I had been top of my class in high school, gone on to graduate from the Ivy League. "Such potential," I imagined him sighing. And though he was supportive of my politics to a degree, he didn't understand the counterculture. When I told him I was moving to Vermont to start the farm he threw up his hands.

"A commune?" His eyes pleaded with me. "Why?" he asked.

He just didn't get it, didn't get me. I wasn't looking forward to the one substantive discussion I knew was coming. He laid it on me after I had been home for almost three weeks. "So what's next? What are your plans?"

I swallowed hard. "Well, I'm thinking I'll go back to Vermont before Christmas, finish out the season on the farm, and apply to law school next year."

I saw his face brighten for the first time since I had been home. "Law school? Now you're talking sense. Where are you gonna go? Somewhere here in the city?"

"Slow down," I cautioned. "I haven't even applied yet. Who knows if I'll get in…"

"Oh, you'll get in," he insisted. "Why back up to Vermont? You can keep helping at the store, earn some money for school."

Although law school was a fiction I had created to make Dad feel better, I was still wondering about the wisdom of returning to the farm. "I can earn some money up there," I lied. "And I've just got a lot of loose ends to tie up, you know? Unresolved business." Which was true.

I had been thinking about how I had left things the whole time I was home, especially since my talk with Brian. I needed to talk to Jill, find out where she was at, if it was really over between us. I also felt it would be wrong to leave the others in the lurch. I missed the farm. I missed the people, but the place really tugged at me too.

I realized how much I loved it. I craved the sky and the woods, the sound of birds in the morning, the smell of the wood fire, and the sunset over Hardwood Mountain. Vermont had gotten to me on a visceral level. I felt the absence of all this and more. I knew I needed to go back, and now, fortified by my weeks of solitude, and with enough money saved to help see us through the winter, I felt ready, to return, and resigned to the fact that I had lost Jill. Besides, I realized what a cruel thing city life was for Ranger, who tolerated it only because of his devotion to me.

I called Brian, and we left a week before Christmas. The temperature seemed to drop every mile farther north we traveled in Brian's VW. The heater gave out altogether when we hit Brattleboro just as the sun was sinking below the hills to our west.

When we pulled off of the interstate in White River Junction, we were in the midst of a snow-covered landscape twinkling under the light of an almost full moon, huge and yellow. As we drove through the Southern Greens it clouded up, and then started to snow shortly after, large flakes falling gently on a light breeze.

Ranger lay on the back seat and I huddled in front under a green army surplus blanket, watching the silent forests and fields roll by, punctuated by an occasional light from a farmhouse, or the street lamps of the small villages we passed through on our way toward the border.

We headed north through flurries, and took the state highway into town, arriving late enough that the general store was closed and the village silent. The hill up to the farm was slippery, but Brian had snow tires, and the little VW clawed its way up.

Ranger was shaking with excitement, and he exploded out of the car when I opened the door, bounding down the path toward the farmhouse. Brian and I followed.

I felt anxiety welling up in my stomach as we approached. Ranger got there first and was dancing in a pool of light that poured out of the open door. I heard Suze say "Ranger!" Then she looked down the path and saw Brian and me walking towards her in the moonlight.

"Dave! Brian! Wow! I wasn't expecting you. Come on in."

She hugged me long and hard when I walked into the kitchen. "How have you been? You're back, both of you?"

"Yeah," I answered. "I just couldn't stand the thought of you suffering through the winter without me."

She laughed. "Well, I'm not going to be suffering through the winter. We're getting ready to leave."

"Huh?" said Brian.

"Yeah," she replied. "Me and Jason. We're leaving, going down to the city."

"What the fuck!" I said. "If you and Jason are leaving who's staying?"

"Um, I guess nobody," Suze grimaced. "I mean, we didn't know you were coming back, and, so much has happened since you left…"

"Nobody! Shit! What do you mean? What happened?" I asked.

"Well you know how rough last winter was, and I'm from the South…"

"Yeah, but what happened?" I couldn't believe it.

"Jill and Mark—I mean all of us decided, we're going to the War Council out in Flint."

"War Council?" Brian queried.

"You know, SDS," I offered. "The Weathermen."

"It's the next logical step, Dave. If you're really serious about the revolution…"

"So you're just leaving? What about the collective? The farm? What about me?" I asked.

"Well, we didn't think you'd be back. The way you left and all…"

"How about me?" said Brian.

"Jason said you were going back to school," said Suze. "Aren't you?"

"Well, I am," said Brian. "But I only told Jason I was thinking about it. Were you just going to leave?"

"Jill says anybody who wants to stay, can stay. But we're out of here."

"Fuck!" I said. "Where's Jason, where's Jill?"

"Jason should be back soon. He went to Newport."

"Where's Jill?" I demanded.

"Hey, don't be pissed at me!" she replied. "Jill's already down in the city."

"With Mark?" I asked.

"With Mark," she said, looking at the floor.

I was already reeling from the fact that the collective was abandoning the farm, but her last bit of news felt like a punch to the solar plexus. I collapsed into a chair at the kitchen table. "You mean I came back to an empty house?"

"Well, we're leaving tomorrow. You're welcome to come down with us," said Suze.

"Or you can catch a ride to Cambridge with me," offered Brian.

I thought for a moment—New York or Cambridge? There was really nothing for me either place. "Thanks," I said. "But I think I'll stay here."

"Really? All by yourself?" asked Suze.

"Dave," Brian sounded concerned. "You don't even have a car. How will you get around?"

"I'll use the farm truck."

"Sorry, the engine blew." said Suze apologetically, and then added, "We never got in any more firewood either, we're almost out."

"Don't worry about me," I said. "I can catch rides to town with Leland, and if I learned anything up here, it's how to cut firewood."

"But you'll be all alone, and you know how long the winter is…" Suze's voice trailed off.

"I won't be all alone. Ranger will be here, and Leland and Mary are right next door. I made a little money while I was away." I surveyed the shelves in the pantry. "And we've got lots of the food we put by from the garden. I'll do just fine."

"Really? You're sure?" asked Brian.

"Sounds crazy to me," said Suze. "Come down to the city. Join us— we're gonna bring the war home!"

"We've had this discussion before. You know where I stand."

"But Dave, the contradictions have never been clearer. Black people are already in revolt, workers and students are next. Don't you want to be in the vanguard? It's coming, shit it's already started…"

"Vanguard?" I cut her off. "We don't need a vanguard. We need a majoritarian movement, and if you think guns and bombs are going to win over the American people, you are truly deluded!"

"Fuck you, Dave! It's happening all over the world! Cuba! China! Vietnam!"

"All Third World countries," I countered. "Do you really think we're facing the same situation here?"

"Come on! Paris, Mexico City, Warsaw! It's happening right here at home too—the Black rebellions, Watts, Detroit, the Panthers, Fred Hampton…are you blind? Look around you."

"I guess we just disagree," I said.

"I guess we do." She paused. "I wish you saw things differently. You should talk to Jason when he gets home. Maybe he can get through to you."

"I doubt it," I replied.

I did talk to Jason, but it was the same old shit. I loved the guy, but to tell the truth I was getting sick of the rhetoric. I had to admit they had developed a compelling internal logic. The problem was with their initial analysis: the idea that Americans could ever be won over by a violent revolution.

Winter 1969-70

THE HOUSE EMPTIED OUT the next morning—Suze and Jason off to join Jill and Mark in New York, and Brian, his car full of his things, on his way back to grad school at Harvard.

"Well, we're really down to the hardcore now. Huh, boy?" I roughed the fur behind Ranger's ears and he whimpered in delight.

The day stretched before me. There was work that needed to be done, but I had no schedule. I just sat at the kitchen table letting the silence surround me. The sun shining through the row of windows over the kitchen sink cast a shaft of light onto the table.

It reminded me that I needed to seal the windows with heavy plastic to cut down on the drafts. I would need to cut spruce boughs to bank the place as well, as Leland had shown me last year.

I wondered how Leland and Mary were doing. I hadn't seen them for over a month, hadn't said goodbye when I left. I had to check in with them. I assumed they would be my closest companions for the duration of the winter, and I was counting on them for occasional rides to Newport or St. J so I could get supplies and food to supplement what we had put by from the garden.

And then there was firewood. The stack on the porch would last about a week. They had already burned through most of what I had managed to cut before I left. That would be a big job. It took a huge amount of wood to heat the house last winter. Maybe I could seal off some rooms to conserve heat.

But I was having trouble getting motivated. I had no sense of urgency as I sat there lost in thought, remembering how full of life the place had always been—too full for my liking at times—and how empty it felt now. I remembered the scramble for coffee on summer mornings when the kitchen overflowed, and the crowd sitting around on the living room floor for meetings. I was having trouble getting my head around the solitude.

Then I looked out the window. The sky was bright blue, reflecting off the untrammeled whiteness that surrounded me. The fir trees that edged the field were a deep, rich green and I heard a crow caw, as if to welcome me home.

My anxiety receded. It did feel like home; emptied of brothers and sisters, but home nonetheless—familiar and comfortable. I rose and filled the insatiable wood stove from the wood box. When I pulled on my boots Ranger went to the door in anticipation. I took my barn coat from the peg in the mudroom, put it on, and stepped outside. Ranger ran in circles around me until he determined that I was walking toward the road, at which point he rushed down the path.

I was headed for Leland and Mary's trailer, my boots squeaking on the fresh snow. Ranger was sitting on their stoop, panting, when I arrived. I knocked on the door and Leland answered.

"David!" he said. "Come on in. Good to see you. It's been a while. Thought everybody left this morning."

"Not everybody," I replied as I entered the tidy little trailer. "I'm staying."

"Oh? Jill told me everybody was clearin' out for the winter. Asked us to keep an eye on things."

"Well, she didn't know I was coming back. I just got here."

"Stayin' by yourself? Don't mean to pry, but…"

"It's okay, Leland. Jill and I broke up, but you know, the farm was always about more than just us. I want to stay. I tried the city again. That's where I've been the past month. I couldn't stand it."

"I can understand that," he said, shaking his head.

Mary walked over and joined us

"How's David?" she asked.

"Hi Mary. I'm fine, glad to be back."

"Is Jill back?" There was a hopeful edge in her voice.

"No, she's gone," I replied.

"Oh." She looked disappointed. "Too bad."

"We broke up," I said.

"I know, and even though it's none of my business, I've got to say I was hoping…"

"Me too, Mary. Me too." My gaze fell.

"So you're back. Well, it'll be good to have a neighbor next door." She was trying to sound cheerful. "Can I get you a cup of tea?"

"Sure, I'd love that." I sat at the kitchen table with Leland while Mary bustled around the little kitchen.

"So what's your plan?" he asked.

"Just get through winter, I guess. No big plans," I said. "Seems like just doing that will keep me busy. They never got in the firewood."

"Oh," intoned Leland. "Well, you know what they say, wood cut in winter heats three times; once in the cuttin', once in the splittin' and once in the burnin'. You let me know when you're ready and I'll come over with the tractor and help you bring it in."

"Thanks, Leland," I replied. "That'll help a lot."

"Just bein' neighborly," he said.

"Care for a cookie?" asked Mary.

The next morning, I caught a ride to Newport with Leland. I got a roll of milky plastic from the hardware store, and picked up felt weather stripping and a box of staples for the staple gun. Sealing up the windows seemed like closing the lid of a coffin from the inside. But it had to be done if I had any chance of staying warm through the winter. It was almost Christmas, and temperatures were dropping fast.

That afternoon I took the saw out into the woods and cut spruce boughs to bank the foundation. The wind had been whistling through the floorboards the night before. The stove kept devouring my meager stock of wood, and I realized I would have to start getting in firewood the next day. Luckily Leland and I had marked some standing dead wood, so it wouldn't all be green.

My supper that night was cornbread that I baked in the cook stove, and a stew I made from our carrots, potatoes and turnips. I got a certain satisfaction from eating the fruits of my own labor. After dinner I cleaned up and settled on the couch in front of the stove with a Murray Bookchin pamphlet called *Listen Marxist!*

The first sentence got my attention. "All the old crap of the thirties is coming again—the shit about 'the class line', the 'role of the working class', the 'trained cadres'...!" from there he went on to denounce the turn toward "vanguards" and centralized politics. He warned about the direction SDS was going, and offered an alternative politics based in participatory democracy, anarchism! I felt like he was saying everything I believed, but had never been able to put into convincing words. I wished I could show the pamphlet to Jill, and talk with her about the ideas, use them to convince her, and win her back.

The date was December twenty-first—the winter solstice, the shortest day of the year. The sun was down by four-thirty, and I'm not sure exactly when I went to bed, but it was early. I stayed in the room I had shared with Jill, lying in our bed. I had grown so used to having her there at my side that it felt empty, beyond empty, desolate. Being there in our bed without her, I missed her more acutely than ever. Ranger must have sensed my despair, because he jumped onto the bed and slept by my side.

When I woke in the morning, I looked out on a gray day, the milky plastic that covered the window responsible for the hue. I made my way downstairs and stirred the coals from the night's fire, added kindling, and finally more chunks of wood to bring it back to life.

I knew what I had to do. The firewood beckoned. I'd sharpened the chainsaw yesterday afternoon, but I wasn't looking forward to getting back out in the woods. I knew how hard the work was, and I was a little nervous about taking trees down by myself. I lingered over another cup of coffee to delay the inevitable, then took a deep breath and pushed away from the table.

I got a regular routine going over the next few days—up early, light breakfast, then out to the woodlot. I dropped and limbed trees in the morning, went home to a big lunch, usually leftovers from the last night's dinner, then back out to the woods.

I spent the afternoons bucking and splitting what I had cut that morning, working at a steady pace. I didn't want to hurt myself out there, so I took my time, and if it was snowing heavily, I planned to stay in the house, cleaning and reading. I didn't want to take any chances with the saw—I remembered what one slip had done to Jason last year.

Ranger followed me out every morning and spent most of the day lying close to where I was working, though when he caught a scent, he would disappear into the woods to pursue some animal or another. I didn't worry about him. He hadn't dragged home any deer legs, and Leland had said that spring was when the deer were vulnerable. Ranger was good company—a quiet presence who always had my back, a companion who made no demands but always reciprocated any attention tenfold.

I found myself appreciating his presence in a different way. We were friends. I counted on his company through the long evenings, which I mostly spent on the couch with a book, or at the kitchen table, writing in my notebook.

It was Christmas Eve, and I had spent the day working in the woods. I dragged myself back to the empty house totally exhausted. The light was fading even though it was only four o'clock or so. I wasn't real big on the holidays, but I found myself thinking about it, missing the hustle and bustle that surrounded it, feeling very alone, and maybe a little sorry for myself. I remembered how, when I was a kid back in the Bronx, my dad would make a big deal every year about us having a Jewish Christmas, which meant that we went out for a meal of Chinese food at a place he liked on the Grand Concourse, and afterward we would go down the block to a fading movie palace and see the latest Hollywood production.

That night I settled for a meal of leftover rice and beans. I didn't have the energy to do anything more than heat up a saucepan on top of the wood stove. I ate sitting on the couch in front of the stove, with Ranger lying at my feet. I wondered what Jill was doing. It seemed unlikely they would be celebrating, but I had no way of knowing.

My holiday would consist of an evening reading and writing, and a night tossing and turning in troubled sleep. I kept dreaming strange dreams, just this side of being nightmares. I remember a feeling more than I do any details. Like I was drowning, getting pulled under by the weight of my own inaction, and try as I might, I couldn't quite get back to the surface.

On Christmas morning I headed out to the woodlot again. I didn't think I could afford to take a day off—the stove was a harsh mistress. I did plan to knock off in the afternoon, though. I had been invited to Leland and Mary's for dinner. I didn't know what to expect, but I was looking forward to it. It had been a couple of days since I had talked to anybody but Ranger.

I knocked on their door at around three o'clock. It had snowed lightly all morning, and I had changed out of my wet work clothes into a clean pair of jeans and a flannel shirt. Mary welcomed me inside.

"Hope you're hungry," she said. "I been cookin' all day."

"Wow!" I sniffed the air. "It smells great in here."

"I'll tell you, Mr. Man, you're in for a treat!" Leland joined us. "Why I haven't seen Mary cook like this for years. Roast ham, sweet potatoes, green beans, apple pie, Christmas cookies…"

"I can't wait!" I took off my jacket and found a seat in the small living room. I saw that the blue Formica table in the kitchen had been covered with a white tablecloth. It made me wish I had brought something to contribute to the dinner.

"We usually don't do a lot for Christmas. No point in fussin' for just the two of us," said Mary. "Havin' a guest though," her eyes twinkled, "makes it a little more special, gives me an excuse to do a little cookin'. He shouldn't eat most of it anyway, but what the heck, it's Christmas."

They both laughed. We spent a few minutes talking about the weather. Then Leland asked, "How's the firewood comin'?"

"I think I've got a wagonload ready."

"Well, good. We'll just have to get out there in the next couple days and bring it in."

"That's a relief," I said. "Thanks, Leland. I don't know how I'd survive the winter without you. The stack on the porch is pretty much gone."

"Oh, you'd do just fine. I'm just bein' neighborly."

"No, really," I insisted. "You're a lifesaver. I don't know how I can repay you."

"Well, truth be told, I've got an ulterior motive," he said. "Hopin' if I help you get your firewood squared away that you'll give me a hand sugarin' again this year."

"Of course," I replied. "You bet. Count me in."

"That's what I was hopin' for," he said.

A few minutes later Mary called us to the table.

RIGHT AFTER CHRISTMAS A nor'easter blew in, dropping about eighteen inches of snow over two days. The wind howled through the old farmhouse like a banshee and I stayed close to the cast iron stove that sat in the center of the main room. Ranger curled up on the couch next to me. I wondered where Jill was. The radio said the huge storm was blanketing the entire northeast. I knew that the SDS conference, the War Council, was scheduled to start. I hoped she wasn't on the road.

And now Jill was putting herself back in the middle of all that bullshit. I couldn't understand it. As the snow continued to fall, I went deeper into my funk. What was she doing? Had she gone crazy, or had I? Was there really a chance that she was right?

The rational part of me recoiled from the idea of violent revolution, but the romantic part of me almost wanted to believe it was possible. Almost. I just couldn't quite make the leap of faith necessary to abandon my belief in nonviolence: no matter the circumstances, I couldn't justify harming my fellow man. Maybe I was just not brave enough, or maybe my natural ambivalence made me cautious. Jill had always been able to commit fully to her beliefs; I, on the other hand, remained skeptical. Our competing natures had always served us well in the past, with me offering a counterbalance to her tendency to jump right in, and her enthusiasm tempering my ambivalence.

But now she had made a leap I was unwilling to follow. It went against my beliefs and my understanding of how change happened. Even in the unlikely event that an armed revolution succeeded, what then? A dictatorship of the proletariat? Like Bookchin said in his pamphlet, it could only end badly, one oppressive elite substituted for another. Yes, we needed a revolution, but not the kind they were planning.

I kept turning these thoughts over and over as I sat there in the house with the blizzard raging around me. I felt lost, isolated, alone and immobilized, a victim of forces much larger than myself. All I could do was wait for the storm to pass, hope for a change in the weather. My actions could have little impact until then. Once things settled down, I would have to dig myself out—carve a path that could reconnect me to the world, and go on from there.

THIS HAS BEEN ONE of the wildest weeks of my life! I was ready to go. None of us minded missing Christmas. The holidays with my parents were always a disaster anyway. But there was a huge nor'easter blowing up the coast, and it just didn't seem like a good time for a road trip. I was as anxious to get to Flint as anybody, but get serious! The roads were treacherous. Mark had his mind made up, though. We had to go, he insisted, and Jason and Suze and I gave in. Tell the truth, I felt a little bullied by him. He shamed us into it: "How are you gonna make a revolution if you're too scared to drive in a snowstorm?"

Well, we went along with him, and we were barely out of New Jersey when we slid off the Turnpike. We waited in the car about three hours before a plow truck came through and rescued us. We got off the highway at the next exit and found a motel.

When we got on the road the next morning, the storm had stopped. It took us a full day to get to Flint. When we arrived, the War Council was already underway. We went to this rundown old dance hall in the Black part of town, really kind of grim. But when we went inside, there were about three hundred kids there. The place was incredible!

One wall had big posters of Chairman Mao, Che, Ho Chi Minh, Fidel, Malcolm X, and Eldridge Cleaver in psychedelic colors. The opposite wall was plastered with pictures of Fred Hampton, who had been shot in his bed by the Chicago pigs just a few weeks before. There was a stage in front of the room with a huge cutout of a machine gun hanging over it.

We got there just as Bernadine Dohrn was winding up her speech. She was talking about the Manson Family, and how they murdered all those people, sat there and finished their dinner, and then stuck a fork in Sharon Tate's pregnant belly. It weirded me out. I couldn't tell if she was serious or not, and then she raised three fingers, like a clenched first salute, and the fork salute spread all over the room.

I looked at Suze and she was shaking her head, but I saw Mark and Jason with their four fingers thrust into the air. "You're kidding, right?" I asked Jason.

"Hell no!" he responded. "Fork you! Off the pigs!" He laughed.

"Right on brother!" shouted Mark.

Whether she was serious or not, she got everyone in the room pretty worked up, that's for sure. The fork salute became a symbol of the revolution, at least for the rest of the War Council.

After that we went over to a nearby church where we were staying and spent the rest of the night partying. The MC5 blasted over a boom box and everyone started to dance. It was wild, like all of the revolutionary energy got transferred into dancing. People were dropping acid and then it got really wild. Pretty amazing.

I saw lots of old friends, folks I knew from other national conferences. It was really hardcore, a room full of committed revolutionaries. I got into it, lost in the music and the crowd. Then, at some point I noticed that everyone was surrounded by a halo of blue light. It must have been in something I drank, but honestly, I don't remember anybody mentioning it. Somebody turned on a strobe light, and I felt like my head was going to explode.

I went out the door for some fresh air and Mark followed me.

"Cool!" he said. "Very cool! I mean these are some down motherfuckers! I can relate to this shit. These people are ready." He put his arm around me.

"Yeah, very cool," I said

"Come on, let's go back in. It's cold out here."

I guess it was, but I didn't notice. I was tripping my brains out by then. The energy in the church was so frenetic, I didn't know if I could take it, but Mark clamped his arm around my waist and half dragged me back in. The acid was coursing through my body, and I felt myself melt into the crowd. Like I felt connected to everyone by a web of energy that was pulsing through us.

At some point I found myself rolling on the floor, naked in a tangle of bodies. I didn't know who was who, or what was what, but there were breasts and cocks and pussies everywhere; fucking, sucking, licking, and touching. It was wild, completely uninhibited, and it felt natural and beautiful. I don't know how long it went on, or who or how many people I had sex with, but it felt great. We really were new men and women, with none of the old bourgeois bullshit. Even though most of them were strangers I have never felt so close to so many people. We were getting ready to go to war. It made sense, we had to trust each other completely, and we couldn't let any of our old hang-ups hold us back.

Everyone crashed on the floor of the church nave that night, lying all over each other. There was hot coffee waiting for us when we straggled into the conference the next day. There were all kinds of events and workshops scheduled. We all spent the morning working on karate moves. That afternoon I learned how to set up a phony ID.

THE THIRD WORLD IS IN REVOLT, *including Blacks in the US, with the Panthers in the vanguard. Our job is to support them by taking heat off of*

them and onto ourselves, bringing the war home so white youth and work-
ers will rise and join us to take the whole racist, imperialist system crashing
down. Then we'll establish a dictatorship of the proletariat, end the war, and
bring real equality, peace, and prosperity to the world.

I feel like I'm finally on the right side of history instead of just playing
catch-up. I can't wait to get to work.

That night we sang together out of a songbook Ted Gold had put together;
"I'm Dreaming of a White Riot", "Bad Moon Rising", "Stop in the Name of
Imperialism", all sung to pop tunes everybody knew. Very clever.

Next day, more workshops; how to get guns, how to avoid the pigs, really
useful stuff.

I got in a big argument with Mark after a discussion on who were righ-
teous targets of revolutionary violence. I mean, I can see attacking the pigs,
and military targets, and corporations, but then they started talking about
white supremacy, and that to really put a stop to it, we might have to kill
white babies! I couldn't see that at all, but Mark seemed to think it was a fine
idea, or at least justified. I thought it was totally off the wall, and luckily, the
leadership agreed with me.

I'm totally prepared to sacrifice and do whatever needs to be done to make
a revolution, but killing babies? Just seems wrong to me.

There were more speeches by the leadership and it seemed like everyone
was trying to outdo each other; really macho, but we have to get ourselves
psyched if we're really going to get serious.

A guy named J.J., who I didn't know but seemed really cool, talked about
how we needed to create chaos, and chaos would lead to revolution. I can dig
that. I didn't agree with everything said, but I have never been so inspired.
It's us against the world, but, like Billy Ayers reminded us, that's the way all
revolutions start.

Fidel left the mountains with just a handful of fighters, same with Mao,

and look what Ho Chi Minh accomplished. We're part of a line of revolution-
aries that goes all the way back to Lenin. By the last day of the conference it
was clear—you're either with us, or against us. Down to the diehard, and it
wasn't just Weathermen. There were White Panthers there, from Detroit and
Ann Arbor, and some RYM II kids, plus some unaffiliated folks. There were
lots of people who didn't come too, but we figure that once we start doing shit,
they'd see the light. Maybe even people like David.

I can't help thinking about him. I can't believe he isn't here with us.
Maybe he'll finally get it. I hope so. I do miss him, even though he can be the
world's biggest asshole.

So in the end it's all crystal clear. We're going underground, closing the
national office of SDS, dissolving it, and starting the revolution! I sort of hate
to see SDS go, I loved that organization, but we don't need a student move-
ment anymore, we need a fighting organization, a revolutionary movement,
and SDS could never be that.

ON THE SATURDAY AFTER Christmas I caught a ride into St. Johnsbury
with Mary and Leland. We squeezed together in the cab of their truck.

"Where to, David?" Leland asked as we turned onto Main Street.

"I'm going to Hatch's, up the hill," I answered. "But I can get out
here and walk. I've just got a little shopping to do."

"Is that that health food store Jill was always tellin' me about?"
asked Mary.

"Yeah, that's it. Only health food store in Vermont as far as I know,"
I replied. "Brown rice, dried beans, stuff like that."

"Don't be giving her any ideas," joked Leland.

"Some health food probably do you some good," she responded.
"We'll see what the doctor says about your diabetes today."

"Doctor's appointment, huh?" I said. "Hope everything's okay."

"Just a checkup," he assured me. "They like to keep track of me, poke me with needles, that sort of nonsense. I keep tellin' 'em I'm healthy as an ox, but nobody listens to me."

"Hush, old man!" Mary admonished. "If it wasn't for the doctors, you'd been dead a long time ago. The way you ignore them I'm amazed you're still around!"

"Don't start that again, Mary." He turned to me. "You see what I have to put up with? Oh, Mr. Man, let me tell you..."

"She's only looking out for you, Leland." It seemed like a good time for me to leave. "I'll get out here," I said as we sat at the only stoplight in town. "Where shall we meet?"

"Meet you at the diner at noon," replied Leland. "Give us time to do some shoppin'. Then we can have some lunch before we head home."

QUEENS, IT TAKES ALMOST *two hours on the bus and subway to get into the city from here. It's really dreary, rows of detached brick houses that go on forever. I didn't imagine going underground would mean cutting ourselves off from everything, but Mark figures nobody would look for us out here.*

We're just starting to get our shit together, and there's plenty to do — logistics. We've got to set everything up—safe houses, new identities, supplies, equipment, ordinance. We need intelligence—we've got to scout targets, plan escape routes, develop contingency plans. It's like a military operation.

We have to compartmentalize and keep things on a need to know basis, so Jason and Suze are going to have to live somewhere else, I don't know where. Mark is the liaison. That way we can't give each other up if something happens. Mark's also looking for a safe house, someplace to run to if we need it.

It will take a while before we are fully operational. Shit, I'm starting to sound like Mark. But we do have to be disciplined and systematic. We're serious, and we're putting it all on the line. It's exciting, and I have to admit, a little scary. We're out here on our own. I wonder what the other collectives are doing. I wonder what the Weather Bureau is saying.

It's only been two weeks since we got back from Flint. I'm still feeling inspired, but I'm not sure exactly how it's all going to work. I mean are we going to do this all by ourselves? At least Mark knows what he's doing. I can't imagine being in this without him. Even the leadership was impressed by him, I could tell.

I wish the feeling was mutual. "Nice bunch of kids, it was fun," he said. "I like where they're comin' from, but they're total amateurs. They've got the right idea, but they'd just slow us down. We're better off on our own."

I don't know what I expected, but I have to admit, Queens is a let-down. After life in Vermont, living like a housewife with Mark in the outer boroughs is a big change. I know it's just temporary, Mark says he wants to go operational ASAP, but first we've got to take care of the preliminaries. I've got to keep reminding myself of that to keep from freaking out. Meanwhile I'm just waiting, and hoping I get a chance to do something soon, to really prove myself.

I know we have to swim in the sea of the people, but couldn't Mark have found somewhere a little bit nicer? I mean, there is no light in here, none at all. And the place is filthy, roach infested. I'll do the best I can, but it's a huge mess. Oh well, we're not here to play house. We've got some serious business to take care of.

I do miss Vermont though. I think about it a lot. But if we're going to make a revolution, we've got to go to the people, and this is where they are. I hope Suze and Jason get here soon. It's hard being alone with Mark. He's so intense, and really moody. It's tough to keep up with his highs and lows. He disappears for days at a time and never tells me what he's doing.

"It's need to know, babe. Better you don't have any details." His standard *answer—like he doesn't trust me or something. I thought we were in this together. I'm every bit as committed as he is. Shit, I'm the one who brought him to Flint. I wish I knew where he was going. No doubt it has something to do with the action he keeps talking about. Hopefully he'll open up more when Suze and Jason arrive.*

I snowed the night before. Leland came up the path with his tractor. He had mounted a set of chains on his rear wheels and he was towing the same sledge we had used for sugaring last spring.

"Ready to go?" he asked me as I met him at the door.

It was a gray day, and the temperature had dropped to zero overnight. I turned up the collar on my barn jacket and jumped on as Leland drove up the path to the woodlot.

I had piles of split wood arrayed along the path, and we stopped at each one and made quick work of throwing them onto the sled. By the time we had reached the third pile I took off my jacket and was breathing hard.

Leland amazed me. He worked at a steady pace, outstripping me as he tossed chunks of wood onto our growing pile, and never breaking a sweat. The guy was almost eighty years old, and once again I couldn't keep up with him.

It took about an hour for us to pick up everything I had blocked and split, and unload it in the dooryard of the farmhouse. Then Leland headed home, and I began to stack the wood on the porch. It was part green, and part pieces of dry standing deadwood. I tried to mix them in the pile, but it was difficult to tell them apart.

I knew it would be tough to get a hot fire with only green wood, but at some point, I would have no choice, as I had a limited amount of dry stuff. I hoped it would last me at least through the bitter cold that was bound to come in January and February. By now whatever moisture was left in the wood was frozen there.

My woodpile wasn't the worlds prettiest, but it stayed up. I set aside a large round of rock maple to use as a new chopping block, and laid a stack of smaller branches to turn into kindling nearby.

Ranger watched the whole operation. He seemed oblivious to the cold and snow, placidly sitting in the yard observing my labors.

By lunchtime I was done, and I stood back to look at what I had accomplished. I figured I must have at least a couple of weeks worth of firewood stacked on the porch, over a cord, and it felt good. One less thing to worry about.

I never imagined myself living in Queens. I haven't even been to the city since we got here.

"Don't call any attention to yourself," Mark said. "Keep a low profile. Pretty girl like you, you'd be noticed in this neighborhood. Better if you just stay inside." So here I am, trying to scrape the layers of grease and dirt from the kitchen, while he's out, who knows where, making plans, or scouting targets, or doing who the fuck knows what.

After the War Council it all seemed pretty clear to me. Form a guerrilla cell. We would move to a working-class neighborhood, establish new identities, disappear into the crowd. Start scouting targets and then begin to bring the war home to those motherfuckers. I was ready then, and I'm ready now. But all this waiting around, and Mark assuming he was the leader. I thought we were a collective, but he's been calling the shots since Flint.

I guess it makes sense. I mean, as he pointed out, he's the only one of us with any real experience. And he does have great instincts, though he doesn't have much theoretical background. Oh shit, now I sound like David. Mark is just the kind of person we need. I guess we've just got to trust his judgment. Anyway, I'm anxious for us to actually get into action. Things may not be exactly what I expected, but we all have to be willing to make sacrifices, to do whatever it takes.

TOSSING ANOTHER CHUNK OF maple on the fire, I was reminded that I was almost out of wood again, and I'd better get some in over the next couple of days or I'd be screwed. If we could get a sledge full, and I thought I'd cut that much, I figured it should last a couple more weeks.

Though I remembered how much wood it took to heat the house last winter, it had grown abstract until I saw how quickly the wood-pile diminished. I realized it had taken over a month to get in last year's supply of firewood. That had been with two of us working, and at a quicker pace. Shit! That meant I would have to spend most of between now and March cutting firewood just to keep up. I thought about sealing off the empty rooms with plastic, and wondered if there was anything else I could do to save heat. I would have to ask Leland.

It was a depressing realization. It was winter, and I wasn't ready. Beyond the firewood situation, I was already going a little crazy. Most of my conversations were with Ranger or myself. I had an almost constant inner dialogue that revolved around Jill. Where was she? What was she doing? How could she be with Mark? How could I rescue her from the huge mistake she was making? How could I win her back?

And that's what I wanted, more than anything—to have her back. Sure, I missed the commune, and I was truly distressed by the political turn things were taking, but most of all it was Jill. I missed her voice, her smile, her touch, our life together. I just didn't feel whole without her.

"Fuck!" I exclaimed, though there was no one else to hear it. Ranger cocked his head in concern and then came to lie next to me on the couch.

He understood, or at least it seemed that way. He could read my moods better than most people.

MARK CAME IN LATE last night when I was already in bed. He was drunk. I asked him where he'd been all day, and he gave me the usual crap, "Very busy, setting things up," but no details. My bet is he made a stop at some biker bar on his way home from wherever. I'd been alone in the fucking house all day. I was pissed.

"Do you really think it's a good idea, getting drunk with a bunch of bikers?" I asked him.

He exploded at me! "How dare you question my judgment? Who the fuck do you think you are?" Shit like that. And he was standing over me with a look of rage on his face, with his fists clenched. It was freaky, I thought he might hit me. I never realized how violent he was. He just barely kept it together. It was a side of him I'd never seen. He scared the shit out of me.

Then, this morning, he acted as if nothing had happened. When I asked if he remembered last night. He was all apologetic, said, "I get that way when I'm drunk sometimes...'cause of the war, you know. Really sorry, never happen again."

I guess I understand, at least as much as anybody who wasn't in the fucking war can understand, but still, I was scared.

I SLEPT IN. LELAND and I had hauled in a good load of wood the previous day, and I figured I could afford to take a day off. But idleness didn't sit well with me. I tended to brood if I wasn't busy. This day was particularly bad. I never considered myself prone to depression, but I soon thought myself into a funk.

What the fuck was I doing? I'd always felt like I had a purpose before—I don't know, ending the war, fighting for social justice, building the collective...all things that made me feel alive and somehow connected to the forces of history. Maybe it was always an illusion, maybe I'd been fooling myself, but I had always found relief in those feelings, never questioned my self-worth, never doubted that in at least some small way I was doing my part.

Now I doubted everything. It seemed like all I was doing was surviving, and what for? What larger purpose was I serving? What was I doing here, geographically, existentially? An isolated existence in a cold farmhouse on a wind-blasted hillside in Vermont. Was that really my fate? Had everything I lived my life for over the past five years turned to shit?

No wonder I was depressed. I stepped back and looked at myself, really looked, and I didn't like what I saw. I thought of all the time I had wasted chasing the ephemeral. I understood then that I really was a utopian, lost in a cloud cuckoo land of dreams, pursuing fantasies that could never be realized.

My stomach churned as these thoughts raced through me, and I found my legs growing heavy and my will slipping away, almost like I had been drugged. What was I doing here? Maybe I should go back to the Bronx and work at the store, save up some bread and go to law school. Why not? It made more sense than toughing out another Vermont winter.

But something within me rebelled at the thought. I wasn't ready to admit defeat, not yet. It was true, the revolution seemed further away than ever to me, but I thought about how far we had come, how much we had already effected—civil rights, sex, music, drugs, a mass anti-war movement...we had transformed the culture and challenged all of America's shibboleths. I had to consider all that. Besides, I had learned that change accrues over time, and who could really say where we were heading?

All afternoon I argued with myself, alternating between hope and despair. I realize now that beyond the abstract arguments was a deeply personal thread, to a large degree about Jill and me, and my sense of loss. I was unmoored on a sea of hopelessness, with nothing to help me keep my head above water.

Everything I cared about and worked for was slipping away. My life was shrinking, my sense of connection disappearing, and in its place, nothing. Or at least not much. I felt worthless and useless. Ranger raised his head from the floor and gave me a quizzical look, attuned to my moods, as always. I realized the longer I sat around, the deeper I sank into the morass of my confusion.

Hoping it would help me clear my head, I decided to go out for a ski. As soon as I brought out the boots, Ranger rose to his feet and began to dance around the door in excitement. I couldn't help but laugh.

I headed down the trail the snowmobiles had packed, and as I fell into the familiar rhythm, I pulled the crisp winter air deep into my lungs, and a kind of peace descended on me. Ranger loped along in front as I glided down the path. Soon the woods were rushing past me on my way towards Hardwood Mountain. I hadn't intended it, but I put on the climbing skins and ended up at the spot on the ridge where Jill and I had stopped for tea the winter before. I took in the view—the frozen lake and Canada to the north, Green Mountains stretching south, and rows of hills fading into the high peaks of the Whites to the east.

It was humbling, staring out over all that grandeur, and it made me realize how little my troubles meant in the larger scheme of things. My troubles, or anyone's for that matter. The mountains will be here long after we're gone, ever changing, full of life, death, decomposition and rebirth. The only importance we have, the only meaning we hold is that which we assign to ourselves. That is the simple truth.

It struck me almost physically. Why this constant search for meaning when we are nothing? What pretense, what conceit, what utter folly. It was liberating in a way, this realization that I could make what I wanted of my life, and it really didn't matter. I was free of any responsibility, bound by no a priorities, able to choose my fate, travel any path I wished. And as I thought about it, I realized that that was exactly what I had been doing. And I had been doing it because it made me feel good. Any thought of returning to the Bronx vanished. I would continue to pursue my dreams, to live a more utopian existence, to seek the ephemeral, to live in a place where I tried to make dreams reality. And I would do it not out of guilt, or shame, or a sense of duty, but because it resonated with my understanding of how things should be and could be—a free choice. Idealistic? Perhaps, but it didn't matter—I was trying to lead an ethical life because that was what made me feel good. I realized that for me it was all about getting closer to people, closer to the land, closer to my own truth. Whatever. I was getting lost in abstractions, and all around me the real world spun on. I took a last look at the vista, called Ranger, who was off somewhere in the woods, and pointed my skis downhill.

SUZE AND JASON ARRIVED today! Thank fucking god! I've been going stir crazy locked up in this apartment alone. Mark is hardly ever here, and when he is, he hardly talks. What is it about men? "So how was your day?" "Good." "What did you do?" "Stuff." I swear it was like pulling teeth to get a word out of him.

So great seeing Suze. I mean, Mark is cool, but clearly not much of a communicator. I can talk to her. She and Jason will be here a few days at least. They're crashing on the fold-out couch in the other room. But Mark says they need their own place. We have to fit in, look normal. Besides we need another safe house. Too bad, I miss the communal thing.

We talked about David coming back to the farm. I can't believe it, after leaving the way he did, not even saying goodbye! There was so much I wanted to say to him, to talk to him about, to explain, to get him to understand. I was sure I could convince him to join us, if he only gave me a chance. But he just left.

I was devastated; I mean we were together for five years. We shared so much. I loved him, still love him, I guess. I know he felt threatened by Mark, but that was separate, completely different. I know I hurt him. But to just leave like that? I could've explained.

I mean I'm a free woman, right? He didn't own me. Why didn't he give me a chance? And now he's up in Vermont by himself. Maybe I should write to him. If I know him, he's wallowing in his misery. Well, let him. But I hate feeling like it's my fault. I didn't do anything wrong. He's the one who left.

At least I've got some company now, and Mark has laid out a job for me. Things are starting to happen. Fuck David.

Finally, something to do! I've been sitting around the apartment for almost a week. Today I went into the city for the first time, to the library, where I checked out twenty-year-old obituaries from the Times, looking for kids who died young, young enough that they never got a social security number. The main branch seemed like the best place to do the research. So many people there—no way anyone would remember me. A librarian pointed me towards the files. She was the only person I had any contact with.

We talked about it at the War Council—the need to establish new identities. In order to survive underground we'd have to cut all ties with our old lives, including our names. In fact, we should each have more than one new name, and papers to back them up—drivers licenses, passports, social security cards.

It all starts with an identity. So I spent the day looking for deaths of little kids who were about the same age as me, Mark, Suze, and Jason. Kind of weird. I found some too: Jamie Larson, two years old; Cynthia Peters, three and a half; Malcolm Black, 1946-1950; Patricia Clark 1948-1950. Enough to get started with. Patricia Clark, I sort of like that name. I wonder how she died; the obit didn't mention it. Could have been polio or anything.

The train ride back to Queens took forever. The whole way back I thought about what we were doing, how momentous it was. We really were the vanguard of the revolution. I looked around the subway car at all the faces, Black, brown, and white. I felt like I was carrying the future, all of our futures, and a chill ran through me. But it was still a secret. They'd find out soon enough, and rise up with us when they did!

The next step took a little longer. I needed to go to the records office and get a birth certificates.

I used the name Patricia Clark to open accounts with Con Edison and the telephone company. Once that was done, I had what I needed. A day later I took the train all the way downtown to the Department of Vital Records, on Worth Street. They made me wait in line all morning, but when I presented the billing information from my utility accounts they issued me a birth certificate. Should be smooth sailing from here on out.

It's kind of exciting, playing the system this way. I mean they seem so all-powerful, but really, the right hand doesn't know what the left hand is doing. I just got issued a birth certificate for someone who died twenty years ago, and they have no idea!

I need to get used to my new name. I think I'll get Mark and Suze and Jason to start calling me Pat, my nom de guerre; Patty Clark, that's me. Kind of amazing, really.

The others need to get their ID together. We've got to rent another apartment to operate out of. I don't know where the money's coming from, but Mark seems to have that side of things covered, at least for the time being. He's got a lot of connections through his biker buddies. I'm sure they're dealing drugs or something, but Mark hasn't let any of us in on the details. Need to know and all that.

I don't really care. We're outlaws, and I wouldn't want to be anything else. We're getting ready for our first action, and I can't wait!

Jason and Suze have been great—they're just as committed as I am, and Mark has them doing stuff too. Suze has been out today looking at apartments, and Jason has a list of all kinds of stuff Mark says we're going to need.

I feel so lucky to be a part of this. The revolution had always been kind of abstract for me before. Now I'm in the middle of it, really doing something. It's like I've been waiting for this all my life. It's hard to explain, but it's as though I've found my destiny. I feel connected to revolutionaries around the world. Mao, Che, Ho Chi Minh; this is how they all got started.

I have no doubts—we're a part of history now. The revolution is coming; we're going to make it happen. It's taken a while, but things are really starting to come together. I only wish David was with us.

HAVING A ROUTINE HELPED the time pass quickly; the daily rhythm of working wood, feeding the fire, cooking, reading, and writing. When the weather was foul I didn't go into the woods—mostly when it was snowing hard. I holed up in the farmhouse, and those days were tough. My thoughts of Jill were with me almost all the time; when I was busy, I could push them into the background, but when I was idle, they welled up in me like a rushing river, threatening to overwhelm me, to wash me away in a flood of sorrow. On those days everything saddened me because everywhere I turned there was a reminder of her.

I learned a lot about myself that winter, some of which I didn't like. I discovered I was prone to depression; maudlin thoughts kept coming to me whenever I allowed myself to relax. Without something to keep me busy, I became lethargic. Some days it was difficult to get motivated enough to get out of bed, or to move from the bed to the couch. The need for firewood was helping to keep me sane.

The next morning, the snow stopped. When I went out onto the porch, I was surrounded by a scene out of Currier and Ives—tree limbs bent by the snow, a blanket of white covering everything, sparkling like mica in the bright sunlight. I stepped off the porch and found myself knee-deep in snow that felt like newly poured concrete; wet and heavy.

I put the yellow chainsaw, my splitting maul, a can of gas and a jug of bar and chain oil onto the toboggan and began to slog through the snow out to the woodlot. It was tough going, breaking trail while dragging the sled behind me, but I was burning through my woodpile at an astounding rate, and I had lost two days to the storm so I had no choice.

The snow came up over Ranger's chest, but he bounded through it effortlessly. I watched his muscles ripple under his fur, and his nose twitch as he took in the altered landscape. He was magnificent, truly in his element, and I took pleasure in his excitement.

I was breathing hard by the time I made it back to where I had dropped a tree the last time I had been in the woods. It was a good-sized maple, but it had disappeared, only a bulge in the snow hinting at its presence. I cleared its surface with a gloved hand, set the choke, pulled the cord, and the saw roared to a start, almost like a living thing in my hands.

I AM GETTING SO sick of lines! I went to the DMV today to get a driver's license and spent the whole fucking day there! At least it was for a good cause. And now I'm all set, Patricia Clark has a license with my picture on it! Except I dyed my hair and cut it. I am now a blonde! It was really all pretty easy, and from here I can get a social security card, a passport, open a bank account, rent a car—whatever I need.

Patty Clark; I like it! Mark likes it too, my new look. He says I look sexy. I feel kind of like a bimbo. I was never into hair dye or makeup, but it's all part of my new identity. I guess I better get used to it.

We aren't that far from Manhattan. I can see the skyline from the elevated platform where I catch the train, but it really is another world out here. Patty from Queens—I look like I could be a secretary working in a midtown office. That's me, at least for the time being. Jason cut his hair short too, but Mark still looks like a biker riding his Harley, but he doesn't wear his colors anymore—they draw too much attention. I think his bike does too. You can hear the thing three blocks away, but he won't give it up.

We argued about it, but he says he needs it. "Gives me a tactical advantage," he says. "They'll never catch me if I'm on my scooter."

Well, maybe, but it's not what I'd call inconspicuous. We also had a fight about his drinking. Lately he comes to bed drunk every night, and he doesn't like it at all when I call him on it. Seems to me like we better keep our wits about us, and seeing him staggering around doesn't exactly make me comfortable. But, like he says, after all he saw in the war, he needs something to dull the pain. It still freaks me out a little.

I'm beginning to realize I really don't know him at all. I mean, we're into some really heavy shit, and honestly, we've only spent a couple of weeks together. I was with David for five years, and we knew each other in and out. Like I could tell what he was thinking, I knew what he was going to say even before he said it. It's not like that with Mark. He's so unpredictable. And his moods…he's fighting demons I can't even imagine.

I wish we spent more time together as a collective though. It's tough, for security reasons, to meet much more than once a week. Suze and Jason are living not far away, somewhere else in Queens I gather, but I don't know exactly where. We've been meeting at this pizza place in Flushing.

Mostly it's just business. Reports on our progress. I wish we could just hang out. I miss them, especially Suze. I really don't have contact with anybody but Mark, and I feel kind of isolated, cut off from everybody and everything. I don't know what I expected, but it wasn't exactly this. Well, nobody said it was going to be easy, and it's not like I didn't make a choice.

BY THE TIME I got home for lunch I was thoroughly frozen and wet. The snow had soaked through my clothes and combined with my sweat so I felt like I had taken a cold shower. I threw on a couple of chunks of dry wood, and huddled close to the stove.

As I stood there, I heard the whine of a snowmobile approaching. Of course, the fresh snow would bring them out, and I listened as a pack of them came up the path from the road, headed to Hardwood Mountain, or Canada, or who knew where. I had grown accustomed to them last winter, but their passage then left me feeling uneasy, almost violated. I was becoming used to being alone and their presence shattered my solitude, and reminded me that there was a still a world out there, and it was not always friendly.

I remembered my last encounter with them on the trail, when I had been run off the path on my skis. Well, they were back, and unless I was prepared to confront them, I realized I had better get used to them. Ranger raised his head and growled as they passed.

Winter was well under way, and there was no turning back. I was here for the duration, and I had to prepare for it; firewood still needed to be cut and stacked, and I needed to face the fact that I had chosen to come back, with all that was implied by that decision.

I called Ranger to my side and scratched his ears and the fur around his neck. He stopped growling and began to grunt in pleasure.

At least with the snowmobiles the path stayed packed down, and there was plenty of snow for skiing. The thought of strapping on the boards pleased me, and added another dimension to winter. Then I remembered skiing to the lake with Jill last spring, our picnic lunch on the shore, and Ranger's bloody deer leg. I kept finding reminders of Jill in every memory; every nook and cranny of my life over the past five years was full of her, and especially there, in the farmhouse.

IT WAS SO EASY! I can hardly believe it. I took the bus and train into the city today. I decided to go to NYU, just because it's familiar, The Loeb Student Center was packed, and it didn't take more than two minutes to spot a likely candidate. She was about my height and weight, hair color and eye color don't really matter, they told us in Flint, that's what wigs and contacts are for. I saw her drop her backpack on the floor near her table. I took a seat at the next table. She had her back to me, talking about some psychology course with a bunch of her friends. I hooked the pack with my foot and slid it over in front of me. I leaned over and unzipped it. Her wallet was sitting right there.

All told the whole thing only took about five seconds. I got up and left. Her name was Nancy Carbone, and I scored her Connecticut driver's license and her NYU ID. They'll work just fine. It's not good for setting up a permanent identity, but I can rent a car or get a PO box with them, or buy a gun.

To tell the truth, I'm kind of proud of myself. I mean I've done plenty of civil disobedience before, broken laws, but I never stole anything. It's for the revolution and all, and Mark says anything goes. We're going underground. We're outlaws now. There are no rules.

If we have to steal, we do it; whatever it takes to bring this fucking war home. It's starting. I'm a little bit scared, but mostly excited. I'm up for this, it's like my real life is about to start.

I can't wait to show Mark. Maybe he'll have more faith in me now. He's never said anything, but I get the feeling sometimes he's not sure I can handle this. I mean the way he keeps me out of the loop. I hate that he's the only one who really knows what's going on. Like I have to prove myself to him somehow, before he can let me in. I guess he is the expert, and it's probably for my own good, but I'm sick of hearing "need to know". I'm as committed as he is, and if you think about it, I have a lot more political experience than he does.

Why are men so controlling? David was the same, in a more passive-aggressive sort of way. It feels shitty to be treated like a little girl who can't handle knowing what's going on. At least David never did that to me. It was more equal. Of course now I'm cadre, and that changes everything. We need to be disciplined, and there's a chain of command.

I thought that being in this together would bring us closer as a couple, but it really hasn't. He's out of the house most of the time, and it's not just that he won't talk to me about the action, he doesn't talk to me about anything, really. He comes home drunk a lot, and he wants to have sex, but he communicates even less than David. Well, I like sex too, and so what if he's not my soulmate? We're comrades, fellow soldiers. I guess I just expected too much of him.

I WAS OVER AT Leland and Mary's to see if I could catch a ride with them, I needed a few things I couldn't get at Mac's general store, a place I tried my best to avoid anyway, plus I hadn't been off the hill for a couple of weeks. Mary told me they were going over to Barre to see her sister the next day, and I was welcome to come along.

We squeezed into the cab of Leland's pickup the next morning and headed down. I had never been to Barre, and all I knew of it was what Leland and Mary had told me about bootleggers and anarchists, so I wasn't sure what to expect. When we entered the town, I saw a sign that said: "Welcome to Barre, Granite Capital of the World."

From my first view of Main Street, the place looked normal enough to me, a small city, like Newport or St. J. But when they parked, and I got out of the truck at the corner of Granite and Main, Barre's true nature was revealed. There were the granite sheds, a vast industrial infrastructure that bustled with activity; huge flatbed trucks loading manufactured granite, mostly gravestones, and unloading giant blocks of the raw material. I could hear saws whirring in the sheds and the sound of metal striking granite.

It was another world, just a block off of Main, and totally unlike anything I had seen in Vermont before. Leland saw me taking it in.

"That's Barre," he said. "No place quite like it. There's the old Labor Hall down the block." He pointed at a red brick building with granite lintels. "Her pa helped build it. That's her house, right across the street, where I first laid eyes on her." He took Mary's hand. "Her sister still lives there. She's pretty sick, else I'd introduce you. Best if we just meet back here at the truck in about an hour. Her sister can't take any more than that." He sounded apologetic.

I continued down the block. A light snow was starting to fall, covering the sidewalk, and turning to slush on the roadway. In a couple of blocks, I reached downtown. I found the hardware store Leland had told me about, sitting alone in a block full of empty storefronts, and I got a set of washers to fix the leaky kitchen sink. Then I walked to a market that Mary said had the venison sausage she fed me for dinner one day, and stopped at a diner for a cup of coffee and a slice of apple pie. Then it was time to head back to the truck to meet Leland and Mary. My big day in town was coming to an end, or so I thought.

Leland and Mary were waiting in the cab for me. "How was your visit?" I asked.

"Oh, not so good," Mary replied. "We just sat with her, I held her hand. Not much left of her. She can't talk. I can't even say for sure that she knew we were there. Likely the last time I'll see her. She's got the cancer."

"I'm sorry," I said.

"That's the way of all flesh; we live, we die. Nothing to be done about it, I guess." Mary sniffed. We sat there in silence for a moment.

"Well now, Mr. Man, how'd you like Barre?" asked Leland.

"Seems like a nice town," I said. "But I only actually only saw a couple of blocks between here and downtown."

"Oh, there's a lot more to it than that. Mary and me were thinking maybe, since we're here, we'd show you the sights, take you up to get a look at the quarries, maybe make a stop over to the Hope Cemetery, so she can pay respects to her ma and pa. That okay with you?"

"Sounds great," I responded. I had wanted to get off the hill, and I was in no hurry to get back.

We drove south out of town and turned off Route 14 where a sign pointed to the left saying "Granite Quarries". The snow started blowing harder as we drove up the hill, through a settlement of rundown duplexes and pulled into a parking lot next to a huge pit. We exited the truck and walked to the edge, which was surrounded by a chain link fence.

I don't know exactly how big the pit was, but it must have been at least four hundred feet deep and a lot more than that in diameter. Sheer slabs of granite protruded in tiers all the way down to the bottom, where a frozen lake sat covered in snow. Wooden derricks towered over the silent quarry across from where we stood.

Shades of gray dominated the landscape; gray clouds in gray sky, overhanging the huge pit of gray granite in the blowing snow; Barre Gray, Leland called it. Forests of gray, bare trees framed the quarry. Somber, even vaguely threatening, the place sent a chill through me.

"'Nuff granite there to last another ten thousand years," offered Mary. "Whole mountain of it. No finer stone anywhere on earth. Why half of Washington, DC is built with the stuff. Used to be, back in the boom times, they worked this quarry with two shifts. Trains full of granite runnin' twenty-four hours a day. Nobody builds with it now, too expensive. Mostly just memorials these days, but I'll tell you, there are graveyards all over the world filled with Barre Gray." There was a touch of pride in her voice.

"Time was," she went on, "Barre had some of the finest sculptors in the world. Why, my pa was one. They came over from Carrerra Italy, where Michelangelo used to work. Started their own art school here, to keep the skills alive. You should have seen the town back then. Folks from all over the world came to Barre to work the stone, not just Italy. Why they had Scots, Spanish, Lebanese, Quebequers…the old Vermonters didn't know what to make of us. It was a lively town, that's for sure."

"So what happened?" I asked.

"Oh, demand went down. They closed most of the quarries. Found out it was cheaper to mine it in places like India and Brazil and ship it up here. They still do the processing here, but mostly imported stuff, not near the quality. Barre went from boom to bust. Used to be plenty of work, between the sheds and the quarries. But with the sheds getting mechanized, and the quarries shut down…" She trailed off.

We stood there staring down into the pit, not talking, as the wind picked up and the snow started falling harder.

"Best we head down the hill if we want to have some lunch and visit the cemetery." Leland's voice broke the silence.

We climbed into the truck cab and drove back through downtown. When we passed the diner, nestled behind a storefront on Main Street, Leland parked the truck. It was the same place I had pie and coffee earlier. There were about a dozen people seated at booths along one wall and another six or seven at the counter.

I was looking at a menu, when Mary gave a start. "Oh my goodness! That's old Mrs. Moretti sittin' in the corner. She was a friend of my mama. Why she must be a hundred years old! She's the one who organized the relief for all those kids who came up here from Massachusetts during that big strike down in Lawrence."

"No kidding," I said. "How cool!"

The old woman was getting up to go, and when she turned, Mary said. "Mrs. Moretti?"

"Mrs. Moretti! How are you?" Mary rose and hugged her. "I haven't seen you in years. We were just here visiting Rosa."

"Poor dear," the old lady commiserated. "I saw her last week. It won't be long now. I'm so sorry, Maria."

Mary looked at the floor. "She had a good life," she said. She looked up. "You remember my husband Leland, and this is our friend, David." She nodded at me. "I was telling him about the old days, when you and Papa and the others were so active."

"Shh!" Mrs. Morretti hissed, and looked furtively around the room. "We don't talk about those times any more. It's not safe."

"But it was fifty years ago!" Mary was astounded.

"Doesn't matter," the old lady insisted. "Remember the Palmer Raids? With all the protests you think they're not still sniffing around? I'm an old lady now, I don't need the trouble. I've got to go." She abruptly turned away.

Mary looked at her, but said only, "It was nice to see you. Stay well."

"What was that all about?" I asked.

"She's scared," said Mary, "Poor dear! A little confused, but still scared after all these years…"

After lunch we squeezed back into the truck and headed out, north this time on Route 14. After we passed through a residential neighborhood we came to a large cemetery at the edge of town.

"Hope Cemetery," proclaimed Leland with a flourish as he drove through an imposing granite arch. The cemetery stretched out in either direction, cut by a network of roads.

As we drove slowly through the forest of granite monuments Mary pointed out some of the more notable ones. "Look over there David," she gestured to the left where a life-sized carving of two beds stood next to each other. A man lay in one, holding the hand of his wife, who lay in the other.

We drove on past a six-foot diameter soccer ball carved from granite. We passed busts carved atop ornate pedestals, and Mary told me that they were memorials for shed owners who had carved their own, or been wealthy enough to have the work done by their employees. The names were all Italian, they all wore suit coats and they all had mustaches. "If you look close you can tell the anarchists from the socialists."

"Anarchist owners?" I asked. "Isn't that a contradiction?"

Mary laughed. "Oh, they started out like everybody else, and some of those sheds were just two- or three-man operations. But, you're right, if they owned one they couldn't call themselves anarchists, they were sympathizers."

We drove past a monument that consisted of two hands, each about six feet tall, cupped, facing each other. We saw a bunch of Jesuses on the cross, countless palm fronds, lilies, and all kinds of other religious symbols.

We stopped across from a life-size statue of a man standing with one leg up on a log. "That's Elia Corti," Mary said. "The fellow I told you about got shot on the steps of the Labor Hall, friend of my father."

We got out of the truck to get a closer look. The statue was finely carved and very lifelike. At his feet lay a granite hammer and chisel, the tools of his trade. "My papa did the lettering on this. Bunch of his friends worked on it. Finest work in the whole place," Mary said with pride.

We lingered a moment in front of the statue, with the snow falling around us, then got back into the cab of the truck and drove on to one of the further rows where we stopped in front of a simple headstone. "My father and mother," said Mary as she opened the door and got out.

We joined her in front of the grave; the stone was small, maybe two feet high. The lettering was carved deep into the gray granite, *Polanyi*, it spelled out her family name, and then beneath that, *Arturo and Angelina* with the dates of their births and deaths. A third line of lettering said simply *Anarchicos*.

Mary stood in front of the grave for several minutes, then she turned, we got back into the truck, and drove home through the thickening snow.

WHAT A BRUTAL NIGHT! We started meeting after dinner. I made spaghetti and opened a jar of Ragú. After I cleared the table the four of us sat there, facing each other.

Mark started things off. "Look, it's crunch time. We're gonna get into some heavy shit now, and I gotta know I can count on you guys. I mean I need to be sure. I've gotta admit, it freaks me out a little that none of you ever has ever really done anything. Like, not anything heavy duty…I've seen a lot of flaky shit from you, and it's time to face up to it."

"What are you talking about!" I responded. "We're here, we're just as committed as you are. We've all been arrested before."

"Yeah, but you're not battle-tested. You're soft. All of you. Really, a bunch of college kids. I gotta be sure you can handle yourselves, that you'll have my back when the shit comes down, 'cause it's gonna."

"What do you mean? You doubt me?" I was angry, he was treating me like a child again.

"Hey, we're talkin' life and death here. Are you really ready for that? You're a little rich girl. You've always had it easy. Are you ready to set off a bomb? Or shoot a pig? This is for real, not some little game you and your roommates are playing. We're done fuckin' around—it's time to get down to it!"

I had to stop to think, but just for a moment. "Yeah, I'm ready," I said.

"You see! That's the problem!" Mark pushed away from the table. "That hesitation, that little moment of doubt! That's what gets you killed in combat. What if we get caught? What if it comes down a firefight? You gonna wimp out on me?"

"Why are you attacking me?" I asked. "We're in this together. I gave up a lot because I believe in what we're doing, I believe in the revolution…"

"Yeah, that's what I'm talking about—you gave shit up! That's your privilege talking. You had shit to give up, and you can always go back to it if things get rough. You and your people are the problem."

"I know," I said, "and I want to be part of the solution. It's what I've been about since I was a kid. It's why I joined SDS." I was pissed. "You know, I actually have a lot more political experience than you do."

"Oh, SDS," he said. "I forgot. Your old college debating society. All talk. Well we're done talking now. If this is gonna work, you better get with the program. This ain't no debate, it's a war, and to win a war you need good soldiers. That means you take orders and you carry them out without question. Can you do that?"

"Of course," I said.

"Really?" he challenged. "'Cause you question me a lot. 'Where have you been?' 'Do you think the motorcycle's a good idea?' 'Should you really be drinking so much?'"

"But—"

He cut me off. "Don't try and defend yourself! It's your class background coming through. You can't stand taking orders from someone like me, you think you know better than anybody. Well, you're full of shit! Who are you to question me? Just a little fuckin' rich girl."

I was practically in tears at that point.

Jason tried to intervene. "Hey, wait a minute, I don't think you're being fair…"

"You!" Mark turned toward him. "You're even worse than she is. You almost blew the whole thing before we even got started! Talkin' to the feds. Weak move man. That's the fuckin' problem with you college kids, too much talking. Just shut the fuck up and listen! I'm sick of this shit! I'm puttin' my life in your hands, and I'm not even sure you won't piss your pants the first time things get heavy! As far as I'm concerned you've all gotta prove yourselves."

Jason looked wounded.

"This is for real, man, not some campus caper," Mark continued. "I want to see if you have any balls before we go any further. As far as I'm concered, you've gotta prove you have some balls."

"Prove ourselves?" Suze looked as freaked out as I felt.

"Hell, yeah!" Mark growled. He was really being an asshole. "Show me you're not a bunch of pussies."

"How?" asked Jason. "We're down and ready. What do you want us to do?"

Mark looked around the table. "We need a car. A late model Cadillac, bring it to this address tomorrow night." He wrote down an address in Queens *on a slip of paper and, smiling, handed it to Jason. "Let's see how badass you guys really are."*

I WOKE AS THE sun came up over the eastern hills. It was one of those glorious clear mornings that sometimes happens in a Vermont winter. By the time I dressed and stepped onto the porch to let Ranger out, the cloudless sky had turned a bright blue, and the sun hung frozen over the range of hills. I took a deep breath and the sudden cold hurt my chest.

I went back inside to make myself some coffee, and when I turned the tap on the kitchen sink to fill the pot nothing happened. I figured that the pipes must have frozen overnight down in the basement. I walked down the stairs and found a torch attached to a small cylinder of propane.

Last winter the pipes had frozen a couple of times when it dropped down to minus thirty or so overnight. After Leland had told us what to do it had been a simple enough matter to thaw them out with the torch.

This time though, when I looked, I couldn't find an obvious spot where they had frozen, so I decided to start where the line came in from the spring and work upstairs from there. It took me an hour or so to thoroughly heat the lengths of copper pipe. Then I went up to the kitchen and opened the tap again. Still nothing.

I had an awful thought. I went back down to the basement and opened the valve where the line came in. No water flowed out. That meant something was frozen outside. I had no idea what to do so I put on my coat and walked over to Leland and Mary's to ask his advice.

Leland was out splitting wood as I approached. When he saw me, he leaned his maul against the chopping block. "How's David?" he asked.

"Not good," I told him. Then I explained the problem.

"Hmm," he replied. "Let's go over and get a look at it. Often times things freeze up at the inlet when it gets real cold. Bring a torch along and we'll see if we can't get you thawed out."

Ranger followed us as we made our way through thigh-deep snow into the woods for a couple of hundred yards till we found the spring. Leland used his arm to clear the top of the spring box of snow, and then removed the cover. Water was flowing through, and the inlet pipe looked clear.

"Well, I don't much care for that," observed Leland.

"What's wrong?"

"Water's flowin' in, but it's not comin' out up to the house. Means there must be somethin' frozen underground between here and there."

"Really?" I asked. "What can we do about it?"

"Nothin' much to be done about it, least not till spring."

"What do you mean?"

"Well, when the snow melts and the ground thaws, hopefully your water will flow again. Unless the pipe burst. Then you'll have to dig it up and fix the break. Come to think of it probably want to dig it up and get it down deeper anyway so this don't happen again."

"But why this winter? What about now? It got just as cold last year." I was near panic at the thought of living in the farmhouse without water.

"You did some blasting up here over the summer, didn't you?"

"Yeah."

"Well, could be that shifted things around some. Don't really know. Good thing is the spring ain't froze. You'll have to haul your water from here, I guess."

"All winter?"

"Till things thaw out."

"Shit!" I exclaimed. Ranger gave me a concerned look.

I took in the full implications of the situation—it was a disaster. Without running water I'd have to haul it in from the spring, which was a long way from the farmhouse. It also meant I'd have to boil water on the stove for washing dishes, or taking a bath.

"Won't be so bad," offered Leland. "I got some five-gallon milk cans you can use. It's how they did it when they first settled up here."

"Thanks," I replied. It was doable, I guessed, but what a hassle. Oh well, between hauling water and cutting firewood at least I would stay busy.

"THE ACTION'S ON?" JASON was excited. "What's the deal?"

"See, that's the fuckin' problem!" said Mark. "Too many questions! Need to know, remember?"

I had no idea how to steal a car. I looked at Jason and Suze in panic.

"What the fuck?" Jason said. "We need some training or something. You're giving us twenty-four hours?"

"Piece of cake," replied Mark. "Just pull out the ignition cylinder and cross two wires. He pulled some kind of tool, a metal shaft with a sliding weight on it, out of the backpack slung on his chair and handed it to Jason. "Slap hammer," he said.

"Slap hammer?" asked Suze.

Mark looked exasperated. "You really don't know anything, do you?"

"We're not auto mechanics," I replied.

"You'll figure it out. You went to college, right?" He laughed. "Just screw it in where the key goes, the rest is obvious. They use 'em to pull out dents. Take you about five seconds to get the cylinder out, then just cross the wires till it starts."

"Great," I said. "Now I feel really prepared."

"Look, if you can't handle this, how can I count on you when the shit really starts to fly?" Mark was angry. "Get it together," he said. Then he rose, turned, and walked out.

The three of us sat there in silence after he left. I was shaken, and I could tell Jason and Suze were freaking out too.

Finally, Jason spoke up. "Let's split up, go out now, walk around the neighborhood and see if we can spot any Cadillacs. Check out the surroundings, see if it looks like it could work."

"We're really doing this?" asked Suze. "It seems insane, and what's it got to do with the revolution? I mean I understand a stolen getaway car, but why a Caddy?"

"It must be that we're going after some ruling-class enclave, somewhere you need a fancy car to blend in. And he's testing us," I said. "I guess it makes sense, at least from his perspective. He's got to know he can count on us, that we won't lose our nerve." I felt like I had to defend him.

"I guess," admitted Suze.

We put on our coats and headed out the door, each going in a different direction. I walked for several blocks and had no luck. Cadillacs were scarce in our working-class neighborhood. Finally, about four blocks away from our place, I spotted a shiny red one parked by the curb. I scoped out the block, and it was quiet and empty. It looked to me as if it could work, assuming the car was there tomorrow night.

I HAULED MY FIRST load of water that morning, pulling the toboggan with two empty milk cans lashed on to it down the slight grade to the spring, over the tracks Leland and I had made on our earlier trip. I removed the cover from the spring box and submerged a five-gallon can in the freezing water. Bubbles rose to the surface as it filled, then I hauled it out and set it on the sled, filled the other one and then pulled the toboggan up the packed snow onto the path that led to the farmhouse.

By the time I got to the house, carried the cans inside and hoisted one up onto the counter next to the sink, I was breathing hard. I had no idea how long it would last, but at least I had enough to boil water for coffee, which is exactly what I did.

While the java brewed, I thought things through. I figured a couple of gallons a day for drinking and washing dishes. I realized I wouldn't be taking any baths until the line thawed, since it would take several sled loads of water to fill the tub. Maybe a sponge bath every couple of days. Flushing the toilet was good for at least three gallons, so maybe I would start using the outhouse. If I did everything I could to conserve water I figured I'd have to make the trip to the spring every other day or so, doable, but a royal pain in the ass.

I savored my coffee as I contemplated the series of disasters I had already faced—my unexpected isolation, the lack of firewood, and the frozen pipes. I wondered what else could go wrong, and as I thought about it, I felt myself begin to smile. It really was kind of funny, when I looked at things objectively. I couldn't allow myself to sink into depression; I had too much to do just to survive the winter. I laughed out loud and put the empty cup in the sink to join the dishes from last night's dinner.

Then I remembered the outhouse and those freezing winter mornings. I was not looking forward to that. What a fucking bummer.

WE WAITED UNTIL ELEVEN. The block had settled down, there was no traffic on the street, and it seemed like if we were going to do it, the time was right. Suze and I stood lookout, and Jason walked up to the car. The red car I had seen the previous night was gone, but Jason had seen this one parked in the driveway of a brick duplex. I watched as he tried the door. No luck. He took the slap hammer out of his backpack and broke the window. I held my breath, waiting for the lights to go on in the house, but they didn't.

Jason reached in through the broken window, unlocked the door and opened it. He leaned in, screwed the slap hammer into the ignition switch, and slapped back the weight. I saw him flip on his flashlight and fumble around under the dash. I held my breath. After what seemed like hours of him trying, the car finally started. He pulled out into the street. Suze and I both ran for the car, and then we were home free! What a feeling! We did it! All we had to do now was meet Mark.

We had mostly empty streets until we hit the Brooklyn-Queens Expressway, and traffic was light there. Suze read the road map and directed us through a labyrinth of little streets that ran under the highway. It was a jumble of industrial spaces, auto body shops, warehouses, lots full of commercial vehicles, even a junkyard. We finally spotted the address, and pulled up in front of some kind of a garage. I jumped out and knocked on the door.

Mark answered, with a big smile on his face. "Alright! I knew you could do it, babe!"

I swelled with pride—he hadn't complimented me in a long time.

"Let's get that thing in off the street," he said, and he pushed a button that opened the door.

Jason drove the car into the nearly dark garage, lit only by a flickering lamp at the far end. He and Suze hopped out. Another guy emerged from the shadows, a truly huge guy wearing a leather vest with patches from Mark's motorcycle gang all over it.

"This is Big Bill," Mark said. "He'll take over from here."

I can't believe it. With all his shit about "need to know", he brought in one of his biker buddies, and without even telling us! It totally freaked me out. And what happened next freaked me out even more.

This guy, Big Bill, went to the side of the garage where a pair of welding tanks sat. He turned some valves and walked over to the car with a torch connected by hoses to the tanks. He lit the torch and started cutting the car apart.

I couldn't believe it. What the fuck! I turned to Mark.

"What, you thought you were ready for an action?" he laughed. "This was a test. You did good."

"But, why cut it up?" I asked.

"Always with the questions. It's worth more as parts than a whole car that's hot. They can't trace the parts."

"This a chop shop," Jason stood watching.

"Clever boy," Mark said.

"But why?" I insisted.

"Duh!" said Mark. "How did you think we were gonna pay for this clambake? Or maybe you'd rather rob banks?"

The torch was throwing off sparks as it cut through the skin of the car, the flickering lamp went dead, and the only light in the room came from the sparks, the flame of the torch and the cherry red glow of metal on either side of the cut. It was one of the most surreal things I'd ever seen. We stood there in silence watching him.

Big Bill drove us home. I didn't say a word the whole time, still trying to figure out how I felt about the situation. This wasn't what I'd signed up for. It took me a while to get my head around it, but Mark had it all figured out.

"It's gonna take some serious bread for us to pull this shit off. I mean we got rent to pay on apartments, we got equipment and supplies to buy. We gotta

eat. It all adds up. We need to bring in some cash. This is a start, but we'll need more. I've got some other ideas, but I gotta know you're with me on this. Can you dig it?"

It makes sense. We were underground now, and digging deeper all the time. Kind of scary, but exhilarating too.

IT WAS SNOWING HARD, and I had decided to take a day off from cutting firewood. I was sitting on the couch reading when I heard a knock. Ranger barked, ran to the door, and started to growl. I soon saw why.

It was the FBI agents, Axton and Terwilliger who had visited us back in the fall. I didn't invite them in.

"Yes?" I said through the partially open door.

"Jason here?" Axton asked, trying to peak around me. "We've got a few more questions for him."

"He's not here, he doesn't live here anymore."

"Really? Where did he go?"

"Don't know."

"You don't know where he's living now?"

"Nope."

"Well, maybe you can help us out a little here, David. It is David isn't it? Answer a few questions for us."

"I have nothing to say," I replied. "I can't tell you anything."

"You're not being very cooperative. You must have some idea where he went. We know he was out in Flint, Michigan with Jill."

"Then you know more than I do. Goodbye!" I tried to shut the door but Axton had his foot wedged in to keep it open.

"If you care about your friends, you'll talk to us. They're in a lot of trouble already, and it'll only get worse. You can help them by helping us;

and if you don't, the grand jury's still in session. We're going to find them anyway. It's your choice."

"I don't know anything," I responded. "And I don't want to talk to you. If you have a warrant, show it. If not, leave me alone, and get the fuck out of here." I pushed the door closed.

I was shaking when they left. What did they mean 'my friends were in a lot of trouble already'? Jill! What kind of trouble? Fuck! I was freaked out. What kind of crazy shit was she into? Where was she, for that matter? I had no idea, but the thought of the FBI hunting her was terrifying. And I was powerless; there was nothing I could do to help her, absolutely nothing.

I WAS PRETTY PUMPED up after we stole the car. I mean, we had pulled it off! I know it wasn't exactly a revolutionary act, but we had crossed some kind of line, and I felt like there was no turning back now. I finally proved to Mark that I was as down and ready as he was, and I'm psyched to see what comes next. We made some money when Bill sold the parts to a junkyard, and we have a little breathing room now.

It's been hard to go back into waiting mode, but that's where things have been at for the last week or so. Mark's been spending a lot of time away from the apartment, so I know he's working on something, but he hasn't told us what yet. I feel like things are coming to a head, like we're on the cusp of a real breakthrough. I am so ready. I was listening to the radio today, and the war is just getting worse. "Secret plan to end the war" my ass! Nixon and Kissinger are even worse than Johnson and McNamara, they're bombing Cambodia! We've got to stop them. Mark's right—the protest marches aren't doing shit. Desperate times require desperate measures, and I'm more than ready to do whatever we need to do.

This country is killing and oppressing people all over the world, and forget about what they're doing right here. Black people are rising up in righteous anger. They're really the only ones fighting back. We have to stand with them and show them they're not alone, and not just by talking. Actions speak louder than words, and I'm ready to act! Nonviolence is no longer an option, not for them or for us.

I'm still angry at David. I've been thinking about him a lot. He's so smart—why doesn't he get it? I guess he's still sitting out in the woods up in Vermont. I feel sorry for him. The revolution is finally happening, and he's not a part of it. I always thought we'd be in it together, but he's so fucking blind he can't see which way the wind is blowing. He's going to be left behind by history.

Sometimes I think that maybe I should write him, try to convince him to join us. It's not too late. But he's so stubborn and self-righteous there's really no point. I miss him though.

IT HAD SNOWED FOUR inches overnight, leaving what looked like a fresh white layer of frosting over everything. The sun was shining, and I had finally gotten a little ahead on the firewood, so I decided to go for a ski. Ranger wagged his whole body in excitement as I strapped on the boards. The path had been packed by the snowmobiles that roared through the night before, and I heard blue jays calling to each other as I glided off into the woods.

Most people think of the forest as a silent place, I know I did before I moved to Vermont. The reality is that if you stop to listen you can hear the sounds of life everywhere—the jays and chickadees, crows cawing, the wind whistling through tree branches, and at night coyotes howling, the occasional scream of a bobcat, owls hooting, and other animal calls I couldn't identify. There were constant reminders that I wasn't really alone, and I took some comfort from these traces of the life all around me.

My initial feelings of loneliness and solitude had begun to give way to a recognition that I shared the hill with others. I could see tracks of deer along the path, and identify the spots in the woods where they browsed the low hanging cedar and spruce. I could tell where they yarded up on the cold nights when the wind howled out of Canada, and sometimes find tufts of fur revealing where they had passed through the underbrush. Other tracks were visible in the snow as well, though I didn't know how to read them.

When I went out in the woods with Leland, he could tell exactly what had passed through the fresh snow. The tracks told him stories that I could only guess at, though in his usual fashion he was happy to share his insights with me. One day he showed me where a fox had tracked a grouse, and we found the place where a pile of feathers and traces of blood spotted the snow to reveal where the hunt had ended. Even in the frozen depth of winter, life and death continued to cycle around me, and gradually I was gaining the skills to be aware of it. The key was to look, really look, and to listen.

I saw Leland and Mary a couple of times a week. He continued to help me bring in sledge-loads of firewood, and she offered me an occasional meal. Just knowing they were nearby was a comfort, and they made a point of telling me when they were going to town, either Newport or St. Johnsbury, so I could tag along and pick up whatever supplies I needed, using the cash I had earned working in my dad's hardware store. I felt like they were my guardian angels, and I looked forward to sugaring season so I could begin to repay the debt I felt I owed them.

As I skied toward Hardwood Mountain, I thought about how things had come to this; I remembered all of the hopes and dreams I had brought with me to Vermont, and how they had all evaporated. But I also reflected on all the gifts I had received, how my life had changed in unexpected ways, and wondered about what would come next. Would I ever see Jill, Jason, Suze and the others again? Would they return with the spring? I doubted it, but who knew?

I tried not to admit it, but I still longed for Jill. I dreamed of her often, and even when I was awake; working in the woods, hauling water, or out for a ski, I couldn't stop her image from coming to mind. She had been a constant in my life for so long that it still felt unnatural to be without her. And there was the added urgency of her in trouble tugging at my heartstrings.

I skied to where the trail steepened to begin the ascent to the mountain's upper reaches, and then, rather than pulling on the climbing skins, I turned and returned to the house. Ranger raced up the path ahead of me, obliterating the track I had laid on the way in.

WAITING. THAT'S ALL I do these days. I've actually started watching soap operas on TV. Fucking soap operas! Ever since the townhouse explosion, Mark said we have to lay low, or at least I have to—he's still out most of the time, still won't tell me what's going on. I do know that everything has changed since the townhouse. What a mess! THREE DEAD! Teddy Gold, who wrote the songbook, Diana Oughton, who I really didn't know, and Terry Robbins, from Columbia. Terry! Such a sweet guy. I still can't get my head around it.

"Sit tight," Mark said, after I saw the story on the TV news. I did, and I still am, and it's been almost two weeks and I still don't know what's going on, and I'm going stir crazy.

I'm not saying I want to quit, or anything like that. Not like those fucking traitors Jason and Suze. We should never have trusted them. They freaked when they heard about it. Just packed up and ran. Mark said if he saw them again, he'd kill them. They know too much. They couldn't handle it. Oh well, at least we know who's for real now, and it looks like it's me and Mark.

I've got to stay strong and trust his leadership. He knows what he's doing. Mark says he knew they'd fuck it up. "Amateurs," he snorted. But he also says the townhouse was a victory for us in a way. It shows the world we're ready to fight, and even die for the revolution. It puts them on notice. He's right, I guess, but three dead? Heavy price to pay. They're the revolution's first martyrs, or at least first white martyrs. And I'm sure they won't be the last.

It's been a confusing couple of months. I mean, after all of the energy in Flint, it seems like we've been mostly just sitting around, or at least I have. Till the townhouse I had no idea that there was even a cell in New York, and now I wonder how many more there are, and what they're planning. I guess I'll find out.

THAT NIGHT I WAS sitting on the couch reading when I heard someone stomping on the front porch. The door opened suddenly and the doorway was filled by a huge man who stepped into the house. "Fuckin' cold out there! I been on the road eight hours. You got beer?" he said.

I was shocked. "Who the fuck are you?" I asked.

"I'm Bill, Big Bill, Mark's friend."

The man stepped more fully into the kitchen, and I got a better look at him. Six foot four or five, three hundred pounds I guessed. A gigantic, tough-looking dude. A biker—at least dressed like one in a leather coat with greasy jeans. He had a huge head covered in long hair and a stubble of a beard covering a chin that looked like it was carved out of granite.

"I guess he never told you I was comin'. I'll be here a couple of days. I got some business to take care of up in Canada. You're Davey Boy, right?" He offered me a ham-sized hand to shake.

"David," I said.

"No beers?"

"Uh, no…" I was still digesting his arrival.

"That's okay—I got some out in the truck." He pulled a fat joint out of the snap pocket in his coat and fired it up, drawing deeply. "Here, real Acapulco Gold, give that sucker a try."

I took the joint and toked on it. I hadn't gotten high in months, not since they all left.

"You said you're a friend of Mark's? Where is he?"

"Down in the city. Hooked up with this foxy little chick, Jill. But I guess you know her, she owns this place, right?"

I sunk into the couch.

"Yeah, man," he went on. "She is some piece of ass. Real classy, I'd like to drill her myself. Mark says he can't hardly keep up with her in bed. Real horny little bitch. He's got her convinced he's some kind of revolutionary. 'Bring the war home' and all that shit. Me? I just want to bring some ludes home. Mark got a contact with a club in Canada. This place should work fine to base out of."

"Quaaludes? Here? I don't think that's a good idea. The feds are sniffing around; they were just here last week. And some nosy neighbors too."

"Don't worry about it. Mark says you know some trail up to Canada. I towed up a snowmobile. Nothin' for anybody to look twice at. The Feds just care about that political shit, and if any neighbors get too nosy…" Bill reached under his coat and pulled out an automatic pistol, making sure I got a good look before he tucked it back into his waistband.

"No, I don't think—" I felt panic rising in me.

"I said don't worry about it." Bill loomed over me. "I got it all covered." He took the joint from me. "Fuckin' cold up here, huh?"

"I'm not sure this is a good idea, the feds said they'd be back."

"What'd they want?" Bill exhaled.

"They were looking for a friend. Jason, a guy who used to live here."

"That pussy?"

"You know him?"

"Met him. Don't see how that'll make any difference to this operation. Like I said, don't worry about it. I'll be gone day after tomorrow. Piece of fuckin' cake."

"I just don't feel comfortable…"

"Fuck that! Mark said it was cool if I used this place, and his old lady owns it. You got a problem with that?" He narrowed his eyes and stared hard at me. I said nothing.

"Good," he said. "You got anything to eat? I'm fucking starving. I'm gonna go out to the truck and get those beers." He walked out the door.

When he returned, he had a six-pack of Budweiser under his arm. I was at the cook stove warming up some leftovers. The big man popped a Bud and sunk back into the couch.

"What's for supper?" Bill asked.

"Rice and beans."

"Fuckin' mush," he said.

"It's all I've got."

"Fuckin' quiet up here," he said. "Where do you go to party?"

"I don't do much partying," I told him. "Nearest bar is about twenty miles away, and I don't have a car."

"Man, I would go crazy here." Bill drank his beer. "What are you, some kind of monk or something?"

"No," I replied. "But I like the peace and quiet, and it's beautiful—a good place for figuring stuff out."

"Don't you get horny?"

I laughed. "Yeah, every now and then."

"I could bring up a chick next time I come," he offered.

"Next time?"

"Yeah, I figure I'll make this run about once a month to re-up. I got some nice pieces of tail I could bring."

"No, that's okay. I get by." I really hoped there would be no next time.

I heard scratching at the door and left the stove to let Ranger in. He had been gone for a couple of hours.

"Ranger!" I said. "Nice of you to come home." He bounded into the kitchen, his wagging tail thumping on the door frame. Then he caught Bill's scent, stopped short, and leaped onto the couch next to the startled biker. Bill recoiled. Ranger sniffed him and then, with a low growl in his throat, sat staring with his nose six inches away from the big man's face.

"Ranger!" I shouted, "Down, boy!"

The dog continued staring with his neck hackles up, as he slowly got off the couch and stood growling at his feet.

Bill looked pale. "Get that fuckin' dog away from me or I'll shoot him," he demanded through clenched teeth.

"Ranger, come here!" I snapped my fingers. The dog reluctantly abandoned his post, glancing back at Bill and still growling, as he came to me and sat by the stove. "It's okay, boy. Leave him alone. Lie down!" He lay at my feet still staring warily at the stranger on the couch, who had relaxed a little.

"You better keep that fuckin' thing away from me. He's vicious. I swear I'll put a bullet in his head if he ever does that shit to me again." Bill had regained his usual bluster.

"He'll calm down. He's very protective, not a trained watchdog or anything. He just reacts to strangers sometimes. Sorry if he freaked you out."

"I don't give a shit. Just keep him out of my face, or he'll get some of this." He patted the pistol in his waistband. Then he relaxed on the couch and stretched out his legs onto the coffee table full of books.

"I'd go nuts livin' up here. Fuck, I've only been here a half an hour and I'm already gettin' antsy. That store I passed on the main road sell meat? I'll go down and get us some hamburger. Fuck that mush you're cookin'."

"Yeah, they sell a little bit of everything, it's a general store. But they're closed by now."

"General store? No shit, like in the olden days, huh?"

"That's why I like it," I said. "Human scale—no shopping malls, no McDonald's."

"Personally," Bill responded, "I can't wait to get the fuck back to civilization. I mean no bars, no broads…"

"Groovy." Sooner the better, I thought; please! Bill's rubbing salt in my wounds about Jill and Mark was bad enough, but the thought of spending another day with him had my stomach churning.

He lit a cigarette and exhaled. "How the fuck do you live up here without a car? How the fuck do you live here at all? I couldn't believe the drive up, there was nothin' at all for miles. It was fuckin' freaky."

"I like the solitude," I answered, which was only half true. I did, but I also missed the company of the others, especially Jill. In my stoned state it felt to me that they had all melted away, like the valley fog burning off in the morning. Smoking pot always put me deep inside my head, thinking and questioning, trying to piece things together. I felt like I was in a zone outside of time, with no history, and no future.

I snapped out of it whein I realized the food was starting to burn. "Dinner's ready," I said.

"Alright, I guess I'm hungry enough to eat your mush. I'll go get us some burgers tomorrow after you show me that trail," said Bill.

I spooned some rice and beans into a brown ceramic bowl with a chipped rim and handed it to Bill, who had moved to the table. Then I served myself and joined him. We ate in silence. I sipped a beer while he downed the remaining four. When we were done, I tipped the jerry can into the sink to wash the dishes.

"You gotta be fuckin kidding me!" said Bill, incredulous. "No running water?"

"The line froze. I haul it in from the spring."

"Then where do I take a crap?" he asked.

"There's an outhouse around the side"

"Fuck that! I ain't shittin' outside, not in this weather."

"What can I tell you? There's toilet paper out there. It's not too bad."

Big Bill thought for a moment, then lit another joint. "No TV or anything, huh? How the fuck do you stand it?"

"I already told you, I like the peace and quiet. I read a lot, I'm getting some writing done, I have some neighbors I visit. I cross-country ski."

"Is that the path, your ski trail?"

"Well, it's really a snowmobile trail. It runs a couple of miles through the woods over Hardwood Mountain, and then across the lake into Canada."

"Any roads over there on the other side?"

"Yeah, there's a road, runs out to a bunch of cottages, but nobody's there in the winter."

He thought for a moment. "Sounds good. No moon tomorrow night. But you don't have a fuckin' phone here, do you?"

"Nope, no phone," I replied.

"Fuck! I've gotta call my guy to set up the delivery."

"There's a phone booth down at the store," I offered. "It'll take a lot of quarters to call Canada."

"All right, you'll show me everything tomorrow," Bill said as he kicked off his boots and stretched out on the couch. "I'll sleep here, close to the stove. Make sure you load this thing up good before you go to bed. You got a blanket or something?"

I found him an old flannel-lined sleeping bag, and filled the stove with firewood. I grabbed *Pedagogy of the Oppressed* from the coffee table and went upstairs into my room.

I had been reading in bed for about half an hour when I heard the stove door open and close, caught a whiff of the smoke that had escaped, and then was overwhelmed by a revolting odor, unlike anything I had ever smelled before.

I flew down the stairs. "What's that stink?" I ran to the door to let in some fresh air.

Bill sat there with a sheepish grin on his face, barely visible in the dim light. "Fuck, I didn't know. It's not my fault. I told you I wasn't gonna shit outside. I had to go, so I crapped in a paper bag. I figured I'd just burn it in the stove. Who the fuck knew? Okay? Don't make a big fuckin' deal out of it, the smell'll clear out."

I went back upstairs and slept until the first light of day made its way through the milky plastic covering the bedroom window. I walked down to the kitchen and started a fire in the cook stove, waking Bill in the process.

"You want any coffee?" I asked.

"Fuck yeah." The big man rose from the couch, stretched, and pulled on his boots. "I got a big day comin' up. Gotta call my man in Canada, scope out this trail, make sure that fuckin' Ski-Doo is runnin' right, and get ready for tonight. How fuckin' cold does it get up here anyway?"

"The thermometer hit thirty below the other night, but we've been having a cold snap. It's usually not that bad."

"Fuck! How you put up with this miserable shit is beyond me. You got something for breakfast?"

"I can make some oatmeal," I offered.

"More mush? Fuck that. Don't you got some bacon and eggs?"

"No, oatmeal is about all I can offer. I could make some toast."

"No restaurants, huh?"

"Well, there's a snack bar at the general store. Greasy eggs, burgers; breakfast and lunch, stuff like that."

"That's what I'm talkin' about!" Bill put on his leather coat. "You said they had a phone booth down there too?"

"Yeah."

"Alright! I'm goin' down to make my call and grab a bite. You can show me that trail when I get back. I'll get some hamburgers for dinner tonight too, and some beers. We need anything else?"

"Not really. Maybe some more milk for coffee and another loaf of bread."

"I'll get my coffee down there with breakfast." Bill lit a joint. "Wake and bake?" He handed it to me, I took a toke, handed it back to him, and he walked out the door.

"I'll be back soon," he said on his way out.

An hour or so later I heard a snow machine bark to life down by the road and Bill arrived back at the house riding a big yellow Ski-Doo.

I stood on the porch and watched as he adjusted the carburetor with a screwdriver until he had it running smoothly. Then he mixed some oil into a red gas can, filled the tank with the mixture, and turned it off.

"So what's the fuckin' deal with this trail?" he asked.

I thought about the path, all of its history, what it represented to

Leland—and now it was all about Quaaludes.

"Like I told you last night, local guys ride their snow machines on it. It runs up and over Hardwood Mountain, then straight across the lake and you're in Canada. This time of year it's really just me skiing on it and the locals going out to ride and drink. I've never seen anybody else use it. It's just one track, no way to get lost."

"Sounds good. Guess I'll check it out. Make a dry run in daylight." He yanked the starter rope on his snow machine and I stood there in a haze of blue smoke as he roared off down the path. I listened as the sound receded into the distance and then disappeared altogether.

I turned to my own yellow two-stroke, the chainsaw, and loaded up the toboggan to head to the woodlot. My firewood supply was getting low again.

I heard him return in the early afternoon, and by the time I came back in for lunch he had already finished a six-pack of beer. He was seated at the kitchen table.

"Got it all figured out," he told me. "It oughta go pretty good. Like I thought, fuckin' piece of cake. All I gotta do now is meet Jean-Pierre at midnight."

"Sounds like a plan," I said.

"What are you up to?" he asked.

"More firewood, do some reading, make some supper."

"Sounds pretty fuckin' boring to me. I'm gonna go to town, see if I can find a bar. You wanna come?"

"No thanks, I better stick with the firewood." I shuddered inwardly, the last thing I wanted to do was spend more time with Big Bill.

"All right, suit yourself. I'll be back in time for supper. See you then."

Darkness came early, enfolding me in the sounds of the forest. There was no moon, just thousands of stars flickering in the freezing night sky. I knew there were moose browsing the spruce that grew on the upper reaches of Hardwood, and Ranger pricked up his ears as a pack of coyotes gave their nightly concert. I reveled in my solitude, relieved to be rid of Bill, at least for an afternoon.

At about eight o'clock Bill stumbled in, half-drunk. "Davey Boy! How's it hanging? Got supper ready?"

I fried up some burgers, and he sat and ate in silence. After dinner he began his preparations. "Fuckin' cold out there. You got, like a sweatshirt, some sweaters, shit like that I can wear? It's gonna be a chilly ride."

I found a sweatshirt that he pulled over his massive head. It barely covered his huge stomach, and I brought him a down vest that Jason had left behind. He put it on, but couldn't zip it, and then pulled on his leather jacket. "You got some kinda hat or something?" he slurred. I lent him a sheepskin bomber hat with earflaps, which he buttoned down. He put on a pair of motorcycle goggles, and headed out the door. He looked both ridiculous and fierce at the same time.

I heard his Ski-Doo bark, and then listened while the noise faded into the distance. Even though he would be late, I couldn't sleep. I kept thinking of Jill and Mark and wondered how Big Bill fit into the picture, an obvious thug without even any pretense of political motivation. He was in it for the money, he made that clear. How could Jill have put me in the middle of this?

I sat at the kitchen table reading until I heard the snowmobile return. Bill burst through the door. "I'm fuckin' freezing! I hope you got a good fire goin'. Holy shit! It's one thing on a nice sunny day, but what is it, thirty below out there tonight? I mean…motherfucker!"

He threw a brown backpack down on the couch and began stripping off layers of clothing. "Except for the fuckin' cold though, just like I thought, a piece of fuckin' cake." He nodded his head at the backpack. "Check it out."

Curious, I picked it up. I was surprised by the weight, and when I unzipped it I saw that it was tightly packed with gallon freezer bags full of blue capsules.

"Mandrakes!" Bill enthused.

"What?" I removed one of the bags to examine it more closely.

"Ludes, you know man, a shit load of 'em. I can get five bucks a piece for 'em down in the city."

"Oh!" Surprised, I looked at the pack again and made some mental calculations. "That pack's worth a small fortune."

"You fuckin' better believe it! Think I'd freeze my ass off for nothin'?" Bill fished a small baggie out of his pocket and tossed it to me. "That's yours, for helpin' out."

"I don't do downers," I said.

"Well then sell 'em. I don't give a shit, but if I lived up here, I'd want to be luded out all the time. Broads love 'em too, make 'em horny as hell."

I put the baggie on the table.

"I'm gettin' the fuck out of here tomorrow morning, thank fuckin' god. But I'll be back up next month. We're gonna get a regular thing happenin' here. Couldn't have worked out any better."

I DON'T KNOW EXACTLY what's going on, but Mark has cooked something up with his buddy Bill, who we met that night at the garage in Queens. He's a scary guy, but Mark trusts him, says he's going to help us make some money. He hasn't said how, but I figure they're bringing drugs from Canada. They had a lot of questions about the house in Vermont and the path that runs through the woods. I thought about letting David know to expect a visitor, but I don't know the timing, and really the only way to contact him is to send a letter, and he doesn't go to the post office much.

He'll probably freak out if Bill just shows up at his door. I know I would—he's kind of creepy. But then again, this whole operation is "need to know" and I'm not even sure what's going on myself. I feel a little bad about it, but this is bigger than me or David.

It feels like things are shifting to a new phase. We made a little money on the Caddy, but Mark says it's not enough—it will all be gone in a month or two. We're going to need more, but Mark said he would handle it from now on. I've just got to trust him.

Meanwhile, we started to scout possibilities for our first action. It's hard to choose: federal offices, Department of Corrections, police headquarters, corporate headquarters, recruiting centers, armories, military bases, banks, Wall Street…there are hundreds of worthy targets within twenty miles of Queens. It's been good to get out of the house and try to figure it out.

We have to weigh a lot of factors: actual impact on the war machine, symbolic value, lots of operational factors like risk, access, escape routes, all that stuff. We'll work it all through and reach a decision soon. I have to say, I feel a lot more confident since we stole the car.

Whenever we go out to scout we wear disguises. I've got a red wig that makes me look like a secretary or something. That way even if we're noticed, nobody will be able to ID us. I feel like I'm finally starting to adjust to life underground. I've had to assume a whole new persona, and honestly, it hasn't been that easy, but I feel like I've really been making progress working on my class privilege and bourgeois tendencies. I've had to rethink and let go of a lot of things, but that's the only way to serve the revolution.

I WORKED IN THE woods all morning bucking up the logs I'd felled the day before, trying to get back ahead on the firewood. I stopped for lunch around noon and went back to the house to heat up some soup.

As I was eating, I was surprised by a knocking at the door. I glanced out the kitchen window to get a look.

"Oh, shit!" I said to myself when I recognized who it was, swept up the baggie full of Quaaludes that still sat on the table, opened the top of the stove and threw it into the fire, then went to the door to greet Axton and Terwilliger.

"Well, Mr. Levinski, how are you today?" Axton was wearing boots this time.

"What do you want now?" I asked.

"Jason around?"

"No, I told you he doesn't live here anymore."

"Oh, we thought maybe he was back. We heard you had a visitor from New York."

"So?" I was surprised they knew.

"We thought maybe Jason came back with him."

"No, just a friend," I said. How did they know?

"Yeah, quite a friend, member of the Saints Nomads motorcycle gang, convicted felon. Didn't know you people were so connected to the common criminal element. Anything you want to tell us about him?"

"Not really. Seems like you know a lot about him already."

"Can we come in and talk?"

"No, I told you last time, no warrant, no entry. And besides I have nothing to say to you."

"You know, you're just digging a deeper hole for yourself. We can come back with a subpoena."

"For what? I haven't done anything."

"You're a person of interest in an ongoing investigation."

I swallowed hard. "Look, like I said, I haven't done anything and I don't know anything, so why don't you stop harassing me."

Terwilliger stepped forward. "If you have nothing to hide why don't you cooperate? We could make it worth your while."

"Like I told you, I have nothing to say."

"Listen, you little prick, I don't like being stonewalled. We've got our eye on you, we will catch up with you and your little gang, and when we do…" Terwilliger narrowed his eyes.

I was scared. How had they known about Big Bill? Apparently, they had a local informant. My guess was Mac, the storekeeper, who had seen Bill the morning before. He must have called in his license number.

I knew it was a bad idea for Big Bill to use the house, and this latest visit from the feds confirmed it.

"I have nothing else to say to you. Don't you have anything better to do with your time?" I responded.

Terwilliger flushed red. "Protecting this nation from scum like you seems like pretty good use of my time."

"I'm done!" I said.

"Don't worry, we'll be back."

I shut the door, shaking.

OVER THE NEXT WEEK or so I managed to block and split enough wood to fill another sledge load, and Leland, as ever, was happy to help. I invited him in for a cup of coffee when we had finished unloading.

As we sat at the kitchen table, he looked around the house. "This old place was in my family for six generations you know. House was built by my great-great-grandpa in 1789, and that was to replace the original log cabin built by his father when they first come to settle the town.

"Come the summer after he got out of the Continental Army. Come up from Connecticut with his brother looking for a place to settle. Built the cabin, went back down, fetched his wife and new baby boy, walked back before the snow flew, pushin' a wheelbarrow with everything they owned in it. This was wilderness back then, virgin forest, full of wolves and catamounts, a hard place to live. Hard as it is now, ain't nothin' next to what they faced. Got their names and dates in the family bible."

I looked around the house with fresh eyes. I had known it was old, but not that old. When we had replaced some rotting clapboards the summer before, I'd noticed the underlayment; planking made of wide boards, some of them more than four feet wide, bearing the marks of the crosscut saw that had made them. I imagined the huge trees that they were born from, and the way an endless forest full of those trees must have looked to his ancestors.

"Yup," Leland continued, "the old home place. Hated to sell, but me and Mary didn't need a big place like this. Once we stopped milkin', got to be too much to keep up with. And the taxes…" His voice trailed off.

It was an old story, all too common in the Northeast Kingdom, evidenced by the abandoned farmhouses and high mowings that dotted the hillsides.

"Lots of history here," he went on, "that's for sure. Hard life back then. Most of 'em left, them that could. Headed west, to New York and beyond for an easier life. Better weather, better soil. Only ones who stayed behind was them that was too stubborn, or too stupid to leave." Leland chuckled. "Not quite sure which I was, probably a little of both, but it's too late for me now. Too old. Just stuck here I guess, like a tractor in the mud."

"But this is a great place to be," I responded. "And you're not stuck, you're rooted. It's amazing your family's been here that long. This is your place. I mean I don't even know where my family was two generations ago, somewhere in Russia, or Poland, or something, and yours was living on the same farm for almost two hundred years. That is so cool!"

"Not cool," replied Leland, "cold, damn cold for two hundred years.

No wonder so many of 'em left. Kind of amazin' anybody stayed, let alone that anybody'd choose to move up here. I admire you kids. I mean when we sold, I figured it to be a summer place for Sy and Claire. But seein' the bunch of you move in…well, that was an eye opener. I'll tell you, last thing I expected."

"Well," I said, "I'm the only one who stayed for a second winter. Like you said, too stubborn or stupid to leave."

"Now I guess that makes us two peas in a pod." Leland winked at me and I laughed.

"I'd like to get a look at that old bible of yours sometime," I said.

"Mostly names and dates, but there's some interestin' things in there 'bout the Underground Railroad and the Civil War. We lost a lot of men. Five brothers went off, only two come back. Old Uncle Seth was still alive when I was a kid. He'd just sit out there on the porch whittlin', never said a word. Oh, we made some sacrifices alright."

Ranger was lying on the couch, twitching in his sleep, dreaming of running in the woods chasing a deer or something. He moaned, and quivered. We looked over at him and Leland said, "Damn fine dog. I like a dog, and you sure got yourself a good one there."

"I do," I said. And it was true.

Ranger was my constant companion, and, at this point my best friend. I don't think I could have made it through the winter without him.

The dog woke, almost like he knew we were talking about him. He rose, stretched, and sniffed the air. The breeze told him stories; the passing of a deer, the coming of a storm, a fire in a stove beyond the next ridge. He walked to the door and waited for me to let him out.

His winter coat had grown in, and the cold and snow didn't bother him. He was in his element here—free to explore the scents that tantalized him, free to pursue his nature. He was half wild, yet bound to

me with an unshakable dedication, born of deep instinct, and reinforced by daily feedings and steady attention on my part. But it went
beyond mere dependency, I was sure of that. There was an indelible
bond between us.

Despite Ranger's undeniable physical superiority, I was the alpha in
our relationship, the leader of his pack. There had been times I wished it
was not so, that I could detach myself from the gray and white shadow
who, when he was not in pursuit of some forest creature, or a bitch in
heat over the next hill, kept me in constant sight.

But this winter, in my despair and loneliness, I was nothing but
thankful for Ranger's presence. He was my companion, and my best
friend, mutely accepting whatever I was feeling, never arguing or dis-
missing me, responding to any gesture of affection, sensing my moods
and offering whatever comfort he could. A good friend, a true friend, and
sometimes, I thought, my only friend.

There were times I found myself talking to him, confiding my
feelings and thoughts. I never truly expected him to respond, but he
commiserated in his own way, and he did his best to comfort me. Maybe
I was reading more into it than was really there, but I swear he understood me better than most people. He read my moods and empathized
as best he could.

Besides Ranger's companionship, and my conversations with Leland
and Mary, mostly I found comfort in my daily routines—bringing in
the firewood, hauling water, cooking and cleaning, reading and writing.
Books were piled on the coffee table in front of the couch, a source of
distraction and pleasure; Marx, Hegel, Marcuse, Kropotkin.

I approached them like a Talmudic scholar, arguing through the
arcana of surplus value and mutual aid; unraveling the logic of the dialec-
tic. And what for? I sometimes asked myself. What was I really learning?

I felt a burning need for clarity. I was searching for the passage, or key phrase that might hold the answer, reveal the true path to revolution. I had drafted four essays so far that winter, trying to clarify my thoughts.

But really, who cared but me? My friends seemed to act on instinct, or defer to the authority of "leadership". But I never could accept received wisdom. I always had to think things through for myself, and I truly believed that without theory to guide us, our actions were doomed to fall short.

The others were disdainful. "Revolution comes from the barrel of a gun, not the pages of a book," were the last words I'd heard from Jason. I didn't care what they said—I needed clarity before I acted, though I had to admit that, despite some important insights, I had yet to find it. In fact, I often felt more confusion than clarity emerging from my studies.

In my experience, uncertainty, ambivalence, and contradiction seemed the central elements of the human condition. How could I reconcile that with revolution? Revolution, for Jason, Jill, and the others, demanded a sense of certainty, an unwavering belief in their own rightness. For them questioning that certainty was fraught with danger—their whole project might unravel.

But the revolutionary vision I embraced was uncertain, tentative, striving to transcend the given and unlock new, unrealized potentials, an open process, not a scientific certainty, a new world, never before realized or even envisioned.

What a shithead I was. Why bother? What was the point? It had all seemed so immediate, not even like: "Change is coming soon." More like: "We're in the middle of change, in fact we're causing it, we embody it, we are it." That sense of urgency and agency, that's what I missed most of all—feeling a part of something that big, that huge, and worldwide. Chances like that didn't come around very often. How could I have let it slip away?

And all of that on top of losing Jill. Fuck! All I ever did was lose.

I should have been used to it—my mom, Jill, the commune, the movement…well, there was no point in feeling sorry for myself. It didn't help.

I WALKED OVER TO Leland and Mary's that morning. The sun was bright, and despite the fact that six inches of snow had fallen the night before, the day hinted at spring, even though it was late February. It was time to start cleaning up the sugarbush to get ready for maple season. I had promised Leland I'd help. I was looking forward to it—I always learned something when I hung out with Leland.

Ranger ran ahead, and when he reached the end of the drive, he rolled in the snow, buried his muzzle in a drift, then stretched out and lay on top of it, soaking up the sun that had already burned through the morning cloud cover and begun to warm up the day. His nose twitched as he caught my scent walking down the path towards him.

He lifted his muzzle from the snow, ears at full attention at the sound of a truck laboring up the hill, wheels spinning in the steep spots. I glanced downhill and saw a red pickup moving slowly on the snow-filled lane, holding to the narrow swath carved out by the snow-plow on its pass up the hill earlier that morning. I wondered who it might be, but figured I would know soon enough, since the road ended at Leland and Mary's. I walked on, and had just entered the barn with Leland to gather what we needed for a day working in the woods when I heard a shot.

"What the fuck?" I exclaimed.

"Sounds like a gunshot to me," said Leland. "Huntin' rifle, pretty close too."

"Who'd be shooting up here? And at what?"

"Don't know for sure."

"I saw a red pickup headed up the hill when I was walking over, figured they were coming to see you."

"Red pickup? Hmm..."

"Oh shit!" I headed out the door. "Ranger!" I called as I began to run towards where I had seen him last.

I was out of breath by the time I reached him. Ranger was lying on the snowdrift, which had been turned crimson by the blood still oozing out of a massive gash in his shoulder. As I drew closer, I could hear him whimpering.

"Ranger! Oh fuck! Ranger!" I fell on my knees in the snow next to him, just barely holding back my tears. The dog's tail gave a feeble wag. "Hold on boy, hold on!" I pleaded.

Leland joined me beside him. He used his red handkerchief to wipe away the blood and get a better look at the wound. The dog gave a start.

"Well, he's still alive," said Leland. "Don't look all that bad, really. Put some pressure on it here." He paced the handkerchief over the wound, and pressed down on it. The bleeding slowed.

"I'll go get the truck, you just keep the pressure on it. We'll get the vet to stitch him up, and he'll be good as new."

I felt my panic begin to subside. "You really think so?"

"Betcha dollars to donuts," said Leland. "You'll see, rugged animal like him. What kind of dirty bastard would do something like this to a helpless creature?"

"Must have been whoever was in the red pickup," I said.

"Mac's got a red pickup," offered Leland. "Wouldn't put it past him."

I put pressure on the shoulder while Leland went for his ancient truck. It took both of us to pick up Ranger and place him on the bench seat between us. I got in the cab, put his head onto my lap, and resumed pressure on the gash while Leland ground through the gears and headed down the hill to the highway.

I sat there, and exchanged Leland's handkerchief for a frayed white towel that had been on the seat. It turned a deep red as it soaked up the blood that continued to seep from Ranger's shoulder.

Leland drove fast, sliding the truck around corners on the snow-covered road as he hurried toward St. Johnsbury and the nearest vet. The dog lay there, half on the seat, half on my lap, and whimpered every time we hit a bump.

"How's he doin'?" Leland asked.

"Okay, I guess. Seems like the bleeding's slowing down."

"That's a good sign. Keep the pressure on till it stops."

My thoughts were racing as we drove on in silence. Fuck! Why didn't I chain him up? It was my fault. That bastard Mac.

"Come on Ranger, hang in there!" I muttered. At the sound of his name the dog's tail gave a weak wag, and I took some solace in that. We hit a frost heave, and he whimpered again.

"Good boy! It's okay; we'll be there soon. They'll take care of you. It's gonna be alright." I wasn't sure if I was reassuring Ranger or myself.

"He's a tough one, he'll be just fine," said Leland. "You'll be amazed how fast he recovers once they get him stitched up. Why I had a dog once, little beagle, got tore up by a fisher cat. I figured she was a goner. Well, three days after the doc fixed her up, she was up and around and by the end of the week she was runnin' in the woods again. Wait and see, I'll bet you a nickel."

"Thanks Leland, thanks for everything."

"Jeezum, I can't believe it. What's wrong with that fella? I mean who does something like that? I knew he was low-down, but I guess I didn't know how low."

We had hit a stretch of the highway by then where the plow had already been by, opening a relatively snow-free lane for travel. Leland quickened the pace, and soon we were on the outskirts of St. J.

"Doc Thurston'll know what to do," said Leland. "He's been the vet 'round here more than thirty years. Used to be he came 'round to the farms, help birth the calves and foals, but now he mostly stays at the office, and it's more dogs and cats."

We pulled off in front of an old farmhouse on the side of the highway. Leland came around to my side of the cab and together we lifted Ranger as gently as we could and carried the bleeding animal into the vet's waiting room.

The room, originally the parlor, was occupied by an older woman holding a cat on her lap, which hissed when we entered, and an old man with a small, long-haired dog of indeterminate origin on a leash. The receptionist, a skinny teenager seated behind a desk, took one look at Ranger. "Doc!" she called into a hallway where a blue door opened. "We've got an emergency!"

Fifteen minutes later, I stood next to Doc Thurston, a small man well up into his sixties, at his stainless steel operating table as he put the last stitches into Ranger's shoulder. The room smelled of rubbing alcohol.

"He should be alright," said Doc. "Good thing you stopped the bleeding. He'll come out of the anesthesia in a couple of hours. Try to keep him quiet for a few days, change the dressing, put that ointment on it as needed, and keep it dry. Keep that cone on his head so he doesn't worry the stitches."

"Okay Doc, thanks, really, thanks a lot."

Leland and I carried the unconscious dog out to the pickup and laid him on the seat. It was noon by the time we headed towards home. I sat silently in the cab, brooding over this latest disaster.

Leland drove a few miles before he broke through my funk. "Well,

I guess he's gonna be alright now, just like I told you. Doc's a miracle worker, see what I mean? Ranger's gonna be just fine."

"Thanks Leland, I owe you big time."

"Oh, nonsense. Got to admit, I got some affection for the big fella myself, so don't you worry about it. Anyway, I'm glad he's okay." He reached over and patted Ranger on the rump.

The whole ride home I kept replaying images of the big dog lying on a pile of snow stained red by his blood.

We turned off the highway and headed up our hill, the truck occasionally working to find traction. Ranger was beginning to stir and he gave a weak thump of his tail.

Leland helped me carry Ranger out of the truck and gently place him on the toboggan I brought from the house. He was slowly regaining consciousness. His legs hung over, dragging in the snow as I picked up the rope and pulled him down the path towards home.

"You come get me if you need help," said Leland as he walked back to his pickup.

Ranger started whimpering in anticipation as we approached the house. When I stopped at the door, he struggled to get up from the sled; unsteady, tentative, but clearly coming back to life.

"Take it easy, boy." I said. I was amazed when he regained his feet and limped up the steps to the porch. I opened the door, and we went inside.

THE NEXT MORNING, I woke early and got out of bed. I heard Ranger's tail thumping on the kitchen floor, where I had made a bed for him using an old blanket. I walked downstairs to care for him.

"Ranger? How's my good boy?" His tail sped up when I spoke.

I squatted down beside him. Doc Thurston had given me a cone to fit over Ranger's head so he couldn't get to the gash in his shoulder; he looked vaguely comical lying there. I pulled back the dressing on his shoulder, and it revealed a raw wound held together by stitches that I cleaned carefully with the rubbing alcohol the vet had given me. Ranger shuddered, but lay there patiently while I finished and applied a fresh bandage. He swallowed one of the antibiotic pills in a piece of cheese in one gulp. I laid a bowl of dog food next to him, but he showed little interest.

I boiled water on the stovetop to made myself a cup of tea. The night before, I had decided to go downtown and see if I could find out anything about the shooting. Though I was positive it was Mac, I couldn't prove it, and saw nothing to gain by accusing him until I could.

I pulled on my coat and laced up my boots. Ranger got up and hobbled to the door to try to join me. I marveled at his resilience and was thrilled to see him up, but I sent him back to his bed and told him he had to stay.

The sun warmed me as I walked down the hill, and I found myself thinking about Jill. Where was she, and what kind of trouble was she in? The drama around Ranger had been a distraction, but not for long. She had crept into my consciousness again.

A truck came slithering towards me down the hill, and when it pulled up next to me, Leland opened the door.

"Hop in," he said, and I climbed into the cab. "Where you headed?"

"Just down to the store," I replied.

"How's Ranger this mornin'?" he asked.

"Unbelievable, he's already up and around."

"Told you he was a rugged one." Leland hesitated. "Hope you're not goin' down there to take it up with Mac."

"I thought I might see if I could find anything out," I replied. "I don't really have any proof it was him."

"No, you don't. Not really my business, but if I was you, I'd just let it lie. He'd just as soon shoot you as the dog. Better to steer clear of him."

"But he can't just…"

"You said you got no proof," Leland interrupted. "And he can 'just'— he always has. Bully, ever since he was a little kid. Oh, he's his father's son alright. Nasty, that one, let me tell you."

"I just thought I'd see if I could find anything out. I'm not going to confront him without proof."

"Now that's a relief. Saw you headed downstreet, and thought maybe you were gonna do somethin' foolish."

"Thanks for your concern, but I'm not sure what I can do anyway, even if I have proof. Maybe talk to the cops about it…"

"Better not to cross him 'less you're ready to see it through."

The truck had reached the state highway and Leland turned into the store's small parking lot. We got out. "Let me do the talkin'," said Leland.

I got a quart of milk and joined Leland at the counter, where he was waiting to pay for a box of matches and some dishwashing soap. Mac gave an annoyed look and put down the gun magazine he had been thumbing through.

He came to the cash register. "Dollar twenty-nine," he sneered.

Leland handed him a dollar bill, a quarter, and a nickel. "Saw you up on the hill yesterday," said Leland. Mac raised an eyebrow.

"Somebody shot my neighbor's dog."

"You mean the one I saw runnin' deer couple nights ago?" Mac glared at Leland. "So?"

"Kind of fond of that dog myself. Nasty business, whoever did that. State Police, generally they frown on that sort of thing."

"What's your point?" Mac growled. "You suggestin' I had somethin' to do with it?"

"Seems strange, you bein' up there and all."

"Who says I was?"

"Well, I saw a red truck," said Leland.

"Mind your own business, old man." Mac leaned over the counter and brought his face close to Leland. "Don't go stickin' your nose where it don't belong, or it might get cut off."

"You threatening me?" asked Leland.

"Can't say it no plainer than that, and I ain't gonna say it again." He stared hard and pushed a penny across the counter. "Take your change."

"Dog's still alive," said Leland. "Guess whoever it was is a lousy shot." Leland pocketed the penny.

I paid for my milk with exact change, and we left the store with Mac glowering at us.

"Well, he pretty much admitted it, and he got a little touchy about it," Leland said when we were back in the truck. "But I guess that don't prove nothin'."

"No, I guess it doesn't." I replied.

We rode along in silence, but as we approached home Leland asked if I was ready to go to work in the sugarbush, and I told him I would meet him after I had a chance to check on Ranger.

I gave the dog fresh water, picked the chainsaw up off of the porch and walked out to the maple grove. Leland and I spent the rest of the morning trimming dead branches and clearing brush. Another few days of work and we would be in shape to drill in the taps and start hanging buckets. We also needed to go over to the local sawmill to pick up the bark covered slabs that Leland's friend Tinker had been saving for him to burn in the sugarhouse.

"Got about a thousand firkins for us to clean up and get ready to go," Leland told me. "*Farmers' Almanac* says it should be a good year for sugarin'. Bet we get our first run right around Town Meetin' Day. I can't wait to start to boil."

While we were working in the maple orchard, washing buckets, and cleaning up the sugarhouse, Ranger continued to recover at an amazing rate. He spent the first couple of days hobbling around the house, but within a week he was out in the woods, and after another week or so the stitches had dissolved and he seemed almost good as new. Once the hair on his shoulder grew back there would be no sign of a wound.

I kept a closer eye on him, calling him to me frequently when we were out in the woods together, making sure he didn't stray too far from home. I tried not to think too much about him getting shot.

Town Meeting was about a week away and we were all set—buckets mostly hung, arch and pans ready to boil. The only thing lacking was wood to feed the fire. That morning Leland drove us down to the village. We turned onto Back Street, crossed the old iron bridge below the dam, and there, on the river, sat Tinker's Mill. The sawmill was housed in a low shed painted barn-red with a rusting corrugated metal roof. The huge saw blade, the planer, and the joiner were all run by belts powered off of a central shaft run by the waterwheel that sat below the dam, where a narrow race carried a steady stream of river water.

Tinker made most of his living sawing thin sheets of cedar that were used to make the round wooden boxes that held the forty-pound wheels of white cheddar produced at the creamery one town over. He also did some custom work, and last year he had sawed out some spruce logs for us.

"Hi fellas!" he greeted us. "Come to pick up them slabs? Mostly well-seasoned by now, ought to burn pretty hot. I can give you a hand loadin' 'em. Not much else goin' on here right now." I looked at the idle equipment.

"They're gonna start usin' cardboard boxes to ship the cheese, that and lots more plastic wrap, stuff like that. Oh well," he lamented. "Nothin' good lasts forever."

There was a huge pile of slabs sitting outside the mill next to a mound of sawdust. The three of us worked steadily loading the pickup until its springs sagged. Leland drove it home and he and I piled the slabs beside the sugarhouse and went back for another load. We worked like that all morning until we had transferred a good part of Tinker's scrap pile, and Leland thought we had enough fuel to see us through sugaring.

WE HAVE A TARGET! *Mark came up with the idea, and I think it's brilliant. An army recruiting center—but not just any recruiting center, the one in Times Square, the crossroads of the world. Talk about high visibility! There is no way they can ignore this. We'll stick it to them in the belly of the beast.*

It's perfect—high impact, a symbol of the fucking war if there ever was one. We'll put a monkey wrench in the war machine too. And we should be able to get in and out without attracting too much attention. Plus, with all the subways right there, getaway should be easy, especially if we plant it at rush hour. We'll just disappear into the crowd.

There's lots of details we still need to figure out, but the plan is pretty clear. Mark will build it, set the timer for late at night when nobody's there, I'll deliver it and plant it. I'll take the train and meet Mark at the house. He came through with a bundle of cash the other day from some deal he cooked up with his buddy Bill, so we won't have to worry about money for a while, and we can set up shop somewhere else and plan another action.

I've never been so excited about anything in my whole life, in fact it feels like my life is really starting now! Yes, I'm nervous, but Mark knows what he's doing and I am so ready for this. All the months of waiting, planning, getting myself psyched up. It's finally happening. I can't believe it. I went out and bought a couple of steaks and a bottle of wine. We're going to celebrate. If I had any doubts at all, they're gone now.

No more protests, no more petitions, no more sit-ins or civil disobedience— this is war; we're really bringing the war home. We're going to bring the paper tiger to its knees, show the world that the emperor has no clothes. And after we show the way, the masses will follow.

It's gonna take a while to work out the details. Mark says we need intel, we need to put together a schedule, a detailed plan, get the makings of the bomb together, all that.

I need to write a communiqué that we'll send to the papers that makes clear what we're about: a declaration of war. They won't be able to ignore us now. This is for real, no more fucking around. I wish David and the others were here, but they just don't get it, at least not yet. Maybe after they see our action they'll come around. I don't know. I hope so, because like Mark says, you're either with us or against us.

It seemed strange to go to Town Meeting without the whole crew, but I caught a ride down with Leland and Mary. Leland took his place at the select board's table, and Mary and I sat together as the town worked through its business—electing town officers, passing budgets, reports from town committees, talking about the school. We ended about an hour after lunch. With no controversial items on the agenda, things moved quickly.

"Well that was pretty uneventful," I commented on the ride home.

"Not much to debate this year," said Mary. "Calm. I like it like that."

The days were noticeably longer, and the temperature was rising.

"Ought to be ideal sugaring comin' up," said Leland. "'Expect we'll get our first run toward the end of the week, weatherman to be believed. We'd best be gettin' the rest of our buckets hung." He looked over at me.

"Just say the word," I replied. "I'm ready."

"Got your seeds started?" asked Mary.

"Not yet. I'm not sure how big a garden to plan, I don't know who'll be around this summer."

"Heard anything from Jill?" Mary sounded hopeful.

"Not a word, I don't even know where she is. I haven't talked to her since November, when I went down to the city."

"Sure hope she's okay," said Mary. "I worry about her. Known her since she was a little girl, and I must admit I've got a soft spot for her."

"Mary, maybe David don't want to talk about her," Leland admonished.

"No, it's okay," I said. "I wish I knew where she was and I wish I could help her. I miss her like crazy, and I'm worried about her too. The FBI was asking about her. I don't know why, but I can imagine, and it scares me."

There was a moment of awkward silence, and I thought I had probably told them more than they wanted to know, but then Mary spoke again.

"Don't worry, David, she's smart, and she's tough, always was real high-spirited. I'm sure she's all right. Probably be back here soon. Home in time to plant a garden this summer."

"Thanks, Mary. Nice thought, but I doubt it. I think she's gone for good, and someplace you can't get home from so easily. We'll see."

The next morning, I heard Leland's tractor churning up the drive towards the sugarbush and I went out to meet him, followed by Ranger, who showed no sign of his recent injury. I hopped on the back of the sledge, which was loaded up with the wooden firkins, stacked one inside the other, that we would be hanging from the spouts in the maples. He stopped in the midst of the towering trees, and we both strapped on the snowshoes he had brought, and each took a stack of buckets, a drill, a hammer, and a firkin full of metal spouts. We began to hang them.

Two days later things warmed up, and by mid-afternoon the sap had started to drip steadily, making a distinct plop each time a drop fell. Soon the maple orchard reverberated with the steady sound coming from a thousand buckets.

Leland was right, it was perfect sugaring weather, freezing nights, and warm sunny days that soon had the sap flowing, and us busy emptying our firkins into the wooden tub on the back of the sledge. We emptied the tub into a galvanized holding tank that sat on the slope above the sugarhouse.

Three days later the weather grew cold again, and the sap stopped running, but we had plenty in the holding tank by then. It was time to fire up the arch and start boiling down.

We filled the stainless steel evaporator pan with sap from the tank, and fed the fire with Tinker's slab wood. As the sap boiled, Leland opened the vent at the top of the sugarhouse, and steam began to billow out, forming a cloud of sweet vapor that hung over us in the still air. Leland was smiling and humming an unrecognizable tune as he danced around the boiling pan of sap.

MARK AND I TOOK the subway into town today and went into the Howard Johnson's across from the recruiting center in Times Square. We sat at a booth with a window that had a good view, ordered lunch and stayed there for a couple of hours watching people come and go. We had finished our third cup of coffee and the waitress was getting annoyed when we finally got up to go.

I had cut Mark's hair for him the night before, and I was wearing my red wig. After a couple of hours gathering intel, we decided to go in separately and scope things out up close and personal. When I walked in Mark was talking with the army recruiter. I looked things over.

It was an odd little one-story building, almost like a trailer or something, set in a triangle between Broadway and Seventh Avenue. There were big plate glass windows full of recruiting posters that looked out onto the crowd. Inside there were desks and a sort of reception areas with chairs. Each service had its own desk and there were racks full of brochures advertising the Army, Air Force, Navy, and Marines. Men in uniform sat behind each desk.

I pretended to look at the brochures and strolled around the room picking up literature. The layout was really simple. After I had a good feel for the place, I asked if they had a bathroom.

"Right over there, miss," the marine recruiter said with a smile. He pointed me toward the southeast corner of the building.

I went into the bathroom and checked things out. There was a sink with a mirror over it, and a toilet. No cabinets or drawers. Nowhere obvious to leave a bomb. Then I looked at the ceiling. It was one of those dropped types, with white tiles suspended by thin strips of metal. When I stood on the toilet seat and poked at one of the tiles it came free. I stuck my hand up into the opening and felt around. There was plenty of room in the space above the tiles, and it looked to me like a perfect place to leave it.

I flushed the toilet, walked back out, then left the building and waited for Mark on the corner. He came by a few minutes later and we went into McDonalds to drink more coffee.

We killed time all afternoon, browsing in pinball arcades and porn shops, until finally, at six o'clock, the guys in uniform filed out, and locked the door. They left the lights on, but I counted that all four of them left. That was the last thing we figured we needed to know about the setup, and we didn't think we'd attracted any attention. So we took a train, and then a bus back to our apartment in Queens.

"I've just got to put a few finishing touches on it, then attach the *detonator. It should be ready tomorrow. I figure we go Friday. Set it, mail out the communiqués, and sit back and watch the fireworks." Mark was amped up—I'd never seen him so excited.*

TO PIG AMERIKKKA,

TONIGHT WE HAVE ATTACKED YOUR RECRUITING CENTER IN TIMES SQUARE. THIS IS THE FIRST SALVO OF MANY IN THE COMING REVOLUTION. YOU HAVE KILLED HUNDREDS OF THOUSANDS OF VIETNAMESE, MURDERED BLACK AND BROWN PEOPLE WITH IMPUNITY, AND OPPRESSED THE NATIONS OF THE THIRD WORLD FOR TOO LONG. THOSE DAYS ARE ENDING. WE ARE DECLARING WAR ON THE EMPIRE!

WE, THE YOUTH AND WHITE WORKING CLASS, ARE STANDING IN SOLIDARITY WITH YOUR VICTIMS. WE WILL NO LONGER ALLOW YOUR CRIMES TO GO UNPUNISHED, AND YOU WILL PAY A HIGH PRICE. THE BUILDING WE ATTACKED TONIGHT IS A SYMBOL OF YOUR POWER, AND OF YOUR VULNERABILITY. WE STAND OPPOSED TO YOUR CRIMES, AND ARE COMMITTED TO A STRUGGLE TO THE END. YOU ARE A HELPLESS, PITIFUL GIANT AND WE, IN SOLIDARITY WITH COMMUNITIES OF COLOR HERE AT HOME, AND PEOPLE THROUGHOUT THE WORLD, WILL BRING YOU TO YOUR KNEES.

DIG IT! YOUR DAYS ARE NUMBERED, KIDS OF ALL BACKGROUNDS—HIPPIES, ANTI-WAR ACTIVISTS, WORKERS, AND STUDENTS ARE HIP TO YOUR BULLSHIT. WE WILL TAKE TO THE STREET IN THE MILLIONS. OUR BLACK BROTHERS AND SISTERS NO LONGER FIGHT ALONE. THIS IS OUR FIRST ACT OF WAR—OTHERS WILL FOLLOW.

THE PEOPLE UNITED WILL NEVER BE DEFEATED! BE AFRAID, BE VERY AFRAID, BECAUSE WE LIVE AMONG YOU. WE ARE EVERYWHERE, AND WE WILL NOT STOP UNTIL YOU ARE CRUSHED BY OUR RIGHTEOUS ANGER.

WITHIN THE NEXT MONTH WE WILL STRIKE AT ANOTHER TARGET THAT PERPETUATES THE INJUSTICE WE OPPOSE. YOU WILL BE HEARING FROM US AGAIN, SOON!

FROM THE REVOLUTIONARY UNDERGROUND.

That says it all! We'll send it off to all the newspapers, TV stations, and radio outlets after we set the bomb. Mark is going to build it so it goes off around three a.m., while nobody's in the building. I'm nervous, sure, but mostly excited. Finally, finally we're fighting back! Those motherfuckers are going to have to listen now, and the ones on the fence will have to pick sides. We're upping the ante for the whole anti-war movement, and I'm betting they'll come on board. People are pissed, they can see the difference between right and wrong. They just need a vanguard to show them the way. And that's us.

Spring 1970

WE WORKED ALL MORNING carrying the sap buckets to the sledge and emptying them into the big wooden tub.

"Them firkins are heavy when they're full," said Leland after a few hours, and it was true. My arms and shoulders were aching by the time we stopped for lunch. I sat on the sledge eating a peanut butter sandwich I had packed and sipping tea from a thermos.

"I guess we got enough to start boiling down again." Leland sounded eager. "I like the whole of sugar makin', but I think my favorite part is seein' it froth up and boil away till all of a sudden it thickens up and turns to syrup. Always seems like magic to me, but it's just chemistry, or somethin'. Anyway, that sweet golden syrup, that's what it's all about. Been makin' syrup for six generations up on this hill. They learned how from the Abenaki, back in the olden times. Some of these trees been producing sap for over two hundred years."

I looked around the grove of maples with new appreciation, especially for the huge trees that dotted the forest, dominating their brethren by their height and girth. I thought about Leland's ancestors laboring in this same sugarbush, probably using the same firkins and the same sledge, though back then it was undoubtedly pulled by draft horses or oxen, not the tractor.

Ranger had been circling around us all morning, sniffing the air, tasting the coming of spring. He seemed as strong and fit as ever.

After lunch we hauled the sledge back to the sugarhouse and fired up the evaporator. I fed the lengths of slab wood into the cast iron arch while Leland watched the sap boil down. The holding tank was full when we started.

"Hope you're ready for a long night," said Leland. "This load'll keep us here for a while. Got some decent runs this season, and it's likely gonna be a busy few weeks. Springs comin' on good and fast now. We'll see, but I got a feelin' this is gonna be a good year for sugarin'."

We drew down an evaporator full of syrup, and around mid-afternoon, Mary started to fill the glass bottles with pints, quarts, half-gallons and gallons of the golden liquid.

"LOOK LIKE A SECRETARY *or something, You wanna blend in." He crushed out his cigarette on top of the radiator.*

"I'm nervous," I said, while I finished putting on my eyeliner.

"Don't worry, nobody's gonna notice you. You're just another worker drone running errands on her lunch hour. Just act normal. Leave the package in the bathroom, like we talked about."

"How big is it?" I asked.

"It'll fit in your purse just fine, forget about it, nobody will suspect anything."

"No, I mean how big will the explosion be?"

"Big enough, but don't even think about it. It won't explode till tonight, when there's nobody there. Don't be uptight, I know what I'm doin'. Just leave it in the ceiling and get out of there. Stay calm, if you look nervous you'll just draw attention to yourself. Trust me, this is a piece of cake, nothing to worry about. Like I said, I've got the details all worked out, all you have to do is hold up your end. It's just a bus ride, an hour on the subway and a short walk, then you're done. Don't freak out on me now. I'm counting on you."

"I'm not freaking out, I'm just a little nervous." I turned away from the mirror and reached for the brown wig that lay on the bed. "Are you nervous too?" I asked.

"Fuck no! Not nervous, just excited."

I believed him. Even though we'd been together over three months, I realized I knew next to nothing about his life—just the bare outlines really. I knew he was an orphan, he'd been in 'Nam, Special Forces, he was into guns and explosives, and he was a revolutionary. But that was about it. Not that I needed to know more, but I wondered. What had really changed his mind about the war? What had he done over there? He dropped hints, but he never really said. And this "need to know" shit. I suppose he's right on a certain level. You couldn't be too careful with the stuff we're getting into. But it still felt like he didn't fully trust me. I wish he'd let me in more. He's enigmatic to point of being downright mysterious.

I put on the wig and looked in the mirror, then turned toward him. "Well?" I said, waiting for his approval.

"Yeah, you look good. Like a real little secretary."

I took the paper-wrapped parcel from the kitchen counter and put it in my bag.

"Wish me luck!" I said.

"Yeah, good luck, babe. See you later."

I put on my peacoat, slung the bag over my shoulder and headed out the door. I walked two blocks to the bus stop and waited.

IT HAD SNOWED THE night before, about six inches of heavy, wet stuff that clung to the branches of the trees, turning the sugarbush into a white cathedral. I wore snowshoes as I trekked from tree to tree, emptying buckets. As the day warmed under a bright sun, rising higher in the sky every day, the sap ran more rapidly. We had already made about eighty gallons of syrup; the days had been busy and the nights had been long. Ranger powered through the fresh snow around us, rooting for field mice and whatever else he could find.

I had taken time early that morning to start some seeds, pressing them into flats that were arrayed on the sills of the south-facing windows of the farmhouse. I guess I was being optimistic, but I planned on a garden that could feed a dozen people. I had no way of knowing who might return, or find their way north for the summer, but, for my own peace of mind, I had to hope for the best. It was hard to imagine being all alone once the winter broke.

Despite the fresh snow, I was now tuned-in enough to the rhythm of our hill to detect hints of spring—noticeably longer days, temperatures above freezing, Ranger's growing restlessness. And I even thought I saw buds beginning to swell on the willows down by the creek.

I was glad to be busy—it helped keep me from obsessing about Jill. I had heard nothing further from the FBI, and figured that their threat to force my testimony before a grand jury was a bluff, and that was a relief. But I still worried about Jill, and what she was doing.

I'd finally heard from her, sort of, a few days before. I had gone to the post office and emptied our PO Box. The usual junk mail—but there was also a large manila envelope addressed to me. I immediately recognized Jill's handwriting, and eagerly tore it open. It contained a pamphlet entitled *On the Need for Revolutionary Warfare: Notes from the Underground.* Written on the front was a short note that read: "Thought you should see this." There was no return address, though the envelope had a New York City postmark, from the main post office near Penn Station. It was signed with a simple "J".

I thumbed through it—the usual rhetoric, what I had come to expect. I searched in vain for a secret message, some additional communication from her, but there was nothing.

THE LIGHT TURNED GREEN *and I stepped off the curb. I crossed the street and walked up to the glass-fronted office, the belly of the beast, I thought. I took* a deep breath and opened the door. Unlike the last time I had been there, the place was relatively empty.

A recruiter came out from behind his desk. "Can I help you with anything, miss?" He was an army sergeant, his uniformed chest full of ribbons and medals.

"Yes," I tried to sound natural, but I knew an edge of anxiety shaded my voice. "My little brother is interested in enlisting. He asked me to pick up some information."

"How old is he?" The sergeant stood in front of me, smiling.

"He just turned eighteen, and he figures he's gonna get drafted anyway, so why not enlist? Get more choices, training, or whatever. Right?"

"He sounds like a very smart young man. I'd love to talk to him about his options in the army. Can I get some contact information for him?" He took a pen from his top pocket.

"Oh," I had a moment of panic. "I don't think he's ready for that. He just wanted me to get some brochures for him. Besides, he wants to join the marines." I was sweating.

"Well, I can give you a brochure about the marines, but I really think he'd be better off in the army. More options, more choices. Maybe he could qualify for officer training. You should encourage him to contact me so we can talk." He shuffled through a rack of literature.

"Here you go, this one is about the marines, but I'm giving you some army material too. He should look it over and come in and see me. Depending on his background, I might be able to get him a nice enlistment bonus.

"You think he's interested in Special Forces? A lot of young guys are really gung-ho about the marines, but they don't realize that all the toughest units are army—Special Forces, Rangers, Green Berets, you know? I'm giving you my card too. Have him call me."

"Okay, I'll do that," I could hardly get the words out, I was practically shaking, and sure it was showing. "Um, do you have a bathroom I can use?"

"Sure, young lady, right over there." He pointed to the far end of the building.

"Thanks," I said, and walked to the bathroom. I went in, closed the door and then locked it. The room was small, and smelled of urine, partially masked by a pine tree shaped deodorizer that hung from a hook in the stall.

I stood there, trying to slow my breathing and calm my heart. I looked in the mirror, and it took me a second to recognize myself. I straightened my brown wig, and then reached into my shoulder bag and took out the paper-wrapped parcel. I stood on the toilet seat and pushed out the same ceiling tile I had a few days before, reached in and found a good place to set the bomb, then replaced the tile, got down and flushed the toilet. I washed my hands, took one last look in the mirror and left the bathroom.

As I walked past the desks towards the exit the army sergeant called after me. "Make sure he gets in touch. You have my card. I can help him make the right decision. Don't forget, have him phone me to set up an appointment."

RANGER SNIFFED THE AIR and ran off into the woods. I was back in the sugarbush with Leland emptying firkins into the transport tank.

"Sap's runnin'. One of the best years for sugarin' I ever seen. We'll be boilin' down tonight!" Leland's eyes were dancing. "Oh Mr. Man, we'll make some syrup, that's for sure."

Despite my anxiety over Jill, his enthusiasm was infectious, and I found myself sharing his excitement. Even though he had been doing this his whole life, he still acted like a kid at Christmas every time we drew off a fresh batch of syrup. The sweet golden harvest, product of our work and sweat, was like an elixir to Leland—restorative, giving him energy, a balm to his aches and pains, and giving me insight into what he must have been like in his youth. The years seemed to drop away, his movements were quick, his face illuminated by a smile, and an edge of excitement crept into his voice. The usually laconic Leland was almost quivering in anticipation at the night of sugar-making to come.

He was fired up, and despite my aching muscles I quickened my pace as well. We were close to topping off the transport tank, which meant about five hundred gallons of sap, which should translate into about twelve and half gallons of syrup. Not a bad day's work, considering syrup sold for around twenty dollars a gallon. I knew that Leland and Mary depended on the money they made sugaring to pay their taxes and supplement their meager Social Security checks, but it was more than potential income that had Leland excited. For him this was another direct connection to the past; his family had been making syrup for over two hundred years from this same maple orchard, if not the same trees. We were using tanks and buckets his great-grandfather had used, and the basic technique for boiling down hadn't changed since Abenaki times. I felt like I was taking part in an age-old ritual; bringing the sweetness promised by the coming spring to fruition; reaffirming that winter really was relinquishing its grip.

Ranger returned to check on our progress, and after I emptied one last firkin into the wooden tank on the back of the sledge, Leland started the John Deere and headed toward the sugarhouse. It was late afternoon, and the sun was obliterated by a menacing bank of clouds as we emerged from the woods into the snow-filled field. More snow started to fall, and Leland surveyed the sky. "Looks like we might be in for something," he declared.

"Franks and beans for supper," Leland shouted over the popping of the diesel. "Best eat something now. Won't be no time once we start to boil. Got to keep an eagle eye on that evaporator. Goes pretty quick, and if it burns in there, awful hard to get that pan clean again."

"Oh, Mr. Man, I like a good hot dog, and Mary's baked beans are just the best. She makes 'em with our own syrup, so you know they're good." He was smiling at the thought.

Ranger walked along beside us as I rode on the back of the sledge, taking the opportunity to rest for a few minutes. My thoughts turned to Jill, as they usually did in moments of inactivity. I hated it, but I couldn't help it. I tended to obsess over things that troubled me, and my recent encounter with the feds combined with the stupid pamphlet that had arrived in the mail had me deeply concerned.

What kind of crazy shit was she into in the name of revolution? My imagination ran wild, and there was nothing I could do about it. I kept flashing on images of her and Mark, with his half-crazed Cheshire Cat grin and his arsenal of small arms. I remembered that day—him leering over her on the firing range—and my stomach started doing flip-flops. How had she let herself be taken in by that guy? But it was the fact that I could do nothing to help that really freaked me out. I couldn't even warn her that the FBI was looking for her.

We had parked the tractor at the sugarhouse, and were sitting at the table in Leland and Mary's trailer. I had already eaten three hot dogs and a plate of beans, but Mary insisted on passing the bowl, swimming in last year's syrup. "Have some more," she said.

"Thanks, but I'm pretty full."

"Nonsense, a growing boy like you needs his nourishment."

I took the beans and spooned more onto my plate. "Thanks, they are awful good."

We ate on in silence until all our plates were cleaned.

"I've got some of those cookies you like, David," Mary offered.

"Well, how could I say no to those?"

"Me too," said Leland.

"Now Leland, you know what the doctor said about sugar."

"Don't care, one little cookie ain't gonna hurt me."

"But, your diabetes…" cautioned Mary.

"Jeezum Crow, woman!" insisted Leland.

The plate of chocolate chips went around, and I took two. Leland took one and glared at Mary when she made a clucking sound indicating her disapproval.

"You could listen to your doctor," said Mary, unable to resist getting in the last word.

"Hmm," he offered as he finished his cookie. "Well, I guess we'd best be getting' started. Sap waits for no man."

"I'm sure it'll wait for a cup of tea," said Mary as she filled the kettle and put it on the range.

IT WASN'T WHAT I expected. I thought I would feel great, powerful, like a warrior, but it wasn't like that at all, Just the opposite, really. I felt like when I was a little kid and did something bad, and hoped I wouldn't get caught. I took a deep breath and stepped off of the curb. No one followed me, and I disappeared underground.

No more than two minutes had passed since I planted the bomb, but it felt like a lifetime. There really is no going back now. I walked through the tunnel that led to the platform for the A train and started to cry. I thought about David, and the commune, and even my parents, and how I would probably never see them again. I walked along with tears running down my face. People gave me weird looks, and must have thought I was crazy. But nobody said anything—it's New York.

I finally got myself under control. What would Mark think if he saw me like that? I had to wait ten minutes before the A to Far Rockaway arrived. Looking around the platform at the mostly Black and brown faces, I remembered why I was there. I had renounced my privilege in order to stand with the oppressed. I was in active solidarity with the Third World.

The train ride went on forever, all the way downtown, Thirty-fourth, Twenty-third, Fourteenth, West Fourth, on and on; then Brooklyn, forever, and finally coming out of the tunnel, into Queens. I sat on the edge of my seat, while the train rattled along above ground past Aqueduct, past Howard Beach, all the way to Far Rockaway. I replayed the whole scene in my head the entire way back. I saw the sergeant; went into the bathroom; remembered the feeling of the bomb in my hands when I took it out of the bag; cool, almost cold; remembered the pattern on the ceiling tiles. It was weird, kind of surreal.

I kept running it over and over in my mind while I waited at the bus stop, and it was still playing while I rode the bus to just a couple of blocks away from our place.

When I was getting ready to turn onto our block, I stopped short. Fuck! Fuck! Fuck! Holy shit! The street in front of our duplex was full of black sedans. I grabbed a lamppost. My knees felt weak and my heart started pounding. At first, I stood in the crowd that had gathered, and while I watched, Mark was led out of the front door and down the steps in handcuffs. Mark glared at Big Bill, who was standing at the bottom of the steps with two guys in blue jackets that said FBI on the back.

I was totally freaked out—didn't know what to do. It felt like I'd been punched in the stomach. I stifled the impulse to run, didn't want Bill to spot me, and ducked into the crowd. Fucking Bill! A rat! How much had Mark told him? I never trusted the guy, not for a minute. Time to go, before they spotted me. But where? I wasn't prepared. I had my Patty ID, but I only had about twenty bucks. No change of clothes, either.

Fuck! I turned and walked away, trying to stay calm and look normal. To make things worse I had to pee really bad. I went to the coffee shop across the street from the bus stop, used their bathroom, ordered a cup of coffee, and sat away from the window but still able to see out. I tried to make a plan while I waited for the bus. When I saw it coming, I went out and climbed aboard with three others. I took a seat in the back.

When we got to the Far Rockaway station, I thought about transferring to the train, but I saw cop cars parked on the street and stayed on the bus, huddling in a back seat. I guess luck was with me. I took the long bus ride all the way back into Manhattan, my mind racing the whole trip.

I replayed planting the bomb at the recruiting station—the look on the sergeant's face when he handed me the brochures, my distress on the way to the subway, how scared I was when I saw the cops, the look on Big Bill's face while he stood there. It totally freaked me out.

And what about Mark? What would they do to him? Would he tell them about the bomb? Did they already know? And finally, what the fuck was I going to do?

Then it hit me—I'd go home! Not my home, I wasn't even sure where that was anymore, but to my parents' place on Central Park West, where I grew up. At least long enough to get some money, a change of clothes, maybe take their car to get out of town. Then up to Vermont and David! David would help me. Set me up with his contacts in Canada and get me across the border. Maybe I could get him to come with me, start over again. I realized how much I missed him.

I got off the bus at Columbus Circle, and turned up the collar on my coat as I walked up Central Park West. The wind gusted and it started to rain. I picked up my pace.

I thought about my parents. Since I'd left for Vermont, I'd had next to nothing to do with them—contemptible liberals who could never understand the urgency of the revolution. Oh, they were against the war, for civil rights, Dad had even taken on a case for the Panthers, but they sat in their big apartment overlooking the park, and they never really did anything, except hold fundraisers. Well, I did something! And it would be all over the news soon enough.

I was thoroughly soaked by the time I got to the front door. When I walked under the awning, the Black doorman, Henry, smiled. He was a great buddy of mine when I was growing up. He swung open the glass door.

"Miss Jill! Why, you're wet through and through. How are you? Haven't seen you around here for quite a while."

I told him I was fine and asked him if my parents were home.

"Well, your mama came back from shopping about half an hour ago. I helped her with some bags. You want me to call up?"

I said no, I wanted to surprise her. I walked through the lobby, all high ceilings, dark wood, and old leather.

I felt my stomach sink while the elevator rose. I got off on the eleventh floor, and used my key to enter the rambling apartment that looked out over the park. "Hello!" I yelled out, then took off my soaked coat, and hung it in the closet.

"Jill?" My mom's voice rang out. "Is that you, darling? My god, it's been so long!" She walked toward me across the living room. "Oh honey, I'm so glad to see you." She hugged me. "How are you, darling? What have you been doing? You're soaked, come in. Let's get you into some dry clothes."

And that's when I really lost my shit. I had been sobbing silently when I hugged her, then she held me at arm's length and my tears came hard and fast.

"What's wrong, sweetie? What happened?

"Oh, Mom!" I bawled. "I'm in trouble, big trouble, and I need your help."

I ATE ANOTHER COOKIE and the teakettle whistled on the range top. Mary poured the hot water into a green ceramic pot filled with dried mint she had grown in her herb garden the previous summer.

"Tea?" she asked.

I nodded, and after a few minutes she poured the steamy infusion into three matching cups. We sipped in silence, savoring it. I looked out the window and noticed the snow falling harder now, having already dropped a couple of inches without any sign of tapering off.

Leland noticed my gaze. "Startin' to look like a real nor'easter. Told you it might amount to somethin'."

"What does that mean for sugaring tomorrow?"

"Well, we'll just have to wait and see what morning brings."

Mom and I were sitting at the kitchen table when my dad arrived. She had called him at his office. "Joan," he called from the foyer. "What's going on? What's the big emergency?"

He walked into the kitchen. "Jill! What an unexpected pleasure! It's been too long, honey." Then he looked at my face, still streaked with tears. "What's wrong? What happened?"

I hesitated.

"Tell him Jilly, tell him everything." Mom looked grim.

"Hey, now you're starting to scare me." He stepped back. "What the hell is going on?"

"The FBI," I choked out the words. "They're after me, Dad."

"Why? What—oh my god, you're not involved in that explosion in Times Square! It was on the radio, in the cab, on the way home—" The color drained from his ruddy face and he collapsed into a chair at the kitchen table. "Oh my god, what have you done?"

"What do you mean? It already exploded? Fuck!" I started to cry again.

"You shouldn't have come here, Jilly. They'll look for you here. You've made me and your mother accessories after the fact..."

"Gary!" Mom cut him off. "It's Jill, our daughter! We've got to help her. We'll get you the best defense money can buy. Your father will know who can handle this."

"Mom, Dad, people may have died!"

"No, Jill!" Mom turned as white as the tile on the kitchen backsplash.

"It was an accident, nobody was supposed to be there. The timer..."

"Shut up, nobody died, lots of people injured, though, dammit!" Dad rarely raised his voice, but he was shouting now. "Let me think! For god's sake, give me a minute!"

"I've got to run, Dad. I've got to get away. Help me! Please!"

"Don't worry, we'll help." Mom glared at Dad. "Won't we, Gary?"

"Of course," he hesitated. "But we've got to get you out of here. This is the first place they'll look."

"I need money, clothes, a disguise...I don't know. We never planned on this. It's not the way it was supposed to go down."

"Goddamnit! I told you, if only you'd listened."

"It was for the revolution, Dad. We made a mistake."

"You've ruined your life, Jill. All your potential..."

"I'm sorry Daddy, I'm so sorry." I was crying again.

"We really don't have time for all of this now, John. We've got to help Jill get away."

"Where, Jilly? Where will you go?"

"I don't know, I really don't know."

I WAS READING ON the couch in front of the stove when I heard a thud. Ranger, who had been asleep next me, snapped to attention at the sound and tilted his head, questioning its source.

"It's okay boy," I reassured him. "Just snow clearing from the roof."

I patted his head.

It had been snowing steadily since dinner time and if the storm continued, I doubted Leland and I would be sugaring the next morning. If it kept coming down like this all night it would take the better part of the next day for us to dig out with the tractor, and open a path into the sugarbush.

I tried to return to Marcuse, who I'd been wrestling with for the past week, but my attention wandered. I thought of Jill. I remembered what it was like when we made love. I wondered where she was tonight, and with a stab of pain, whether she and Mark shared similar moments.

Ranger sat up and licked my face, bringing me back to reality. I scratched him behind his ears and he wagged his tail, thumping it on the couch. I stared out the window at the falling snow, so thick now that it was a complete whiteout, as if the whole world had been sucked into the swirling vortex of the storm. I felt helpless, at the mercy of forces I couldn't control—the storm, Jill, history—it was as though they were all conspiring against me and I was powerless. Wait and see, that's all I could do, a victim of circumstances I couldn't influence.

The dog nuzzled me, trying to console me, or maybe push me out of the funk that was starting to overtake me. I felt like I was being buried alive, but the snow kept falling, and the memories kept coming. Why couldn't I forget her? It was over, she had made her choice, I needed to let go. But I couldn't, and Marcuse didn't offer enough to distract me.

I WAS BEHIND THE wheel of my father's big Jaguar sedan on I-95, just north of Bridgeport when the heavy rain began to freeze and mix with snow. Between the downpour and the muck being thrown up by the other traffic on the road, I could hardly see the car in front of me. When an eighteen-wheeler went past,

I was blinded till the wipers cleared the windshield.

By the time I reached Hartford the storm had changed over to a steady, heavy snow, and traffic on the interstate slowed to a crawl. I noticed cars off the road every few miles, and even the trucks had slowed down. I thought about leaving the highway and holing up in a motel until the storm died down. Mom had given me a couple of hundred bucks, all they had in the house. But when I thought about it, it seemed like a bad idea. Too risky.

Once I got past Springfield, farther north, I left the interstate and took the Mass Pike. The towns and cities gave way to long stretches of emptiness, and the traffic thinned out to the point where I was almost alone on the highway, creeping along for what seemed like hours the rest of the way to Boston. The snow was steady, and heavy, almost blinding, the whole way. Even though the drive was stressful as hell, I felt a little calmer—at least I wasn't freaking out.

I eased up to the curb behind Brian's VW in front of an old Victorian in Cambridge, half a mile from Harvard Square. I was happy to see his car, 'cause I wasn't sure he'd be home. I took a deep breath, opened the car door, and walked toward the house. Snow swirled, and the wind howled in my ears while I walked to the front porch and rang the bell for his apartment.

"Who is it?" I barely recognized Brian's voice over the tinny speaker.

"Jill," I answered. He buzzed me in and I heard a door open at the top of a narrow stairway.

"Wow, Jill!" Brian hugged me when I got into his small apartment. "Didn't expect to see you. What a surprise! Hey, you're covered with snow. Give me that wet jacket."

I took off my peacoat and handed it to him. He hung it on the back of a chair in the kitchen.

"I didn't know you were in town. How the hell are you?"

"I just got here."

"Just, as in now?"

"Uh huh."

"In this mess? You drove?"

I grimaced, and he noticed.

"What's wrong? What's going on? I thought you were with Mark, in New York."

"Something happened," I looked at the ground, not sure how to tell him.

"Well, you're better off without him. I mean..."

"No, not that. It was a political action."

"What kind of political action? What are you talking about?"

"Things are fucked up, Mark got busted, and I'm sure the pigs are looking for me by now."

"For a demonstration?" he asked.

"We set off a bomb, the timer fucked up..."

"Oh, shit! A bomb? You went all in. That's heavy, fuck. That's really heavy." Brian was pacing around the kitchen. "And you came here?"

"I didn't know where else to go. I need your help. I've got to get away, up to Canada."

"My help?"

"Yes, please!" I started crying.

"Okay, Jill, okay." he gave me a hug, and patted my back. "Of course I'll help."

I blew my nose in a paper napkin I took from the kitchen table.

"But won't they be looking for you? I mean how..." I could hear a note of fear in his voice.

"Sorry to drag you into this, Brian. I made a mess, I really do need your help, though."

"Yeah, sure, okay, but how?"

"I've got to get rid of my parents' car, and then get up to the house in Vermont."

I hardly slept at all on Brian's couch that night, and when I got up the next morning the sun was shining and beginning to melt the snow, the sixteen inches that had fallen.

A sense of impending doom had been at the back of my mind, or maybe in my stomach, ever since I'd left the apartment in Queens carrying the package in my shoulder bag. It came in waves, sometimes lapping at the edge of my consciousness and sometimes, like now, cresting and breaking big, roiling, rolling and threatening to drown me.

I'd never really felt this way before—out of my depth, completely vulnerable and so, so small.

I got out of bed and Brian handed me a cup of fresh-brewed coffee. But as I sipped it, it turned sour in my stomach, and I tasted bile as it rose in my throat.

"We've got to get out of here," I said. "They'll be looking for me. They know we're friends. Shit, I'm sorry, I didn't mean to bring heat down on you. I shouldn't have dragged you into this, I just didn't think…"

Brian cut me off. "Don't worry about it. They're not that smart. It'll take weeks for them to make the connection. You're safe here. At least for now."

"No! I've got to go. Just help me get to Vermont."

"Well, we can't go anywhere just yet. It'll take 'em hours to clear the roads. I don't even know if the interstate is open. Let's check."

He turned on a radio that sat on the kitchen counter and tuned it in to an all-news station. They spent five minutes listing local school closings, and then moved on to report on travel conditions, urging drivers to stay off the roads and let the highway crews do their work.

"In other news, police in New York City, with one arrest already made, are seeking Jillian Levy, an anti-war activist, for questioning regarding yesterday's bombing of an armed forces recruitment center in Times Square. She is believed to be affiliated with …" The radio died when I unplugged it.

"I'm going to go crazy just waiting here." I tried to stop shaking. "Can't we do something?"

I LEANED INTO THE snow scoop. Leland and I had been moving snow for half an hour. Almost thirty inches had fallen before the nor'easter had blown offshore, and it was heavy, wet snow, not the fluffy powder of mid-winter. Sugar snow, Leland called it, not because of its consistency, but because of its timing. We worked together in silence, breathing hard. A fuzzy, bright spot appeared in the sky, and Leland squinted up at it.

"Startin' to burn off, might have a sunny day after all, that'll get them firkins fillin', yep, it's the sweet season, alright."

We both looked up at the sound of the town snowplow rumbling down the road towards us. The clatter of tire chains and a plume of snow marked its passing. The cut that served as a drive to Leland's trailer, which we had dug out fifteen minutes before, disappeared, buried in the wake of the plow. The plow driver turned around in Leland's dooryard and waived to us on his way back down the hill.

"Shit!" I leaned on the handle of my scoop.

"Oh, don't pay it no mind," Leland shrugged. "Won't take but a minute to clear with the tractor."

I PACED AROUND BRIAN'S book-lined living room, glancing out the window, listening for the sound of a snowplow, anxious for the street to be cleared. We had to go! I felt trapped in the apartment, like the world was closing in around me. Questions kept popping into my mind. Where was Mark? What had they done to him and what had he told them? Why had Bill ratted us out? I'd never trusted him. Why had I listened to Mark to begin with? Why had I let myself get so involved with him? Who the fuck was he, really?

The whole thing had been his idea. He set it all up—he got the explosives, he built the bomb, he set the timer. Had he known? Had he planned it to go off with people in the building? I suddenly doubted the whole thing. What an idiot I had been to trust him. I shuddered, and felt a sudden chill.

"Are you okay?" Brian asked. "You're shivering. Here, take this," he handed me a sweater that had been draped over the back of a chair.

"I'm sorry, I'm freaking out." I put it on.

"Yeah, me too. A bomb, I still can't believe it. It just doesn't seem like your kind of a deal."

"Desperate times—desperate measures," I said. "But I didn't want anybody to get hurt. That wasn't the plan. You get it?"

"I'm not sure I do," he responded. "I mean, I understand the sentiment, but…"

"Don't start! Please. I had this conversation a million times with David, and I can't handle it right now."

"Sorry, I didn't mean to, I just don't—"

"Stop! I need to focus on getting out of here."

There was a moment of silence and then Brian said, "Vermont, huh? Makes sense, I guess. You think David's still there? I haven't heard from him since I dropped him off, right before Christmas. Jason and Suze were leaving. He was all alone. I wonder if he stuck it out."

I froze. I hadn't even considered the possibility that he wasn't there. I was counting on him. I'd hoped he'd come with me. I'd hurt him, I knew that. I felt bad about it, really bad, but it was for the revolution, he must have seen that. Did he hate me for it? I mean, he'd always been there for me. Solid as a rock. I couldn't believe that had changed. I knew him too well to doubt him now. But was he still there?

"I can get across the lake on skis even if he left," I said to Brian. A bit of false bravado. I chilled at the thought of David's not being there.

RANGER ROLLED IN THE snow, buried his muzzle in a drift, then stretched out, soaking up the sun that by mid-morning had burned through the clouds and begun to warm the day. His winter coat was shiny on his dappled gray flanks and broad white chest. His nose twitched as he caught my scent.

The snow, despite its depth, didn't trouble the big dog as he ran toward me. When he stopped he sat and lifted his head with his ears at full attention.

A few moments later I heard the sound of a truck struggling up the hill, wheels spinning on the final steep section. When I turned, I saw it was our neighbor, Caleb. He came slowly up the snow-filled lane the plow had cleared earlier that morning. Leland joined me and we waited together for him to arrive.

He stopped in front of us and rolled down his window. "Howdy, neighbor," he said. "I was just down to the post office, and I saw somethin' I thought might interest you." He passed Leland a sheet of paper.

Leland looked it over and then his arm fell to his side. "Oh my word! This is not good. Jeezum!" He looked away as he handed me the flyer.

Or rather, the poster, because that's what it was; a wanted poster, with Jill's name written in bold letters across the top. I recognized the picture. It was the mug shot they had taken when we had been arrested after the occupation of the Dean's Office back at school. I couldn't believe it.

"Oh shit!" I muttered, "Oh shit!" I felt Leland and Caleb's eyes on me. "What a mess!" I said as I turned toward them.

I WAS FINALLY IN the car. The streets of Cambridge were beginning to come back to life, shopkeepers were shoveling the sidewalks, and the students, acting like grade schoolers let out for a snow day, were staging a huge snowball fight in Harvard Square. It was good to be moving. I felt a wave of relief piloting the Jag through the slushy mess that covered the roadway. I was thinking more clearly, felt more in control.

When I looked in the rearview mirror, I saw Brian right behind me in his green VW. We wound our way through the city streets and finally entered the tunnel that took us directly to Logan.

The longterm parking lot was straight ahead, and the airport was eerily quiet, still digging out from the storm. I guess flights had been canceled until they could get the runways cleared.

I pressed the button and got a ticket for the lot as the gate opened. Brian stopped outside with the VW, idling there with steamed up windows while I eased my Dad's Jaguar in at the end of a row of snow-covered cars. I left the key in the center console.

My feet got soaked as I walked across the slushy parking lot to the waiting car. I got in next to Brian and sighed. "Next stop, Vermont."

"Yeah, I guess," Brian sounded less than enthusiastic. "I'm a little freaked out, to tell the truth."

"Me too," I offered, "I'm sorry, I really am, I just didn't know who else I could trust."

"It's cool, don't worry about it. It's for the revolution, right?"

We retraced our path back through the tunnel and over the bridge. I-93 was moving slowly; the plows were still opening up lanes, and traffic consisted mostly of eighteen-wheelers, with an occasional car bearing a ski rack mixed in. It took over an hour to get past Concord, but as we headed farther north into New Hampshire, traffic began to thin out. By the time we left the interstate, past Manchester, we were practically alone on the road.

I sat quietly next to Brian in the Bug, my mind reeling as I thought about the last few days. I wondered about Mark. How was he? Had they hurt him? What would happen to him? Then a vision of shattering glass washed *over me. Fucking Mark! Why had I trusted him? I thought about my mom, crying, with my father's arm around her shoulder as the elevator door closed. Would I ever see them again? And what could I expect in Vermont?*

When I thought about David, I had a moment of panic. Would he be glad to see me? Would he help? Of course he would—he was David, the one person I'd always been able to count on. Why had I ever left him? Would he forgive me? He'd been right all along about Mark, about everything. Why hadn't I listened to him? After all our time together, everything we'd been though, how could I have just walked away? I was overwhelmed, lost, and really, really scared. I started shivering.

"Can you turn up the heat a little?" I asked Brian.

"Actually, it's not working," he said sheepishly.

I FELT LIKE I had just had the wind knocked out of me, seeing her picture there, staring at me from the wanted poster. "I knew they wanted to talk to her, but this?" I was still having trouble believing it. "What am I supposed to do?" I had no idea, and I didn't really expect an answer from Leland or Caleb.

"Not much you can do." Leland looked at me with sympathy. "Mary's gonna be awful upset," he added. "But nothin' any of us can do, not now, not here, 'cept maybe hope for the best. Poor girl…that fella she started hangin' around with, figured him for trouble right from the start."

"It's crazy," I said. "I didn't think…" I stopped. Ranger had loped over to where we stood, sensing that something was wrong. He looked up at me, his gaze anxious. "Shit!" I said again. "Shit."

I felt like I should be rushing into action, but I was at a loss. Ranger was whimpering now, tuned in to my distress.

"Maybe we ought to take a break," offered Leland, "go up to the house, have a cup of tea or somethin'."

"Yeah, good idea," I answered. I felt woozy, like I might pass out.

Caleb said his goodbyes and got back into his truck. Leland and I walked back to the trailer, and I stumbled up the wooden steps like a sleepwalker. When we entered the little kitchen, I fell into a chair.

"Done already?" inquired Mary, in her usual cheerful manner. Then she caught sight of me. "What's wrong? What happened?"

Without a word Leland handed her the poster.

"Oh, no!" she said after glancing at it. "Those bastards! Why it's Barre all over again. Poor Jill! Girl must be terrified!"

I was in shock, my mind racing, full of possibilities, but unable to sort things out, to think clearly. It was like my worst nightmare had come true, and I was at a total loss.

I heard Mary through a fog. "Oh David, I'm so sorry. She's a good girl. Tryin' to help…and the damn government, I wouldn't put it past them to set her up. Jill! Oh no…" Mary started to cry.

"Now, Mary," Leland tried to comfort her. "No tears, that won't help. They ain't caught her. She's gonna be all right, wait and see. She's a smart one, that Jill."

Leland was right. She was still free, for now at least. That was something to be thankful for and hopeful about. But I could find little solace in the thought of her on the run. Where was she? What was she thinking? Where would she go? Hard to say, but Jill *was* smart. And she was resourceful, and tough. The feds would have a hard time catching her. I was sure of that. And at that thought my panic began to subside.

WE CROSSED THE CONNECTICUT *River into Vermont at White River Junction and headed north on Route 14, following its twists and turns, skirting the peaks of the Green Mountains and the high passes, mostly closed because of the snow. We went through picturesque towns that looked like ads for country living; Sharon, Royalton, Bethel, Randolph, Williamstown, villages neatly arrayed around a town common punctuated by white-steepled churches. We crossed covered bridges, passed farmhouses with peeling paint, and faded barns with elaborate cupolas that spoke of a different era. We stopped for gas, and cups of steaming coffee in Barre, and then headed up into the Northeast Kingdom.*

I sat shivering under a green army blanket, and felt like I was traveling through time; slipping back into another century far away from Queens and Times Square, a place where life was simpler. And as we headed north, I found myself thinking more and more about David, about how it would be seeing him again.

We were stuck behind a state plow truck when we turned onto Route 5. It was slow going, but at least we had a clear lane of travel. I let out a sigh.

"What's up?" asked Brian.

"Just thinking. I hope David doesn't have a heart attack when he sees me."

"I just hope he's there," said Brian.

"Oh, he'll be there, I know it." It was inconceivable to me that he might have abandoned the farm. I knew David, and he was nothing if not stubborn. I was counting on it. He had to be there. I could cross the lake without his help, but the thought of heading into Canada without friends, or contacts, without David, was devastating. I began shivering again.

As usual, a cup of tea with Mary and Leland made me feel better. I still felt a knot in my stomach, but I was beginning to sort out my thoughts. I had no idea where Jill was; there was nothing I could do to help. She probably didn't want to be "rescued" anyway. She had chosen her path, she was committed. In fact, she and Mark were probably celebrating.

They had struck their first blow against the empire.

She was really underground now, so deep I would probably never see her again. I just hoped she could stay there, out of sight, and out of their clutches. The thought of Jill in a prison cell seared me like a hot knife. It was hard to imagine her huge spirit confined to a cage.

I was obsessing about her as usual, but at a level of anxiety I had never experienced before, as if the knot in my stomach was a living creature, gnawing away at me from the inside.

Leland glanced out the window at the bright sun, and then turned to me. "What do you think, you feelin' up to it? I'm a little concerned them firkins maybe overflowin' less we get out there soon."

"No, I mean yes, I'm ready. Probably do me some good, get my mind off—" I choked up, couldn't say her name. "Let's go."

We went back out to the barn and finished freeing the doors. But even the shoveling didn't ease my anxiety. Leland started the tractor and pulled out. He used the bucket loader to clear the way out to the sugarbush. I rode on the sledge and ranger loped along beside us. It was mid-morning and the sun shone brilliantly in the bright blue sky, melting the snow that draped the branches of the maples, a glorious sight, but it brought me no pleasure.

Leland was right—the buckets were full. The sap was running heavy—not just dripping, but actually flowing, and some of the firkins were starting to overflow.

THE VW MADE IT up the hill, wheels spinning most of the way. We came to a stop next to a snowbank that blocked the drive to the farmhouse. Brian and I got out. It was about five and the sun was low in the sky, shining on the ranges of hills to the east with a flat light. I took a deep breath. We scrambled over the snowbank together and I saw footprints on the path.

"Signs of life!" I said.

"Great," replied Brian. "I guess Dave is still here."

We trudged through the wet snow until we reached the farmhouse porch. Out of breath, I looked at the eaves dripping with melting snow, and sighed.

"Home," I said quietly, and I realized it was; home in a way the flat in Queens had never been, home in a way my parents' place had never been. My home. I was relieved.

We walked into the mudroom and I opened the kitchen door. "David!" I called out. My voice echoed through the empty house.

I collapsed on the couch, in front of the wood stove radiating warmth.

"Wonder where he is?" Brian mused. He picked up Reason and Revolution *from the coffee table and started to thumb through it.*

"Well, wherever he is, at least he left a fire," I observed.

"Yeah," said Brian putting down the book and walking over to the stove. He lifted the lid and looked inside. "It's burning down, I'll throw in some more wood." He went out to the porch and came back with an armful of firewood.

We sat there in silence together on the couch. Brian started thumbing through Marcuse again. I was staring around the house, remembering my time there with David. On top of everything else, I was nervous to see him again. Would he forgive me?

I got up and began walking around, revisiting familiar territory. I wandered up the stairs to our old bedroom. When I looked on the dresser, it was all I could do to not freak out. I picked up the poster and took a close look.

It was me—my mug shot from the Dean's Office. Fuck! Another kick to the stomach. How had they got it out so fast? What a fuckup this whole operation had been. A disaster. But the poster meant David knew, anyway.

I went back down and showed it to Brian.

"Oh, fuck," the color drained out of him. "I bet they'll be sniffing around

here soon enough."

"I'm sorry, Brian. You should go. I shouldn't have dragged you into this. What a shitshow."

"Maybe I'll get back on the road," said Brian. "I want to head back before it gets too late."

I EMPTIED THE LAST bucket into the wooden tank mounted on the sled. The sun was sinking, but my distress hadn't abated. We had worked steadily all day, with only a short break for lunch. I'd gone back to the house, but I couldn't eat anything. My stomach still churning with worry, I'd spent the time staring at the wanted poster sitting on the dresser in what had been our bedroom.

My muscles were sore from our day's labor, and that usually brought me a kind of peace. Endorphins, or something like that, I guess. But I found no peace that afternoon. Nothing seemed to quell my anxiety, the foreboding that consumed me.

"Well, I guess we'll be boilin' down tonight," said Leland. "Yes sir, Mr. Man, we'll make some syrup! Pretty much the best run I ever seen."

"Great," I offered with all the enthusiasm I could muster, which was not much.

"Won't do any good frettin', you know. Nothin' you can do to help."

"I know. I just can't stop thinking about her."

Leland was silent for a moment. "Me neither," he said. "And I know the missus is worried too, but life goes on, you know, and she's a real smart girl. Be surprised if they ever catch up with her. Don't know if it helps, but try to keep that in mind."

We headed back to the sugar shack with the wooden tank sloshing, and me riding, standing on the sled behind the tractor with Ranger trotting along beside us.

We transferred the sap to the holding tank, using a garden hose to siphon it off. Then Leland filled the evaporator.

He started a fire, the dry slabs of softwood caught quickly, and soon a roaring fire was blazing under the evaporator.

"Let's go up the house and see what Mary's got for dinner," suggested Leland.

"Sure," I answered halfheartedly. "Though I don't have much of an appetite."

We walked over to the trailer and climbed the wooden steps. The windows were steamed over from a large pot of boiling water that sat on the stove.

"Spaghetti and meatballs," Mary announced as we entered the kitchen.

"I like a meatball!" declared Leland. "Mary makes about the best spaghetti you ever tasted, I can guarantee you that."

While we seated ourselves at the table, Mary drained the pasta and put in a large bowl. "That's my homemade tomato sauce," she said. "Canned it up right from the garden."

She served me a huge portion, and then Leland and herself as well. I stared at the steaming mound of spaghetti that filled my plate.

"Go ahead and eat," she encouraged me. "Need some cheese?" she offered me a container of grated parmesan.

"Sorry Mary, I'm just not very hungry."

"Nonsense!" she said. "Young fellow like you, after a hard day's work. You've got to eat something, David."

I forced myself to take a forkful of pasta and then cut into one of the meatballs. "Delicious" I said, and it was. But all I could manage was a few more bites. While Mary and Leland ate, I mostly pushed the spaghetti around my plate and brooded about Jill.

We didn't linger long over dinner. Leland was anxious to get back to our boiling pan of sap.

"Best head back over," he said. "That fire'll need feedin', and pretty soon it'll be time to draw down some syrup." We got up from the table. "Probably be back pretty late," he told Mary as we walked out the door.

I WAITED ALONE IN the house, wandering around like a ghost; passing from memory to memory. Every room had a story, a feeling, a snatch of a song, a familiar smell. Everything had meaning.

I threw a log into the stove, then went to wash the dishes David left in the sink and discovered there was no running water. I filled the kettle from the milk can on the counter, and put it on top of the stove. Upstairs, in our old room, I brushed my hair with his old brush, and looked in the mirror. I was a mess—red-eyed, dirty, deeply furrowed brow, with a haunted look in my eyes.

I hardly recognized myself. It was the first time I'd really looked, been confronted by my new being since I left the bomb. And I did feel new, brand new, but not in a good way. Mostly I felt less. Gone was my confidence, gone was my certainty, gone was my whole life before the bomb went off.

My hair was full of tangles, and I brushed slowly, from the bottom, to get them out. I imagined I felt the blast in my solar plexus, like I had been punched and couldn't quite catch my breath.

When would David get home? Where the hell was he anyway? He didn't have a car; barely knew how to drive a stick, though I'd tried my best to teach him in the Volvo. It was hopeless; he kept stalling it every time he let out the clutch.

He couldn't have gone too far. He lit a fire to keep the house warm, so he was definitely coming back. I lay on the bed and looked around the room, and then out the window. I saw the last of the remaining daylight shining on the next ridge. I shivered, pulled a blanket over me, and closed my eyes, suddenly exhausted. Memories faded into dreams, almost peace, and then, a blast, a shower of glass, screams, and I was wide awake, shivering under the blanket.

The kettle had boiled, and I went downstairs, made a cup of chamomile tea, then used the rest of the hot water to wash David's breakfast dishes. I listened to the empty house—floorboards creaking as I walked to the couch, logs popping in the wood stove, the wind occasionally rattling a window. I saw the manifesto I'd mailed David sitting on the coffee table and picked it up. "Revolutionary Vanguard"; "Armed Struggle": "Bring the War Home". Well, we had, we'd done it.

But now it all sounded empty. The triumphant, righteous feeling I'd anticipated had never come. Mostly I felt guilty, alone, and scared. But mostly guilty. How could I have put lives at risk? I didn't want to hurt anybody. That wasn't part of the deal. What had gone wrong? Fucking Mark! He'd convinced me, he put it all together, he built the bomb.

Dusk faded to darkness and I added more wood to the fire. I stood there for a minute, soaking up the heat. I was hungry—I hadn't eaten anything since early that morning. I checked out the fridge and found a pot of rice and beans I reheated on top of the wood stove. It filled my stomach, but didn't stop the feeling of dread that had been haunting me. I cleaned up after myself and waited for David.

LELAND AND I WORKED until almost midnight, boiling down the sap until it was a rich dark syrup, and then drawing it off to fill the gallon jugs we lined up on the shelves of the sugar house. Ranger waited patiently, lying on top of a snowdrift until we were done.

"Well, pretty good day's work, I guess," said Leland. "Thanks. Back at it again tomorrow, best rest up."

I glanced at the shelves full of syrup. "Yeah, a good day's work," I agreed, thankful for the distraction the work had offered. But now I was heading home to what would likely be a sleepless night as I wrestled with thoughts of Jill.

Ranger ran on ahead as I walked back home. The moon was high in the cloudless sky, full enough to cast shadows on the path. I saw smoke curling from the chimney, and noticed a light on in the kitchen. Funny, I didn't remember leaving on a light, but Ranger sat on the porch, waiting for me with his tail wagging wildly.

"Hey, what's going on, boy? What's got you so excited?" I walked up the steps, stomped the snow off of my boots, and stroked his fur. Then I heard the mudroom door open. I looked up, and there was Jill, backlit by the bare bulb that hung behind her.

"David!" She threw her arms around me, and squeezed tight. I was momentarily speechless. I hugged her back, hard, like if I let go, she would fall off the edge of a deep chasm. Ranger danced around us. She pulled me into the mudroom, still clinging tightly.

"Jill! Are you okay? What…"

"Shh, wait," she tightened her embrace. "I'll explain everything. It's just so good to see you!"

I HADN'T REALIZED HOW much I'd missed him until he was there. His arms felt so good around me, so right. I relaxed and felt the old feelings of comfort, familiarity, a deep understanding that I was home, a feeling of safety. I pulled him into the house, and we sat next to each other on the couch.

Ranger tried to wedge himself between us, but I couldn't let go of David.

He was my anchor, or maybe my life preserver.

"What's going on? The feds…" he tried to talk, but I leaned over and kissed him. I hugged him again, and then took a deep breath.

"I have so much to tell you. I need your help. I'm in trouble, big trouble," I said. And then my story poured out.

David furrowed his brow while he listened, and when I was done, he got up and started to pace around the room.

"We've got to get you across the border," he said. "You're not safe here. The feds have been nosing around, talking to people in town. Anybody see you arrive?"

"I don't think so," I answered.

"Good, this is gonna take a day to set up."

"Can't we just go now, tonight?"

"Go where and do what?" he said. "I've got to get our friends to meet you with a car. Tap into the support network. I've got to get down to the pay phone, make some calls. If nobody saw you, we're probably okay."

"They're looking for me," I said.

"Yeah, but it's a big country, as far as they know you're still in the city. We'll get you out tomorrow." I could see him thinking, trying to formulate a plan, think things through. Typical David. I knew I could count on him. I started to calm down.

"David," I looked at him. "I'm sorry, I'm so sorry. I know I made a mess of it. I was wrong, I…"

"Hey, don't worry about it. That's the last thing you should be thinking about now. And you're here. Let's just concentrate on getting you out of this."

There was an awkward silence, then David turned and went to the porch for another armful of firewood to feed the stove.

"Well, we should probably get some sleep. It's gonna be a big day tomorrow." He rose and walked to the stairs, looked back at me over his shoulder *and said "Goodnight."*

I watched him from the couch, and then I got up. "Wait, I'm coming with you. I mean if it's okay."

He turned, took my hand, and led me up the stairs. I pulled on a flannel nightgown that I'd left in the dresser and joined him under the covers.

"Hold me," I said, and I spooned up against him. It felt good. I sighed and felt something close to peace for the first time since the bomb exploded. That's how we fell asleep, and when the sun rose, I was still there, snuggled in the crook of his arm.

I woke up the next morning and could hardly believe it when I looked over at Jill, lying next to me. I had been fantasizing about her return all winter, aching for her, and now she was beside me again, sharing the same bed. I realized she was desperate, and it wasn't necessarily love that had brought her back. Not exactly the return I had hoped for, but at least she was here. I heard Ranger's tail thumping on the floor. The sun was barely up, a hazy blur on the horizon, trying to burn through the fog that blanketed the hills.

Jill stirred, opened her eyes, and shifted beside me. "Hey," she said, and she threw her arm over my chest.

"Hey, yourself. How'd you sleep?" I asked.

"I slept," she answered. "No bad dreams. That's something, but I could use some more. What time is it?"

"Early. Go back to sleep. I'll make some breakfast." I tried to rise, but she hugged me tight. "I should get up," I said. "Big day ahead, lots to do."

She loosened her grip. "Okay, I guess. I'll get up too."

"No, you can sleep a little more. I'll call you when the coffee's ready." I went downstairs and stirred the glowing embers, then placed kindling over the coals gradually adding larger pieces of wood until the stove was full and the fire roaring. I thought about her lying upstairs, and all the pain she had put me through.

I filled the kettle with water and put it on the stovetop. As the boiling kettle began to whistle, Jill made her way down the stairs to the kitchen. She warmed herself by the stove as I poured the steaming water into the french press. Neither of us spoke.

Jill knelt down and ruffled Ranger's fur. "How's he doing?" she asked.

I handed her a cup of coffee. "Unbelievable," I responded. "Like he'd never been shot."

"Shot?"

"Yeah, his whole shoulder was blown open. That asshole down at the store. I've got no proof, but he practically admitted it to Leland. Ranger made an incredible recovery though. He doesn't even limp. Hard to believe after all the blood, but none of it seems to bother him."

"He's tough," she said, scratching him behind the ears. "No doubt about that."

I scrambled some eggs in a frying pan on top of the stove. We both tore into them.

"It feels good to be here," said Jill.

"Well, don't get too comfortable," I responded. "You'll be leaving soon, hopefully tonight. I'll go down to the phone after breakfast and see what I can set up. Best if you just lay low till then. Don't let anybody know you're here."

"Really, not till tonight?" She sounded anxious, scared.

"Yeah, too risky in the daylight, somebody might see us. Snowmobilers, or ice fisherman on the lake. Better to wait for dark."

I got up to go, and she reached over and squeezed my hand.

"Hurry back," she said.

I pulled on my plaid wool hunting jacket and laced up my boots.

"You look like an old Vermonter," she teased.

"After this winter I feel like one," I said as I headed out the door. The day was already warming up, the sun had burned through and snow was dripping from the eaves of the house. A good day for sugaring, I thought, as I glanced up the road toward the sugarhouse. I felt a momentary pang of guilt, Leland would be counting on my help today, but I had other priorities.

I went to the trailer and knocked. Leland came out. "Ready to go?" he asked.

"Sorry, something came up," I said. "I need to take the day off."

"Need some help?"

"No, I've just got to take care of something for my dad," I lied. "Get back to it tomorrow."

"Okay," Leland said. "Thanks for letting me know."

As I walked down the road, I saw that muddy ruts were forming and rivulets of snowmelt were running down the hill in the ditches at the sides. The sun warmed me as I walked on.

I went to the small parking lot shared by the post office and the general store and crossed to the phone booth. I weighed a change purse full of dimes and quarters in my hand and hoped I had enough for the call. I pulled a folded piece of paper from my pocket, dropped a dime in the slot, and dialed a string of numbers.

An operator came on the line. "That will be three dollars and fifteen cents, please. I counted out the coins, and realized I didn't have it. I hung up, walked to the post office and dug into my pocket. I pulled out a wad of singles flattened out two and slid them across the counter.

"Change please." I waited while the postmistress counted out eight quarters. Then I turned and opened our PO box, crammed full of junk mail as usual. I threw it all away in a wastebasket that sat in front of the bulletin board.

I counted out the correct change, redialed the number, deposited the coins and then waited while the phone rang. I was just about to give up when I heard a sleepy voice on the other end. "Jed, it's David. I wondered if you could help me out...ASAP. Yeah. Tonight, eleven, same spot. All right. Merci, my friend, see you then."

Done; easy enough. I tried to hold my growing panic in check as I trudged back up the hill to share the news with Jill. Tonight, and none too soon.

The feds were already circulating wanted posters, how long before they showed up looking for her? I remembered their previous visits, and their quizzing the neighbors. Had anyone seen her arrive? I doubted it, or the FBI would have already been to the house. Still, I was scared. Night seemed like a long way away. Maybe we should cross sooner. I weighed the options as I walked home.

Calm down, I told myself. Nobody knows she's here. In a little while she'll be safe in Canada. I thought about Jimmy, the kid I had helped across that first summer, and the others we had simply driven across; no hassles, no problems whatsoever. Of course, they weren't wanted by the FBI.

I remembered the hidden room in the basement that Leland had shown us. He'd told us about the Underground Railroad, runaway slaves, their last refuge before crossing to safety.

Shit! Why was I driving myself crazy? Odds were good nothing would happen. Freaking out wouldn't help, would it? I had to calm down, be cool. I didn't want to get Jill any more worked up than she already was. She seemed on the edge of panic already, like a different person from the self-confident Jill I knew.

I WAITED FOR DAVID, sitting on the couch in front of the stove, petting Ranger, who lay beside me while I replayed the last four days in my head. Wherever my thoughts began, they always ended in a shower of glass. It was a picture I couldn't make disappear, no matter how hard I tried. I felt trapped in that moment, destined to replay it for the rest of my life. That one imagined moment, raised in high relief from a lifetime of memories.

I tried reading to get my mind off things, but the words quickly faded away, replaced by images of shattered glass and screaming people. The steady drip of snow melting off the roof was like a ticking clock. I put down the book and stared out the window. So beautiful—untouched ridges, marching on into Canada, my new home. I shuddered, and the dog shifted on the couch. I got up and threw another log onto the fire.

The sun had burnt through the last of the clouds, and the sky was blue, the light bright and piercing, leaving dust visible in the shafts of sunlight that streamed through the kitchen window. I heard footsteps on the porch and waited while David stomped the snow off his boots.

"Getting warm out there." He announced when he came in the house.

"Well, what's the deal?" I asked. I'm sure he heard the anxiety in my voice.

"Tonight, he'll be there tonight."

"Really? Tonight?" My shoulders relaxed. "Oh, Dave! Another chance for us." I got up and squeezed him tight.

"Us?" he sounded puzzled, like it was a new thought, like he had never considered that there was still an us after all that had happened.

"Of course, us. What did you think?"

"Don't know," he said. "Wasn't really thinking about us, I mean I thought about us all the time, just not this way, I mean in another context."

I looked away, averting my face, but he could see the tears beginning to form in my eyes.

"Jill," he said. "Wait, don't, I—"

"It's okay, Dave," I sniffled. "I understand."

"No, it's not that. I just need time to think about it. I mean Leland and everything…I never expected…it's all happening so fast."

"Sure, think about it." My shoulders were shaking. "We've got till tonight, right?"

He put his arm around me. I'd imagined us together—exiled to the frozen north, but together, building a new life side by side. That vision had sustained me, had made the whole thing seem possible, but now…I was flooded with dread at the thought of going on without him. Was it the idea of losing David, or the fear of being alone? Probably a little of both, but whatever it was I was terrified, blubbering like a baby.

"Hey, calm down," he said. "I just, I've got to think. This is brand new for me, I mean, Canada." He pulled a blue handkerchief from his pocket and handed it to me.

I wiped my eyes and blew my nose. "It was stupid of me to think, you know, after all the shit I put you through…"

"No! It's not like that, I don't care, none of that matters. I still love you Jill. This whole thing is crazy; it's like everything's changed. I don't know."

"I know it's crazy! I'm sorry. Please, just come with me, David. I need you. I love you. I don't think I can do this without you." I clung to his arm.

I HAD NEVER SEEN her like this; frightened and needy. I had trouble reconciling this scared, clinging girl with the Jill I knew so well. This might be the first time I'd ever seen her express doubt, or fear, for that matter. She had always kept her cool, whatever the situation.

Leave with her? Why not, I thought. What was I giving up, really? Family? All I had left was my father, and the old man didn't need me, didn't seem to need anybody. Friends? I'd been alone for months, hardly talked to anyone but Leland and Mary. Leland was counting on me, sure, but then, so was Jill. All my friends from the commune had drifted away. Ranger? What about Ranger? I looked over at the dog sitting on the couch. He could come with us. Why not?

No, there wasn't much keeping me there, well, except for Leland. But I'd missed Jill so much, spent months aching for her. Now that she was back, within my reach, I couldn't let her go again, send her off into the unknown all alone. I had to help her, had to be there for her. I looked at her, hanging on my arm. She seemed small and vulnerable, like a lost little girl.

"Well, I guess I better throw a few things in a backpack." I said.

"You're coming?"

"I can't let you go alone."

"Oh, Davey!" I could see the relief in her face. She squeezed my arm. "I knew I could count on you. You're always there for me. Even when I fuck up."

I took her hand and squeezed it, forcing a smile. Shit, what was I doing? I looked around the old house, my home for almost two years, my books and papers, my growing woodpile, visible on the porch through the kitchen window. I thought about sugaring with Leland. It would all be gone, made superfluous in an instant, supplanted by a new reality, more urgent and compelling.

I felt like I had awakened from a long sleep—energized, aware of everything around me. I looked into Jill's brown eyes and kissed her.

"Come on, we need to get ready," I said, though there really wasn't that much to do.

I climbed the stairs to our bedroom and went through the small chest of drawers, choosing things I thought I would need—underwear, red union suit, socks, a green flannel shirt and an extra pair of jeans. That was about it.

I had a couple of hundred dollars left from the money I made working at my dad's hardware store. That should be enough to get us started. There was a big community of resisters in Toronto. They would help. Maybe Jill had some money too. I couldn't worry about all that, though. We just had to get away before somebody came to the house looking for her.

After I finished packing, I went to the mudroom and got out her skis. Mine were already on the porch. I scraped off the old wax and applied a base of glide and a middle section of Klister. I got out two pairs of climbing skins to throw in my pack. We would need them to get up and over Hardwood Mountain, the only obstacle I could see standing in our way.

Canada—a new life. I was still trying to get my head around it. Life with Jill—what I'd been dreaming about all winter, pining for, aching for, though I had never imagined it would come this way. Still, at least we would be together, have a chance.

THE DAY DRAGGED ON FOREVER. *I felt a little calmer now, tried to focus on what was coming. I distracted myself as best I could, scrubbed the counters and mopped the floor, tried to make the time go faster. I could tell David was anxious too.*

Finally, I spoke. "Can't we go now, Dave? I just want to be there."

"Probably better if we wait, otherwise we'll just be standing around in the cold. Besides, there's less chance somebody will see us if we wait for dark."

"Who would see us?" I asked.

"I don't know, Jill. But come on, let's be smart here. Just be safer to wait."

"Yeah, you're probably right. I'm just feeling antsy."

"Me too," he said.

When the sun finally moved across the sky enough to lengthen the shadows, I brewed a pot of tea. David and I were sitting across from each other at the kitchen table, sipping steaming mugs in silence.

David got to his feet. "I'm going over to say goodbye to Leland and Mary. Let them know I'm leaving."

"You sure that's a good idea?" I asked.

"I owe them at least that much," David answered. "They kept me going all winter. If I just disappeared...I'll tell them I'm headed back to the city. They're cool. They won't ask any questions. You know, when the feds came around, they never said a word about anything. Besides, it's not like I'm going say anything about what's going on, and even if I did...they really love you Jill, and they're worried. I just want to say goodbye, that's all, and thanks. They really are great people. They've been my lifeline. You don't know... well, I'll tell you some other time, but the stories I heard from them—incredible, really incredible." He pulled on his jacket. "I won't be long."

I felt a wave of panic, and he must have seen it on my face because as he was leaving, he said, "don't worry, I'll be back soon."

I KNOCKED ON THE trailer door and I heard Mary call out, "come in." I entered and saw her and Leland seated at the kitchen table.

"Everything okay?" he said, giving me a quizzical look. "Had a decent run this mornin', but likely only a few more days for collecting. Trees are gonna bud up, saps no good after that. Just a little more gathering, boilin' down, then some cleanup. Call her done for the year."

Leland had a wistful look on his face. "Don't know how many more seasons I got left in me."

"Leland!" Mary gave him a disapproving look.

"Well it's true, woman. Ain't getting any younger, neither of us."

I shuffled my feet and looked down at the floor. "I'm sorry Leland, but I'm done."

"What do you mean?" he asked. "There's still a solid three, four day's work."

"Something's come up. I've got to get back to New York, I'm leaving tonight."

"Oh?" Leland raised a bushy eyebrow.

"Sorry, it's important, my dad…I just came over to say goodbye, and thanks. You too, Mary, thanks for everything."

"Are you alright? Anything we can help with?" Mary sounded concerned.

"No, you've already done so much for me. I've just got to tie up some loose ends at the house." I turned back to Leland. "Hope I'm not leaving you in a lurch."

The old man snorted. "Got along just fine before you come, guess we'll be alright without you."

"Don't be mad, Leland. I—it's an emergency. You understand."

Leland's tone softened. "Course, it's only…well, it's the end of the season anyways. Me and Mary can finish up." He rose and put a hand on my shoulder. "I guess we had a pretty good time, didn't we. Enjoyed workin' with you. You did pretty good too, for a flatlander."

I grinned and offered him my hand. "I'll miss you Leland, you taught me a lot."

"Oh, Jeezum, I don't know about that." He shook my hand. "Well, I hope we see you back here soon."

"Probably not," I hesitated. "I've got some things I've got to take care of." I thought of Jill waiting back at the house. "Maybe sometime, though."

"Well, good luck to you," he said. "And if you ever want a job in the sugar woods you know where to come."

"Thanks Leland. Thanks Mary. Take care of yourselves." I started toward the door.

"Here," said Mary who had been bustling around the kitchen. She handed me a brown paper bag. "Some of those cookies you like. For your trip."

I leaned over and hugged her. "You're too much!"

I opened the door and turned for one last look at my neighbors. "Bye now, take care." Then I swallowed hard and walked out into the sunlight.

When I got back to the house Jill was sitting on the couch, absently shredding a piece of paper.

"How did it go?" she asked, looking up at me.

"Okay, fine, I guess. It was weird, but they didn't question me or anything. I was letting Leland down, I mean sugaring and everything. But what the fuck, you know, priorities."

"Yeah, it's not like we have a lot of options," she shrugged.

"Think you remember how to ski?" I asked, changing the subject.

"Of course," she laughed. "It's like riding a bike."

"Yeah, but it's been a while. We're gonna have to skin over Hardwood. It's a workout."

"Well then we better get an early start," Jill tossed her head. "How long will it take?"

"Figure an hour or two, to be on the safe side, maybe three. Sure you can handle it?"

"We don't have any choice, do we?"

"Not really."

"Then I'll handle it."

"At least it's not gonna be real cold tonight."

"Good," she said.

An uneasy silence descended on the room. We sat together on the couch, each lost in our own thoughts. I thumbed absently through an old copy of *Rolling Stone,* wondering what was to come, and Jill scratched Ranger behind his ears, The sun sank lower in the west until it disappeared behind a far ridge, leaving us to sit in the gathering darkness.

I looked around the house, my gaze wandering in the shadows. Nothing much to leave behind—a couple of shirts, my books and my journals. I thought for a moment about bringing the journals. The spiral-bound notebooks would fit in my backpack, but what was the point? Just notes, mostly, from my readings. There were a couple of tentative essays, but they didn't amount to much.

Oh, what the fuck, who was I kidding? I wouldn't need them. I didn't know what my new life would bring, but I doubted that my musings on politics and philosophy would be a part of it. I might as well burn them. No, too dramatic, just leave them, leave everything. I felt a sudden emptiness at the thought.

Jill turned on a light. "Getting hungry?"

"A little," I said. "We should probably eat something before we go. I can make some beans, there are still some soaking from yesterday."

"No, I've got it." She added some water to the pot and placed it on top of the wood stove. "No point in starting a new fire. We'll be out of here soon enough."

"I guess," I said, watching her while she stirred the beans.

"The last supper," she laughed, but I could see the tension in her shoulders, and her laugh seemed forced.

I went back to brooding about the journals while Jill kept an eye on the beans to make sure they didn't burn. We were both startled by the bark of a snowmobile coming to life.

"What the fuck?" Jill looked at me, her eyes wide.

"Don't know," I looked back at her. "Probably just Mac and the boys going riding. Nothing to worry about." I tried to reassure her. But I had my own questions. We always heard them approaching up the hill, but not this time. Who? And why?

We saw the beam of the headlight approaching up the path, and then it came to a stop near the house.

"David?" Jill's voice rose an octave.

"You better get downstairs, to the basement. Let me handle this." My heart felt like it was going to tear a hole in my chest.

She walked to the door at the head of the basement steps and opened it. I called after her as she headed down the stairs. "Go to the secret room, behind the shelves, I'll get rid of whoever it is."

I heard heavy footfalls on the porch, then in the mudroom. The kitchen door swung open, and Big Bill stood silhouetted in the doorframe.

"Yo! What's up, Davey boy?" he bellowed. "You miss me? Here to re-up, just like I told you." He walked into the kitchen. "You still up here jerkin' off all by your lonesome?" The big man slowly looked around the open room and then walked over to warm himself at the wood stove.

"Still here," I said as I stood beside him at the stove, blocking his view of the basement door. "Didn't expect you back so soon. It's not a good idea. The feds were here again. They know about you."

"No shit? Fuck! Well, don't worry about it. I'll be out of here tomorrow."

Ranger came downstairs and was on alert, standing beside me with his hair bristling, and a low growl in his throat. "Ranger!" I grabbed him by the collar.

"Shit," Bill startled. "I told you last time to keep that fuckin' mutt away from me."

"Sorry," I took him firmly by the collar and led him to the door. "Out!"

I insisted, and Ranger slunk away, looking back over his shoulder at Bill.

When I went back inside, the biker was sitting on the couch, pulling off his boots. "Still a shitload of snow up here, huh? It melted off right away down in the city. Hey, heard anything from that chick, Jill? Her and Mark got into some heavy shit. She disappeared."

"No, not a word," I said. "I don't expect to either. What happened?"

"Man, you really are fuckin' out of it up here. She bombed that army thing in Times Square. Recruiting office. FBI's lookin' for her, wanted criminal."

"What about Mark?" I asked.

He hesitated for a moment. "He's still around. He's lookin' for her too."

"He's not wanted?"

"Fuck no, he skated. Let the chick do the heavy lifting. That's Mark all the way, man. He's got a way with the ladies. Thought maybe she'd head up here."

"This is the last place she'd come," I said.

"Uh huh." He sounded unconvinced.

I WAS SHIVERING, CROUCHED in a corner of the little room hidden behind the basement cupboard. I had heard someone come into the house. Who was it? And what did they want? I'd been just pulling myself back together, calming down a little, and getting ready for the ski over Hardwood. Now I was in panic mode again, my mind racing to find an answer that didn't freak me out even more. A leaden feeling washed over me, making every breath an act of will. Everything that had happened over the last few days came back—the bomb, my parents, the drive north. I began to sob softly. I couldn't help it. I tried to stop shivering, to stop crying, to pull it together, but I couldn't.

I felt my heart beating like a hummingbird in my chest. We were so close, almost there. I couldn't give up hope now, couldn't afford to fall apart. I had to get myself back under control.

"So WHAT THE FUCK you been up to?" Bill was sitting on the couch with his feet up on the coffee table. "I mean I don't get it. Still no car? What, you just sit around here all day? I couldn't take it. No way. No fuckin' way! This all out of whack man, like it's the eighteen-hundreds or somethin' up here. I mean, shit...no people, no chicks, nothin'! It's like a total escape from reality."

"Suits me just fine." I got up to stir the beans. "Reality sucks, and besides I don't have to deal with other people's bullshit here, just my own." I thought of Jill, hiding in the basement.

"Yeah, I guess I can dig that, but still, I mean, no chicks? No, not for me, man. Hey, you got some beers? I could use a cold one right about now." He gave me a hopeful look.

"No, sorry, no beer."

"Hey, what you cookin there? I'm hungry."

"Just beans."

"Oh shit! I forgot, you're into that health food crap, right?"

"Well, I try to eat healthy, and it's cheap." How could I get rid of him?

He provided the answer. "Ah, fuck that! That store still open? I'll go down and get us some steaks and a couple of six-packs."

"Yea, he's open till eight. You've got time."

"Fuck, I was just gettin' comfortable here." He leaned over and pulled on his boots. "Well, what the fuck. You need anything else while I'm down there?"

"No, but if you want coffee in the morning..."

"Yeah, alright." Bill put on his leather jacket. "I'll be back in a flash with the stash."

I offered him a thin smile. "Take your time, I'm not going anywhere." I watched as the biker walked out the door and slammed it behind him. I heard the snowmobile cough, waited until the sound started to recede, and then opened the door to the basement.

"JILL!" I HEARD DAVID call down into the basement. I made my way up the stairs.

"Who was it? What did they want?" My voice cracked and I made no effort to hide my anxiety.

"Some fucking biker buddy of Mark's, up here to bring a load of Quaaludes in from Canada."

"Bill? Big Bill??"

"Yeah, that's him. He came up once before."

"Oh shit! He's with the FBI."

"That guy? Come on, he's a drug dealer."

"I saw him with them, when they took Mark. He's a rat. He set us up. He's here looking for me."

"Shit, the feds knew all about him. They must have busted him and turned him after his last trip up here. He did ask about you, but he said Mark got away."

"We've got to get out of here!" I was panicking. "Now, right now!"

"My thought exactly," said David. "He went down to the store. We've probably got twenty minutes, a half hour at most. It's enough time to give us a decent start."

While he was talking I ran upstairs and grabbed my backpack. David was lacing up his ski boots by the time I got back. I joined him and we went out through the mudroom to the front porch where we clamped into our three point bindings, grabbed our poles and kicked off onto the snowmobile track heading for Hardwood

Mountain. David wore a headlamp that spread a pool of light ahead of us.

I hadn't been on skis for over a year, but it all came back to me and we established a rhythm that carried us down the path.

Ranger was with us, loping ahead, disappearing into the woods and then reappearing to check on our progress. The woods were silent—no sounds except our skis on the snow and my breathing, growing heavier as we kicked and glided our way up the gentle slope that led to Hardwood.

My thoughts were racing. Bill, the fucking rat! Had he been working with the Feds all along, or had they turned him, like David thought? I'd never liked Bill, never trusted him. He was a thug, didn't even pretend to be political. It was weird that Mark brought him in, especially given all of his need to know bullshit. Had the whole thing been a set up?

I was breathing hard by then, out of shape from my months sitting around the apartment in Queens, almost panting trying to keep up with David. When he noticed I was falling behind, he stopped.

"Just a quick break," he said. "Probably time to put on the skins anyway. It gets steeper after that big white pine up ahead."

I was thankful for a chance to catch my breath. David took the climbing skins out of his backpack and handed me a pair. We both pulled them over our skis. Ranger came back and sat in front of us while David drank water from a wineskin he'd filled when we left the house.

He handed me the water. "We're almost there. Just this steep section up to the ledge, then it's all downhill."

"Thank god," I said, still panting. "I don't know how much more I can take. This stretch almost killed me."

"Oh, you'll make it. We've got time." Then he looked up. We both heard the sound of a racing engine off in the distance, "Snowmobile," he listened for a moment. "Stopped, probably at the house…"

Fear shot through me like an electric shock.

"We better get moving," he said, clamping back into his skis. "Don't worry, we can always bushwhack if we have to, he can't get a snowmobile through the trees. We can always get away."

I hoped he was right. We kicked off and began the climb to the ledge. The trail hugged the side of the mountain, winding steeply toward the ridge. We were both breathing hard. We climbed steadily. The skins kept us from slipping backwards, but it was hard work.

Sweat beaded my forehead and upper lip. I was panting, and felt my heart racing and my legs burning, but the sound of the snowmobile, which started again after a few minutes of silence, kept me going. We rounded a corner and I could see the exposed rock shelf, wind-blown and bare of snow, not too far ahead.

I LOOKED BACK OVER my shoulder at Jill. She was struggling, but so was I, breathing hard, huffing and puffing my way up the mountain. I'd skied up once before this winter, on a sunny day with a thermos of tea and a cheese sandwich in a daypack; a relaxed excursion with all the time in the world to make my way to the ledge.

I heard the snow machine drawing nearer. And when I looked back, I saw a headlight below us cutting through the night in the distance, and racing toward us at a good clip. The sound was getting louder, and I figured it wouldn't be too long before it caught up.

Jill was tired. She could barely slide her skis forward, I could see her panting, but she forced herself to keep going. She had to. It couldn't end like this. If we could just make it to the ledge...I knew that from there it was a downhill run as the path snaked its way through the trees to the lake shore.

Now only one last steep pitch stood between us and the ridge, but when I turned to see how Jill was doing I saw the headlight through the trees, not far behind and closing fast. The bark of the snowmobile cut through the night like a screaming banshee, and I knew we'd never make it to the ridge before it caught us.

I took off my skis, and told Jill to do the same and follow me into the woods. I stopped behind a clump of spruce about a hundred feet or so off the trail, out of sight and waited for her to join me.

She was gasping for breath. "Take it easy," I said. "We'll wait here, let him pass." My breathing was starting to return to normal, and I was thinking more clearly. We stood together, screened from the path by the night and the clump of trees. The whining two-stroke drew closer by the moment and then the headlight cut the darkness with a yellow shaft of light.

I held my breath, but the snow machine never slowed as it raced past us up the mountain.

"Holy shit!" exclaimed Jill. "What now?"

I thought for a moment. "Don't know. Not sure, I mean we've got to get across, and now he's between us and the lake. I guess we'll have to bushwhack. Shouldn't be too tough if we stay parallel to the trail."

"What if he comes back?" I could hear the fear in her voice.

"Well, we'll hear him, won't we?" I was fairly certain he would come back once he realized he had passed us. And it would be easy enough for him to see where we had left the path by our footprints.

"Ready to go?" I looked at her and saw she was still breathing heavily.

"I guess." She clicked back into her skis and was leaning on her ski poles.

I pushed off up the hill. The slope was steeper here and it was tough going through the ungroomed forest. As we climbed, the undergrowth slowed us down and blowdowns grew thicker where a big wind had come through leaving a tangle of downed trees in its wake.

"No way through here." I looked up and down an irregular line of splintered trunks and tops that paralleled the trail. "Maybe we better get on the path. We'll hear him if he comes back. We can duck back into the woods then."

Jill barely acknowledged me. She was panting, and it was all she could do to slide one ski in front of the other. She looked beyond exhaustion, like fear and adrenaline were all that kept her going.

We backtracked, traversing the slope we had just climbed to get back to the path. We were still a few hundred yards shy of the ledge, and it was the steepest pitch of the trail.

I stopped and realized that the sound of the snowmobile, which had been receding into the distance, was gone. I waited, catching my breath while Jill caught up. Ranger came bounding out of the woods, and sat in the snow with his head cocked, like he was waiting for instructions. "Good boy, Ranger, stick close. We'll be there soon," I told him.

Jill pulled up beside me, gasping for breath. "What now?"

"Let's take a break. Have some water." I passed her the wineskin and she squirted a stream into her mouth. "Catch your breath, then one more climb and we're there."

She drank again, and then handed the skin back to me. "Where's Bill?"

"Don't know. I can't hear him. Can you?"

"No, not anymore."

"So maybe he's gone. Maybe he's picking up some ludes in Canada. Maybe he crossed the lake." I was trying to reassure her.

"You don't believe that, do you?" She shifted on her skis.

"It doesn't really matter, does it? We've got to get across either way. If he comes back, we'll deal, you know?"

We spent a few more minutes resting and then started up the trail again.

"My thighs are burning," Jill said, and before too long she was panting again. "This backpack is killing me. It feels like it's full of cannonballs." She kept her eyes on the tips of her skis, not wanting to see how far we still had to go.

I was lost in the twists and turns of my head. I knew the biker was there, up ahead somewhere waiting for us. He grew to monstrous proportions in my imagination—a massive, menacing presence lurking somewhere in our immediate future. And what to do? How to cross to safety?

I was breathing hard myself, but I saw the exposed ridge just ahead now, one final push and we would be there.

The trail left the shelter of the trees, and the wind racing along the ridge, though tempered by the coming spring, still cut. Jill was about ten yards behind me when I pulled up in the shelter of a granite outcropping.

I waited, protected from the wind, catching my breath and thinking about what came next. Jill reached me, breathless and exhausted. She dropped her pack onto the snow, released her bindings and collapsed on her backpack behind the sheltering rock.

"Holy shit!" she gasped for breath. "I forgot how fucking steep it is." She put her head between her legs and tried to regain her composure. "It's downhill from here, right?"

"Yeah, a piece of cake." I tried to sound optimistic. "No snowmobiles, we're practically home free."

"I've got to rest."

"Sure, take your time." I glanced at my watch. "Jed won't be there for another few hours." I passed her the wineskin, and she squeezed a steady stream of water into her mouth. The only sound was the whistle of the wind through the trees and along the ridge. A light snow started to fall. I had a momentary pang of guilt, thinking of Leland and Mary.

Ranger, who had been sitting patiently, thrust his twitching nose into the air, catching the scent of Canada blowing up the mountain. He looked at me impatiently.

"It's okay boy, we'll get going in a minute." The dog shook himself, and wagged his tail, anxious to be off.

I waited until Jill's breathing returned to normal. "Ready for the downhill? Better take off the climbing skins. Remember how to snowplow? Don't want to get going too fast."

"I remember," she said. "It's got to be easier than getting up here."

"Sure thing." I put both pairs of skins in my pack. Jill got up and I helped her clinch her pack at her hips to take some of the weight from her shoulders. She clamped back into her skis.

"Ready?" I pushed back onto the path.

"Here goes nothing," she followed me.

The trail hugged the side of the mountain as it snaked down toward the lake; fairly flat runs, where we kicked and glided or poled our way, interspersed with steeper sections where we let our skis run or snowplowed to control our speed. The beam of my headlamp illuminated the way, the snow sparkling in the light.

Jill was keeping up now, gravity urging us on as we made our way down the mountain. She took a fall on the first steep section, but after she regained her feet, she remembered how to snowplow. The downhills were almost exhilarating, but given the circumstances we couldn't really enjoy them. The trees flashed by and every minute brought us closer to our goal.

I searched the trail ahead for signs of Bill, but I saw nothing and heard nothing. We skied through a clearing, an old woodlot full of saplings and the stumps of departed giants. I was able to see through the forest here to the lake below, an expanse of white, reflecting the light thrown by the moon. I stopped to take in the view, and Jill pulled up next to me.

"Well?" She tugged at her jacket.

"Looks good. I don't hear him, or see him. We've just got a little ways to go now, down and across." I looked at her and saw her jaw clench.

"Let's go," she said, and then she followed me down the mountain.

We were getting close to the path's end now—one more turn, then a straight, gentle downward slope that would deposit us on the lake's shore. We made the turn and were letting our skis run when we heard an engine bark to life and a headlight shown across the path not thirty feet ahead of us. The yellow snowmobile leapt out of the woods, Jill fell and I snowplowed to a halt.

Big Bill killed the engine, got off the snow machine, reached under his jacket and pulled out his pistol. "Figured you'd come this way. Fuckin' A. I was right, knew you'd run up here. But guess what? You ain't goin' nowhere. FBI is on their way."

"What do you want? Let us go, I'll pay you!" Jill's voice was shaking as she picked herself up, and I could see tears starting to well up in her eyes.

"Nah, I don't think so," sneered Bill. "I'm already gettin' paid. And besides, I hate you fuckin' commies. Better dead than red, that's what I always say. So why don't you just turn around and we'll go back to the house and wait for the feds to get here from Burlington. Won't be long now." He gestured back up the path with his pistol.

"I called 'em from the store. You really think I bought your bullshit about bein' all alone? I saw two pairs of skis on the porch. I knew she was here. Didn't figure you'd be dumb enough to try to run."

"I can't believe you're a fucking rat." I was incredulous.

"Let's just say after the last trip we made an arrangement. None of your fuckin' business anyway, you red bastard. If it was up to me, I'd shoot you right here."

"But—"

"Shut the fuck up and get going!" Bill jerked his pistol in the direction of the house.

Without a sound, a gray shadow launched itself from the woods. Ranger's leap knocked the biker to the ground, and he had Bill's forearm clamped in his jaws. The gun went flying and the dog was tearing at Bill's lower arm The biker was pounding at the dog's head with his free arm, but as if with no effect whatsoever. I heard the sound of something breaking, and Bill howled with pain. When Ranger let go, I saw a bone sticking out between Bill's glove and the cuff of his jacket, and blood squirting out of the wound.

I yelled at Ranger to stop, and he did, but only long enough to gather himself with a low growl, and then lunge for the big man's throat. Bill tried his best to protect himself with his good arm, but the dog was in a frenzy and there was no way Bill could fend him off for long. Ranger tore at his sleeve and came away with a mouthful of leather, fabric, and flesh. Bill was screaming, and Ranger kept at the arm that tried to hold him off.

Jill and I were watching in shock. I looked down at the snow and saw the pistol lying there.

I bent and picked it up. I felt the weight of it in my hand. For once, I didn't think. I stepped toward them, pointed it, closed my eyes and pulled the trigger.

Ranger yelped, and then flopped onto his side with blood pouring out of a wound in his chest.

They were both lying there on white snow turning crimson as blood flowed out of both of them. Bill was passed out now, shock I figured.

"Oh, shit!" Jill said. "Let's go! Let's get out of here!"

I stood there in silence, stunned by what had just happened. I looked at Bill, blood pumping out where Ranger had torn open his arm. Ranger lay there whimpering with blood flowing from his chest wound in a steady stream. The big dog raised his head, gave a final huge sigh, and collapsed.

"You go," I told her. "I can't leave him. I've got to try to help."

"But you heard him, the feds are on their way!"

"If we leave him, he'll die. I'll try to keep him alive until they get here." I rummaged around in my pack, found one of the skins and used it as a tourniquet to slow the bleeding from his forearm. "I'll take him back on the snowmobile," I said.

"But David…"

I couldn't believe she wanted me to leave him. "You go," I said. "Get out of here! Now! The fishing access, Jed'll be there in an hour or so. You'll be safe, he'll take care of you."

"What about us? Our new life?"

"I can't just leave him, Jill."

"But he's a pig! He was gonna turn us in. They'll arrest you! Fuck it! Leave him!"

I looked at Bill oozing blood past the tourniquet, and knew he wouldn't last long without help. And, despite my love for Jill, I knew what I had to do.

"You gotta go…"

"Not without you!"

"You've got to, right now!"

"I can't—I need you David."

"Go now! The feds are on their way…"

"David, please," she begged.

"He'll die if I leave him. I'll come find you in Canada."

She turned to me and we embraced, hugging each other tightly, neither of us speaking.

I could see tears welling up in her eyes

"Go on!" I implored.

She picked up her ski poles and tentatively slid one ski in front of the other, like she was moving underwater, slow and deliberate. While tightening the tourniquet on Bill's bloody arm, and looking past Ranger's still body, I watched Jill through my tears as she skied out onto the virgin snow that covered the lake.

About the Author

Dan Chodorkoff, co-founder of The Institute for Social Ecology, lives in northern Vermont with his wife. He is the author of *Loisaida*: a novel, and T*he Anthropology of Utopia*.

Author photo by Rick Levy

Fomite

More novels from Fomite...

Novels

Fomite

Diane Lefer—*Confessions of a Carnivore*
Diane Lefer—*Out of Place*
Rob Lenihan—*Born Speaking Lies*
Colin McGinnis—*Roadman*
Douglas W. Milliken—*Our Shadows' Voice*
Ilan Mochari—*Zinsky the Obscure*
Peter Nash—*Parsimony*
Peter Nash—*The Perfection of Things*
George Ovitt—Stillpoint
George Ovitt—Tribunal
Gregory Papadoyiannis—*The Baby Jazz*
Pelham—*The Walking Poor*
Andy Potok—*My Father's Keeper*
Frederick Ramey—*Comes A Time*
Joseph Rathgeber—*Mixedbloods*
Kathryn Roberts—*Companion Plants*
Robert Rosenberg—*Isles of the Blind*
Fred Russell—*Rafi's World*
Ron Savage—*Voyeur in Tangier*
David Schein—*The Adoption*
Lynn Sloan—*Principles of Navigation*
L.E. Smith—*The Consequence of Gesture*
L.E. Smith—*Travers' Inferno*
L.E. Smith—*Untimely RIPped*
Bob Sommer—*A Great Fullness*
Tom Walker—*A Day in the Life*
Susan V. Weiss —*My God, What Have We Done?*
Peter M. Wheelwright—*As It Is On Earth*
Suzie Wizowaty—*The Return of Jason Green*

Writing a review on social media sites for readers will help the progress of independent publishing. To submit a review, go to the book page on any of the sites and follow the links for reviews. Books from independent presses rely on reader-to-reader communications.

For more information or to order any of our books, visit:
http://www.fomitepress.com/our-books.html

CPSIA information can be obtained
at www.ICGtesting.com
Printed in the USA
LVHW112040120622
721099LV00003B/553

9 781947 917811